What the critics are saying...

4½ Stars! "Fans of the vampire genre will be well entertained. Alyssa and Christian were compelling characters and their chemistry will keep the reader glued to the pages. Robin's has penned a winner to be sure." ~ *Romantic Times BOOKclub*

5 Hearts! "Vampires, elves, and gargoyles? oh my! After Sundown: Redemption by Eden Robins is well versed tale of the paranormal...a perfect story for the avid vampire lover in us all." ~ *The Romance Studio*

9 Gargoyles! "Utterly amazing! After Sundown is a breathtaking new world with familiar places and legendary/mythical creatures, it holds the promise of many more tales. Redemption is beautiful. Robins creates a heroine women can relate to with the same fears all women have when falling in love. Danger, suspense, a villainess you love to hate, gorgeous males and a love to melt the hardest of hearts, Robins promises much and delivers a hundredfold. Plus, she paves the way for future tales in the After Sundown world. Do not miss!" ~ *In the Library Reviews*

"A gripping story full of action and multifaceted characters, Eden Robins pulls readers in with the heightened sense of danger that surrounds Alyssa, and the sensual vampire who has been assigned to protect her. I, for one, am eagerly awaiting the next installment in the After Sundown series by Eden Robins, and no doubt many others will too!" ~ *Romance Reviews Today*

4 Angels! "After Sundown: Redemption is a very interesting and exciting novel. Just when I thought I had everything figured out, Ms. Robins threw in a great plot twister that knocked me off my feet. I congratulate Ms. Robins on a marvelous job with her first installment in the After Sundown series and I look forward to reading Book 2." ~ *Fallen Angel Reviews*

Eden Robins

After Sundown
Redemption

Cerridwen Press

A Cerridwen Press Publication

www.cerridwenpress.com

After Sundown: Redemption

ISBN #1419953265

Edited by Mary Dawson
Cover art by Syneca

Electronic book Publication May 2005
Trade Paperback Publication March 2006

Cerridwen Press is an imprint of Ellora's Cave Publishing, Inc.®

About the Author

ꟷ

Eden Robins hears voices in her head. Her characters' voices, that is. She loves creating new worlds and complex characters that always seem to find their way into one sticky predicament or another. She enjoys helping them get untangled from these situations, only to find themselves entangled in love affairs that will last for all time.

Eden welcomes mail from readers. You can write to her c/o Ellora's Cave Publishing at 1056 Home Avenue, Akron, OH 44310-3502.

After Sundown:
Redemption

ᘐ

Dedication

ℬ

To my friend, Steven, who made me realize that tomorrow may never come, so I need to make the most of today. You'll always be in my heart.

Chapter One

ᘛ

Almost there. Just a little farther. Alyssa's heart was hammering so fast she thought it might burst from her chest. But she had to keep going. She spied the door leading from the parking garage. Still a long way to go. Why had she parked so far away? Was that a breath she felt at the back of her neck? Fear engulfed her. She tried to pump her legs faster. Her muscles shot daggers of pain upwards in protest. They'd almost reached their limit.

She could make it, almost there— Something pulled at the back of her blouse and then lost its grip. She finally reached the door, gave it a good push. It was unlocked. Slipping inside, she slammed the door behind her. Alyssa sagged against it in relief. People were all around her. She trembled all over in an effort to get her breathing back to normal. Safe. For now. Other than losing her shoes, she was fine.

The man had attacked as she approached her car. She swung her purse hard enough at his head to momentarily disorient him. Then brought her knee up and centered it where he was most vulnerable. He doubled over with a groan. She began her race. Her high heels had impeded her speed, so she kicked them off. Ignoring the pain from the bits of rocks and debris she stepped on as she ran for her life, she silently thanked her mother for pushing her to do track while growing up. Despite the fact that her father had always said she "ran like a girl", she knew she had been one of the fastest runners in her school—boy or girl.

Gradually Alyssa got her breathing back to normal. Everything would be okay now. But what about the next time? Whoever was stalking her—yes, she finally admitted that's what was happening—wasn't going away. This was the third speaking engagement he had shown up at and despite the heightened security precautions she'd taken, he didn't seem to be slowing down. This time, it felt like he'd been just steps behind her. He'd never been that close before.

Her publicist was right. She had avoided his suggestions to hire personal security. Now she knew she couldn't put it off any longer. She had assumed that, like everything else in her life, she could handle this herself. She was wrong. The situation was getting out of hand. Whoever was after her wasn't giving up. As much as she hated to admit it, it was time to ask for help.

* * * * *

The next evening, after much persuasion by her publicist, Alyssa Edwards walked into the office of Sundown Security Agency. Her conversation with the agency's owner, Vlad Maksimovitch, started out well. Although she had thought it strange that the agency only opened its doors after sundown, her publicist had assured her that this company was the best in Arizona. They specialized in security for evening functions and since her three remaining motivational workshops were at night, that suited her purposes perfectly.

Vlad, as he asked her to call him, offered her herbal tea as they sat in his office discussing her situation. The light scent of chamomile relaxed her frayed nerves. Also there was something about his tone of voice, which left her at ease. He had an almost lulling cadence to his speech. Despite the fact that he was one of the most attractive men she had ever met, his warm smile and easy manner made her comfortable almost immediately.

Then he mentioned the "B" word.

"A bodyguard? No way!" Alyssa bolted off her seat and almost stormed right back out the door. "Mr. Maksimovitch, when my publicist set up this appointment it was to acquire some additional personal security, not provide me with a babysitter. I know how to make safe choices. I don't need anybody to tell me how to do that."

"I disagree."

Alyssa swung around at the sound of the unfamiliar male voice behind her. The man was leaning negligently against the doorframe leading into the office. His arms were folded casually across his chest and he appeared very relaxed. His eyes challenged her and he wore a mocking smile on his face. For some reason that smirk irritated her.

"Excuse me? Who are you?" She lifted an eyebrow arrogantly.

"Miss Edwards, this is Christian Galiano," Vlad explained. He rose from his chair and gave Christian a warning look. "He's the specialist that I assigned to guar-uh, work with you."

Christian pushed away from the doorway and strode towards her. His mocking expression suddenly changed to intense interest. Alyssa felt something new replace the irritation she had felt only moments before. Everything seemed to move in slow motion as the man drew closer. His body moved in a way that seemed unnaturally graceful, as if he were almost gliding towards her rather than walking. Her eyes rose to his and she couldn't drag them away. His gaze drew her in, endlessly tugging at her. She felt herself falling into their mocha colored depths.

"Christian!" Vlad yelled.

Christian maintained eye contact with Alyssa until he stood close enough to touch her. He slowly raised his hand to her face. Caught up in his captivating gaze, she had no will to stop him.

"Cristobal! No!"

This time, Christian heeded Vlad's words. He broke eye contact and Alyssa stumbled backwards. She would have fallen against the desk if he hadn't reached out at a speed so fast it blurred to grab her arm and steady her. What had just happened? She felt as if she had been in some sort of daze.

Realizing Christian still held on to her, Alyssa's irritation returned. She tried to pull free, but he didn't release her. Instead, he slowly slid his hand down her arm, over her elbow, skimming his fingers on her wrists before gently enveloping her hand in his.

"It's a pleasure to meet you," he said.

His lilting Spanish accent and light touch left her momentary nonplussed, but she quickly shook it off.

"Nice to meet you, Mr. Galiano. Now if you'd let go of me?"

She looked pointedly down at their clasped hands, then back at him.

"Of course, but please call me Christian," he said, releasing her.

Alyssa stepped back, putting some space between them before turning back towards Mr. Maksimovitch.

"I appreciate your efforts to protect me, however, a bodyguard is not exactly what I had planned," she reiterated.

"You need to change your plan, Ms. Edwards," Christian responded.

"I don't think so," she countered. The man was *really* starting to get on her nerves. "I don't need a man following me around wherever I go, telling me where to go, what to do, or how to do it."

Christian looked like he was about to argue, when Vlad interrupted.

"Miss Edwards. Our business is security. We understand your reluctance to hire a bodyguard, however, it sounds to me like your problem has become more than just a case of an avid fan wanting your attention. Last night you were attacked. Your physical well-being was threatened. You managed to escape, but next time you might not be so lucky."

Darn it, the man was right. If he hadn't just voiced her own concerns, she would have been able to refuse their services. Whoever attacked her last night wasn't playing around. She only had two more days until her next speaking appearance. Pride had no place in this. Her life might be at stake.

The two men waited silently for her to make her decision. Christian's expression mocked her, Vlad's looked earnest, concerned. She knew what she had to do.

"Fine," she agreed through gritted teeth. She really didn't like this. "*But,* no offense Mr. Galiano, I'd prefer that you handle my case, Vlad."

Christian's smile remained firmly in place, but Alyssa noticed it now looked like little more than a baring of teeth. Well, that was just too bad. She felt comfortable with Vlad and definitely uncomfortable with Christian. Something about him screamed a silent warning that said, "Stay far away".

"Regretfully, Miss Edwards, that's not possible," Vlad explained. "I'm working on a high profile case of my own at the moment and won't be able to handle yours as well. Also, please understand that I choose the specialists to work each case based on the specifics of the circumstances. After looking over your situation and talking to your publicist, I knew that Christian was the one to best handle your needs. I promise you, you'll be satisfied with him and his protection."

Vlad looked pointedly at Christian.

"Isn't that right, Christian?"

Christian looked like the cat that swallowed the cream. His smile widened to wolfish proportions as he met Alyssa's gaze.

"I can definitely satisfy your needs, Miss Edwards. As long as you do as you're told."

Alyssa fumed. The man was just too much! Placing her hands on her hips she met his gaze squarely.

"I don't take orders very well, Mr. Galiano. *And,*" she paused to rake her gaze scathingly over him from head to toe, "my satisfaction is not so easily fulfilled."

When her eyes returned to his face, she could tell by his clenching jaw that he was not amused. Their gazes met and clashed.

"We'll see," he said, before turning to look at Vlad. "I'll leave the details to you, as usual. Just fill me in later."

Christian turned and left the room without a backwards glance.

"Yes, we will," Alyssa, hissed under her breath.

She turned to Vlad with a smile that was most definitely forced.

"I'm sorry, Ms. Edwards. Christian is usually not like this. I promise you, he'll handle your case with the utmost professionalism and courtesy. He is very good at his job. You'll feel safe in his hands," Vlad guaranteed.

"Thank you. I appreciate your confidence in your employees. As you mentioned before, this situation has gotten way out of hand. Everything I've tried up until now hasn't helped.

"Let's go over the events one more time. Tell me everything, from the first time the stalker appeared until now," Vlad requested.

"Of course. It all started after my first motivational talk since being back in Arizona. As you know, I've been traveling around the country promoting my new life therapy book, *Balance*. I scheduled six appearances around the state. I thought it was fitting to finish out my ten-week tour in my home state. Anyway, I was at the Grady Gammage Auditorium in Tempe, when the stalker first contacted me. Everything was going as usual when…"

* * * * *

In his office down the hall from Vlad's, Christian paced restlessly back and forth. His acute hearing allowed him to hear every word Alyssa Edwards spoke. When Vlad promised her that he would behave with professionalism and courtesy, Christian smiled coldly. Vlad knew he was listening and that was his way of warning him to behave.

Christian ran his hand through his hair and exhaled loudly in frustration. He wasn't quite sure why he had acted that way with the human woman. She was pretty. He'd give her that. Her straight, raven black hair hung loose down to the small of her back. She had delicately arched eyebrows, crystal blue eyes, creamy white skin and full, berry-red lips. Her ample and voluptuous curves also kept drawing his gaze. But he had seen many more exquisitely beautiful women during his two hundred year lifetime and none had affected him like this.

Most women tried to attract his interest. Alyssa had done just the opposite. She had acted like she wanted nothing to do with him. That surprised him. Even when he had tried to mesmerize her, she had struggled against it. Her strength of will amazed him. She had fought him up to the moment he had released her from his mental embrace. That was unusual.

Despite all that, what most intrigued him had been her ability to ignite his emotions. Most humans only mildly affected him, but she had actually made him feel several ways. Challenged, interested, irritated and yes, attracted. Something about her appealed to him, made him feel alive, but he couldn't quite place what it was, yet.

Though he knew what had happened to Alyssa up to that point, Christian listened attentively, careful not to miss any unusual cadence changes or hesitations in her voice. He had learned through experience that it wasn't always what the person said that answered your questions. It was more often how they said it. He knew she was scared by the last attack, as she should be. But he could also tell she didn't like asking for help. She was very independent. That was an admirable trait, but it could present a problem if she wasn't willing to cooperate with him. He had a job to do and he would succeed, with or without her agreement.

He was sworn to protect the humans he had easily killed so long ago. Almost a hundred and fifty years had passed since he let the vampire in him take control of the person he was. The man now ruled the vampire, not the other way around. And his duty to protect was what he lived for. It was the only thing that kept him from walking into the sunlight and ending his existence.

He delved lightly into Alyssa's mind, careful to keep his search delicate so that she remained unaware of his probing. He couldn't stop the satisfied grin that spread across his lips. She was wondering about him, even as she said goodbye to Vlad. Good, she wasn't as unaffected by him as she pretended to be. That would help.

"Did you get it all, my friend, or have you been in here the whole time, daydreaming about our beautiful new client?" Vlad asked as he walked into Christian's office.

"I heard it. And I agree, she is quite attractive, but that's not what worries me. Ms. Edwards is very independent and really doesn't want to deal with us. I skimmed her mind lightly, as I'm sure you did and despite her fear over the situation, she was trying to figure out a way not to use our services, even as you walked her to her car and she drove away."

"Nevertheless, she will use our service. Her publicist insisted and she has already given us a down payment." Vlad smiled, before he turned serious again. "You have a new client, Christian. But please refrain from any more open displays like the one in my office earlier. We don't want to scare our customers away. Our business has grown substantially in the last few years and we're establishing a good reputation. I want to keep it that way."

"Don't worry. I'm sure Ms. Edwards and I will come to an agreement," Christian said with a wicked smile.

"That's what I'm afraid of," Vlad muttered, shaking his head. He placed a file on Christian's desk, then turned to leave the room. "Take a look at Ms. Edwards' file. She's going to meet with you here at the office tomorrow night, so that you can go over procedure and layout. Her next speaking engagement is the night after next."

"Thanks. Where are you off to in such a hurry?" Christian asked with a knowing grin.

Vlad stiffened and glared over his shoulder.

"You know perfectly well where I'm going. If I'm not at little miss princess's house by a certain time, her daddy gets very unhappy," he said with a grim smile. "And with the amount of money he's willing to pay and his large crowd of friends that are just the kind of people who could be our future clients, I'm willing to speed up my pace a little. Dealing with his daughter, of course, is a totally different matter. I don't know how much longer I'm going to be able to put up with her."

"Good luck," Christian snickered before his friend slammed the office door on his way out.

* * * * *

Alyssa drove through the drive thru, grabbing some Japanese fast food from Teriyaki Now! on her way home. Her apartment was finally starting to feel like home again. After being gone for so long, it was hard to settle back into her place. As she set her keys and food down on the counter, a big black fur ball jumped onto the kitchen table and meowed loudly.

"Finally forgiven me, huh?" she asked, petting her cat. When she scratched his head, he closed his eyes and began purring loudly.

"I missed you too, Jonathan, but this speaking tour was something I needed to do. I know Aunt Joyce took good care of you while I was gone. You certainly don't look deprived," she added, stroking his substantial belly. In response, he turned and gave her hand a little nip.

"Okay, so I'm not totally forgiven. How about some dinner?"

Alyssa opened a can of cat food and poured it into Jonathan's bowl, then set it on the floor by his water. He jumped off the table and sniffed his food. She sat down, pulled her dinner out of the bag and began to eat. When she was about halfway through, Jonathan jumped back onto the table and sat down in front of her. He waited patiently, watching her chew each bite and occasionally sniffing the air.

"No. The vet said I have to stop giving you treats. I know teriyaki chicken is your favorite, but I can't do it," she explained.

Jonathan meowed sharply, then proceeded to pace on the table in front of her.

"Nope. I'm not giving in this time. You need to be healthier," she said firmly.

Jonathan stopped and emitted a small pitiful meow, then lay down on the table and rolled over onto his back. All the while he watched her eat.

"No, I can't—"

The doorbell rang at that moment and Alyssa got up to answer it. Jonathan let out one more meow and she gave up.

"Fine. Here's the rest. I'm done anyway." She set the bowl in front of him before walking to the door.

She started to open it and then remembered what had happened the night before. She needed to be more cautious, make safer choices. She peeked through the peephole and then opened the door wide.

Her Aunt Joyce breezed inside.

"Hi. Jonathan and I are just sharing our dinner, again," Alyssa explained.

"I thought he's on a diet?" Her aunt hiked one eyebrow.

"He is, but I figured a little chicken wouldn't hurt him."

"Honey, 'a little chicken' is what got him where he is in the first place. Admit it, Jonathan is one spoiled cat and you'd be unhappy without him."

"He was a stray found, end of story. He had no place else to go. And what am I supposed to do? He has to eat," Alyssa replied.

"And he has to have his special kitty bed, his kitty blanket, his kitty toys, his fish shaped bowl and don't forget his little kitty sweater for those especially cold days when you take him for a walk in his kitty halter leash. That cat is one of the most spoiled animals I have ever met," her aunt complained.

"He was so incredibly difficult while you were gone, Alyssa. He didn't want to eat, didn't want to use his litter box and didn't want to take his daily walk. I had to feed him like a baby and carry him around outside, just so he could get his fresh air. Honestly, I don't know how or why you put up with him," her aunt complained.

Alyssa smiled. She knew that despite all the complaining her aunt was doing, she absolutely adored Jonathan.

"I'm sorry he was such a bother. Thanks for taking care of him for me while I was gone. I don't know what I would have done without you." Alyssa hugged her aunt.

"I was glad to do it for you, Aly," her aunt replied softly, hugging Alyssa tightly before pulling away and taking her niece's face in her hands. "Let me look at you, girl. You were gone too long. I missed you."

"I missed you too, Aunt Joyce." Alyssa smiled. "Now come into the kitchen with me and we'll have some tea."

Alyssa poured two glasses of iced tea and sat down across from her aunt at the kitchen table. The kitchen was one of her favorite rooms in the apartment. She had decorated it with yellows and light blues, as well as some plants, to make it warm and inviting. She loved sitting at the table chatting with friends and family. It was one of the things she and her mother had done when Alyssa was a child. Though her mother was now dead, she still enjoyed the tradition.

Her aunt stayed for a short time. They talked about Alyssa's trip and her appointment at Sundown Security.

"So you're meeting with Mr. Galiano again tomorrow?"

"Yes, we're supposed to go over plans for my last few motivational talks. He'll suggest some ways to secure each location," Alyssa replied.

"It sounds like this man knows what he's doing. That's good. I don't want anything to happen to you. If you're obligated to finish your tour, at least I'll have the comfort of knowing you'll be safe."

"Hmmm," Alyssa replied noncommittally.

She really didn't want to think about how safe she might be with the arrogant Mr. Christian Galiano. But later on, after her aunt left and Alyssa lay in her bed, her thoughts kept wandering back to him. The rest of the night she tossed and turned, dreaming of dangerous attackers and a handsome, mocking stranger saving her each and every time.

By morning her dreams had her completely irritated with Christian. She didn't know how she could possibly wait until evening. She just wanted to get everything clarified and organized in her mind so that she could concentrate on other things.

Like her upcoming speaking engagements. No matter how many times she spoke in front of a crowd, she always needed to prepare. Once she had done enough preparation, she had no trouble speaking in front of large groups of people. Millions even, as she had done when she appeared on The Good Day Show with Ellie Tyler. She had watched Ellie for years and felt comfortable with her. But the fact that so many people were going to be watching the interview worried her, so she had prepared extensively for it. By the time she went on TV, she felt ready and answered each question appropriately.

Despite the fact that the she had a lot of work to do, the day dragged on forever. Before sunset, Alyssa was already in her car, heading into downtown Phoenix, on her way to meet Christian. She pulled into the parking lot just as the sun was disappearing over the horizon. She enjoyed the scene for a few minutes. Arizona sunsets were incredibly beautiful and this one was no exception. The pinks and oranges that streaked across the sky seemed too bright to be real. It was almost as if someone had painted them there. When the colors faded and twilight fell, she got out of her car and headed for the Sundown Security office. She knocked on the door, but no one answered so she tried the lock. It was open. Slowly, she twisted the knob and pushed the door inward.

"Oh good, dinner. Just in time too, I'm famished."

Alyssa stopped short in the doorway. The woman standing inside didn't look friendly. In fact, she looked downright unfriendly. Alyssa slowly counted to five. She just wasn't in the mood for this.

"Look, you'll have to find your own meal. I'm not here to deliver dinner," Alyssa said irritably. "I'm here for an appointment."

"Who said anything about delivering dinner, my dear? You *are* dinner." The woman smacked her lips, giving Alyssa a leer that revealed sharp, elongated teeth. When she strode forward, Alyssa retreated backwards through the doorway, her heart pounding in sudden alarm.

Chapter Two

ß

This wasn't good. There was something not right, something strange about this woman. Fear replaced the irritability Alyssa had been feeling only moments before. This stranger meant her harm. The urge to turn and run was strong, but Alyssa somehow sensed that she would never make it. She just kept slowly backing up out the door and into the parking lot. Just as the woman was about to reach her, Alyssa bumped into something solid. Swinging around she saw Vlad Maksimovitch standing there. Without looking down at her, he gently pulled Alyssa behind him.

"Bazhena, it's been too long. What brings you here?" Vlad asked the woman.

"Hello, Vlad. I was in the area and thought I'd stop by. It has been a long time hasn't it? At least four hundred years by last count. Of course it's still not long enough for me to forgive you for that little misunderstanding we had."

Despite the fact that the conversation seemed pleasant and mundane, Alyssa felt the emotional undercurrents all around her. These two people hated each other. She was sure of it. Four hundred years, had she heard that right?

"Bazhena, you killed someone I cared about. And I tried to kill you because of it. I'd call that more than a little misunderstanding, wouldn't you?"

"Whatever, Vlad. You just hold onto your little human moral code and I'll do my own thing. Now if you'd turn over that delectable little morsel behind you I might be willing to forgive you."

Alyssa stiffened in fear. This strange woman was talking about her like she was a piece of meat. What was going on here?

She peeked around Vlad and found Bazhena's gaze slide immediately to hers. She leered at Alyssa and smacked her lips again.

"Come out, sweet, I only want a little taste."

"You touch her and you'll be walking into the sunlight sooner than you planned, *Wendigo*."

Alyssa swung around and saw Christian striding towards them. Fury made his eyes glow and his muscles bunch rigidly with each step he took. He looked like a dangerous predator Alyssa wouldn't want to be the wrong side of. He walked right up to Bazhena and towered over her. She seemed unconcerned even though her petite size was no match for his. Her mouth had hung open in shock when she first saw Christian. But she smiled in amusement now as he towered over her. Alyssa noticed Bazhena's smile never reached her cold eyes.

"Cristobal! I truly never expected to see you again. What are you doing here?"

"He works with me," Vlad interjected.

Bazhena looked back and forth at the men with an amused smile.

"The two of you are friends? How droll!" Bazhena laughed in a way that sent chills up and down Alyssa's spine.

Bazhena was incredibly beautiful. Her red, formfitting mini-dress clung to her in all the right places. She was petite, maybe five-feet three-inches tall. Her shapely body perfectly matched her height. She had golden hair that hung in loose shiny waves down her back. Her eyes were the blue of a crystal clear summer sky. Full lush lips that were the deep dark red of cherries contrasted with her almost alabaster skin. Except for the two, long, sharp incisors sticking out below her top lip, most men she knew would drool all over this woman. Vlad and Christian acted as if she disgusted them. She definitely needed some orthodontic work, but that didn't account for the look of repulsion on both men's faces. Who was this woman?

Bazhena didn't seem to notice their distaste. She smiled seductively up at Christian. He stiffened in response. Chuckling, she skimmed her index finger down one side of his face. "Don't tell me you have become a fanatic like this one, Cristobal?" She motioned towards Vlad. "After I turned you we had—"

"That's enough!" Christian roared, pushing her away from him. Bazhena stumbled back, but immediately righted herself.

"Leave now or I'll make you leave. And I can promise you it won't be pleasant," he warned.

Anger flared in Bazhena's eyes, then her gaze turned calculating.

"Fine, I'll leave. You two are about as fun as a wooden stake. If you'll just give me my little snack, I'll be on my way."

Unease slid over Alyssa. This was not good. Bazhena was referring to her as a snack.

"You will not touch this woman," Christian growled. "She's under my protection."

Bazhena's eyes widened in surprise, then narrowed dangerously as she turned her gaze to Alyssa.

"I thought you would have learned the folly of getting too attached to humans by now, Cristobal. Obviously I didn't teach you well enough."

"I've learned more than enough since you ruined my life. If you touch her, you'll regret it."

"Are you threatening me, Cristobal?"

"Definitely." Christian's stony expression gave no quarter.

Bazhena looked like she was about to protest when Vlad left Alyssa's side and stood next to Christian.

"Will you leave now, or must we exert force?"

Enraged, Bazhena turned her furious gaze to Vlad and shrieked, "*You* will force me to do nothing!"

Before Alyssa knew what was happening, Bazhena grabbed the front of Vlad's shirt with one hand and lifted him off the ground. Then she flung him across the hall. He hit the wall with such force Alyssa thought he would have been knocked unconscious. Instead he stood up, brushed off his clothes and strode back towards Bazhena as if nothing had happened.

"Tsk. Tsk. Very childish, Bazhena. But so like you," Vlad said with a condescending smile.

Bazhena slowly retreated. Christian advanced on her. Vlad followed close behind.

Glaring back and forth between them, she shouted, "This is far from over!"

Then Bazhena turned away and disappeared amidst some gathering fog.

Relief washed over Alyssa. That horrifying woman was gone. What happened? How had Bazhena just disappeared into the mist? Since when was there fog during the dry Arizona summer? She studied the place where that woman, or whatever she was, had just been. Why had she wanted to taste Alyssa? And what did she mean by *taste*? The woman's incisors had been incredibly long and sharp and she had looked at Alyssa with a kind of hunger she couldn't, no, didn't want to understand. Dizziness assailed her as questions rampaged through her mind. Her knees gave way beneath her and she sank to the ground. She held her head in her hands as the endless questions and inconceivable answers bombarded her.

"Alyssa."

Her thoughts scattered. Alyssa looked up at the sound of Christian's voice. He and Vlad slowly approached her. The look on their faces was wary, carefully watching her. The two incredibly handsome men affected her as they strode side by side towards her. They both moved with a predatory grace that belied their size and each had a kind of magnetism that kept her eyes glued to them. Yet it was Christian who interested her most.

She had to admit it. He was beautiful to look at, but definitely all male. Well over six feet, lanky, but also muscular. His masculine beauty was undeniable. It took her breath away.

He had a very pale complexion, full sensuous lips and sharply chiseled features. Thick, arched eyebrows topped his mocha-colored eyes. And his dark brown hair hung loose past his shoulders. Alyssa wanted to twine her fingers in the silky-looking tresses. Christian's eyes held hers and she couldn't look away. As if he kept them connected by his will alone.

His gaze called to her in a way that made her think of things she thought long buried. The image of black silk sheets, candlelight and two intertwined lovers lying on a huge bed in the center of a room, filled her head. She lost focus for a moment and swayed. Christian's firm grasp kept her from falling as he helped her up. But it also broke the seductive spell that had enveloped her.

She snapped her head up and stared at his face. He stood so close she could see the gold flecks sprinkled throughout his eyes. Her gaze ran down his strong nose to his mouth. His lips were curved into that knowing smirk she now knew signaled his amusement. Once again, that smile rubbed her the wrong way. She stiffened and yanked her arm out of his grasp.

"Would you mind keeping your hands off of me?"

Christian's amusement turned cold.

"Gladly."

Alyssa watched him walk away and head into his office without another word.

Vlad cleared his throat and she swung her gaze back to him.

"Miss Edwards. Won't you come into our offices?" Vlad asked gently. "The three of us need to talk."

He motioned for her to go ahead of him and they proceeded to Christian's office. Alyssa saw Christian standing behind his desk facing the window. She thought he was lost in thought as he gazed outside into the darkness.

She was wrong. He was well aware of their presence.

"I'll tell her, Vlad. I know that you have an appointment that you, uh, can't be late for," Christian said, still facing the window. He tried, unsuccessfully, to keep the humor from his voice. "So feel free to go. I'll talk more with you later."

Christian turned slowly. Though his words were for Vlad, his eyes narrowed on Alyssa's face.

"Fine," Vlad said. "Ms. Edwards, I leave you in Christian's capable *and* professional hands. I'm sure he'll be able to answer whatever questions you have."

With one last warning glance at Christian, Vlad closed the door softly behind him.

Nervous, Alyssa sat down. She was alone with a man she didn't feel quite safe with. The air grew thick with awareness. Christian continued to stare at her broodingly. The silence finally became too much for her. She was not into playing childish games.

"What?" she demanded.

Christian lifted one eyebrow and gave her that smirk she was beginning to really, *really* dislike.

"I was just wondering how you managed to get yourself into trouble just by showing up at our offices. Does this happen to you a lot?"

Alyssa knew by the twinkle in his eyes that he was teasing. She was not in the mood. She needed answers. Things were getting a little too creepy for her.

"Who was that woman? Why was she so interested in me? How did she disappear, turn into mist?"

Christian hesitated. He wanted to tell her the truth, but she wasn't ready for that yet. He felt her frustration, her fear. He would tell her what he could.

"She is a vampire."

"A *WHAT*?" Alyssa shot up from the chair and placed her hands on her hips.

"Very funny. I've had enough teasing tonight, Mr. Galiano. Now please be straight with me. What is going on?"

"You want the truth?" Christian advanced slowly. His face became solid granite, his gait aggressive. He had stopped playing, but Alyssa didn't know if she liked that. This was a different side of him, one she hadn't seen before.

He drew closer. The air around her became electrified. The hairs on her arms stood on end. Her heart beat rapidly. Her breath grew short. Filled with the primitive urge to flee, she struggled to stand ramrod straight as Christian reached her. Her body started to tremble. She couldn't control it. She wanted to turn and run away, but suddenly felt paralyzed. Frozen to the spot. She lifted her eyes helplessly to his.

Christian smiled down at her. But it was not a comforting smile. Instead, the predatory grin made her more afraid. She was in danger. Of that she had no doubt. Then he opened his mouth slightly. Fangs like she had seen on Bazhena appeared from below his top lip. Horrified, her gaze fixated on his mouth. He growled low in his throat. Surprised by the sound, her eyes snapped up to meet his. She gasped, barely holding in the shriek of fright that filled her. His eyes glowed with a red light.

Engulfed by horror, Alyssa felt her legs give way. She fell forward, unable to stop herself. Christian's strong hands caught her.

"I'm sorry I had to do this to you, *palomita,* but your disbelief left me little choice. Now you see me for what I am. I, Cristobal Galiano y Pumarada am a vampire. Just as Vlad Maksimovitch and Bazhena Galichanin are vampires. We do exist. Don't ever doubt it. Even as we speak, I smell your fear and I hear your racing heart. The blood singing through your veins calls to me. Makes me hunger for you in ways you can't imagine."

Christian leaned closer. His lips brushed her neck. Shivers of awareness ran through her body.

Alyssa felt his warm breath tickle her ear. "The difference between Bazhena and I is that she kills humans and I protect them. That is the only thing that keeps me from taking you right now," he whispered.

Alyssa struggled to tamp down the fear that threatened to engulf her. Just as she had always done when she was a child. He was a vampire! Her whole body shook. Her heart beat out of control, her breathing grew shallow and her hands became soaked with sweat. She closed her eyes and thought of that sunset scene she so often visualized in her mind when she felt like she was losing control. The image calmed her almost immediately. The shaking stopped and her heart slowed to a more reasonable pace.

Okay. The man was a vampire. A *vampire*!

Calm down. She forced herself to put that thought on the back burner until later. Right now she needed to get this situation into some sort of manageable form. Christian looked much too threatening for her liking. Falling back on her training as a therapist, she tried the one approach that had helped her in the past.

Christian knew his words were harsh, but she had to hear them. He wouldn't tell her everything right now. But she had to know what he was. It was the only way he could do the job he was hired to do. Maybe now she would understand and accept that.

It had taken him a while to get over his shock at seeing his creator. Bazhena had made him into this creature over two hundred years ago. He hadn't wanted it. Hadn't asked for it. Nevertheless, it was his own fault that he'd been turned into a vampire. And he would never forget that.

Bazhena had told Vlad that she was in the area and had just stopped by for a visit. Christian knew she lied. Vampires are not social creatures. If they had one or two real friends they were lucky. Stopping by to visit a vampire you hadn't seen in over four hundred years did not ring true. And what did Alyssa have to do with all of it? He would have to find out Bazhena's real reason for showing up tonight. But he could deal with that later. For now, he needed to calm Alyssa down and then go over her case. Now, more than ever, he wanted to know exactly what had been happening to her.

The only problem was that he couldn't calm down. The adrenaline that had made his eyes glow and his fangs elongate had also had affected him in other ways. Alyssa's scent intoxicated him. The sound of her blood rushing through her veins excited him. And the feel of her silky skin beneath his hands made him long to run his fingers up and down her body. She called to him in a way no other ever had. Frightened by his own admission, he released his hold.

Alyssa righted herself before she fell against him. She shook her head as if trying to clear her mind. Squaring her shoulders, she met his gaze with her own curious one. Her next words were not the ones Christian expected.

"So why did you say your name was Christian?"

"Excuse me?" Christian was dumbfounded by her query.

"Well, everyone I've met recently calls you Cristobal. Why did you tell me your name was Christian?"

He remained speechless. She didn't look the least bit frightened! And of all the questions she could have asked, this was not the one that came to mind. He was momentarily sidetracked. Her intelligent eyes intrigued him. He lost himself in their lively depths, only to have her soft chuckle bring him back.

He frowned. He was on very unfamiliar ground here. He usually didn't have personal conversations like this with his human clients. "What's so funny?"

"You look like I asked you the hardest question in the world. All I want to know is why you told me your name is Christian, when it isn't."

"It is, uh, I mean it isn't." He blew out an exasperated breath. "What I mean is that my birth name is Cristobal, but over time I adopted the name Christian."

"Why?"

"It's a modern version of Cristobal and since I work with a lot of humans, it was easier for them."

"I see. How old *are* you?"

"Over two hundred years old."

"*That* old?"

Alyssa asked him in a way that made him feel as if he should be using a walking cane and residing in a senior citizen rest home.

"Yes, *that* old," he replied irritably.

"And which name do you prefer?"

Again, her change of topic and unusual question unnerved him. No one had asked him what he preferred for a very, very long time. Momentarily bemused by her questions, he gave himself a mental shake. He had to get back to business.

"That really doesn't matter, Alyssa," he said brusquely. "The point of this conversation is that I am a vampire and my job is to protect you. Do you understand that?"

"Of course. I understood that the first time you told me. Do you repeat yourself often?"

Frowning, Christian studied Alyssa's face. Her dimpled smile and the amusement in her eyes were unmistakable. The minx was teasing him!

He couldn't resist the answering grin that spread across his lips. He was surprised, but also glad to see this side of her personality. She had a sense of humor and she was stronger than she looked. He liked that.

Alyssa didn't know where the questions came from. She had used this technique before when she was on unfamiliar ground. Asking ordinary questions usually managed to calm her and the other person down. She settled down immediately and was glad to see Christian also relax. He was puzzled enough by her query that his fangs withdrew and his eyes returned to their normal color.

Relieved and feeling more in control of her situation, she said, "Okay. So you and that woman Bazhena and Vlad are vampires. But you're also a bodyguard. And you plan on protecting me from this stalker. Is that correct?"

He gave her an indulgent smile. "Yes, *palomita,* that is correct."

"What does *palomita* mean?"

"Full of questions aren't you? I think I'll let you find that out for yourself. Now let's get back to business." Christian moved back around to his side of the desk, sat down and opened the file in front of him.

He motioned for Alyssa to sit across from him. "Please sit down. We have a lot to cover before your speaking engagement tomorrow night."

Alyssa remained standing.

"One more question before we start, Mr. Galiano. Do many other people know you're a vampire?" She'd been dying to ask that, because the whole situation was just so weird.

"I'll answer that on one condition."

"What?"

"That you sit across from me and that you call me Christian, not Mr. Galiano. I think it will make things easier and more comfortable for both of us. Agreed?"

Alyssa nodded her head and sat down. After all, he and Vlad had just saved her life. She figured that she at least owed him that. This side of Christian intrigued her. He wasn't mocking her and instigating her anger. They were actually having a civil and somewhat friendly conversation. Pleased by his easy-going manner, she nodded her head.

"Agreed."

"Good." Christian's lips spread into a much too satisfied smile and Alyssa wondered if she had agreed too quickly. "To answer your question, no, not many people know what I am. Think about it? Who would you tell? And more importantly, who would believe you? Today's society is based on science and facts. Luckily, it's that narrow mindedness which allows us to operate Sundown Security and keep our anonymity. Our group is diverse and talented, but we all have one thing in common.

We can all be categorized as unexplained or unsubstantiated phenomena."

"You mean there are others like you working here?" she asked, unable to keep the shock from her voice.

"Well, I wouldn't say 'like me'. We all have our own special talents," he explained vaguely. "But let's get down to business. I see from your file that the first incident—"

Christian looked up as somebody opened his door.

"Hey, Christian. Who does a vampire fall in love with? The girl *necks* store. Get it? The girl—uh, sorry. Hmm. I didn't know you had a client. Talk to you later."

Christian's door quickly closed.

Alyssa was too stunned to speak. The man who had just stuck his head through the doorway had the face of an angel, a perfect Adonis, with long golden hair. Weren't there *any* ugly men working here?

Frowning, Christian returned his attention to her.

"Sorry about that. Where were we?"

"Was that, um, I mean, was he—like you?" Alyssa tentatively asked.

Christian chuckled. The low seductive sound of it sent a tingle up and down her spine.

"A vampire? No. He's an elf."

"An *elf*?" Alyssa thought about the cookie commercial with the happy, little elves running around baking. "But I thought they were, uh, little people?"

"Think *Lord of the Rings*. Did you see Orlando Bloom as the elf, Legolas?"

Alyssa nodded her head, remembering the tall, gorgeous elf on screen. The face that had peeked in Christian's office a moment ago, would have given Legolas a run for his money.

"Elves come in different sizes," he explained. "Now let's continue going over your file."

Alyssa didn't respond at first. She was trying to digest all of this, but it was way too much. Out there in the 'woo woo zone' too much. Fine. She would think about it later. She had to get through this meeting first.

"Okay, I'm ready."

Christian nodded his head.

"You're finishing your ten-week motivational and book promotion tour back in Arizona. The stalker has appeared at your first three engagements in the area, but the last one was the first time that he actually tried to physically attack you. Is that right?"

"Yes." Alyssa shuddered, remembering the terrifying fear she experienced while being chased through the parking garage.

"At your first engagement, he left a threatening and disturbing note in your dressing room. The second appearance, he left another note and stole some of your personal items—some of your undergarments. Correct?"

"That's right." Alyssa's face flamed with embarrassment. The fact that the stalker stole her panties sickened her. The fact that he snooped through her belongings angered her.

Christian kept his head down as he wrote notes in her file. He must have sensed her embarrassment because he suddenly stopped writing and glanced up at her. She saw anger flare in his gaze for a moment. Then compassion filled his eyes. Reaching across the narrow desk, he laid his hand softly over hers. Alyssa was startled by the gentle act. But the feel of his hand enveloping hers was comforting, so she left it in his grasp.

"I know this is difficult for you." He gave her hand a light squeeze. "We're almost done. I just need to get a few more facts down. You decided to take some action after the second incident? What did you do?"

"I asked my publicist to speak to the security personnel working at the next speaking location. He set up some additional measures to keep all but my closest people from getting too close to me or my dressing room."

"If that's the case, how did this guy get to you?"

"After I was finished and things went so well, I felt pretty comfortable. One of the security guards started to walk me to my car. I began to feel silly. I kept thinking about how I was no superstar celebrity. I'm just a counseling therapist who wrote a book that helped people. About halfway to my car, I told the man he could leave. I never dreamed that whoever was stalking me would even think about physically attacking me. Up to that point, all he had done was leave notes and take some of my things."

"Then what happened?"

Christian continued to question the events that lead Alyssa's publicist to approach their agency for help. She looked at her watch. An hour had already passed since she had entered his office. She needed to stand up. Sitting for this long made her restless. Or maybe just being this close to Christian made her feel that way. Despite the fact that he was asking her questions in a very business-like manner and she was answering him in a professional way, the chemistry between them kept flaring up when she least expected it.

Alyssa stood and began pacing the room. She couldn't sit still any longer. Christian watched her with his potent gaze, leaving her hot and bothered. She was tired of his questions. And she was starting to feel like the bad guy instead of the victim.

Releasing her pent-up breath in a long exasperated sigh, she asked, "Didn't Vlad tell you all of this?" The irritation in her voice was unmistakable.

"Yes. But I need *you* to tell me." Christian's expression was too intense.

She felt like a bug under a magnifying glass. He was studying every word she said, every movement she made, every facial expression, every breath she took. She couldn't stand much more.

"Fine. But this is the last time," she said. "I had just reached into my purse when he grabbed me from behind. Luckily, he lost his grip when I stepped back and stood on his toe with my stiletto heel. I was able to twist around and hit him with my bag. Before he could recover, I kneed him. Then I kicked off my shoes and ran as fast as I could back to the door leading into the lobby. End of story."

Alyssa slumped back into the chair. She was emotionally exhausted. It was like she had actually gone through the experience again as she retold it. After her harrowing experience with Bazhena, Christian's revelation about being a vampire and his probing questions, she was just plain worn out.

"Thank you, Alyssa. I'm sure that wasn't easy for you. But I had to hear everything from you. It helps me understand the situation better. I just have one last question, then we're done," he said softly. Rising from his chair, he walked around his desk.

Alyssa watched Christian's progress, wondering what he was doing. He stopped behind her seat. He scooped up her hair and placed it over one shoulder. Then he laid his hands gently on either side of her neck. Alyssa stiffened, but didn't pull away. He began massaging her tense muscles. It felt so good. She didn't have the will to stop him. Closing her eyes, she leaned her head forward. His fingers rubbed the back of her neck. Up to the base of her scalp. Down to her shoulders. As each muscle he touched reveled in his ministration, her tension eased.

After a few minutes, Christian slid his fingers up, along her jaw to just under her chin. He tilted her head back, supporting it with one hand while tracing the contours of her face with the other. Alyssa's eyes fluttered open. She watched his eyes caress each feature of her face, until they finally rested on her own gaze. She found herself entranced by the desire in his stare. His fingers tightened in her hair, holding her in place. His head lowered towards hers. A yearning like she had never experienced before consumed her, but she tried to fight it.

"Y-you have one more question for me?" she asked in barely more than a whisper.

"Yes." He drew closer. His hair fell forward and its silky texture slid over her cheek. It was as soft as she had imagined. Alyssa couldn't hold back the moan of pleasure that contact gave her.

Christian's eyes flared, then darkened with hunger. "Are your lips as soft as they look?"

Then his mouth closed over hers.

Chapter Three

ജ

Alyssa's supple lips tasted better than Christian had imagined. He groaned aloud when she opened her mouth, inviting him in. He deepened the kiss, suddenly so ravenous that he could barely restrain himself. She had been too much of a temptation to resist. Although he had tried, the vulnerable look on her face and the need in her eyes pulled at him. His questions had pushed her to the limit. But he had no other choice. If he was going to protect her, he needed to know everything.

The thought of a stranger going through her belongings, touching her intimate items angered him. One thought roared through his head. *She is mine*! He tightened his hold, unconsciously squeezing her hair. She gasped against his mouth. Realizing what he had done, he wrenched his lips from hers and stepped away.

He would not lose control. Long ago he had learned that without it, he was nothing more than a monster. Now was neither the time nor the place for this. Walking over to his office window, Christian once more stared out into the darkness. He ached to turn around and look at Alyssa, but he needed to calm himself first. What was happening to him? This possessiveness he felt was new and not altogether comfortable. No other mortal had affected him like this since before he had been become a vampire. Why did she?

Elena.

Just the name of his ex-fiancé brought pain and guilt rushing back to him. Although over two hundred years had passed since he last saw her alive, time hadn't changed those feelings. That's what must have drawn him to Alyssa so quickly. Her straight dark hair, pert little nose, plump lips, intelligent eyes and delicately arched eyebrows reminded him of Elena. Other than the fact that Elena had brown eyes and Alyssa had blue ones, they looked almost exactly alike.

Relief coursed through him. Now he knew why he had been acting out of character. The two women looked so much alike that his ability to behave professionally with Alyssa was impaired. That was about to change. From now on, it would be all business between them. He would get her through her last three speaking engagements. Protect her from harm. Say goodbye. That would be that.

Alyssa floated in a sea of passion. Christian's lips moved expertly over hers. Sensations tingled from her mouth, down her body, all the way to her toes. She felt so alive. Every one of her senses became heightened. The feel of his warm hands massaging her neck, the tickle of his silky hair brushing her cheeks, his spicy male scent and the intimacy of his mouth as it explored hers. It all became too much. When his hand tightened in her hair, pulling it slightly, she initially only felt the pain. But as she tilted her head back, so that he could take her mouth more deeply, the pain turned into pleasure. She gasped from sensory overload.

Christian moved away. Without his touch, she felt cold. Slowly, the overwhelming feelings passed. She lifted her head and opened her eyes. The room came back into focus. She found Christian. He stared at her from across the room. The hot desire in his gaze was gone. Now she looked into a face made of granite and eyes as cold as ice.

"Alyssa—"

"No." She didn't want to hear whatever he was going to say. How embarrassing! She had been totally moved, no, *shaken* by their contact, while he obviously had felt very little.

"I need to go." She gathered her things as quickly as possible and headed towards the door. "I'll see you tomorrow as planned, right?"

Without giving him a chance to answer, she dashed out the door. He caught up with her just as she reached the parking lot and grabbed her arm.

"Alyssa, wait a minute."

Dreading the confrontation, but seeing no way to avoid it, she raised her gaze to his.

Christian looked almost as miserable as she felt.

"What happened back there was my fault. I apologize. I shouldn't have let that occur."

"You shouldn't have *let* that occur?" Alyssa repeated dumbfounded. "Well, I guess that's one way to look at it."

"I shouldn't have let myself lose control like that. I'm a professional and I usually have no problem acting like one."

"Christian, it's really no big deal. We kissed. There wasn't much else to it. Let's move on."

"No big deal?" Christian's eyes narrowed dangerously. "So you weren't at all affected?"

"Not really," she lied. "I mean there was a little spark, but nothing much."

"Right." He studied her intently.

"I'm sure you can be a professional when you want to be. So let's just go on that premise. From now on, it'll be just business between us. You'll protect me and I'll give my motivational speeches, okay?" she asked.

Alyssa saw Christian hesitate. Anger flashed in his eyes, then he shuttered his expression and slowly nodded in agreement.

"Works for me. I'll come by your house tomorrow night and look over your home security. We'll go from there to your speaking engagement."

"Fine. See you then," Alyssa said over her shoulder as she walked the remaining distance to her car, got in and drove away. She felt Christian's shrewd gaze following her. Sure enough, when she looked in her rearview mirror he was still standing in the parking lot, watching her.

* * * * *

Walking into her apartment, Alyssa enjoyed the rush of cool air. Though the sun was already down, the current heat wave had made her car feel like an oven. She popped a low fat frozen dinner into the microwave and poured herself a diet soda. As soon as she sat down at the table, Jonathan hopped up and began pacing back and forth in front of her.

"No, Jonathan. Not this time. I know you're always hungry, but you are *not* getting my dinner tonight. Go eat your cat food, buddy. You have a ton of it in your bowl."

Jonathan's only response was a low, pitiful meow. Alyssa petted him, but refused to budge.

"Don't do this to me. I will not feel guilty. You need to eat healthier. Look at me. I'm eating a low fat meal. I know, I know. It's filled with artificial everything and ingredients I can't even say, but it's *light*!"

The cat continued to stare at her. She ignored him and ate almost everything. Then guilt took over. She left one small piece of chicken on the plate and pushed it towards him.

"Here. That's all I can give you. Take it or leave it."

Jonathan began nibbling the morsel before Alyssa even finished her sentence and then licked the tray.

"Sheesh. If anyone came in and saw you right now, they'd think I don't feed you. Aren't cats supposed to *like* cat food?"

Jonathan licked up the last drop of gravy, swished his tail and jumped off the table.

"You're welcome!" she called as the feline sauntered out of the kitchen.

Alyssa washed the few dishes in the sink and wiped the table. She spent the next couple of hours going over her speech for the following night. When she felt prepared enough, she put her papers away and picked up the romance novel she was currently trying to read in her spare time. But she just couldn't concentrate on it. A problem arose every time she came to a love scene in the story. She kept imagining someone other than the character. Someone who had dark brown hair, mocha eyes that made her melt and a body that made her drool. The man screamed the word sexy, just by standing there. His name was Christian and he was a vampire.

The enormity of that finally hit her. Up to this point, she had been operating on autopilot. She put the book down and sat in stunned silence thinking about him. The man was a vampire! How was it possible? Why didn't people know they existed? And what about that hunky elf that popped his head in the door of Christian's office? Didn't he have pointy ears or something that gave his identity away? How could such creatures exist without being exposed?

Alyssa's thoughts rambled as she got ready for bed. She lay under the covers with the lights off, trying to remember how Christian had looked with glowing red eyes and two sharp, pointed teeth. The image wouldn't come. Instead she saw a gorgeous man with long dark hair that felt like silk, hands that made her body come alive and a mouth that knew just how to tempt her. She fell asleep, dreaming about him wearing a knight's outfit, charging to her rescue on a white horse. He was trying to save her from an unseen monster that chased her. The oddest part was the end of the dream. When the monster finally appeared, he turned out to be Christian.

* * * * *

When Christian arrived at Alyssa's condo the following night, he did a quick study of the outside perimeter, then rang the doorbell and waited. How was he going to handle this? He couldn't go into her apartment unless she invited him in. That was one of the few vampire myths that was actually true. Vampires could enter any public building without a problem, but entering a person's home was a different story. Humans had powers of their own when it came to their personal dwellings. No one seemed to understand how or why, but that power kept vampires from going into people's homes until they were invited. He needed Alyssa to do that, but wasn't sure how. When she opened the door, his worry instantly dissolved into male appreciation. He couldn't keep the wide grin from spreading across his lips. His gaze lingered over her from head to toe.

She was dressed in some sort of business suit. But it was like no suit he had ever seen. A pair of pants and a buttoned jacket, that's where the business part ended. The material looked soft, like silk and the color was a deep red rose. She wore no shirt beneath the jacket and the scooped neckline shifted his imagination into overdrive.

When his stare finally rose to her face, it looked flushed. She licked her lips nervously and he fixated on her pink tongue. She pointedly cleared her throat a second time and he finally realized she was talking.

"Please come in. I'm just about ready."

Christian followed her inside. Satisfaction coursed through him, while the predator he was roared in triumph. She had invited him in. Now he could enter her home whenever he wished.

He hoped the rest of the evening went as well, for both their sakes. But if not, he would be ready. He had made sure that he fed well before coming to Alyssa's house, for two reasons. The first was so that he would be at full strength in case of trouble and the second was so that Alyssa would not tempt him.

The three young men who had supplied him with sustenance would only remember drinking too much and passing out outside the bar they liked to frequent. Vlad had taught him long ago how to feed gently and replace a human's memory with one he planted for them. Christian had come a long way from the creature who used to rip out the throats of his victims as he fed, with little thought for them or their lives.

"I need another minute or so," Alyssa said. "Please sit down and I'll be right out."

Christian sat on the couch Alyssa motioned towards. He watched her walk away. The soft sway of her hips beneath the sensual material mesmerized him. His body's reaction was immediate and demanding. So much for feeding well so she didn't tempt him. It was obvious his body wanted more than just blood from her. Too bad it wasn't going to get it. He was here to protect her. Period.

Alyssa shut the bedroom door behind her. She leaned against it for support. No man had the right to look that good! The image of Christian standing there when she opened the front door was branded on her mind. His black button-up shirt stretched across his chest. Charcoal gray pants were tailor-fit. Expensive-looking black shoes matched his belt. His hair was tied at the back of his neck. She had to curl her fingers into a fist to keep from reaching out and setting his silky mane free. Somehow he looked professional, dangerous and incredibly sexy at the same time.

She got the impression that he was completely in his element as he stood in the semi-darkness among the shadows, just out of reach of the hall lights. The night seemed to embrace him, reluctant to release him as he stepped into her well lit apartment. When he brushed by her, his scent assaulted her sanity—spicy and seductive. Her stomach clenched in an effort to control the irresistible magnetism she felt towards him.

Why did Christian affect her like this? She usually had no problem dealing with men, gorgeous or otherwise, because she was in no hurry to establish any kind of serious relationship with them. Most men she knew sensed that immediately about her, or she told them flat out and they got the message. She had too much going on in her life at the moment to deal with a serious relationship.

For some reason her common sense approach wasn't working with Christian. The minute they were in the same room everything else faded in comparison. Her whole body focused on him.

It had to be the vampire thing. He must be using some sort of power over her. Didn't vampires have that kind of power? The kind that was difficult, if not impossible to resist? Great, just what she needed—another control freak like her dad. Well, vampire or no, she would keep things focused on business only.

In the bathroom, she began brushing her hair. She had planned to wear it loose tonight, but now she knew that would never do. Professional. She must look professional. Sweeping her hair up, she quickly fastened it into a bun. After applying lipstick, she stood back to take one last look in the mirror. Light makeup, hair in a bun and a business suit, understated and business-like. Just the message she wanted Christian to get. Grabbing her purse, she headed out of her room.

Christian had just managed to get himself under control when Alyssa reappeared.

"I'm ready. Shall we go?"

His gaze focused on her upswept hair and the way her graceful neck was exposed. He barely managed to hold in a groan as his body sprang to attention once more. Frustrated by his inability to control his reaction, his response came out much more harsh than he had planned.

"Let's get some things straight before we go anywhere. Sit down."

He knew his tone didn't sit well with Alyssa. Her posture stiffened. Anger and rebellion flashed in her eyes. She looked as if she was about to refuse, then changed her mind. She sat on the couch as far away from him as possible. Though she waited silently for him to say something, her eyes shot sparks. He smiled. She looked like she was about to scold him. His amusement must have annoyed her further, because she shot to her feet and glared down at him.

"I find nothing amusing about this! I'm prepared to listen to what you have to say, even let you tell me the best way to protect myself, but I will *not* be treated like a child!"

Christian's eyes roamed over her from head to toe and then back up again. When his eyes met hers once more, he didn't try to hide the hunger he felt. Alyssa's eyes widened in surprise and she gasped. She started to back away, but he shot his hand out and gently gripped her wrist.

He held her gaze with his.

"I think of you in many ways, *palomita,* but a child is not one of them." He ran the pad of his thumb over the pulse at her wrist. It was beating rapidly. Satisfaction ran through him. Good. She wasn't as immune as she pretended to be.

"Please sit down." He gave her wrist a slight tug. "We need to discuss some issues before we leave."

Alyssa allowed him to pull her down close beside him. When he released her, she scooted as far away as the couch allowed. But not before her enticing scent washed over him. He inhaled deeply. She smelled like sunshine and apples. Neither of which he had experienced for a very long time. A longing, unlike any he had known since turning immortal, swept through him. To be human again, to walk in the sunlight, find love and share his life with another.

No! He was undead, a creature of the night. There was nothing else. He had to live this way because of Elena's murder. She had been killed because of him. Therefore he was a murderer. He accepted and lived with his guilt. Alyssa was light and life. He was darkness and death. The two would not mix, he wouldn't, no couldn't, let them.

"First of all, tell me more about what you do. Understanding what you speak to people about may help me understand your stalker. And it might help me figure out what he plans in the future."

Alyssa didn't answer him at first. She studied him warily, as if she wasn't sure what he would do next. He couldn't blame her. He wasn't so sure himself. Especially where she was concerned.

She finally spoke.

"What do I do? Well, I talk to people about issues that directly impact their lives and ways to deal with those issues."

"Like what?"

"Stress, for instance. It's a very big problem in today's society. Not only can it cause relationships to end, marriages to break up and families to become dysfunctional, it also results in more frequent illnesses and trips to the doctor. Although it is an emotional response, it's also very physical as well. And a continual bombardment of stress on the body can and will result in physical sickness."

"So, what do you tell people to do?"

"I don't tell them to do anything. I just talk about how people can decide to do certain things that will improve their quality of life. I also talk about how some choices change lives in a negative way. It all comes down to choice. And balance."

"*Balance*, that's the name of your book. Is this what it's about?"

"Yes. Basically it's about how people get consumed with the negative and then forget to find time for positive moments in their day-to-day existence. That leads to a stressful life, emotionally and physically."

"What made you write it?"

"I was seeing a pattern, sort of a trend in what people were coming to talk to me about. A lot seemed to have problems rooted in a stress-filled environment. It was causing everything from depression, to eating disorders, to couples not having intimacy in their relationship. The effect of prolonged stress on people is enormous. And most of the individuals who come to see me don't even realize it's happening. It's an insidious problem. It creeps into a person's life and grows if not addressed."

"So you teach people how to be less stressed out?"

"What I try to show people is that stress doesn't have to be a controlling agent in their life. They can manage and contain it, if they dedicate themselves to making the right choices. They need to get in touch with themselves and what they want in their life."

Christian's admiration for Alyssa grew as she spoke. She was intelligent, beautiful and so full of light. It wasn't just the words she said, either. It was how she said them. The warmth in her voice was unmistakable. She cared about people, about what they were feeling and what happened in their lives. And she wanted to help them. He could see how people would get lost in her voice, mesmerized by the hope in her words. She didn't have to be a vampire to do that, either. She did it all on her own.

Christian shook his head. Cleared his mind. *Focus. He needed to concentrate on the business at hand. She was a mortal, nothing more.* He cleared his throat. All business.

"Let's go over the plan for this evening."

He pulled a folded sheet of paper from his pocket, opened it and laid it on her coffee table. It was an architectural diagram of the Grady Gammage Auditorium in Tempe, the location of her speaking event that evening. All the entrances and exits as well as the various rooms were clearly outlined, some areas crossed off and others highlighted.

He pointed as he spoke. "We'll go in this side entrance. You'll stay very close to me as we walk through here and follow all directives I give. Here's the room that's been set up for you to wait in. You'll let me go in first to check it out, then, when I signal you, you may come in. I've spoken extensively with the security team there and they're going to work with us as much as we need. But keep in mind one thing. You must trust no one but me tonight. If they say jump up and I say get down, you need to follow my orders first and foremost. Your life is completely in my hands tonight. Do you understand that?"

"Yes."

That was all she said. It surprised him. He had expected a fight and right now he felt ready for one. His body was screaming for something he refused to give it, but he needed some way to relieve it.

"Fine." He gritted his teeth. Control. It was all about control. He took a deep breath and slowly released it as he glanced around the room. "I'd like to review the interior security in your apartment before we go. I checked the outside, but need to see the inside before I can make recommendations."

Confusion marred her brow. "What recommendations?"

"Alyssa, your life is in danger. If someone is willing to attack you, they also may consider invading your home to get to you."

Alyssa said nothing, yet her stunned expression indicated that the thought of someone coming to her home hadn't entered her mind. As much as he didn't like to see her fear, he felt that she needed to know what could happen. That was one policy he maintained with all his clients. He was upfront about the potential threats against them, measures they could take to protect themselves and ways in which he would strive to protect them.

"But I live in a gated apartment complex," she protested. "Surely that must offer some protection against this type of thing?"

"Only minimal. Do you mind if I take a quick look around?" Without waiting for her answer, he started towards her bedroom. "I'll start in here."

Alyssa was still trying to digest his disregard for the security offered by her apartment complex when she realized where Christian was headed. She sucked in a gasp, then let out an ear-splitting shriek.

"No, wait!"

Not her bedroom! She definitely didn't need a good-looking and totally sexy vampire in her bedroom right now. Besides, her bedroom was in a state of chaos, with undergarments strewn everywhere. She had to do something to stop him.

Racing past him, she blocked the doorway before he could go through. He stopped inches from her, a little too close for comfort, but she held her ground. Their gazes met. He lifted one eyebrow in question.

"Is there a problem?"

His voice brushed against her senses like a feather. Chills ran up her spine. She tried to ignore it.

"Yes, there *is* a problem," she said. She lifted her chin proudly. "I don't want you in my bedroom, thank you very much. If you want to look around the rest of the apartment you may, but please stay out of this room."

Alyssa could swear that she saw a twinkle of amusement in Christian's eyes, but then it was gone. Had she only imagined it? His eyes did little more at the moment than reflect her face in their milk chocolate depths.

"I need to look over the whole apartment, *palomita*. That includes your bedroom." His tone was quiet, but adamant. He was going to look in her room whether she wanted him to or not.

Christian tried to move past her, but she slid in front of him, once more blocking him.

"Wait," she said again, this time breathlessly. Christian was so close to her she felt his clothing brush across hers. Tingles of awareness ran up and down her spine.

He didn't seem to notice. His face turned stony and his eyes narrowed.

"Alyssa, we don't have much time. We need to leave soon so that we arrive early enough to go through the security procedure I laid out to you. Move away from the door so I can check out your room."

"No."

"No?" His eyebrow lifted arrogantly.

Her no sounded firm. But when Christian said no, it sounded threatening. And the brooding expression on his face was no comfort. Somehow she needed to diffuse this situation—quickly.

"My room's a mess. I need to pick up a couple of things first. Why don't you look through the other bedroom and the rest of the apartment? By the time you're done, I'll be ready for you to come in here, okay?"

Christian looked like he was about to argue, but then gave her a curt nod.

"I'll be right out." Alyssa slammed the door in Christian's face, but was too worried about the state of her room to think much about it.

How was she going to get this place presentable in a couple of minutes? She picked up all the clothing on the floor and dumped it into the hamper. She was *so* behind on laundry! Next she picked up books lying open on her desk and bed and carefully stored them on the shelf in her closet. She had checked out books about vampires at the library earlier in the day, but she didn't want Christian to know she was investigating him.

She scanned the room. With the clothes and books put away, it didn't look half bad, but she still wasn't happy with it. A second later, Christian gave the door a cursory knock and then strode in without waiting for her to open it. He walked directly to her window and checked it thoroughly. He scanned the rest of her room, an intense expression on his face and then headed back towards the door.

What had she been so worried about? Alyssa's sigh of relief got caught in her throat as Christian stopped short before walking out of her room. Slowly, he reached towards something hanging on her wall.

When Alyssa saw what it was, her eyes widened in shock. She moved forward. Trying to reach it before he did but couldn't. Her world suddenly changed to slow motion. His hand wrapping around the object became her whole focus, as if a camera was doing a close-up shot. He turned towards her and she cringed at the amused curiosity in his gaze.

He raised a large strand of garlic up in the air.

"Planning on doing some Italian cooking? In your bedroom?"

Chapter Four

ꟹ

Alyssa wanted to crawl under a rock. The whole idea of buying the garlic had seemed good when she was at the grocery store earlier today, but now it just seemed really, really dumb. The books she read had all said garlic was good protection against vampires! Yet it seemed to have little effect on Christian as he turned around and hung it back on the wall.

"Don't believe everything you read, *palomita*." He turned and left the room, but not before she saw that irritating, knowing smirk spread across his mouth.

Darn it! The man was just too smug for his own good.

"I'm ready to go now," he called from the other room.

"Fine. I'll be there in a minute."

Alyssa took a little bit longer than necessary, just to annoy Christian. So what if she was acting childish? So what if this went against everything she spoke to people about? It felt good! Thinking about speaking made her realize that she needed to get a move on. She didn't want to be late.

"Ready!"

Alyssa left her bedroom and found Christian waiting impatiently by the open door. Finally having her chance to irritate him, she let mischief get the best of her common sense. With an extra sway in her hips, she brushed by him and smiled seductively. She could have sworn she heard a soft growl as she passed him. But he said nothing as they entered the elevator.

Not until she pushed the first-floor button and the car started to descend, did she realize she was in trouble. Christian reached over and held the *Door Close* button, suspending them between floors. He moved closer, until he towered over her.

Trying to gauge his mood, Alyssa looked into his eyes. They were dark and unreadable. Placing his free hand at the base of her neck, he began drawing little circles with his fingers. Sparks of pleasure shot throughout her body. When he moved so close she could feel his hard chest pressed against hers, her heart sped out of control.

"I don't like to be teased, Alyssa."

Christian lowered his mouth towards hers. When he spoke, each word brushed air against her lips. They tingled in response, ached for something more. As if sensing her need, he ran his tongue lightly over her bottom lip, then her top. He blew softly. His actions inflamed her. Alyssa wanted more. Leaning forward, she tried to touch her mouth to his, but he pulled back. She attempted to move forward again, but he gently grasped the back of her neck and held her in place.

She gritted her teeth in frustration. Suddenly she wanted the contact more than breathing. She needed, no she *had* to touch him. Now. Her self-control disappeared as he shifted his body. His chest brushed across hers, leaving her nipples sensitive and swollen. She couldn't hold back her needy moan. Christian smiled knowingly. He knew she was his for the taking.

"You must never forget, *palomita*, that two can play this game. And I have had much more practice than you."

Christian released her, let go of the *Door Close* button and moved to the other side of the elevator. Although he appeared cool and calm, he was anything but that. Back in her apartment, when she had looked so seductive and tempting, he had wanted to slam the door shut and take her then and there, damn the consequences. He barely controlled himself as she passed by, the scent of apples following in her wake.

She was teasing him and that he would not tolerate. The monster stayed leashed inside him because he chose to keep it there. It had not been a problem for a long time, but if she continued to play with him, he knew the beast would come out. And he was sure it would frighten her.

She looked scared now, as the elevator stopped and the doors opened, but he didn't think it was because of him. He had a feeling Alyssa had her own beast inside that wanted to break free. That scared her. He already knew she valued being in control, so he understood how she must feel right now. Nevertheless, she needed to know he would not stand for her teasing. It could easily turn dangerous for them both. He needed to concentrate on her protection. She needed to concentrate on getting through her next three speaking engagements—and staying alive.

The evening started out as planned. Alyssa was very quiet as they drove to the auditorium in his car. He didn't interrupt her silence. He kept his mind where it belonged—*on the job.* Once they arrived, he escorted her to the room they had prepared. He had scanned the building while they walked, but didn't see or sense anything out of place or unusual.

He checked her room thoroughly. Satisfied that she was safe in the small waiting room, he said, "I'm going to do one more scan of the building. Lock the door as soon as I leave and don't let anyone but me in. Understand?"

Alyssa hadn't spoken since they left her apartment. She acted startled by his voice. Her far-off gaze shifted and focused on him.

"What?" She looked confused, disoriented.

What was she thinking about? Her eyes looked vulnerable, they called to him— No. He was here to do a job. Nothing more.

"I'm going to check out the building. Stay here, lock the door and don't let anyone except me in." His voice was gruff and unyielding, even to his own ears.

Her lips thinned and her brow furrowed. He knew that look. She was irritated.

"Fine," she said.

That was her only reply before turning away, as if he no longer existed. Then she began rummaging through her bag.

"Fine," he said through clenched teeth. He slammed the door a little harder than necessary as he left the room.

Alyssa's shoulders slumped. She released a loud sigh as Christian left the room. Her body was shaking from the effort not to cry. She would not let this happen. She had seen what it had done to her mother and promised herself she would never live that way. Waiting expectantly for a man to come home, revolving her whole life around him, basing all her decisions, big or small, on what he thought. That was no way to live. Her mother's suicide was proof of that.

Back in that elevator, for just a sliver of a moment, she had wanted to do exactly that, whatever it took to please Christian. To forget who she was and try to be who he wanted her to be, to make him desire her as much as she desired him. She had lost her self-control.

Shame washed over her. She had never let this happen before. Why him? Why now? It had to be the uncertainty of her situation. The fact that she had so little say in what was going on. But one thing she knew for certain, it wouldn't happen again. She couldn't let it. She would keep her distance from Christian. That was the only way. And when her last motivational speech was done, she would say goodbye to him forever.

She spent the remainder of her time alone studying her speech. It still amazed her that she had ended up using the speaking circuit to promote her book. She had always hated talking in front of people. One on one she was fine, but when it came to public speaking, she froze up like an icicle. Somehow that changed when she met her publicist. He told her she had to do these motivational talks if she wanted her book to sell.

He helped her realize that the anxiety she felt about speaking wasn't worthy of her time. That she needed to put her energy towards more productive activities, like helping people by selling her book. Once she looked at it that way, her perspective changed. Her publicist gave her some tips on public speaking and she had no problem after that. Once she concentrated on what she was saying rather than the setting she was in, her anxiety disappeared.

Someone knocked on the door. She got up to open it and then remembered Christian's warning.

"Who is it?" she asked quietly.

There was no response. Yet there was. She saw the doorknob slowly twist. Someone was testing the lock. The room's temperature dropped substantially. She began to shiver from the cold. An overwhelming sense of discord hit her like a slap to the face. The doorknob rattled. She took an unconscious step back. Somehow she knew. Whatever was on the other side of that door was evil. And it meant her harm.

Alyssa stared in horror at the doorknob. It stopped rattling. Then she heard it. It was a subtle but distinct sound, carried on the wind. The fact that there was no wind inside a building meant nothing. She heard it and that wasn't all. It was someone whispering her name, someone calling to her. And it pulled at her. It reached inside her. She had to go to it. The wind brushed against her, pushed her forward. She didn't question it. The voice needed her. How could she say no?

Her legs propelled her towards the door before she was aware of thinking about it. She reached it in no time. She grasped the doorknob. In that moment the smell washed over her. Sweet, that was her first thought—sweet, yet something more, too much more. It permeated everything. Made her dizzy. Her thoughts clouded, then suddenly cleared and crystallized into one idea. She had to open the door, now.

She began to unlock it. She needed to get out. The voice kept whispering, endlessly pressing her on. There. It was unlocked. Alyssa slowly twisted the knob. The door began to open.

The whispering in her head abruptly stopped and the wind brushing against her ceased. The sickly sweet smell disappeared.

The urgent need to open the door was gone. Fear and shock instantly replaced that need. Then she heard it.

A screech so loud it ricocheted throughout her head. She covered her ears. Yet the sound was just as loud. She realized then that she wasn't hearing the sound, it was coming from inside her mind. Her knees buckled and she went down hard. Then everything went black.

* * * * *

Christian scanned the auditorium. People were starting to file in. It looked like Alyssa was going to have a full house tonight. He was looking forward to hearing her speak. Whatever she was saying got people's attention and they liked it. He had done some investigating and found out that Alyssa and her new book, *Balance,* were a hot item right now. She had made a number of the bestseller lists. Her down-to-earth, back-to-basic approach to getting your life in order and trying to live a personally productive and meaningful life was striking a chord with the stressed out, "no time to stop", "have to climb to the top of the corporate ladder" population of today.

Of course, some people didn't like that. They didn't like change. They didn't like someone stirring up the waters. Christian thought that was the type of person stalking Alyssa. She had somehow disrupted someone's life and that person resented her for it. It seemed the logical explanation.

He remembered how the disruption of his life had affected him. In one night his fiancée was brutally murdered and he was turned into a vampire. He wasn't happy with the world in general at that time and especially not with Bazhena. During the short duration that she had kept him on her leash, his only thought was murder. He wanted her dead and he would do whatever he could to accomplish that. She had altered his life forever and killed the woman he loved. At that time it hadn't mattered that he caused his own troubles by questioning his love, and lusting after Bazhena. She was to blame and he wanted to make her pay for it. He went crazy from the rage and rational thought was not part of his life for a time. He took revenge often, wherever and on whomever he felt like.

Alyssa's stalker hadn't reached that stage, yet. But he was getting closer to it, closer to her. And as his anger and frustration grew, so would the severity of his actions. So far, Alyssa was the only one at risk, but others could be hurt. If they got in the way, they could be killed. And once that step had been taken, there was no turning back.

He remembered the first time he had killed someone in his anger to get back at Bazhena. Although he had no power over her at that time, he had power over mortals. He fed and killed. He was vicious and cruel, causing his victim as much pain as possible. It had been intoxicating. Addicting. It had momentarily satisfied him. If Alyssa's stalker got a taste of that, there was no telling how many people he would kill.

Christian did one more check of the perimeter, then talked to the on-site security team. They said everything was going as planned. Nothing unusual. But Christian wasn't satisfied. Something wasn't right. He couldn't place it, but he felt the disturbance in the air. As he headed back to Alyssa's room, the feeling got stronger and stronger. When he realized the implication of that, the awareness hit him. He could feel the danger and he could sense Alyssa's fear. He raced forward, using his mind to scan what he couldn't see.

Bazhena. He would know her sickly sweet, cloying smell anywhere. She was trying to get to Alyssa. Christian slammed his mind into Bazhena's, jamming her thoughts with his own. Because she had created him, they had a mental bond that was difficult to break. He had forgotten how sick her mind was and almost recoiled from the evil he felt. But he held on, pushing at her, diverting her attention from Alyssa. Bazhena was surprised by his presence. She had been giving her full concentration to Alyssa. This gave him a momentary advantage. Before she could switch to him, Christian sent Bazhena a violent mental push. It was designed to wreak havoc with her brain and cause incredible pain.

He heard Bazhena's mind scream, then her presence was suddenly gone. He knew she would be out of commission for the rest of the night. He reached Alyssa's door and pushed it open. He found her crumpled on the floor, unconscious.

Alyssa slowly opened her eyes. It hurt too much. Seeing could wait. She shut them again.

"You must open your eyes some time, *palomita*."

Her eyes opened wide at the sound of Christian's amused voice and she grimaced in pain. His softly teasing tone sent tingles up and down her body. She realized two things at once. She was lying on the floor. And Christian was holding her. The first fact left her curious. The second made her downright confused. She looked around, studiously avoiding Christian's eyes. She already knew what those eyes did to her. She didn't need any more confusion at the moment.

"What happened?" She tried to sit up, but Christian kept her in his arms.

Her gaze swung to his then. What was going on?

"I'm not sure. I think you must have gotten dizzy and fainted. I found you lying on the floor when I walked in," he said.

"Fainted? I don't faint." She quickly dismissed his explanation. Her brow furrowed in concentration. Why couldn't she remember?

"The last thing I remember is going over my speech. Then waking up on the floor. In your arms." Alyssa looked pointedly at his arms around her.

The feel of him holding her was starting to take its toll. Although she didn't know what had happened, her body was very aware of what was going on right now. Christian held her so that he supported her head, the upper half of her body cradled in his lap. His hands lay just below her breasts. All he had to do was move them up an inch and she would probably lose it. Right there in the dressing room. Lose control and attack him.

The desire burning in his gaze didn't help matters. It scorched her. She shifted her body restlessly and encountered something very hard pressed against her back. She froze. Christian's eyes narrowed dangerously and he started clenching and unclenching his jaw. He looked like he was in pain.

This time when she tried to sit up, he didn't stop her. She scrambled to her feet. Dizziness overwhelmed her. She had to steady herself by grabbing the nearby chair. After a minute or so, the feeling passed and she let go. Christian was watching her warily, cautiously, as if he wasn't sure what she would do.

Ignore it. That's what she would do. She was not about to acknowledge the fact that the man made her knees weak. Stick to the business at hand. That's what she had to do. She jumped slightly when Christian interrupted her little internal pep talk.

"How are you feeling?" he asked.

Other than the fact that she wanted to jump his bones, she was feeling much better.

"Better." That was all she could manage.

"Why don't we cancel your speech for tonight?" he suggested.

That got her attention back to business.

"No," she declared. "Those people bought my book. They came tonight to hear me talk. I need to do this. Don't worry. The dizziness has passed and I'm feeling much better. It was probably just nerves."

"Are you sure?"

"Yes. Positive."

Christian studied her silently until she felt like squirming, then he nodded his head. Alyssa released the breath she hadn't known she was holding.

"Fine, but take it easy out there. I'll be to the right of you, backstage if you need me. Just look my way and I'll come to you," Christian said.

"Okay. I'll keep that in mind."

Alyssa's talk went flawlessly. She put her whole self into it like she usually did and was exhausted by the time Christian helped her gather her things and drove her home. The positive energy in the theater had been strong. For some reason, whenever she gave these speeches she picked up on the audience's feelings. Not each and every person, but the group as a whole. Most people had been very open to her speech. She hoped she had touched someone's life in a helpful way tonight.

As Christian walked her to her door, she felt relieved. She was glad the stalker hadn't appeared. She felt confident that Christian would have handled the situation if something had happened, but the experience would have shaken her. Maybe his presence alone would keep the creep away. She hoped so.

Christian hadn't said much to her after her speech or on the drive home, so the sound of his gruff voice came as a surprise when they reached her apartment door.

"I need to do one last walk through before I go. I'm sure everything's fine, but I want to make sure."

Alyssa didn't want him in her apartment again. It was unsettling. She was exhausted and just wanted to crawl into bed and go to sleep. But when she looked into Christian's eyes she knew that wasn't going to happen. He wasn't taking no for an answer. She gritted her teeth in frustration. Sometimes the man reminded her of a pit bull! Not letting go of something until he was good and ready.

"Fine. Let's get this over with so I can get some sleep."

She opened the door and he followed her inside.

"Jonathan, where are you?" she called out.

The next moment was a blur. Christian grabbed her arm, swung her around and hauled her up against him.

"Who's Jonathan?" he snarled.

The anger in his eyes left her speechless. She couldn't find the words to answer him because the ferociousness of his gaze was such a shock. His eyes narrowed to slits. He grasped her shoulders and gave her a little shake. It didn't hurt, but it got her attention, as it was meant to do.

"I asked you a question, Alyssa. Who is Jonathan? Your boyfriend? Your *lover*?" As Christian spoke his voice grew deeper and deeper, until it sounded almost like a low growl.

Alyssa remained frozen in shock until the meaning of his words finally penetrated. Then a wide smile spread across her lips. Christian thought Jonathan was a man. A soft chuckle escaped her lips.

She started to tell Christian who and what Jonathan was, but didn't get the chance.

"I see nothing funny about this situation, *palomita*. I want an answer from you now, do you understand?" His voice didn't sound like his own. It was deep and gravelly and the growl was now definitely in his voice.

Christian grasped her chin gently, but firm enough that she knew she couldn't break his hold without a real struggle. He tilted her face up to him so that their eyes met.

"I sense no other human presence in your apartment. I will ask you one more time. Give you one more chance to answer of your own free will. Who is Jonathan?" His gaze was penetrating and demanding.

Alyssa couldn't answer if her life depended on it. She got lost in Christian's mocha eyes. She felt like he was drinking her with his gaze and she didn't want him to stop. When he bent his head, her reaction was immediate. Her lips tingled for his kiss. Her breasts swelled and her nipples pebbled against his chest. A pulsating ache started in the pit of her stomach and moved lower to settle permanently at her core.

His lips touched hers, almost, but not quite. She groaned and strained upward. He held her in place.

"Do you want me, Alyssa? Do you ache for me?" He whispered each question against her lips. Each word affected her like he was physically touching her. "I feel your breasts tightening against my chest. Do you know what I want to do to them? I want to worship them with my hands, mouth and tongue. I want to savor your nipples like sweet summer berries. Draw on them until I've had my fill. Would you like that, Alyssa? All you have to do is answer my question, *palomita*."

Her knees felt weak. She was lost in a haze of desire. What was the question again? Her world suddenly narrowed down to one thing. She had to feel his lips on her, had to feel his sexy mouth against her body. What was that damn question? She couldn't remember.

"Who is Jonathan?" Christian repeated.

Right, that was it. She could answer that question.

"My cat."

"Your cat?"

"Yes. You know, my pet?"

"I see. Your cat."

His voice sounded tight now. Then nothing. He continued to stare deeply into her eyes, but that was it.

Alyssa squirmed restlessly against Christian. She had answered his question. Why didn't he kiss her? She had enough of waiting. She needed him now. She placed her hand behind his head and pulled him closer. His lips touched hers and she practically screamed with satisfaction. His mouth moved gently, expertly over hers. When she tentatively touched her tongue to his, he groaned and deepened the kiss.

Christian was stunned. He couldn't believe what had just happened. He had never felt jealous over another man in all his long existence. But the thought that Alyssa had been with someone else had incensed him to the point that he would have killed the man if he had been in the same room. One thought ran fast and furious through his head again and again. *She is mine.*

He had been so enraged that he used mind control on Alyssa. Took away her free will. When she told him Jonathan was her cat, his sanity returned. As he looked down into her passion-glazed eyes, he pulled back mentally and waited. Nothing changed. She was free of his thrall. She should have pulled away from him, come to her senses. But she didn't. Alyssa was still straining to get closer to him, pressing against him. When she pulled his head closer to hers and kissed him, he didn't argue. This was not his doing. She wanted him. Savage satisfaction filled him. Good. He wanted her too. He was tired of fighting it.

Christian explored her lips, enjoying their softness. When her tongue touched his, desire hit him like a punch to the stomach. He growled low in his throat. He delved between her lips, enjoying her sweetness. His senses were enflamed by her enthusiastic response. He pulled her closer. He couldn't get enough.

Alyssa's hands wandered restlessly over him. She was telling him without words how much she wanted him. Each touch of her fingers left him struggling for control. It had been so long since he let someone this close. He tried taking deep, cleansing breaths to slow his need. He didn't want to hurt her. Since his change, his physical reactions had become stronger, more intense. He wasn't sure she'd be able to take the full brunt of his passion, yet.

When her hands slipped under his shirt and played over his stomach, he almost lost it. Enough! He couldn't hold back any longer. He needed, no, had to touch her now. Placing his hands over hers, he slid them around her waist behind her back. He held her hands there with one hand and used his free hand to unbutton her suit jacket. Kissing her deeply, his tongue engaged hers in an intimate dance again and again. Alyssa moaned. She strained against his hold, tried to press closer to him. He groaned in relief when her jacket finally came free. Sliding his hand over her soft stomach, he felt it quiver from his touch. Christian smiled against her lips. He liked knowing she was so sensitive to his touch.

Slipping his hand up along her rib cage, he encountered the edge of her bra. Alyssa pulled away, drew in a sharp breath and held it. She was waiting. His fingers played along the lacy edge. She shuddered. Christian found the front clasp of her bra and deftly undid it. No matter what the time period, he and women's lingerie had always worked easily together. Her full breasts sprang free. Alyssa broke their kiss and leaned her head on his shoulder. She was struggling to catch her breath. He paused, his hand hovering over her breast. Did she want him to continue or stop?

Christian held onto his control by a thin thread. He had to be sure she wanted this. If she said no after this point, he didn't know if he could stop.

"Touch me," Alyssa gasped.

That was all the encouragement he needed. Covering her breast with his hand, he savored its soft fullness. A perfect fit. He ran his thumb back and forth over her nipple. It pebbled and tightened from his touch. His mouth watered at the thought of that sweetness in his mouth. He rained kisses down her neck. He pressed his mouth against her pulse, ran his tongue over the spot. Another kind of hunger took over. He smelled her blood, smelled her life force and fought against sinking his teeth into her soft flesh.

Alyssa arched her back and made a soft mewling sound. He dragged his mouth downward. Her body was calling to him. He let that guide his hunger. He leaned forward, making her arch her back. Her jacket parted and her breasts thrust upward, offering him a feast he couldn't resist. He suckled each breast until her nipples were bright red and swollen, stiff and wet from his worship. Alyssa's moans were getting louder. Her need was driving him crazy. Her desire was slamming into him at two levels, physical and mental. Not only could he see and hear her body's reaction to his touch, he could feel the desire consuming her mind. Her thoughts reached him in erotic wave after wave.

Christian slid his mouth over her stomach and ran his tongue over her soft curves. Delving into her belly button, he felt another shiver overwhelm her. His lips traveled lower, to the waistband of her pants. He couldn't resist running his tongue back and forth under the fabric. This time, Alyssa's stomach jumped from his touch. He only realized he had released her hands when he felt her fingers running through his hair, urging him on. Grasping her hands, he lifted his head to meet her desire-filled gaze.

Christian knew, without a doubt, he could take her. He could seduce her body to the point that she was pleading with him to make love to her. But he didn't want it that way. Not with Alyssa. He had to know she wanted him.

"Alyssa, are you sure? Tell me now, *palomita,* because if we continue, I won't be able to stop. Do you understand?"

Alyssa nodded, but he waited patiently. He wanted to hear her make this decision. Say the words. Her eyes pulled at him, the heat in them screaming her desire.

"I need you to tell me, Alyssa. I won't go on until I know for sure that this is what you want."

"I want you, Christian. Don't stop." Her voice was throaty, filled with passion.

He needed no other urging. With a growl he let the predator in him loose. Alyssa was his.

Chapter Five

ꟃ

Christian slowly worked Alyssa's pants lower. Her skin felt like the silky material of her suit. He splayed his fingers over the soft curve of her stomach. The image of a baby growing inside her came crashing into his consciousness. His hands stilled their exploration. His body shook as unfamiliar emotions washed over him. He had never thought about children before. Why now? How did this mortal affect him so profoundly?

Alyssa squeezed her fingers tightly in his hair. She made needy sounds in her throat. He hardened to the point of pain. His thoughts reverted to only hunger and need. She pulled his head to her body. The scent of green apples and sunshine filled his senses. Wrapping his hands around her waist, he pulled her closer. He skimmed his lips and tongue over her skin, savoring the taste of her. Moving lower, he got lost in the delights of her body.

The sound didn't reach him until he felt Alyssa stiffen. The persistent rap rubbed him the wrong way. He raised his head and glared at the sound. Someone was knocking on Alyssa's apartment door. Christian growled. He pressed closer to her and his hold tightened possessively. *She Is Mine!* That thought pounded over and over in his head as the beast threatened to overtake him.

Not now. Not *now*! Alyssa needed this, needed Christian in a way she had never experienced before. To stop would be difficult, even painful. The feel of his mouth, lapping at her, his hands holding her tight, his silky hair beneath her fingers. It was too good.

She thought about ignoring the knock. Maybe whoever was pounding on the door would go away. The knocking continued, louder, until it became a frantic staccato that she feared would never stop.

"Alyssa? Honey, are you in there?"

Alyssa's shoulder's sagged in resignation. She had to answer the door. She had forgotten that she promised to meet her aunt here after her speech. And knowing her aunt, if she didn't answer the door, it wouldn't be too long until she called the police. Ever since Alyssa's mother committed suicide, her Aunt Joyce had become the proverbial protective mother hen. Most of the time, Alyssa appreciated her aunt's concern, but now was definitely not one of those times.

With a groan, she reluctantly pulled her hands from Christian's hair and tried to push away from him. His only response was a soft growl. She looked down as he slowly raised his head. She gasped. The black pupils of his eyes had become red. Dilated to the point that almost no white showed. Nobody she knew was in those eyes. They were cold and empty. A shiver slid down her spine. Two elongated teeth protruded when his lips curled into a snarl. Alyssa stood as still as possible. Knowing somehow that if she moved, it would make things worse.

A loud knock sounded at the door again. She almost jumped. Christian's gaze narrowed warily, watching, waiting for her to try to bolt.

"Alyssa, are you there? It's Aunt Joyce. Open the door. Is everything okay?"

Christian's gaze swung from hers to the door. She felt his whole body shudder. Then he slowly loosened his hold. It seemed hours before he finally dropped his hands to his sides. Alyssa felt relieved and bereft at the same time. Slowly she backed away. Christian continued to watch her with cold eyes. She feared he might jump up and grab her again. Instead, he dropped his head into his hands and groaned. The sound was filled with pain. His face was now hidden behind the strands of hair she had ruffled with her fingers. It fell around him like a silky curtain. She had the urge to go to him. Run her fingers through his mane. Make the pain go away.

Another knock broke the spell.

Alyssa adjusted her clothing and strode towards the door.

"Just a minute, Aunt Joyce," she called out.

She placed her hand on the doorknob, but didn't turn it. She took a deep breath. Counted to ten, then turned back towards Christian.

He was gone. Startled, she did a quick sweep of her apartment, but found no sign of him. He had left her apartment through some way other than the door. That chilled her as she let her aunt in.

"Alyssa, why didn't you—look at you! You're shivering! What's going on?"

Her aunt's concern warmed Alyssa somewhat, but she still couldn't shake the feelings created by Christian. It was like he had become something else, something not quite human. She knew, of course, on a conscious level that he had already admitted to being a vampire. But that knowledge and seeing the actual phenomenon were two different kettles of fish.

Without answering Alyssa turned around and walked away. Her legs suddenly felt shaky. She collapsed on the couch with a loud sigh. Too much had happened too fast. She needed to get a handle on things, but she wasn't sure how. Her aunt closed the door, sat down beside her and placed her arm comfortingly around Alyssa's shoulders. The warmth and love Alyssa felt encouraged her to talk.

"Christian just, uh, left."

Alyssa wasn't prepared to explain exactly how.

Her aunt's expression turned shrewd and a little smile played on her mouth.

"Christian? Oh, Mr. Galiano."

"Yes, he brought me home a little while ago."

"I see."

That was her aunt's only comment.

Alyssa continued.

"The evening went fairly well. Except for the fact that I fainted."

Her aunt's brows furrowed with concern.

"Fainted? You've never fainted in your life, sweetie. What happened? Are you feeling ill?"

"No, I'm fine. And the strange thing is I don't remember what happened. All I recall is being by myself in my room at the auditorium, then waking up in Christian's arms."

Her aunt raised one eyebrow and her smile widened.

"You woke up in Mr. Galiano's arms?"

"Yes."

Her aunt said nothing. She merely waited silently, with an expectant smile on her face. Alyssa resisted saying anything more, but when her aunt kept smiling and waiting, she finally gave up with an exasperated sigh. Her aunt wasn't going anywhere until she filled in her experience with some details.

Alyssa told her the rest of the story, except for the most intimate parts and the part about Christian's disappearance. She wasn't ready to analyze either of those events, yet. It was always like this with her aunt. Even though Alyssa was the trained therapist, her Aunt Joyce always knew how to get her to talk.

From the time she was a small child, her aunt had been there to help her through the rough times. Not her mother, who was often "sick" in her room with one malady or another. Not her father, who thought being a parent meant criticizing his only child for the things she wasn't good at, and trying to force her to do what he felt she should. Her Aunt Joyce had always been the one who took time to listen and understand.

Even after her mother's suicide, when Alyssa had closed herself off from the rest of the world, her aunt had managed to get through to her. Alyssa had become numb after her mother's death. Too scared to let her feelings in because she knew they would be filled with pain and guilt.

Pain because her mother was dead. Pain because she hadn't loved her daughter enough to stick it out in this world. And guilt. Because Alyssa hadn't seen what was happening to her mother. It didn't matter that she was a teenager, it didn't matter that her mother was the adult. She should have seen what was happening and helped her mother before it was too late. But she hadn't. And Alyssa had known that if she let those feelings in, they would eat away at her, until she didn't know what would be left. So she blocked out the rest of the world—her friends, her overbearing father and even her beloved aunt.

Her withdrawal lasted three months. Her father had tried yelling at her, over and over. But that only had made her withdraw further. Alyssa didn't do her schoolwork. Her grades dropped. She never went out with her friends or had them over. After the first two months, all but a couple of them stopped calling. She just sat in her room, trying to hold back the tidal wave of emotion that was building inside of her. Whatever it took, she was determined to keep everything inside, until she felt like she was going to explode. But she refused to let herself lose control. That's what her mother had done. And look what happened to her.

Her aunt had left Alyssa alone during that initial period. Looking back, she wasn't sure why. Maybe her aunt felt she needed the time to adjust, or maybe she just wasn't sure what to do. Either way, at the end of three months her aunt had had enough. She stormed into the house and told Alyssa's father to get out and only come back when she called him. He had refused. Alyssa sat in fascination, watching their exchange. She would never forget the look on her aunt's face as she gently led Alyssa to her room and quietly asked her to stay there until she came to get her. She had never seen her aunt look so angry.

She closed Alyssa's door and her aunt and father had a monster of a fight. Alyssa had tried not to care. Tried to keep herself in that numb world she had found, but her aunt's furious face and raised voice had caught her attention. She couldn't hear much of the argument, but she did manage to catch her aunt yelling the words "jackass" and "incompetent" in the mix. She was shocked by the fact that her father hadn't put up much of a fight. He was a born and bred drill sergeant. Talking softly wasn't one of his fortes.

But that day he was pretty quiet. He yelled back a couple of times, but mainly it was a defensive statement like, "I did no such thing" or "That's not true". And that was that. Not too long after, Alyssa's father came to her room and mumbled something about going out for a while and leaving her with her aunt. He gave her a kiss on the cheek. As he pulled away, she saw the one thing that made her forgive him for some of the wrongs he had done in the past and the ones he would do in the future. A tear slipped from his eye and ran silently down his cheek.

Before that day, she had never seen her father cry, or show much emotion other than anger. Even after her mother's death. Alyssa had always thought it was because he was a drill sergeant and they just didn't do that. But in that second, as that tear fell, she discovered something. Her father was human. And for some reason, that helped her feel a little better.

Her aunt did the rest. After her father left, she coaxed Alyssa from her room and into the kitchen, which was the one place where Alyssa and her mother had spent the most time together. She sat Alyssa down at the table, poured them both a glass of iced tea and sat across from her. Her aunt reached across the table, took her hand in hers and gave it a light squeeze.

"I miss your mother, Alyssa. I miss her so much my heart hurts. She was my sister and I loved her dearly. But she had a lot of problems. Problems that had nothing to do with you or what kind of daughter you were. Those issues had been with your mother even before you were born. She had been offered help in the past, but chose not to take it. Only she could have helped herself. Not you, not me, only her."

After that her aunt kept quietly holding Alyssa's hand. Saying nothing. Just looking at her with the love and concern that had always been there for her.

Alyssa's carefully fortified damn broke. It started quietly with silent tears running down her face. Next the tidal wave rolled over her. Her shoulders shook and she sobbed uncontrollably. At some point her aunt came around the table and put her arms lovingly around her. She didn't say anything, didn't try to shush her, or tell her everything was okay. She just silently held her, until Alyssa couldn't cry anymore. Until she felt like she had poured everything that had been bottled up inside of her out onto that kitchen table.

Alyssa would never forget what her aunt had done for her. She had saved her from herself. A piece of her soul had disappeared the day her mother killed herself, but her aunt had helped her keep the rest.

* * * * *

Christian was not happy. In fact, he was damn uncomfortable as he drove back to the office. And not just in the physical sense, although he did have to keep adjusting his slacks during the drive. His body did not want to calm down. It had been on full alert with Alyssa at her apartment and getting it back to normal proved difficult.

He was disgusted with himself. Mentally, he had lost it. He had lost control of the beast. It had only been a few minutes, but it was enough to wreak havoc in him. Unleashed in that way, the vampire he was became elemental. Only two thoughts prevailed, hunger and the need to satisfy it.

Something happened as he was holding Alyssa. His desire for her had transformed into the beast. He had become vampire without willing it. That had not occurred since he was a fledgling.

It should not have transpired. He was too old for it.

Luckily, Alyssa's aunt had continued knocking on the door. That was the only thing that had kept him at bay. The worry and concern in the woman's voice had somehow penetrated his thoughts enough to let him withdraw. It had been excruciatingly painful, to the point where he almost hadn't been able to do it. But slowly, inch-by-inch, he had moved away from Alyssa.

After taking a few seconds to collect himself, he had gone into Alyssa's room and jumped easily out of her apartment window. He'd transformed into fog and floated to his car. His body should have calmed down by now. But he was still wound tight. He wanted Alyssa. He wanted her now, under him, as he plunged again and again into her sweetness, making her completely and utterly his.

He pulled into the parking lot and turned off the engine.

"Dammit!"

Christian smacked the steering wheel with his open palm. He needed to get his mind on his job and out of his pants! He stalked into the Sundown Security office and groaned when he saw Vlad. He didn't need an interrogation right now.

Vlad looked up from the papers in his hands. His eyes narrowed as he gave Christian a quick once over. Then his mouth spread into a sardonic grin.

"Frustrating, isn't it? Join the club, my friend."

Christian gave him a cold, blank stare. The one he had practiced using on his clients over the years.

"I don't know what you're talking about." He tried to sound casual, but because his gritted teeth punctuated every word he uttered, it was not very convincing, even to his ears.

"Whatever you say." Vlad shrugged.

Christian glared at him, but the mocking smile remained on his boss's face.

"Unpleasant wanting something you can't have, isn't it?" Vlad asked as his eyes became haunted. "My little miss princess is turning out to be much more of a handful than I anticipated. And a tempting handful at that."

Christian wasn't moved by his friend's admission.

"I'm sure *you'll* handle your situation, Vlad. Just like *I'll* handle mine."

"Right," Vlad replied.

But Christian wasn't so sure. He still felt edgy and restless and he knew just who the cause of that was. Alyssa. With her crystal blue eyes and long raven hair. He focused on his friend. Tried to get his thoughts back to where they belonged.

Vlad didn't comment. He walked into his office, motioning Christian to follow.

"Come sit down. Tell me how the case is progressing. Anything new?"

Christian relayed what had happened at the auditorium with Bazhena.

Vlad frowned. He looked worried.

"Are you sure you incapacitated her for the rest of the night?"

"Yes. Her mind was completely open to me. No blocks, no defenses. I slipped right in." Christian's face filled with disgust as he recalled the evil and twisted caverns of Bazhena's thoughts.

"Bazhena was directing everything towards Alyssa when I hit her with my mind. I could sense how much pain she was in. She won't recover until the next sunset."

"This is the second time she's gone after Miss Edwards," Vlad noted. "The first time, I thought she was just in the wrong place at the wrong time, but now I know it's personal. Bazhena wants Alyssa for some reason, but why? Can you possibly enlighten me, Christian?"

"She's the *Wendigo,*" Christian muttered.

"The what?" Vlad looked confused. He remembered Christian calling Bazhena by that name the other night. When she tried to attack Alyssa. But he didn't know what it meant.

"Nothing. A memory just came to mind."

"Tell me about this *Wen*—what is it?"

"*Wendigo*. You know the Native American tale don't you? I remember hearing it, while I was stationed as an officer in St. Augustine. Mostly from the Ojibwa or Cree Indians who came down to Florida from up north."

"I've never heard about it."

"I'm surprised. The *Wendigo* is a story that men have spoken of since even before I became a vampire. Legend tells of a half beast, half phantom creature that has supernatural strength and speed and moves faster than the human eye can follow. It is supposed to be able to blend into the trees and winds. It can change shape at will. Some say the *Wendigo* can scare its victims to death with a single look. It's also said to whisper into the wind, calling its victims, luring them to their death."

Christian rose from his seat and walked over to Vlad's window. He peered out into the darkness. This story was bringing back unpleasant memories. Still he continued.

"Its name can be roughly translated as 'the evil spirit that eats mankind'. And that's what it's purported to do. It can devour its victims in more than one way. Either by feasting on their flesh and blood, or stealing their mind, turning them into a cannibalistic zombie, devoid of all personality. It's also said that if a person is in the presence of, dreams about, or is bitten by a *Wendigo*, they will become one."

Christian turned from the window and stared intently at Vlad.

"Any of this sound familiar?"

"Of course. It sounds like you're describing a vampire. What's your point, Christian?"

"Nothing really. It's just that when I was still mortal, I heard that tale pretty often. And when Bazhena claimed me for the first time, with Elena's bloody body lying dead in her arms, it was all I could think of. Even today, when my thoughts turn to her, I imagine her as the *Wendigo*."

"You actually believe that rubbish?"

Christian glanced towards the door. The man who interrupted his story looked perfectly human, perfectly normal. Of course, just like everyone else at Sundown Security, he wasn't. He was tall and muscular, with shoulder-length brown hair and gold eyes. Not brown or green with gold specks, but the kind of true gold that glows in the night when light reflects off it. That was the only clue hinting at his true nature. He was an immortal of magic and legend. He was a dragon slayer.

"This cynicism is coming from you, Eric?" Christian asked. "Someone who spends his days chasing dragons? Isn't that somewhat hypocritical?"

Eric grinned and shrugged his shoulders carelessly.

"Maybe you have a point."

"Did you need to talk to me about something, Eric?" Vlad asked.

"Yes, but it's not urgent. I can wait until the two of you are done telling each other children's tales."

Shooting Christian one last smirk, Eric closed the door on his way out.

"That guy can be really irritating." Christian grinned and shook his head.

"Maybe. But he's damn good at what he does."

Vlad's serious tone held Christian's attention. Vlad looked worried. His boss was an old vampire. That meant he was very powerful. If he was worried about Bazhena, then there was something to be concerned about.

"Any suggestions on how to deal with her?" Vlad asked.

Christian could think of many gruesome ways to deal with Bazhena, but he knew that's not what Vlad meant. There was a rule against vampires killing each other without cause. And up to this point they had no cause.

"I'll ask around. See if anyone's heard anything. Bazhena usually isn't discreet when she travels. She's as flamboyant as she can be without catching too much mortal attention. And she likes to talk about herself. That could help us. I'll keep a closer eye on Alyssa, spend every evening with her or close enough that I'll be able to pick up on any disturbances."

Vlad nodded.

"I'll find out what I can also. And remember, Christian. Although Bazhena isn't as old as I am, she's still very powerful."

"I know."

Christian strode towards the door. He'd start investigating tonight.

"Be careful, my friend," Vlad called to him.

"Aren't I always?"

He could still hear Vlad's loud guffaw as he left the office.

* * * * *

Christian drove over to Twice Charmed. It was one of the few nightclubs open all night and it was unique. It catered to and attracted the paranormal types like vampires, werewolves and elves, among others. This wasn't a fact that was openly discussed. It just was. There was an aura around the place, a sense of dread the creatures that inhabited it perpetuated. Except for the occasional groupies or lost tourists, humans seemed to naturally stay far away from the club.

Despite this, there was one fast and steady rule everyone had to adhere to. No harm would come to humans while they were at or in the vicinity of Twice Charmed. The owners made this rule from the beginning and everyone involved knew why. If humans started dying at or near the club, people would get suspicious and curious. And none of the patrons of Twice Charmed wanted that. This was one of the few places where their kind could be themselves without hiding it from others. Everyone wanted to keep it that way, so they obeyed the rule, most of the time.

On those occasions when the rule was broken, harsh punishment resulted and the perpetrator was never allowed to return to Twice Charmed. No exceptions were made. Everyone knew that. So most behaved themselves. Except for the fighting. There weren't any hard and fast rules about that. Especially when it involved two different species.

The owners didn't allow fighting in the club, but they had no qualms about brawling in the back parking area. Especially since bets were often made on the winner. And the owners always demanded a cut of the winnings. Since the parking area was enclosed with high block fencing, they knew it wouldn't attract much attention from outsiders. But the fights always drew curious onlookers from inside the club.

Christian approached the entrance and allowed himself to be searched. No weapons of any kind, magical or otherwise were allowed. The large, well-muscled man who checked him with detached thoroughness was a gargoyle. Most people couldn't tell what they were when they were in human form, but since one of Christian's co-workers was also a gargoyle, he knew just what to look for.

Gargoyles were in high demand for security jobs for several reasons. One stood out above all the rest. An innate dislike and wariness of any creature other than one of their own kind. Caution and suspicion was their natural mode of operation.

The gargoyle let Christian pass with little more than a grunt and a wave of his hand. People often made the mistake of assuming gargoyles were stupid. In actuality, they were, on the whole, very well spoken, intelligent creatures. They just didn't like to talk to any but their own species.

Inside the club, Christian looked around. He had to fight the rush that flowed over him. A gathering of such beings was always filled with high energy. Patrons enjoyed the freedom to express their true selves, to the point that everyone grew more and more excited as the night progressed. Sometimes that energy stayed positive. Sometimes it didn't. It was the latter that caused fights out back.

Positive energy flowed over Christian tonight. A beautiful woman entered the club and strolled by him. Her dress clung to every curve and her hips swayed seductively as she walked. She was tall and thin, with firm breasts and a behind that had just the right amount of jiggle. He knew that most of the males in the room were watching her with appreciation and anticipation.

He had seen her at the club many times before. She was a mortal human, a groupie who liked to be with magical creatures. He had seen her with various people over the last few months. She had never caught his interest. But tonight was different. Since she was here so often, she might know something about Bazhena. He needed to act quickly, before another decided to take her.

He sent a mental message to her. It projected hunger and promised passion.

She stopped walking. Swinging around, her gaze narrowed as she searched the room. She finally found him. Her face registered surprise, but then she smiled. When he returned her smile, she sauntered over.

"Hi." A seductive smile played across her full lips. An invitation was written all over it.

Christian's body responded immediately. Good. Maybe tonight he would be able to accomplish two goals. Find out more about Bazhena and get Alyssa out of his head.

"Hello." Christian gave her a heated look. Then he smiled in a way that brought her closer.

It always brought them closer.

Chapter Six

෴

"I'm Amelia, but you can call me Amy." The woman held out her hand.

"I'm Christian."

Christian took her hand, but instead of shaking it, he brushed his lips across the back. His stare never left her face. He could see her eyes widen in surprise. He purposely grazed her skin with his teeth. The minute he did so, the surprise in her stare flared into desire. He kept her hand clasped in his. Rubbing his thumb on the soft inside of her palm, he watched her eyes darken with passion.

Her next word came out breathless.

"You look familiar. Have you been to Twice Charmed before? I know I wouldn't forget a man who looked like you."

"I've been coming here for a long time." Christian didn't want to give away too much information. He didn't know if Bazhena had mentioned him to anyone else.

The woman licked her lips as her gaze ran over him. He could hear her heart speed up and her body tightening. He gave her another mental push, just enough to help her close the distance between them. He didn't want anyone listening to their conversation.

Amy looked up into Christian's face. Her hunger was blatant. She wanted him. She didn't try to hide it. Couldn't hide it. She was his until he chose to release her.

Walking her to a secluded corner of the club, he held her close and whispered each question into her ear. They looked like they were being intimate as she rubbed herself against him, moaning with need, but she answered each and every question he asked. Amy held nothing back. He wouldn't let her. Afterwards, he sent her home with the thought that she had not met anyone interesting at the club that night. If they met in the future, she wouldn't remember him either.

Christian sat down at an empty table and pondered what Amy had told him. But he couldn't concentrate. He was perplexed. He had had this beautiful woman in his arms, begging for him to take her. But he couldn't. He kept thinking about Alyssa. Every time Amy rubbed against him, he imagined Alyssa rubbing against him. Every time Amy kissed his neck, he imagined Alyssa kissing his neck. As he pulled Amy closer and felt her softness push against him, he thought of Alyssa's voluptuous body pressed against his hardness.

In the end, he knew he couldn't take Amy. He wanted only one mortal woman. Alyssa. This disturbed him. He had never had this kind of problem before. Women were attracted to him. Even without using his powers, he never had a shortage of women willing to sleep in his bed. When he was interested. Which wasn't often. He liked women, respected them and enjoyed their company, for a little while. But his solitary existence was a necessary part of his job, so he had never pursued any woman seriously.

* * * * *

After her aunt left, Alyssa lay in bed, tossing and turning. She tried to sleep, but was too restless. She called out to Jonathan, but he didn't come. Usually he slept on her bed at night, his purring lulling her to sleep, unless he found a juicy bug or rodent to play with for a while. He must have gotten lucky tonight. Giving up, she kicked the sheets off and got up out of bed. She stood in front of her bedroom window and stared through the open curtains, out into the moonlit night. But she saw nothing. Instead, the image of Christian looking up at her with hungry, glowing red eyes appeared. Fear burned in the pit of her stomach. She thought she had it together. She thought she could deal with this. She was wrong. *Way* wrong.

What had she been thinking? The guy was a vampire for crying out loud! He bit people's necks, sucked blood from their bodies, slept in coffins! This was not just the dangerous bad boy-type that so many women liked to get entangled with. This guy wasn't human. He wasn't even alive. Was he?

Alyssa remembered the empty, cold look in Christian's eyes earlier. She had seen that look only one other time. She had never forgotten it. While in high school, her class had gone on a field trip to the Phoenix Zoo. She had moved ahead and approached the black jaguar exhibit. In awe of its beauty, she stood close to its cage. The cat turned its stare to her and a shiver of dread had run down her spine. His eyes were dead. There was no other word for them. The jaguar's eyes told her that he would kill her and eat her if he could. There would be no sympathy or compassion. There would just be death. Hers. Looking into Christian's eyes had been like reliving that experience.

The memory cleared, replaced by another. Christian kneeling on the ground, bent over in pain. Struggling with an agony she couldn't imagine. Didn't want to imagine. She remembered the way his body had shaken with effort.

She had wanted to go to him, to touch him. To wrap her arms around his kneeling form and help him. She didn't know how, but she had wanted to try. Wanted to make all the pain go away. So that he could be free, free of it all.

Alyssa shook her head. Tried to clear it. What was she thinking? She didn't even know what he was going through. Had no idea how to help him. And what if she had gone to him? What if he had looked up into her eyes? Mesmerized her with his glowing red gaze. Then sank his teeth into her neck and sucked every last drop of blood from her body, until she was nothing but a dried up corpse.

Alyssa shivered. She was starting to creep herself out. When had she begun thinking about dried up corpses? She went back to bed, pulling the covers over her head like she used to do when she was a child. Foolishly thinking that if she lay perfectly still it would keep the monsters at bay. She knew better now.

Still, she kept the blanket over her head. She practiced using the breathing technique that had helped her calm down so many times before. Concentrated on inhaling—one, two, three, four, five and exhaling—one, two, thre—what was that? Alyssa held her breath and listened. When she heard nothing, she thought she had only imagined it. She started to relax. Then stiffened in fear as she heard it again. A scratching noise, not loud, but definitely there.

She listened carefully. It was coming from the area by her bedroom window. What should she do? What if it was Christian? What if he had come back to…to what? Finish her off? Tear his teeth into her neck? Suck all the blood from her body?

Or make love to her? She got only a glimpse of what if would be like and she knew her body hungered for more. She wanted to press her soft curves against his hard angles. Needed to feel his strong hands exploring the contours of her body. Craved to have him inside of her, filling her in a way she knew only he could.

Alyssa was hot, too hot. She threw the blankets off again. She couldn't take it anymore! Storming to her bedroom window, she opened it wide. She never saw the shadow until it flew at her. It hit her squarely on the chest and she lost her breath. Falling backwards from the impact, she felt a sharp pain as something pricked her neck. It was too late. She should have listened. She should have stayed under the covers like the child inside her had told her to.

Alyssa screamed. She landed on her back with a loud thud. The impact knocked the breath out of her.

"Meeoow."

Her eyes shot open. She knew that meow! Her cat lay on her chest, his claws stuck into her as he held on for dear life.

Alyssa caught her breath.

"Jonathan? What were you doing outside?"

At the sound of her voice, his nails retracted.

She petted him, trying to calm both of them down. Alyssa was shaking and couldn't seem to stop. When Jonathan began to purr, she knew she could move without risking more injuries from his sharp claws. She wrapped her arms around him and sat up. Her head swam then slowly cleared. Jonathan squirmed in her tight hold so she released him. Settling down on her lap, he repositioned himself until he was comfortable. She continued to pet him and talk in a soothing voice. Calming down with each passing minute, her heart beat eventually slowed.

"Now why were you outside, Jonathan? You're a full-time inside cat. You don't do outside. And I don't remember opening my window—"

Then it hit her. The window. That was how Christian left her apartment earlier. And he must have left it open long enough for Jonathan to climb out onto the ledge. No wonder she couldn't figure it out. She was on the second floor and nobody could jump from her window without getting seriously hurt. Nobody human, that is. A vampire, on the other hand, could probably do that. They had supernatural strength.

Alyssa gently set Jonathan off of her lap and walked into her bathroom. Taking off her nightshirt, she surveyed the damage. She had four good size cuts on her neck and chest. Jonathan had really been holding on. He must have been frightened, being outside on the narrow ledge by himself.

She cleaned her cuts with antibiotic spray and put Band-Aids on each one. After closing her bedroom window, she went to bed with the bathroom light on. She couldn't fall asleep right away. She tried to imagine Christian jumping from her window. What powers did vampires actually have?

She fell asleep picturing Christian flying through the sky.

* * * * *

Alyssa woke up late the next morning, around ten. Even then, she felt like going back to sleep. Usually a morning person, this surprised her. She blamed it on the events of the night before. Thoughts about the previous evening made her remember her decision to find out more about vampires. She had already been to the library. Today she planned to hit the video store.

By the time she rented the videos it was early afternoon. Earlier in the day she had put the ingredients for beef stew in the slow cooker. The delicious smell filled her place as she cleaned her apartment. After a quick bowl of cereal, she had showered then gone to the video store. Luckily they had the movies she was looking for.

Alyssa made some microwave popcorn, poured herself a large cup of diet soda and plopped down on her couch. Sometimes she loved being a couch potato. The first movie she watched was the most recent version of Bram Stoker's *Dracula*. After that she began watching Ann Rice's *The Vampire Lestat*. One of the characters reminded her of Christian. His dark skin, shoulder-length, midnight-black hair and intense eyes were incredibly similar to her new bodyguard's. It's what made the actor so popular with women.

Beside the fact that Christian was taller and a little more muscular, the two could have been brothers. Maybe not twins, but definitely related. They even had the same Spanish lilt to their voice that made her skin feel like it was being caressed with silk every time she heard it.

Great. So not only did Christian have the power to make her want him, the guy also looked like one of the hottest stars around. That was *so* not fair. She didn't need this in her life right now. Professionally, things were going so well. She was independent and in control of her life. She didn't need a bossy vampire taking it over.

Despite the fact that her thoughts kept drifting back to Christian, Alyssa somehow managed to finish watching *The Vampire Lestat*. She got up and stretched. Viewing two movies in a row, with little more than a few bathroom breaks, left her stiff. After wandering around her apartment and stretching her legs she headed into the kitchen. Jonathan joined her and they shared a big bowl of beef stew. Even though it was the middle of a hot Arizona summer, Alyssa still loved eating homemade soups and stews. They were her favorite meal.

The sun had set by the time she finished the dishes. Alyssa tried to go over the speech she was giving tomorrow night, but she couldn't focus. She felt restless and just couldn't sit still. Finally giving up, she got up and paced her apartment.

Maybe she would go out for a walk.

The minute that thought hit her, she could think of nothing else. So what if it was dark, her mind kept telling her. She lived in a safe neighborhood. She would be fine. Just put on your shoes and go for a walk. It will be fine. Just pick up the keys and walk out the door. It will be fine.

Alyssa listened to the voice in her head. How could she not? Yes, she needed a walk. It was just the thing. She would feel better after she went outside. It will be fine. That's it. Unlock the door and walk out. Just do it. You want to do it. You need to do it.

Yes, she had to get out. Needed the fresh air. Hurry. There wasn't much time. She had to do it now. Alyssa unlocked the door and opened it. She stepped out and ran into something large and solid. Glancing up, she saw Christian staring down at her with amusement on his face.

"Going out, *palomita*?"

Christian knew from the dazed look on Alyssa's face that Bazhena had gotten to her. She had whispered in Alyssa's mind, like the legendary *Wendigo,* lulling, then luring Alyssa outside. If he hadn't picked up on Bazhena's thoughts, Alyssa would have become another of his creator's victims. Carelessly used and discarded.

The thought of Bazhena using Alyssa infuriated him. He clenched his fists tightly by his sides and then projected his thoughts outward.

She is mine.

He heard Bazhena's soft laughter in his head. It should have sounded light and airy. It didn't. It sounded evil and slightly crazed. And it mocked him. Of that he had no doubt.

We will see, Cristobal. We will see.

Then Bazhena's presence was no more. He could no longer perceive her thoughts. She had either gone a great distance away or blocked her mind from him. Only that would affect his ability to read her. Though vampires and their creators had a mental bond, each could stop the other from reading their mind. As a fledgling he hadn't known how to. But over time he had learned to completely close off his thoughts from Bazhena. She had been furious about it, but helpless to prevent it.

Alyssa slumped against him and slid to the ground. She had fainted again. Bazhena had released her. Scooping Alyssa up in his arms, Christian carried her into her apartment and slammed her front door closed with his foot. He walked into her bedroom and carefully laid her on her bed.

Sitting down beside her, he studied Alyssa. He had felt her mind fight Bazhena's control. She had struggled against it longer than any human he had seen before her. Vlad had warned him about Bazhena, but Christian didn't need the warning. He knew what she was capable of. Had seen firsthand the control Bazhena could exert over not only humans, but also other vampires. He was amazed by Alyssa's strength of will. How could someone who looked so fragile be so strong?

She reminded him of a bird. That's why he called her *palomita,* the Spanish word for little bird. Her long, silky black hair feathered around her, beautifully framing her heart-shaped face. Her creamy white skin looked soft as rose petals. His finger itched to stroke it. And her full, lush, berry-red lips. He groaned as his body responded. That mouth was made for him. He could imagine the feel of it against him, all over him.

Christian shot to his feet. He began pacing the room. He knew Alyssa would wake up soon. She would open her eyes and look up at him. He could get lost in those eyes. Lose himself in their crystal blue depths. Forget about everything. Forget about what he was, forget about all the wrongs he had done in the past and forget his debt to humanity. His body tightened. Thickened to the point of pain. He felt his teeth elongate as the beast threatened to rise.

No! Christian swung around and strode out of the room. He had to get himself together. When Alyssa woke up, he would be in control. She needed his protection. That was the plan. His body could wait.

Focusing on his breathing, Christian slowly calmed down. He sat on Alyssa's couch. He started to flip through one of the magazines on her coffee table when he spotted the video jackets. Curious, he picked one up. A grin spread across mouth. So, his *palomita* was interested in vampires? Interesting. Using the remote, he turned on the movie she had been watching. He had never read Ann Rice's books on vampires. So many had tried to tell the vampire's story. He wondered what her take on his kind would be.

* * * * *

Alyssa found Christian sitting on her couch an hour later. She woke up disoriented. Why was she lying on her bed with her clothes on? What time was it? She got up and walked out of her bedroom. She needed something cold to drink. Her mouth felt drier than a desert. Stumbling into the kitchen, she poured herself a glass of cold water from the fridge. She drank all of it, then poured another. She was so thirsty!

Carrying her glass into the other room, she noticed for the first time that her TV was on. Had she left it on and gone to sleep? The last thing she remembered was eating some stew with Jonathan. After that things were fuzzy.

Then she saw Christian. The glass slipped from her hand and crashed to the floor. She would never forget the look in his eyes as he swung his head towards her and shot to his feet. For just an instant, his gaze looked haunted with pain and suffering. She barely held back the urge to run to him and hold him close. Whatever he was watching on the television had profoundly affected him.

Then it was gone.

"Surprised to see me, *palomita*?"

Christian shuttered his eyes so that they held nothing but casual interest. Alyssa wasn't fooled. Forgetting about the broken glass, she took a step forward, then gasped when a sharp pain shot through her foot.

"Don't move. I'll get you."

As he closed the distance between them, Alyssa couldn't help but notice how Christian looked. It almost made her previously dry mouth water. She forgot about the pain in her foot. He wore his hair loose. It spilled in dark shining waves around his shoulders. She really, *really* wanted to run her fingers through it. He wore a charcoal-gray, ribbed T-shirt that strained against the wide expanse of his shoulders and clung to his muscular chest. She had to swallow as her gaze lowered. His black jeans hugged him in all the right places. She could almost see the play of muscles in his powerful thighs as he drew close. Her thoughts scattered as he picked her up and brought her to the couch. He set her down gently and then hovered over her. His eyes were glued to her foot. Alyssa followed his gaze.

Uh oh. Blood. Vampire. It took Alyssa a second to figure it out, but the minute she did, she stood up and started to limp quickly towards the bathroom.

"I'll go clean this up. Then we can talk about why you're in my apartment."

She tried to make her voice sound calm, relaxed. Instead it came out a high-pitched squeak.

"Stop."

It was only one word. But Christian's compelling voice pulled at her. Made her want to listen. She hesitated and then fought against it as she tried to move forward.

"Now."

That was it. Her feet stopped. She wanted to get to the bathroom, needed to close the door and lock it. She didn't want to see Christian's eyes glowing red or his teeth grow.

"Don't move."

His voice lured her, enticed her. Made her want to do whatever he asked of her. Before she realized it, he was standing directly in front of her. She stared at his chest, refusing to look up. Christian tilted her chin up with his finger. She closed her eyes tight. *She didn't want to see the vampire…she didn't want to see the vampire…she didn't want to see the vampire.*

"Look at me, *palomita*."

It was a command. She knew that now. He asked and she wanted, no needed to obey. Still, she fought it as long as she could.

Her eyes fluttered open. She met Christian's stare and saw only his rich mocha eyes. No red. No glowing. Just Christian's desire-filled eyes. The breath she had been holding came out in a rush. This she could deal with.

"I could never hurt you, Alyssa. Do you understand that?"

She silently nodded her head. She believed him. Knew in her heart that his words were true.

His head descended and their lips met. She forgot the rest—the pain in her foot, the glowing red eyes, the teeth. None of it mattered as they touched. She wrapped her arms around his neck and pulled him closer. Gently worshipping her mouth, he told her without words that what he said was true. He wouldn't hurt her.

After what seemed like only seconds, Christian broke their kiss. She moaned her protest. She wanted more. Wanted him.

He scooped her up and cradled her in his arms as he carried her to her bathroom. Alyssa kept her arms wrapped around him. Savored their closeness and the feel of him holding her. No one had carried her this much since she was a child. She wasn't a lightweight either. Even if they wanted to, most men wouldn't find carrying her an easy endeavor. Yet Christian held her as if she weighed nothing. Made her feel delicate and cherished.

He set her on the edge of her bathtub. The image of the two of them in the bath together blossomed in her mind, wet and soapy, their hands sliding over each other. She would wash his back and—

"Where do you keep the tweezers, Alyssa?"

Christian's question broke her seductive reverie. She looked blankly up at him. What had he asked?

One of Christian's eyebrows rose and a mischievous grin spread across his mouth. His eyes danced with amusement and something else, an arrogance that she didn't want to examine too closely. One that told her he knew he could take her there and then and she would welcome it.

"Your bathtub is very big isn't it? It could easily fit two people, don't you think?"

Christian's grin spread to wolfish proportions. Alyssa felt herself blush. She never blushed! But she suddenly felt like she had been caught with her fingers in the cookie jar.

"I-I never really thought about it," she lied.

She tried to act nonchalant, as if his words hadn't sent fingers of desire throughout her body.

Christian threw back his head and laughed. It was a joyous sound. It made her feel better, just hearing it. But she was so shocked by it that she forgot about her embarrassment. She could only stare at him in wide-eyed wonder.

His laughter slowly died down. But the smile remained as he shook his head.

"*Palomita,* you truly please me."

Alyssa couldn't help herself. She smiled. His words pleased her.

"Now, let's take care of that cut. Where are your tweezers?" Christian asked again.

"In the medicine cabinet behind you. Why do you need them?"

Christian retrieved the tweezers, antiseptic spray, gauze pads and bandages from the cabinet.

"In case there's still some glass in your foot. That's why I didn't want you to move. If there was glass in your skin, it might have become too deeply embedded to pull out. Do you have a clean washcloth?"

"Yes, under the sink."

He took out the cloth and turned on the hot water. He plugged the drain, squirted some soap into the sink and filled it with the hot water. After soaking the washcloth in it for a minute, he wrung it out and brought it over to where she sat.

Christian knelt down in front of her and gently grasped her calf. His touch made her flesh burn. When he lifted her leg up and slid his fingers towards her foot, tingles of pleasure shot through her. Shehad a thing about her feet. She loved to have them massaged. She could sit for hours enjoying it.

He held the heel of her foot in his hand, while gently washing the area of the cut with the other one. Alyssa had to bite her lip to hold in her groan of pleasure. She was forced to lean back slightly as he lifted her foot higher. He examined it closely.

"I don't see any glass. I'm going to press lightly on the area. Let me know if it hurts when I do."

Why did Christian's voice sound deeper all of a sudden? She looked at his face, but all his attention was focused on her foot. She forgot about it a second later as he probed her cut lightly with his finger.

"It's tender when you touch it, but I don't feel any sharp pain."

"Good. That's good."

That was all Christian said. But it was enough. She could hear the roughness in his voice. She could feel his hand tighten around her. Something had changed. He had changed.

Before she knew what he was going to do, Christian dropped the washcloth and grasped her calf with his free hand. He slowly pulled her foot closer to his face, closer to his mouth. She tried to pull away, but his hold on her was firm. It didn't hurt her, but she wasn't going anywhere until he released her. She steeled her body for whatever was going to come next.

"What are you doing?" she asked in a shaky voice.

"Your sweetness calls to me. I have to taste you."

His breath tickled the bottom of her foot as he spoke. The hoarse sound of it slid over her like honey to her senses. Soothing her fear while leaving waves of pleasure in its wake. Her thoughts grew fuzzy and unfocused.

"Don't worry, *palomita*. You *will* enjoy it. I promise you that."

Alyssa watched in frozen fascination as Christian touched his mouth to her foot. At first she felt nothing. Then his tongue flicked lightly over her cut, once, twice and again. Its hot roughness burned her. His teeth grazed her injury. Then his mouth pressed tightly against it, while his fingers played along her calf, caressing it.

It should have hurt. Somehow she knew that. But it didn't. Instead, the pull of Christian's mouth sent lust crashing through her. The feel of his fingers running up and down her leg, the sight of his head bent over her, the silky curtain of his hair covering his face and brushing against her. It was too much. Desire climbed up inside her. Alyssa tilted her head back and closed her eyes tight. She tried to fight it. Tried to deny what was happening to her. But it was no use. She was helpless to stop the wave of pleasure that crashed over her. She splintered into a million pieces.

* * * * *

Christian carried a still unconscious Alyssa to the couch and laid her down on it. He didn't trust himself in her bedroom right now. She was too much of a temptation. He quickly applied the antiseptic to her foot, although he knew it wasn't necessary. Like all vampires, he had something in his saliva that promoted fast healing. Alyssa's cut would be healed by morning.

She looked peaceful in sleep. Content. He smiled at that. Content. That's exactly the opposite of what he felt right now. He had thought one taste of Alyssa would satisfy him. He should have known better. Instead it had increased his hunger tenfold. Although her sweetness had tasted like nectar, his true pleasure came from watching Alyssa lose herself in his touch.

Since joining up with Vlad, Christian always used mental transference on those he drank from. He made the experience comfortable for them and then left them forgetting it ever happened. But he had never taken it a step further. The way Bazhena had done with him, that first time. Leaving him gasping with pleasure, begging for more as she brought him over. She did this with her "special" victims. Bringing them intense pleasure while draining them completely, until their heart stopped beating.

He had always made those he fed from comfortable, but this was the first time he had let himself go. Let his power bring pleasure. He had taken Alyssa. Not in the traditional human sense, but nevertheless they had shared something. And it had been incredible. He had felt every emotion she did. And when she finally let go, let him bring her to her peak, he had almost lost it.

He stood up in an effort to make himself more comfortable. His body was strung too tight, to the point of pain. Pacing back and forth, he struggled to get himself under control. Once he calmed down, he sat in a chair facing Alyssa.

After what he had learned last night from the mortal woman at Twice Charmed, he knew he needed to watch over Alyssa as long as possible, until the sun was close to rising. Bazhena meant to have her. Christian would never allow that.

Alyssa was his.

He wished he could stay longer. Wished he could watch the sunrise with her, share the day with her, not just the night. But he knew that was impossible. Apples and sunshine. They were no longer part of his life. Now only darkness and death belonged to him.

* * * * *

Alyssa's eyes fluttered open. She looked around in dismay. Why was she lying on her couch? She could tell by the light pouring through her front window that it was morning. Why had she slept on her couch all night? She sat up slowly, gently removing Jonathan from where he lay on her chest and noticed that the TV, showing nothing but static, was still on. She tried to clear the fuzz from her brain. What had happened last night? She looked down at the coffee table in front of her and saw the video cases. That's right. She had spent the evening at home, watching a video vampire marathon.

Vampire? Christian! Now she remembered! Grabbing her foot, she pulled it onto her lap. She searched the bottom of it. Where was it? There was no cut! How was that possible? Had it just been a dream? No, it had been too real. She jumped off the couch and ran to the kitchen. She looked in the garbage can and saw the shards of glass in there. It had really happened.

It all came rushing back. Christian was in her apartment. She dropped her glass and cut her foot. That's when things got strange. He carried her to the bathroom. Then he…he—she couldn't even admit to herself what she'd let him do. And more to the point, how she reacted to what he had done.

She had sat there like a helpless ninny and allowed Christian to take what he needed from her, even wanted him to take it from her. Without an argument or fight. And if that wasn't enough, she had not only lost control of the situation, she had also lost control of herself. Just like she had always promised herself she would never do. Just like her mother had always done, letting Alyssa's father take over her life completely. Memories of her mother's dependent behavior filled her head.

Shame washed over Alyssa.

Then anger.

She would not let this happen! She was stronger than that. She could handle the situation. It was a momentary lapse, nothing more. And she would tell Christian that when she saw him tonight. The thought of looking into those seductive mocha eyes and hearing his husky voice made her heart race.

No. It wasn't going to be like that. She would be in control of herself. He was a vampire. Yes, that was very unsettling and kind of freaky, but she needed to get over that. Move on.

Alyssa had one more engagement after tonight and then she would be done. Hopefully between now and then, Christian would find the creep responsible for stalking her and put a stop to it. Those two issues should and would be the focus of her relationship with Christian from now on. She would concentrate on getting through her next two speeches and he would protect her from her stalker, possibly discovering who it was.

That's all she could handle right now. That's all she would deal with. She was not her mother. She would never be her mother. She was an intelligent, independent woman, who was doing just fine on her on. She made that her mantra over the next hour while she ate breakfast, then showered and dressed. As she was brushing her teeth, the phone rang. Spitting out as much toothpaste as possible, she raced to the phone.

"Herro?"

"Alyssa? Is that you dear?"

Her aunt's voice sounded confused.

"Yesh. Hode on."

"What?"

Alyssa ran back to the sink and quickly rinsed the rest of the toothpaste out of her mouth. She heard her aunt asking, "Hello? Is anyone there? Alyssa? Are you there?"

Drying her mouth she put the receiver back up to her ear.

"Yes, it's me. Hi, Aunt Joyce. Sorry about that. I was brushing my teeth."

"That's all right, sweetie. Are you almost ready?"

"Ready?"

"Yes, you know, for our shopping trip? Remember you and I are going to hit the secondhand shops today to find that special dress for the reception tonight?"

As her aunt spoke, Alyssa remembered about tonight's speech. Her aunt had set up tonight's engagement with the Arizona Women's Chapter Against Domestic Abuse. Women from all over the state would be coming and then a cocktail reception was being held afterwards.

Alyssa had wanted to wear one of her usual business suits for the speech, but her aunt insisted that she wear something dressier for the reception afterwards. She had explained that many of the women in this group were prominent business, political and social leaders. This event was a black tie event so Alyssa had to dress accordingly.

"Oh, no! I forgot to mention this to Christian. He's going to feel out of place if he's not wearing a tuxedo. Aunt Joyce, I need to call the agency and leave a message for him—"

"Don't worry, Alyssa. It's taken care of. I called your publicist yesterday and got Sundown Security's phone number. I spoke to a Mr. Maksimovitch and mentioned it to him. He'll make sure Mr. Galiano is properly dressed."

"You talked to Vlad, uh, Mr. Maksimovitch?"

"Well, yes. I had a few questions for him."

Alyssa tried not to let the irritation come out in her voice. Sometimes her aunt still treated her like a child.

"That really wasn't necessary, Aunt Joyce. I could have called myself."

"I know that, dear. But you have to humor me sometimes. You're always so busy and I worry about you. After all, you are my only niece. I just wanted to make sure they were taking good care of you. That's all."

Alyssa irritation melted away at her aunt's caring words.

"Thank you for taking care of that, Aunt Joyce."

"You're welcome, dear. Now, are you ready to shop?"

"When am I not ready?"

"Isn't that the truth?" Alyssa's aunt chuckled. Shopping was an activity they enjoyed doing together.

Twenty minutes later her aunt picked her up at her apartment. Alyssa loved to browse at secondhand and antique stores down in the Willow District. That area of downtown Phoenix was revitalized with little antique and clothing shops as well as galleries. She liked the atmosphere and selections available, especially when it came to dressing for special occasions. She always managed to find clothes that were more to her tastes, instead of the latest fashions.

They spent almost all day shopping, with only a small break for lunch at Willow Bakery. The fresh breads and pastries were always a temptation that she and her aunt had a hard time resisting. After lunch, Aunt Joyce managed to pick out several outfits. Alyssa bought a beautiful antique pillbox at one shop, but no outfits until the very last shop they visited.

Her aunt discovered the dress first and rushed over to show it to her.

"This would be perfect for tonight."

"It's not very professional looking."

"You aren't supposed to look professional tonight," her aunt reminded her. "Just try it on. Please?"

Alyssa looked at the frothy creation and doubted she would like how it fit. Her full figure made her very particular about which outfits she wore. But she would try it on for her aunt. She went into the dressing room and started undressing. Her aunt passed a pair of shoes and sheer scarf under the stall door.

"Here, try these too. They'll match perfectly."

The minute Alyssa put the ice blue, floor-length dress on and looked in the mirror, she knew she would buy it. It was soft and feminine, while being sleek and sexy at the same time. It hugged her shape with a fabric that looked and felt lighter than air. The scooped, cowl neckline layered softly down, barely showing the rise of her breasts, which were pushed slightly up by the cut of the bodice. The waistline of the dress cinched in, making it appear small, then flowed along her body's curves all the way to the floor. And her aunt was right, the light blue shoes and chiffon scarf she had found later perfectly complimented the dress. She loved it.

Her aunt dropped her off at home later and told Alyssa she would see her tonight at the Scottsdale Plaza Hotel. The women's group she was speaking to had rented a banquet room at the luxury resort. The whole event would be a fundraiser for women's shelters and assistance. Alyssa was not charging for her appearance tonight. It was a cause she believed in strongly.

As she dressed that evening, her thoughts returned to Christian and the events of the previous night. She reminded herself of her resolutions. Concentrate on the goals. Get through the speeches. Let Christian protect her. That's it. No more intimate and strange moments. Professional, professional, professional. She gave herself a final pep talk right before her doorbell rang. She was ready. She could handle this, could handle him. After a quick glance through the peephole, she saw Christian. Taking a deep breath, she put on a forced smile and opened the door.

Her smile faltered and she sucked in her breath. Christian stood in the doorway wearing a tuxedo. Her gaze roamed hungrily over him. It stopped at his lips. Focused on them. Alyssa remembered the feel of them pressed against her skin. She shivered. But it wasn't from being cold. Her insides went up in flames. One totally primitive thought entered her mind, negating every other.

I Want Him Now.

Chapter Seven

ꟾ

Apples and sunshine.

It was all he could think about when Alyssa answered the door in a sexy frothy blue dress that matched her eyes. He let his eyes travel the length of her, lingering on the low scoop neckline. Knowing how sweet she tasted made the sight of her exposed flesh an exquisite torture. The fact that her dress clung lovingly to her ample curves didn't help.

The soft color and material haloed her body, while the design fit her to perfection. Like its wearer, the dress was a mix of innocence and seduction. And he craved to explore both. He wanted to taste her innocence and plunder her until he found satisfaction. He looked at her face and groaned softly. She wore her hair up again. Tendrils curled around her delicate neck. A neck, he noticed, which was swathed in a sheer blue scarf the same shade as her dress.

The dress enhanced Alyssa's bright blue eyes, making them shine like jewels. But the slightly dazed way she was looking at him made him wonder if Bazhena was nearby. He opened himself to his surroundings but picked up nothing. No, it wasn't Bazhena. Why did Alyssa look glassy-eyed?

Christian grinned as he watched Alyssa slowly peruse him from head to toe. That was why. She was as affected by him as he was by her. After a minute or so, she raised her gaze to his. His smile widened when he saw the look in her eyes. She was hungry…hungry for him.

He liked that.

He moved forward, through the doorway. That broke her stupor. She took a step backwards. Her eyes widened in alarm.

"I-uh-I forgot something. I'll be right out. Please come in and have a seat."

Alyssa scrambled away into her room and slammed the door behind her.

Keeping his eyes firmly on the seductive sway of her hips as she retreated, he closed the door and strode into her apartment.

He felt too restless to sit. Instead he wandered around, looking at the pictures scattered about the place. But he didn't really see them. His mind was still trying to process what he had learned over the last couple days. Since the woman at Twice Charmed had been human, he had managed to get a lot of information out of her. Currently she was a vampire groupie. She belonged to one of the vampires who frequented the club. Amy wanted to become immortal, but hadn't been transformed yet.

She knew all about Bazhena. Amy's boyfriend was apparently very impressed with Christian's creator and was acting as her "guide" through the city. It seemed Bazhena was searching for something having to do with a very old legend. She had found an ancient book during her travels around the world, which described how to transform into the most seductive woman on earth, completely irresistible to both humans and legendary creatures.

The legend stated that whoever acquired three specific items and then recited the incantation, would become the most desirable creature on earth. No one would be able to resist her. Amy claimed that Bazhena was in Arizona looking for the third and last item. But she didn't know what that was. The vampire Amy belonged to was very close-mouthed. The only thing he mentioned was that Bazhena was looking for The Light.

Christian had no idea what The Light was. After Alyssa's function tonight, he would speak to Vlad. Find out if he knew anything. Since Vlad was older than Bazhena, there was a chance he would know the legend. There were hundreds of stories circulating throughout the world about vampires. Some true, some not. When Christian had watched Ann Rice's movie about vampires in Alyssa's apartment last night, he had been awed and truly moved by the accuracy of her portrayals. Many had tried to show the vampire's life, but Ms. Rice's storytelling ability had been the most accurate he had seen thus far. She showed both the gentle and violent side of their lives.

Christian glanced at Alyssa's coffee table. The videos were gone. Alyssa must have returned them. He wondered what she had been feeling when she watched the movies. Fear? Disdain? Had the taking of blood completely repulsed her?

Last night's events came back to him in a rush, the taste of Alyssa, the feel of her beneath his fingers, her abandoned reaction to his touch. It hit him like a punch to the stomach. He struggled to tamp down a wave of desire. Looking around for something to take his mind off the pressure in his pants, he spotted a picture he hadn't noticed before. He calmed down almost immediately and a wide grin curled the corner of his lips upward. It was one of Alyssa's childhood pictures.

The photo was of Alyssa as a teenager and another woman, who must be her mother. The similarities in physical appearance were obvious. But what caught his attention was Alyssa's smile. She had the same smile today, carefree and warm. The kind that made a person want to share in its brightness and smile right back.

Alyssa leaned her head back against her closed bedroom door. She needed to get a grip. Yes, Christian was hot. But so were a lot of other guys. The vampire thing. It must be the vampire allure. She had read about it and seen it in the movies she had rented. Vampires had the power to control others with their mind. Christian was manipulating her. That was all. That was why she had such strong reactions to him. She just needed to remember that what she was feeling wasn't real, not truly. She ignored the little voice inside her that whispered otherwise, the one that told her that her feelings meant something more than she wanted to admit.

She took several deep breaths to calm down. When she felt ready, she moved away from the door and opened it. She walked back into the other room and stopped in her tracks. Christian really did look incredible in that tux. Some people wore tuxedos and they just didn't seem to fit. He looked like he was born to wear one. His actions, the graceful way he moved. It all fit in with the image he presented tonight—suave and debonair and very, very sexy.

Her quick perusal ended abruptly when Alyssa noticed that Christian was holding a picture of her and her mother. It was one of the few pictures that had survived over time.

He studied it intently.

Alyssa felt her face flush with embarrassment. That picture showed her as the plump tomboy she had once been. Her hair was scraggly and she had the type of childish carefree grin that showed practically every tooth in her mouth. What was he thinking as he looked so closely at it?

"Ready to go?" she asked.

"You have your mother's eyes and her mouth. She's a very beautiful woman."

Alyssa didn't want to hear that. She didn't want to hear how similar she was to her mother. Not now. Not with everything going on between her and Christian.

"My mother is dead."

Alyssa wasn't sure why she told him that. It just popped out of her mouth before she could stop it.

"I'm sorry."

"Don't be. It was a long time ago."

Her voice came out cold and unfeeling. She couldn't help it. Her mother was a topic she didn't share easily.

Alyssa walked to the door and opened it wide. She turned back to Christian and pasted a smile on her face.

"Shall we go?"

Christian froze. A small knife was stuck into the outside of the door and there was an envelope attached to it. Alyssa hadn't seen it yet. How had someone managed to put that there without him hearing? His senses should have picked up something.

Instead they had been focused on Alyssa. Her smell, the way she looked and the way she moved. He was so involved in her that he was neglecting the real reason he was there. To protect her from harm.

He strode towards her, his long legs eating up the distance between them. He could see the fear in her eyes, but that couldn't be helped. He needed to get her away from that envelope as quickly as possible. He finally reached her and without a word, picked her up and placed her directly behind him.

"Go into your room and don't come out until I tell you," he commanded.

"What? Wait a minute. I—"

Christian swung around and pinned her with his sharp gaze.

"Your life is in my hands, remember? Do what I say now, or I'll take you to your bedroom myself. And I don't think you'll like the consequences, Alyssa."

Alyssa's eyes widened in surprise, yet she still looked like she was about to argue. Then her gaze finally found the knife. Her mouth formed into a perfect O. She took an involuntary step back.

"Go, Alyssa." The quiet warning in his voice was obvious.

She tore her stare from the door and fixed it on him.

"I'll go, Christian. But I expect you to tell me the truth about what's in that envelope."

"Agreed." He nodded his head towards her bedroom. "Now go."

Alyssa took one last look at the door and then went into her room.

Christian studied the envelope and the small knife. He feared there might be some sort of explosive, or chemical inside, but he couldn't sense anything unusual. Walking into Alyssa's kitchen, he grabbed a dishtowel. Placing it over the handle of the knife, he carefully pulled it out. He wrapped it up and placed it on the table by the door. The police would have to be notified and the knife checked for fingerprints.

The envelope fell to the ground. Not wanting to get his own fingerprints on the document, he got a paper towel, then picked it up and turned it over. The flap had not been sealed. He lifted it slowly. Nothing happened. Good. He pulled the sheet of paper out and scanned the letters that had been clipped from the newspaper. The words didn't surprise him. He had seen this type of letter before—threatening, but not specific. It read—

YoU ARe DEAD.

yOU ARE dEAD.

YOU arE DeaD.

YOu WiLl PaY.

Her stalker had found out where she lived. He had taken the next step. The danger to Alyssa was now doubled. And it was his fault for not catching it. He needed to focus on protecting her. That was his job.

He would bring the knife and the letter down to the police station for them to analyze. He knew this was going to upset her, but he agreed to be up front with her about everything. He would keep his word.

"Alyssa, you can come out now."

Alyssa stopped pacing the length of her room when she heard Christian's voice. It was about time! She needed to know what was going on. It wasn't everyday that she had a knife stuck in her door. It frightened her, but at the same time it left her angry that once again someone had violated her personal space.

She noticed the opened letter in Christian's hand immediately. Walking up to him she attempted to take it from him. He held it high above his head. Just out of reach. She felt like stomping her feet in frustration. But never got the chance as Christian's soft touch scattered almost all thoughts from her mind.

"Before reading this, I want you to know something, Alyssa." Christian placed his free hand under her chin and tilted her face up to his. His eyes were intense as they stared into hers.

"This letter changes nothing. I am still here to protect you and I *will* do that. Do you understand what I'm saying?"

Alyssa squirmed under the intensity of his gaze, but silently nodded in agreement.

"Yes, now please let me see the letter, Christian."

He brought it down to her level. Careful to touch the paper towel, not the paper, she took the document from his hand and read it. The words impacted her like a punch to the stomach. Her hands began to shake as she felt fear run up and down her spine. Christian was wrong. Things had changed. It was no longer a matter of someone trying to invade her privacy. Someone wanted her dead.

He took the letter out of her hand without a word and placed it back in the envelope before putting it next to something wrapped in one of her kitchen dishtowels. She knew it was the knife. Christian walked her to her couch and sat her down beside him. She stared across the room at the dishtowel, as if waiting for it to move and come flying at her on its own.

Someone wanted her dead. But who? Why?

"Look at me, *palomita*."

Something in Christian's voice cut through the shock she was feeling. It drew her eyes to his. Once there, she couldn't look away.

"No harm will come to you. I promise this," he vowed. "But maybe you should cancel tonight's speech."

"I can't. These are my aunt's friends. I can't let her down."

"I think she would understand, considering the circumstances."

Alyssa frowned and lifted her chin stubbornly.

"I'm going, Christian. You said you would protect me. I believe you."

Christian looked like he was about to argue, but then stood up and walked to the door.

"Very well. Let's go."

The drive to The Plaza was tense. Alyssa's thoughts kept returning to the stalker's note. Christian wasn't talking much either. In fact he barely said anything. His silence was making her nervous.

She tried to make small talk to ease the tension.

"I'm glad my aunt spoke to Vlad about this function tonight. I hope you don't mind getting dressed in formal clothes."

"It's fine."

"We don't have to stay long at the reception. I wouldn't even attend the party afterwards, but my aunt asked me to. Belonging to this organization for the past twenty years, she is very involved in it. My aunt can be very persuasive when she wants to be. She doesn't give up easily. She's a fighter."

"Is that where you get it?"

Alyssa was confused.

"Get what?"

"Being a fighter. Is that where you get it, from you aunt? Or from your parents?"

Alyssa tensed. Mention of her parents always did that to her. Even as a grown woman, her parents still affected her. Christian's voice sounded casual, but she detected something. He was asking about more than her aunt. He wanted to know about her parents.

"I never really thought about it. I am who I am."

"What was your father like?"

How had this conversation gone from impersonal and light to personal so quickly? Alyssa was uncomfortable, until she remembered that it was too late to go back to polite conversation. The man had drunk her blood! You can't get much more personal than that. Well, maybe you can, but Alyssa *so* didn't want to go there right now. She quelled the image of them in a hot embrace.

The drive to The Plaza would take about twenty more minutes. Plenty of time to get down and dirty personal. She made her decision. She would answer his questions, then he better answer some of hers.

"My father was a drill sergeant in the marines. He's a pretty tough nut. You know the type. Doesn't show much emotion, very strong-willed and controlling. Was he a fighter? I'd have to say yes and no."

"What do you mean?"

Alyssa took a deep breath. Ready—set—go.

"As I said, my father was a tough nut. And he liked to control everything in his life. That included my mother and me. My mother was not a fighter. She was a codependent. Everything my father told her to do, be, wear, think, she did without an argument. Her life revolved completely around him and his needs. Even after I was born, every decision was based on what Daddy wanted, what Daddy told us we should do, what Daddy liked. As a child, I would wonder why my mother never did what she wanted to do. And as I got older I couldn't imagine her existing without my father. He was her world. He made her who she was. And she gladly accepted that. "

Alyssa took another deep breath and released it before continuing.

"When my mother died, I realized that everything was not what it seemed. Yes, my mother depended on my father, but my father also depended on my mother. He needed that worship, that compliance, that complete devotion to be happy. Without it he was lost. He didn't know what to do with himself, or me. Though I was devastated by my mother's death, my father couldn't break out of his own shell of shock and grief to comfort me. I guess he didn't know what to do with a daughter who refused to revolve her existence around him. Who wanted to live her life in her own way and be an independent person. So my father did nothing. He chose not to fight for me, his own daughter. He chose not to fight for our relationship. So in that sense, I'd have to say he was not a fighter."

"How did your mother die?"

Alyssa knew Christian was going to ask that. Nevertheless it still shocked her. She wanted to clam up, not say another word. But she had gone this far. It was pointless now to stop.

Maybe he needed to hear it. Maybe then he would understand why she couldn't be with someone like him. Not just because of the vampire issue, although that was a biggie, but because of his need to control her. She could never and would never allow that to happen.

"My mother committed suicide. She couldn't deal with the fact that she wasn't able to make my father completely and utterly happy. Or so she thought. She lived her life for him, yet he always managed to criticize her. He complained about everything. Her hair, her body, her clothes, her friends, her cooking, her cleaning. He even criticized her for having a daughter, instead of a son, after the doctors told her she couldn't have any more children. It didn't matter that she almost died having me. It wasn't what my father wanted."

Alyssa fought against the tears welling up in her eyes. She should be over this by now. Why did it still hurt so much? Swallowing hard, she stared out the car window, avoiding

Christian's knowing gaze. She jumped when he placed his hand over hers where it rested on the car seat. She swung around to look at him. He kept his eyes on the road as he drove, but also gave her hand a reassuring squeeze. The comfort from that small contact helped her continue talking.

"What my mother never realized and what I figured out as I got older, was that my father *was* happy. He was happy with my mother, just the way she was, needing and depending on him. Letting him control everything in her life, including her emotions. That power over another human being was an addiction to my father. And he knew that as long as my mother thought he wasn't completely satisfied with her, she would continue to make him the center of her universe. In the end, I think my mother just lost it. She couldn't take it anymore."

"I'm sorry, *palomita*."

Christian's words were filled with regret.

He released her hand. Alyssa wanted his touch back. She felt desolate without it. He gently wiped a tear from her cheek with his fingers. Surprised she lifted her own hand to her face. Her cheeks were wet with tears. How long had she been crying? She had been so lost in her memories, that she didn't even realize it.

Alyssa swiped the tears off her cheeks and tried to get back under control. Christian said nothing else as she got herself together. He moved his hand back to the steering wheel and away from her. She wanted it back, wanted his touch. But she wouldn't ask him. She couldn't let him see any more of her vulnerability. He would only use that to control her, just like her father had always tried to do.

Raising her chin proudly, she continued.

"So, to answer your original question, was my mother a fighter? No. She gave up on her own life and she gave up on her only child. Obviously she loved neither enough to fight for them. I think you were right the first time around. If anyone taught me to fight, it was my Aunt Joyce. She's taught me a lot. I'll always be grateful for that and for her."

Alyssa clamped her mouth tightly closed. That's it. She was done. True confessions from the therapist who was supposed to have everything together were now over. Time to turn things around. It was Christian's turn. She had some questions for him.

"Enough about me. Tell me about you."

She saw Christian stiffen.

"What would you like to know?" he asked warily.

"Tell me about Bazhena. Tell me how you became a vampire. And tell me about Elena."

Christian swung his shocked gaze around to look at Alyssa. She was staring calmly out the front window. How could she possibly know about Elena?

"If you don't keep your eyes on the road, I'm going to get nervous." Alyssa said without looking at him.

Christian's turned back to the street. He frowned, his eyes narrowed dangerously and his jaw tightened. Alyssa was good at making him lose focus. Too damn good. He needed to concentrate.

"How do you know about Elena?"

Alyssa looked like she was about to speak, then she hesitated.

"I need to know this, Alyssa."

"I know. I'm just trying to figure out how to say this. Okay. When you, uh, when you were, um, taking care of my foot, blood wasn't the only thing we shared. I could feel you in my head. Feel what you were experiencing. And I picked up certain images. I saw a woman who looked a lot like me, but wasn't me. Then the name Elena popped into my head. Who is she, Christian?"

She had picked up his thoughts? That had never happened to him before. Maybe because he had projected pleasure so strongly to her, she had gotten glimpses of other images and feelings as well.

He thought about telling her nothing, just clearing her mind and changing the subject. But he wouldn't do that. Alyssa had just shared something of herself with him that was so personal, so painful that he could not keep this from her.

"Elena was my betrothed. It was the year, 1785. We were going to be married. I lived in St. Augustine, Florida at the time. I was a Spanish soldier stationed there during Spain's short second occupation. Then a strange woman came to town. My life changed completely and Elena's ended."

Christian tightened his hold on the steering wheel. The memories always came back so strongly, as did the pain.

"Bazhena. She was the mysterious woman who came to our town that summer. And she was the most beautiful woman I had ever seen. The minute I laid eyes on her, I could think of no other. I became crazed, obsessed with her. Elena and I had known each other in Spain, before her family immigrated to Florida. We had grown up within the same circle of friends and family. So we knew each other well. She could tell something was wrong. She tried to talk to me about it several times, but I wouldn't listen to her. I wouldn't discuss it."

"In one breath, I told Elena nothing was wrong and in the next I set up a discreet assignation with Bazhena. We met a few times, each more intense than the last. I couldn't get enough of Bazhena. I felt like I was losing my mind and she was taking it over. Which, looking back now, was exactly what was happening. She was slowly making me hers. I think, with enough time, I would have gone to her willingly. I would have betrayed Elena, a woman I had known all my life and had fallen in love with, just to be with Bazhena. Unfortunately for Elena, it didn't happen that way."

Christian got lost in the memory. His mind wandered to those last couple of days before Elena was killed. Just as he had done a thousand times before, he desperately wished he had handled things differently. Maybe it would have made a difference. Maybe Elena would not have been murdered.

"Christian? Are you okay?"

Alyssa's concerned voice broke through his thoughts.

"Yes, I'm fine. Where was I? I went to see Bazhena one evening. I arrived a little early. I must have entered without her hearing me, because I know she would not have wanted me to see what I saw. At that point, I didn't realize she was a vampire. I was so lost in her spell that I only thought of her as an incredibly beautiful, desirable woman who made me mad with need."

"What happened next?"

"I entered her room and saw her with someone else. Another man. The man was on his knees in front of her. Bazhena was bent over him, her hands holding his shoulders, but I couldn't see her face because it was buried in the crook of the man's neck. His arms were wrapped tightly around her waist, his head thrown back. The man's eyes were closed and his face was contorted with a mixture of pain and pleasure. His body was convulsing as if he was having an orgasm and he was gasping Bazhena's name over and over again. Jealousy and rage overcame me. I strode towards them, intending to break them apart. Bazhena must have heard me because she raised her head and looked at me."

Fury swept through Christian. He remembered what Bazhena had done to the man embracing her. And how he could do nothing to stop it.

"Her eyes were glowing red and her elongated incisors shined against the blood covering her lips. I stopped at the sight of her. Frozen to the spot in shock. The corner of her lips turned up into a smile. That smile, which I had found so enchanting, now looked grotesque and evil. My eyes traveled back and forth in shock between the two of them as if my mind couldn't quite process what it was seeing. The man moaned and turned slightly towards me. As he did I saw the side of his neck. It had been torn open. Blood pumped out of the wound and down his body. Yet his eyes remained closed and his moans were ones of pleasure. He even pulled Bazhena's head back to his neck."

Christian would never forget how she laughed when her victim had done that. It had been a low, throaty laugh. One filled with intense satisfaction.

"She gladly complied and continued to drink from the man, swallowing his life in great noisy gulps. His movements slowed and the moans coming from him ceased. Replaced by loud, gasping breaths as he struggled for life. I finally broke out of my frozen stupor and tried to move towards them. I knew the man would die if I didn't reach him. I tried, pushed myself with everything I had, but I couldn't move. I was paralyzed. Bazhena's eyes stayed on me, intense and watchful as she fed. I knew she was holding me back somehow. Controlling me. I could only watch as the man's hold on her went slack. She released his shoulders and he slid slowly down her body to the ground."

Christian paused to get himself under control. To tamp down the anger and frustration he had felt that night over two hundred years ago. His gaze slid to Alyssa. She still looked straight in front of her, out the window. But he could see by the frown on her face, that she was uncomfortable. His story was affecting her also.

"Alyssa, I don't have to finish. I can stop n—"

Alyssa turned away from the window and honed in on his face. She searched his eyes. What she was looking for, he wasn't sure. Then she shuttered her gaze and turned back towards the front window.

"No, Christian, finish. I need to hear it all."

Her voice sounded toneless, without feeling.

What was she feeling? He could delve into her mind, but he didn't want to do that. She had to tell him of her own free will. He would wait until she was ready.

"I learned Bazhena was a vampire that night. She killed the man. Then let his drained body drop to the ground. She walked right over him towards me, as if he were just another piece of furniture she needed to maneuver around. She took a handkerchief and daintily wiped the blood from her lips. Her callous attitude towards it all made me realize that this wasn't the first time she had done this, and it wouldn't be the last. As she approached, I regained the ability to move. I backed away from her in horror. Tried to keep some distance between us. Her eyes flared with anger. She asked me where I was going and I told her I didn't want to see her ever again, that I was getting married. That Elena and I were going to spend the rest of our lives together. I told her it was over between us."

"What did she do after you told her that?"

"Something that should have warned me of upcoming trouble. She did nothing. She stopped following me and let me walk out. All the while she continued to smile at me in a way that wasn't normal. She looked cold and calculating. Over the next couple of days, I tried to forget that night. Tried to concentrate on Elena and me. Tried not to remember the horror I had seen. I shouldn't have done that. I let my guard down and Elena died because of that."

"What happened?" The dread in Alyssa's voice was obvious. She knew that whatever he was about to say, it wasn't going to be good.

"Bazhena came to my home two nights after she killed that man. And she wasn't alone. Elena was cradled in her arms. Dead. Completely drained of blood."

That image of Elena, dead in her arms, rose up like a monster. Bile rose in his throat as he remembered how Elena had looked, so still and pale. Small spatters of blood on her cheeks marred her beauty. Then Bazhena moved the scarf around Elena's neck aside. The gaping wound was horrendous. It looked as if someone had gnawed their way almost completely through her neck. Christian tried to erase the image of Elena from his mind. He tried to forget the savage satisfaction on Bazhena's face as she held his dead fiancée in her arms. But it stayed with him.

He knew Alyssa was waiting for him to continue, but he didn't. He was done. It was enough, for now.

He was grateful Alyssa didn't push him to continue. Neither of them spoke. Silence stretched between them until they reached their destination. The Plaza Hotel's lights shined bright, making the building stand out like a beacon against the dark desert mountains. The people walking into the hotel were just as bright. Women were adorned with jewels and sequined dresses and the men decked out in tuxedos. Christian pulled the car around to a lesser-used entrance and parked. He got out, walked around to Alyssa's side and opened the door for her.

Alyssa didn't get out.

He waited a minute or so, but nothing happened. Curious, he bent forward and looked into the car. Alyssa sat stiffly in her seat, looking straight ahead. Not moving, not looking at him. Nothing. Just sitting there, staring out the front window.

Chapter Eight

❧

Alyssa could see it all.

Everything Christian was telling her.

She didn't know how—she didn't want to know.

She just wanted it to stop.

The images bombarded her mind. Uninvited. She couldn't get them out.

Elena lay so still. Her head tilted to the side at an odd angle, leaving her neck exposed. It looked half eaten away and blood still dripped from it. Her eyes were open, but unseeing. Dead.

Bazhena laughed, satisfaction written all over her face. An evil leer curved her bloodstained lips. Discarding Elena like a piece of trash, Bazhena dropped her on the ground. Then she went after Christian. Her movements were too fast. One minute she was standing over Elena's dead body, the next she had Christian in her hold. Alyssa felt his disgust, his anger, his sadness and his fear. Bazhena pulled him to her. Her mouth opened and her sharp incisors drew closer to his neck. He struggled with everything he had, up until the moment her mouth touched his neck. Then everything changed. Desire and pleasure like nothing he'd ever felt before exploded inside Christian. Instead of pushing Bazhena away, he grabbed her head and pulled her tighter against his neck—

Christian touched Alyssa's arm. The images shattered into a hundred pieces then skittered away. No! She wanted the pleasure back. Yearned for it. How could she live without it?

"Alyssa. What is it? What's wrong?"

Christian's voice brought her back to the present. The sound of it soothed her restlessness. Helped her focus on his face. The concern she saw was a comfort. It would be okay now. She'd be okay. Taking a deep breath, she counted to five and then exhaled. Again. She started to relax a little. The tightening in her body slowly loosened.

"It's okay, Alyssa. You're going to be okay."

"H-how did you do it?" Alyssa gasped.

Christian's eyes grew wide, his face tightened. Alyssa could see it. He knew what she was asking. He knew what she had felt, but he pretended not to.

"Do what?"

"Make yourself leave Bazhena. Live without that kind of pleasure?"

His eyes turned cold. No emotion showed. It was as if he just turned himself off.

"I had to. I couldn't let someone control my whole life. I couldn't belong to someone with everything I was."

Alyssa stared deeply into Christian's eyes.

"Neither can I," she said.

Ignoring his outstretched hand, she got out of the car and walked away.

She knew Christian would have to catch up with her, guard her tonight and protect her life. But afterwards, when all of this was done, it was over. That yearning to belong to someone, like she had felt in Christian's memories, scared her more than her father's overbearing, controlling ways ever had. She could not, *no*, she would not let someone take over her life like that.

And Christian was capable of doing just that. The way he took her the other night. The way he made her feel. That had been only a taste compared to what Bazhena had done to him. And that had blown Alyssa away. If she let Christian stay in her life, there was no way she would escape. She wasn't strong enough to fight that kind of pleasure. After a while, she wouldn't want to fight it.

Christian got to her before she entered the hotel. Grasping her arm, he turned her around to face him. He searched her face.

She struggled to maintain a calm facade. She kept her expression blank, waiting for him to speak.

He opened his mouth and then clamped it shut again. After a minute, he finally spoke.

"Let's go in. Stay behind me."

Christian turned away from her and with one last glance behind his shoulder, walked into The Plaza. She followed close behind. He had explained the procedure, tonight he was mother duck, she was duckling. She followed where he walked, when he walked, never veering to the side, back, or front unless he did.

The picture Alyssa created in her mind of Christian as a mother duck brought a very unladylike snort from her. She couldn't help it. He was about as un-mother duck-like as anyone she had ever met. The analogy worked in terms of procedure, but otherwise it was just too ridiculous.

She watched him work. Though she was behind him, she knew he scanned the area constantly. Periodically he glanced back at her to ensure she was okay. Every movement he made was calculated. His body completely blocked hers. If someone tried to approach her, he stopped them.

"Ms. Edwards can't talk to anyone until after the speech."

People took one look at Christian and obeyed. Alyssa realized that those around them cleared a path for Christian. It didn't seem to be a conscious action. It was as if they did it through instinct. She noticed a group of people talking in front of them. As she and Christian drew closer, the group didn't look their way. They all just sort of shifted to one side so that the two of them could pass. It was almost as if they all got the same mental suggestion to move at the same time. Alyssa wondered how much of that was due to Christian using his vampire powers and how much of it was due to the fact that he was an intimidating man.

He stopped abruptly and Alyssa barely avoided running into him. She saw his back stiffen and he clenched his fists tightly to his side. Curious about what could have caused this reaction in Christian, she peeked around him.

It wasn't a what, it was a who.

Aunt Joyce stood directly in front of Christian. Hands on her hips as she gave him the once-over, then studied his face with interest. The speculative gleam in her eyes wasn't lost on her. Her aunt thought every man might be a perfect candidate as a husband for Alyssa. If only she knew about Christian.

"Well, Alyssa? Aren't you going to introduce me to your young man?" Joyce impatiently said.

"He isn't my young man. This is Christian Galiano. He's the security specialist handling my speaking engagements. Christian, this is my Aunt Joyce."

Aunt Joyce held out her hand.

"Hello. Please call me Joyce. It's so nice to finally meet you, Mr. Galiano. I've heard so many good things about you from Alyssa."

Christian looked at Alyssa. He raised one eyebrow and a knowing smile spread across his lips.

"Really?" The amusement in his voice was obvious.

Alyssa wanted to wipe that smile off his face, but instead smiled sweetly back at him.

"Of course. You've been such a gallant gentleman. What could I possibly have to say about you that my aunt would find displeasing?"

Christian's eyes narrowed dangerously. Warning her. She chose to ignore it.

"Christian has protected me just like he's been paid to do. He's very good at his job. Isn't that right, Christian? And once my last speech is over, he can go protect someone else and I can get on with my life."

"Alyssa!"

Her aunt's shocked voice made Alyssa cringe inside. Why was she goading Christian? She was being rude and it wasn't fair. Maybe it was the frustration. Maybe it was the knowledge that she wanted him, but couldn't allow herself to have him. Before she could even think about apologizing, Christian spoke.

"That's right. Once you get through your last engagement, I won't need to babysit you anymore, will I, Alyssa?"

Alyssa was steaming. Babysit? How dare he?

Christian bent close and whispered. The feel of his breath caressing her ear sent shivers of pleasure up and down her spine. Then the meaning of his words hit her and she stiffened.

"Until that last engagement, you are mine, *palomita,* to do with as I choose. Don't forget that." Christian grasped her arm. His hold didn't hurt, but she wasn't going anywhere until he was ready.

"I need to take Alyssa to her room while she waits to go on, Joyce. She will be much safer there than the middle of the room. If you'll excuse us?"

Alyssa wanted to resist, but knew if she did, it would only cause a scene. She didn't want to do that to her aunt. Not in front of so many of her aunt's friends.

Her aunt looked confused for a minute, but then she nodded her head and smiled.

"Of course. Nice meeting you, Mr. Galiano, and I'll see you both later."

Alyssa calmly let Christian lead her to her room.

But the minute Christian closed the door and released her arm she slapped him, hard, across the face. Or, at least that was her intention. Before her palm even touched him, he caught her hand and pushed it behind her back. He did the same thing with her other hand and held them together with one of his hands. Christian pulled her against him. She shivered when she noticed how good her softness felt pressed against the hard contours of his chest.

"Now where were we? That's right, you were telling me how to do my job, weren't you? And I was telling you that I owned you until my job was done. Do you have a problem with that?"

The deep timbre of Christian's voice told Alyssa he was angry. That and the furious look on his face. Well, too bad. She was angry also. Angry and frustrated about, well, everything.

"Yes, as a matter of fact, I do have a problem with that." Alyssa lifted her chin and met his gaze without a flinch. "Nobody has, nor will anybody ever *own* me. You *work* for me, period. End of story. Please don't forget that."

Christian moved his face so close to hers that she could make out each individual eyelash on his beautiful mocha eyes.

"Forget it? How can I forget it? Every time I see your lush lips, I have to remind myself that this is a working relationship, so I can't kiss you senseless. Every time I see the sensuous way you move your body, I have to remember this is business only, so I can't explore your voluptuous curves. Every time I hear your husky voice, I have to remember that you're a client, so I can't let the sexy sound of it make me so hard I want to explode."

Christian's last word came out a growl. He stared into her eyes, demanding everything. Asking for nothing. His admission ignited a fire of desire. It hit her like a locomotive, making her shake with need.

He lowered his mouth to hers. She rose up to meet him. She was tired of fighting it. Tired of denying herself. She wanted Christian with everything inside her. She wanted him naked and pressed against her. She craved his touch everywhere on her body. She yearned to feel his hardness plunging deep inside her.

I want you too, palomita.

Christian's voice in her mind added kindling to the fire of her need. She strained against him, opened her mouth and invited him in. His tongue engaged hers in a dance that turned her insides out. She struggled to free her hands, until he finally released his hold. She had to touch him—*now*.

Christian couldn't get enough of her mouth. He explored every corner, until they were both moaning. He felt her hands at his back, then under his jacket, then pulling his shirt out of his pants. The feel of her fingers sliding up his body made him groan.

He tore his mouth from her lips and trailed it down her neck. He unwrapped the scarf she wore, exposing her creamy white skin to his hungry gaze. Laving and sucking her pulse point, he let the hunger build in him, then moved lower. He traced the outline of her collarbone with his mouth, taking small nips of her skin and then soothing it with his tongue.

Alyssa was breathing hard, each breath pushing her breasts up against the scoop neckline of her gown. Grasping her waist Christian lifted her and brought the low-cut plunge even with his mouth. Her cleavage called to him. He ran his tongue in the crevice between her breasts, savoring the sweet taste of her, the feel of her soft skin against his mouth and the enticing smell of apples. Then he followed the neckline, teasing it with his tongue.

Alyssa was making small noises of pleasure that made him want to lift her dress and take her there and then. She started squirming against him. Christian let her slowly slide down his body until her feet once more touched the floor. As she did, he moved one hand to her thigh and slipped it under her dress. He thought he would explode when he felt a garter holding up the smooth stocking she wore. Growling with need, he moved his hand higher. He reveled in the feel of her velvety skin under his fingertips.

Christian could feel the heat emanating from her core. He had to touch her. As his hand drew closer to her center, Alyssa widened her stance and tilted her hips forward. He needed no other invitation. She wanted him, wanted his touch. He read the need in her body's reaction to him and in her thoughts. She was crying out with need. And he was only too happy to satisfy her.

Slipping his fingers under her panties, he felt her moist heat. He parted her lips and his fingers became soaked with her wetness. Her body was weeping for him, calling to him. He ran his fingers over her sensitive nub, again and again. He felt her knees give way. He held her up with one hand at her waist.

Alyssa's moans grew louder. Christian captured her lips with his own, taking each moan into his body. He thrust his tongue inside her mouth at the same exact moment he plunged his fingers into her hot core. Once, twice, again and again.

Come for me, palomita. Let yourself go.

The minute Christian projected his thoughts to her, Alyssa's body tightened then convulsed with pleasure. He ran his tongue from her mouth down to her neck so he could hear her gasps of pleasure. The sound of it rolled over him, satisfied the beast in him. Made him want to roar with triumph. He brought her this pleasure. Only him. She was his.

Alyssa eventually climbed out of the fuzzy haze of her release. She opened her eyes and found Christian looking intently at her. She couldn't read his expression, other than the fact that it was serious, very serious. He was looking at her with such intensity, as if he were searching for an answer in her face.

"What?"

Her voice came out a whisper. She had to ask. Needed to hear him speak. What they had just shared had been, well, fantastic. No one had ever made her feel like that. Being able to touch each other physically and mentally had been an incredibly sensual experience.

Christian shuttered his eyes and released her. She was unsteady at first, but then found her balance. He moved away from her. Put distance between them. His face looked cold and emotionless.

"Christian?"

Alyssa cringed at the sound of her own voice, vulnerable, unsure and needy. Just like her mother.

"Alyssa, I think—"

A knock sounded at the door.

Alyssa had never been more thankful for someone interrupting a conversation as she was tonight. She would make a fool of herself if this continued.

"I'll get that," she said a little too brightly.

She turned around to open the door, but just as she placed her hand on the doorknob, Christian's hand wrapped around hers.

"No. Just ask who it is. Don't open the door." His breath tickled her ear as he whispered to her.

The feel of his hand over hers, his hard chest pressed lightly against her back felt so good. She just wanted to lean back against him and close her eyes. Enjoy the closeness they shared.

Another knock at the door broke through her dreamy state.

"Ms. Edwards, are you there?" an unfamiliar male voice asked.

She felt Christian's chest rumbling against her back. Was he—? It sounded like he was growling! Surprised by the sound, Alyssa attempted to turn around and look at him. She didn't get very far. He wrapped his free arm around her waist and brought her up hard against him. She started to protest, but the feel of his hardness against her bottom left her speechless.

"Answer him now, Alyssa." Though he was whispering in her ear, Alyssa couldn't mistake the serious tone of his voice.

"Y-yes. What is it?" She sounded shaky, even to her own ears.

"You're on in five minutes. I need to take you to the stage area in two."

Alyssa had trouble focusing on the man's words. Christian's proximity was distracting her.

"Okay. I'll be right out."

Christian released her.

She didn't turn around immediately. What would she say? What could she say? She had never been in this kind of situation before. She wasn't sure how to handle it.

"Turn around, *palomita*."

His sexy voice pulled at her. Made her want to do whatever he asked. She swung around to face him.

Their gazes met. His mouth curved up in amusement. But his eyes looked sad and so lonely. She wanted to go to him, but fought it. No. She needed to settle this once and for all.

"Christian, I know we just shared something intensely intimate. You made me feel incredible, but I—"

"No. Don't say it." Christian shook his head and his eyes narrowed dangerously. "I don't ever want to hear you say that."

He looked angry, really angry and she didn't know why.

"Say what?"

"Don't say that you regret what just happened. Don't deny what we have between us, Alyssa. I didn't want this to happen either, but it has. Deal with it like an adult, not a child."

Now it was Alyssa's turn to get angry.

"How dare you? You don't even know what I was going to say."

Quietly, so quiet that Alyssa almost didn't hear him, he broke through every wall she had built up around herself over the years.

"Yes, I do know. I felt you, heard your thoughts in my mind, just like you're starting to feel mine. We're developing a bond. You didn't ask for it. Neither did I. But it's there. And we need to decide what to do about it."

He heard her thoughts? Could it be true? How was it possible that even as he spoke, she could feel the honesty, frustration and anger in his mind? He was telling her the truth, but he wasn't happy about it. Neither was she.

"Listen, I can't deal with this at all right now. I have a speech to make and I need to do a good job because my aunt is depending on me. This is important to her. I can't disappoint her." Alyssa rummaged through her bag and pulled her notes and bottled water out before continuing.

"I'm not sure what we're talking about here, but whatever it is will have to wait. We can discuss this afterwards, okay?" she asked.

Alyssa walked back to the door and opened it. Before walking out, she looked over her shoulder at Christian.

"Ready?"

Alyssa could see the turmoil swirling in Christian's soulful eyes. Then he blinked and it was gone. His face became a calm, confident and cold facade. He tucked in his shirt, then walked towards her and held the door open.

"After you."

He sounded polite and emotionless. That's what she wanted, didn't she? All business, no emotions? She should be happy.

But she wasn't. She didn't like it. Not one little bit.

* * * * *

Christian struggled for composure as Alyssa gave her speech. He scanned the room once more, checking for anything or anyone unusual. He had to concentrate on keeping her safe. Instead he was thinking about how many different ways he could wring her pretty neck. The little fool really didn't understand what was going on. Or she was pretending not to understand.

Alyssa needed control in her life. Their relationship, up to now, had been more out of control than anything else. She was having a hard time dealing with it. He could understand that. He wasn't handling it in the best way possible either. Just remembering what happened between them in the backstage room made him want to take her to some isolated location and make love to her until neither of them could breathe. That was in no way close to being in control.

Considering how much discipline he used to contain his beast this should be laughably easy. But it wasn't. Christian wanted Alyssa in a way that stripped everything away, all the civility, all the expectations and all the rights and wrongs. He needed to make her completely, totally and irrefutably his. And the urge was getting stronger and stronger.

Unfortunately, so was the beast. The vampire he was wanted to break free. Craved to take her in the way of their kind. Needed to taste her sweet life force while he plunged deeply into the welcoming warmth of her body, over and over again.

"Mr. Galiano? Is everything okay?"

Christian was shocked back to reality. Alyssa's aunt spoke softly, but still she had surprised him. That never should have happened. If he hadn't been daydreaming, he would have heard her approach. And what about Alyssa? He searched the room, his gaze resting briefly on her. She was safe. He released the breath he had been holding.

"Mr. Galiano?"

Christian turned to Alyssa's aunt. Her concerned expression urged him to calm her fears immediately.

"Everything's fine. I was just checking out the room. Your niece is safe. I'm watching over her."

"Good. It's about time somebody did," she muttered.

Christian didn't think she had wanted him to hear that, but he had.

"What do you mean?"

Joyce look startled for a moment, but then she chuckled softly.

"My niece is just too darn independent for her own good. She's always been scrappy like that. Even as a young girl. She's a very goal-oriented, focused and well disciplined person. But she's also very stubborn."

"I never noticed." Christian struggled to keep the amusement from his voice.

Joyce chuckled and gave him a doubtful look.

"*That* she got from her mother. And that stubbornness gets Alyssa into trouble sometimes. But most of the time those traits have helped her get through some pretty rough spots. She's come to depend on them in everything she does. That's why she's had such a hard time finding a man. They all say they want a strong woman, but when they get one, they don't know what to do with them. Do you, Mr. Galiano? Do you know what to do? Do you know how to keep a strong woman?"

Christian wasn't sure exactly what Joyce was asking, but he suspected it was more than the words she was using. She was trying to help him understand something about Alyssa. So he stayed quiet. He didn't try to answer her question. He knew she was going to answer it for him.

"The way a man keeps a strong woman, Mr. Galiano, is to let her figure out that she needs to keep him."

Alyssa's aunt gave him a satisfied smile.

"Keep up the good work. I like you. And I trust you to take care of my niece. Considering she's the one person I care most about in this world that should tell you something."

Then she walked away.

Now Christian knew for sure. He knew whom Alyssa took after. It wasn't her mother or her father. She definitely took after her aunt.

* * * * *

Alyssa finished her speech to enthusiastic applause. She had tried to stay focused as she spoke, but it had been difficult. She kept thinking about what had happened between her and Christian earlier and the resulting conversation. If he pushed her about this she knew she wouldn't handle it well. She wasn't ready to deal with her feelings right now. As a therapist, she knew this wasn't the healthiest attitude in the world, but she couldn't help it.

Where Christian was concerned, she couldn't seem to think rationally. She had glanced at him periodically throughout her speech. The sight of him made her heart flip-flop like a fish out of water. His devastatingly handsome face was serious as he checked out the people listening to her. She could have told him that the energy in the room was only positive tonight, but she wasn't sure he would believe her. And she didn't know if she was ready to share her ability with him.

He scanned the room constantly. Searching for something amiss. He looked tense, ready for anything. She remembered the feel of his muscled back beneath her fingers and his hard chest pressed against her. He was a male in his prime. He would have no problem handling any situation that arose.

His eyes had touched on her briefly during her speech and she stuttered over a word or two. After that, she tried to ignore him and concentrate on what she was saying. She hadn't been completely successful. His dominating presence made him stick out like a wolf among sheep. But she had managed to complete her speech without any more stumbling.

When she walked off stage, Christian met her at the edge and guided her back to her room backstage. He didn't speak as he went in first. She followed close behind and watched him do a quick check of the room. Then he turned without a word and left.

Alyssa didn't know what to do. He hadn't said a word to her. She had expected him to start the discussion where they left off before her speech. But he hadn't. What was he up to? She quickly freshened her makeup and hair and then opened the door. Christian stood stiff and unyielding with his back facing her.

He turned at the sound of the door opening.

"Are you ready to go to the reception?" His face held no emotion. His voice sounded polite, professional and distant.

Alyssa didn't know how to react to him. She was relieved he didn't push her about their relationship. But she was also disappointed for some reason. She knew it was irrational, but couldn't help it.

"Yes, I'm ready," she replied just as coldly.

If that's how he wanted it to be, then she would go with it too.

As they walked together to the reception, neither of them spoke. Yet Alyssa felt the tension between them fill the air. She was relieved when they entered the room and she saw her aunt standing right by the door.

"Alyssa! You did a wonderful job." Her aunt gave her a big hug. "Please come meet some of my friends."

Alyssa spent the next hour talking to her aunt's friends. She felt Christian constantly by her side. But he wasn't the only one. Women were gathered around him like bees to honey. Engaging him in conversation and flirting outrageously. She could see he was trying to maintain his distance from the group, keep an eye on her. But every once in a while a woman would lean towards him, say something quietly to him and they would both laugh. That irritated her. His husky laughter was a pleasure that she wanted to be the only one to enjoy.

If they had all been her aunt's age, it probably wouldn't have bothered Alyssa as much. But they weren't. The women who seemed to find him the most fascinating were young, some younger than her. Alyssa tried to get Christian's attention a couple of times, but every time he glanced her way, her aunt would grasp her arm and steer her towards someone else she wanted Alyssa to meet.

She tried to ignore it. Tried to put all her energy into her conversations with various people, but it was no use. Her irritation rose to the point where she felt like yelling and pulling her hair out. She wanted to tell all Christian's admirers to get lost. He belonged to her. She had the primitive urge to yell, "He's mine!"

After about an hour, she was tired of talking. And she was sick of seeing all those women fawning over Christian. She glanced at the dance floor and saw a few couples dancing. She had an idea. Despite her aunt's protests, she excused herself and walked to where Christian stood with his harem. She pushed her way through the crowd until she stood facing him.

His face still held no emotion as he looked at her, but she didn't care. She wanted to be with him at that moment and nobody was going to stop her. Not the throng of women around him, not even him. She lifted her chin proudly and held her hand out.

"Dance with me."

Chapter Nine

ꝏ

Christian wanted to throw back his head and roar in triumph.

Yet he held everything inside. He kept his face a blank as Alyssa approached him. He had been excruciatingly aware of her as she moved around the room, talking with various people, and not just because he was trying to protect her. His eyes were drawn to her without thought, without will. He just couldn't get enough of looking at her. That was a pleasure he refused to deny himself.

The women around him paled and faded into nothing. Their inconsequential conversation and flirting meant absolutely nothing to him. Mortal women were always attracted to him, wanted to be near him. He had accepted that long ago. It mattered little to him. *Until now*.

He watched the sweet sway of Alyssa's hips as she approached him. The dress she wore made his mouth water. She shimmered with beauty, seduction and innocence, all at the same time. And she called to him. Maybe not consciously, but it mattered little. He felt it, heard it. Her mind and body were shouting out her message loud and clear.

Alyssa wanted him. Nothing else mattered. The other women seemed to sense what was going on. They slowly moved away, until it was just he and Alyssa facing each other. She held her hand out to him. Christian's chest tightened. His breath grew short. Still he waited. He held back a moment. Continued to stare at her, exhibiting no emotion. He needed her to remember this moment. Remember how much she wanted him. And remember that it was her choice.

She asked him to dance.

His expression changed. Christian let his desire and hunger burn in his eyes. Let her see the beast's face as it pinned her with its powerful gaze. Alyssa's eyes widened. Her lips parted in a gasp. She started to back away. He seized her hand before she could move. He led her to the dance floor. Once there, he didn't give her a chance to escape. Instead, he pulled her against him. He knew she could feel his desire. Feel his body tighten with hunger. He moved to the slow music, keeping her soft curves pressed against him.

His movements were meant to entice and seduce. She didn't fight it. She clung to him, her body wrapped around his. He knew she finally understood. He had lain in wait and she had come to him. He was the predator and she the prey. Alyssa had been well and truly caught.

Alyssa was panting. There was no other word for it. She would like to think she was just breathing hard or taking quick breaths, but that wasn't the case. The feel of Christian's hard contours rubbing and sliding over her sensitive body made her pant with desire. And she could do nothing to stop it. She didn't want to stop it. She had asked, no, practically begged Christian for it.

She had requested a dance. But they both knew she was asking for so much more. Jealousy had consumed her while she watched Christian talk with the other women. Alyssa had never felt that kind of jealousy and anger, ever before. It had taken hold and given her a good, hard shake. But it had also made her admit how much she wanted Christian. Needed to feel him inside her and all around her as they made love, over and over again. That thought alone filled her mind as she had approached him.

The responding *roar* she heard coming from his thoughts told her everything. When she saw his eyes suddenly flare with desire and a hunger so strong it left her breathless, she knew. He wanted the same thing she did. Tonight. Nothing would stop them. Tonight they would satisfy the lust burning through them like a wildfire.

Slowly, Christian moved them towards the door. In the hall outside the reception room, he backed her up against a wall. He took each of her hands in his and held them on either side of her head. His actions surprised her. She broke eye contact and looked around. The hall was empty. Everything became blurred as Christian kissed her neck. She leaned her head back to give him better access. He nuzzled her, then ran his tongue over her collarbone. Her knees grew weak and she started to slide down.

She felt his knee lift up against her leg. He nudged her thighs apart and pushed his knee against the fabric of her dress until it pressed between them. His leg held her up, but the feel of it pressed against the center of her made her gasp with need. He moved his mouth back up to hers and plunged his tongue inside her parted lips. He stroked her again and again, plundered every corner of her mouth, demanding her response. He moved his leg slightly and she whimpered. The friction against her hot core felt too good. She tilted her hips forward, then back again. The movement built her flaming passion into a roaring fire.

Christian stiffened. He tore his mouth from hers and released her hands.

"Someone's coming."

Alyssa struggled for composure. Christian grasped her shoulders and slid his knee from between her legs. Alyssa smoothed her dress down and steadied herself while he held her in place with his hands. He waited until she gave him a nod. Then he released her and took a step back, putting some distance between them.

A few seconds later, a couple walked out of the reception room. Alyssa gave them a friendly smile, then turned back to Christian as if they were in the middle of a conversation.

"That was a little too close for comfort," she said, trying to ignore the flames of desire burning in his eyes.

Christian nodded and gave her a lopsided smile. Her heart did a little flip-flop. It was the type of grin she would have expected to see on a younger Christian, one who was not a vampire. She couldn't resist smiling back. They were like a couple of kids who had gotten caught making out at the school dance.

Christian's smile faded as he stared into her eyes.

"I want you, *palomita*. So much my body hurts. What do you want?"

Alyssa's image of two kids dissolved. They weren't kids. And what she wanted from Christian was utterly and completely adult.

"Let me say goodbye to my aunt and I'll be right back."

"I'll go with you."

Christian walked beside her.

She turned and held her hand up.

"No. If you come, I'll have no excuse to leave. I'll explain that you're pulling the car around front and will be waiting for me, so I have to leave."

"I will not leave this building without you, Alyssa. It's not safe for you to be so far away from me. Especially after what happened in your apartment. I'll wait here, where I can keep my eye on you."

Alyssa started to argue, but knew he was right. Plus the stubborn look on his face made her realize the futility of it. She nodded in agreement.

"Fine, I'll only be a minute."

She turned away and walked into the crowded room.

She found her aunt a few minutes later and said her goodbyes. Aunt Joyce wasn't as disappointed as Alyssa thought she'd be. In fact, she agreed with Alyssa's decision to leave very quickly.

"Oh, I understand dear. You two run along and do what ever it is you need to do," her aunt said with a smile. "Have a nice time."

The speculative gleam in her aunt's eyes made Alyssa wonder what she was up to.

A crashing noise caught Alyssa's attention. She swung her head towards the sound. She was shocked to see one of the waiters drop his tray of drinks and start running in her direction. As he did so, she noticed him pull something from his jacket. Her heart skipped a beat when she saw that it was a large dangerous-looking knife. He raised it above his head as he drew closer and closer. Everything moved in slow motion after that—the waiter running towards her with the knife, the shocked looks on the faces of the other guests as they stood frozen in terror.

Alyssa finally broke out of her stupor. She turned and began to run, too late. He was so close by then she was sure she had little chance. This was it. This was how it would end. The image of Christian's face swam before her. No! She wasn't ready for it to end. She wasn't ready to lose him. She had just found him. She pushed herself harder, but tensed her body in anticipation of that wicked blade tearing into her flesh.

A blur of movement caught her eye. Her heart almost burst from her chest. He was almost on top of her. She would never get away. She was dead. It was over. Suddenly, she was pushed from behind. Flying forward out of control, she hit her head on one of the tables. Everything went black.

Christian barely held onto his control. He kept his fists tightly at his sides. His beast struggled to be set free. To tear. Kill. Destroy. He glared down at the unconscious man who had dared to try and hurt Alyssa. He lay helpless at Christian's feet. It would be so easy to rip his neck apart. One or two bites and the man would never see another day, or night.

Instead he removed his belt and secured it around the man's wrists. If he woke up before the police came, Christian wanted him secure. He had seen the hatred, the intense loathing on his face as he tried to attack Alyssa. The man would not have hesitated to kill her.

Christian had been so stupid. He had let his guard slip. Let himself get lost in his feelings for Alyssa. Because of his weakness, she could have been killed. He stepped over the man and went to where Joyce was sitting with her niece.

Joyce looked up and Christian felt guilt wash over him. He had promised to protect her niece. Alyssa's aunt said nothing, but he knew she must be very angry.

"Has she moved at all?" he asked.

"No. It's like she's in a deep sleep. I can't wake her up."

Joyce's voice cracked and Christian saw tears well in her eyes.

"I'm sorry I didn't do a better job of protecting her."

Surprise registered on Joyce's face.

"What do you mean? If it wasn't for you, my niece would be dead." She reached out and gave his hand a squeeze. "I don't know how you got from the doorway to her so quickly. Frankly, I don't care. All that matters is that you saved her life. I'm grateful for all you did and will remember it always."

Christian remembered hearing the scream in his head, hearing Alyssa calling out to him in a fearful, frantic voice. He had run into the reception room, using all his speed and strength. He had pushed her aside just as the stalker's knife was about to tear into her back. Then Christian turned on the man. His fist connected with the assailant's face. The sound of flesh hitting flesh and bones cracking had given Christian great satisfaction.

Staring down at Alyssa's still face, all the energy, all the power he had felt faded to nothing. He knelt beside her. Skimming his fingers over her forehead, he gently pushed her hair out of her eyes. He called to her softly. Entered her mind in a careful effort to awaken her. At first he heard no response.

Then he heard something. Soft at first, he almost missed the sound of her voice in his mind. He called out to her again, urging her to talk to him. She said his name. It was barely a whisper through his thoughts, but it was there. Relief washed over him.

Palomita, I hear you. Please wake up. We're worried about you. Your aunt is distraught. She doesn't know what to do first. The ambulance and the police are on the way.

Ambulance? Am I injured? Did that waiter stab me?

No. But you hit your head on the side of a table when I pushed you out of the way.

You pushed me?

I had to. Otherwise he would have sunk that knife into your sweet flesh and that I would not allow. If anyone sinks something into your flesh, it will be me.

Christian could hear her soft laughter like a caress through his mind. She sounded weak. But her laughter reassured him somewhat.

"Wake up, palomita. I need to look into your beautiful eyes."

Christian waited.

Nothing.

Alyssa?

His call was soft, but insistent.

Then it happened. Her eyes fluttered open and focused right on his face.

Their eyes met and held.

"Thank goodness. You gave us quite a scare, dear." The relief in Aunt Joyce's voice was unmistakable.

Alyssa turned her head to glance at her aunt and cringed.

"Ouch. I feel one monster of a headache coming on."

"If it wasn't for Mr. Galiano, you might not be feeling anything at all right now. That maniac was too close to you, dear." Her aunt gave her a hug. "I'm so glad you're awake."

The paramedics and police arrived at the same time. Alyssa's health was addressed first. The police took the unconscious stalker into custody and questioned other guests while she was being cared for. She was checked for a concussion. Luckily she had none. Then the paramedics poked and prodded her head to see if she needed stitches. She had a cut on her head, but it only required a couple of butterfly bandage strips. They told her to take it easy and if she had any other symptoms, like nausea or vomiting she should contact her doctor immediately.

"I'll watch over her tonight. If I see any of those symptoms, I'll contact her doctor," Christian promised. He'd watch over Alyssa. Take care of her needs.

Pulling him aside, away from the paramedics still examining Alyssa, Joyce gave Christian a speculative stare, then a wide smile spread across her face.

"So you're going to stay with my niece tonight? I had planned on doing that myself, but I think it would be better if you did. I'll come by in the morning to see how she's doing. These old bones aren't up to pulling an all-nighter."

Christian gave Joyce a doubtful look. Alyssa's aunt looked pretty healthy to him. And he didn't remember Alyssa saying anything about her being ill. Interesting. That meant Joyce wanted him to spend the night with her niece. Good. That made two of them.

Alyssa thanked the paramedics for their help. As soon as they left, the police approached her. Christian walked back to her side and stayed there.

I'm here with you, palomita.

I'm fine. You don't need to hover.

Nevertheless, I will.

Despite her thoughts, she was comforted by Christian's presence, both physically and mentally. His imposing presence was hard to ignore.

The policeman took notice immediately.

"I'd like to speak to Ms. Edwards alone."

"I'm Ms. Edwards' bodyguar—"

Alyssa cleared her throat loudly.

Christian looked exasperated, but continued.

"I'm in charge of Ms. Edwards' personal security. I'm with Sundown Security."

"Sundown Security? Yeah, I've heard about you guys. You're good. Helped us out with some of our high priority cases. Were you involved with this incident, Mister…?"

"Galiano. Yes, Ms. Edwards was under my protection when the stalker attacked."

Christian went on to tell the officer about the events that had occurred up to that night.

"Do we have any of this on file?"

"Yes. Ms. Edwards' publicist as well as my boss, Vlad Maksimovitch, have helped to keep law enforcement up to date on the various incidents."

"Thank you, Mr. Galiano."

"Ms. Edwards, I still need to ask you some questions. Are you feeling up to it?"

"Yes, go ahead."

The officer asked if she had ever met the man who had attacked her. She had avoided looking at him, but realized that she had to do so now. She glanced over to where he sat handcuffed at a table with another police officer. He wasn't very tall, wirier, than muscular. His hair hung down in greasy strands around his neck. His face looked worn. He had black smudges and bags under his bloodshot eyes. As if he hadn't slept for a long time. He was awake. His eyes caught and held her attention. He glared at Alyssa. The hatred in his eyes burned bright. As she met his eyes, Alyssa felt it like a physical attack.

She looked away. Turned back to the policeman speaking with her.

"I've never seen him before."

"Do you know why someone might be stalking you?"

"No. As a therapist, I work with couples and families. Help them resolve issues. I've never had a problem with any of my patients."

Alyssa saw movement out of the corner of her eye. She turned in time to see the other police officer stand up with her attacker. As the man stood up, he kept his angry eyes burning into hers. Then he started yelling.

"You bitch! You and that stupid book you wrote ruined my marriage. Made my wife leave me. You wrecked my life. I'd kill you right now if I could. Just like I tried to kill her for daring to walk out. If this cop wasn't holding me back, I'd wrap my hands around your neck and squeeze—"

Before he could finish ranting, the other police officer jerked him around and pulled him towards the door. The man didn't resist. But he kept glaring back over his shoulder at Alyssa.

Alyssa sat in shock. Each hateful word the man had spoken was like a physical blow. The next thing she saw was Christian's back. He stepped in front of her, blocking her view. Then she heard him growl. Christian wasn't a happy camper. His fists were clenched tightly at his side and his body was stiff and tense.

She knew he was preparing to launch himself across the room at the man. Could see it in his body posture. Feel it in his mind. This would not be good. He could get into trouble with the police. Unable to think of anything else to divert his attention, she reached out and gave his behind a light squeeze, more like a caress.

It worked. Christian swung around and looked down at her with an incredulous look on his face.She smiled sheepishly and shrugged. The transformation on his face would have been humorous, if it hadn't singed every relevant body part she owned. His eyes turned hot and smoky, his lips parted into the sexiest smile she had ever seen.

Alyssa's mouth went dry. She imagined him as a tall, cool drink, the only thing able to quench her thirst. Then the image of him caressing her bottom shot into her mind. Except in this case her bottom was bare. And his hands were everywhere.

She knew Christian had to be projecting this picture to her. She bit down on her bottom lip to keep from moaning with pleasure.

With one last heated look, he turned back to the police officer.

"Is there anything else you need to know?" Christian asked as he moved aside once more.

Immediately, Alyssa noticed that her stalker was gone.

"No. That's it for now," the officer responded, handing him back his belt. "But Ms. Edwards, I will need you to come down to the station tomorrow and fill out some additional paperwork."

"I'll do that," Alyssa agreed.

After the officer left, Aunt Joyce joined them again.

"Are you all right, Alyssa?"

"Yes, just a little tired. I think I'm ready to go home."

"I understand, sweetie. There's just one problem. The press seems to have gotten wind of this incident. They're waiting for you outside."

"The press? How did they hear about this so quickly?"

"I don't know, but somehow they did."

"I'll get Alyssa home safely. Without encountering the media," Christian said.

Alyssa knew without a doubt that he would do just that. She wasn't sure about her emotions, but when it came to her physical well-being, she trusted him completely.

"I'll go with Christian, but what about you, Aunt Joyce? Are you going to be okay?"

"Me? Of course— I have a perfectly capable companion who'll get me home in a flash," Joyce said, looking behind her at a handsome elderly man standing nearby. "You just worry about you and let Mr. Galiano keep you safe. I know you're in good hands."

She gave Alyssa a hug and Christian a meaningful look over her shoulder.

"I'll plan on seeing you bright and early tomorrow morning, Alyssa. But if you need anything before then, please call me."

"I will. Thanks."

Christian took Alyssa's hand and led her to the double doors leading out of the reception room. Then, instead of taking the elevator down to the parking garage, he led her back to her backstage room.

"Why are we here?"

"I'm taking you home."

Christian slid a chair across the room and opened the second story window. He took a quick look outside.

"Good. This window faces the back of the building. No one will see us."

"See us do what?" Alyssa asked, totally confused.

Christian climbed onto the chair and held out his hand to her.

"Come up here. We don't have much time. I hear voices in the hallway getting closer."

The light bulb suddenly went on in Alyssa's head. She slowly shook her head and started backing away from the window.

"I don't think so."

Christian frowned down at her.

"You trust me with your life, remember? Don't make me come down there and get you."

Her eyes widened at his threat. Then she folded her arms across her chest and lifted her chin stubbornly.

"There is no way I'm going out that window, Christian."

His eyes narrowed dangerously. He stepped off of the chair. But didn't come close to her.

"Are you sure?"

"Yes, I'm sure." She met his gaze squarely.

In the blink of an eye, Christian stood inches from her. Her head snapped up to look at him. He gave her that knowing smile that rubbed her the wrong way. It should have warned her. Before she could say a word, he picked her up as if she was as light as a feather and threw her over his shoulders. Though he did it gently, the breath was momentarily knocked out of her body and she saw stars.

She eventually regained her breath, but the stars remained. She looked around her in shock and amazement. She was flying through the night sky! Clouds floated above them. The moon lit up everything. Alyssa enjoyed the wind brushing over her in a sweet summer caress. She knew she should be scared to death, but she wasn't. Instead she felt peaceful and free, like she was floating in a wonderful dream.

She could see the lights below her marking each structure. She saw Scottsdale Road. Busy as ever despite it being summertime. The cars driving back and forth along it looked like toys. She saw the lake at McCormick Ranch reflecting the moon off its smooth surface. And the swans, white and shining like beacons in the darkness. Some taking flight and rising into the air.

She couldn't look around fast enough. The action made her cringe in pain from her head injury. She had completely forgotten about it. It all came back as dizziness assailed her. She closed her eyes, wrapped her arms tightly around Christian's back and held on for dear life. This was no dream. She was flying through the air!

"It's all right, *palomita*. I won't let you fall." The amusement in his voice was unmistakable.

She kept her eyes tightly shut. Anger replaced some of the fear Alyssa was finally feeling.

"I don't find this funny, Christian. I'm flying through the sky on your back. This doesn't happen to me everyday."

"Here. Let me make it better by taking your mind off of it. Remember that image of me rubbing your sweet backside?"

Alyssa lost her breath again as Christian's hand slid up the back of her leg, under her dress and rested on her bottom. Her panties were not much of a barrier. Though he was only laying his open palm on her, his touch made her skin tingle with pleasure.

He started drawing slow circles. They got bigger and bigger, until he slid his fingers over the edge of her underwear. He ran his fingers along the elastic band and delved underneath. Alyssa's breath caught in her throat as he caressed her skin. She forgot about the stars. She forgot about the night sky. She forgot about flying through the air. Christian's touch. It was all she knew. All that mattered in that moment. He began tracing the crease of her behind. She stopped breathing altogether until he removed his hand and laid it back on her thigh.

The next thing she knew, Christian slid her off his shoulder, down the front of his body, until her feet touched the ground. The ground? Her eyes flew open. Alyssa held onto Christian's shoulders for support. She looked around her in amazement. They were standing right behind her apartment complex. She glared up at him.

"That wasn't fair fighting, Christian."

"I know. Unfair, but extremely effective and enjoyable."

He chuckled softly. The low, sexy sound sent tingles throughout her body. She ignored it, but the tingles returned when he took her hand in his.

He led her to the front of her building. She went with him, but knew this discussion was far from over. She had flown through the sky! Looking above her, she still couldn't believe it.

They took the elevator up to her apartment. Christian released her hand to press the floor button. Alyssa was glad because she couldn't help remembering what had happened between her and Christian the last time they were in the elevator. She struggled to think of something else as her body grew warm. She stared at everything but him. Neither of them spoke on the ride up to her floor.

The elevator bounced as it came to a stop. The jarring action brought Alyssa's headache roaring back to life. Without a word, Christian placed his hand at her elbow as they walked down the hallway. It was such an old fashioned gesture that Alyssa was too surprised to comment. Pulling out her keys, she opened the apartment door. Once inside, Christian released her elbow. Dizziness and fatigue overwhelmed her. The events of the evening were catching up to her. She walked over to her couch and sat down. Closing her eyes, she laid her head back and exhaled loudly.

Her eyes flew open again when she heard Christian close and bolt her door. He walked over to where she sat. Helplessly her eyes stayed glued to him. The man had a way of moving that drew her attention no matter how awful she felt. He sat down beside her.

"Didn't the paramedics give you something for your headache?"

The concern in his voice warmed her.

"Yes, but I forgot all about it. They told me to take these pain relievers as soon as possible. The pills are in my pocket."

Alyssa pulled out the packet. Christian walked into her kitchen.

"I'll get you a glass of water."

"Thanks."

She opened the packet. When Christian returned with the water she popped both pills into her mouth, sipped the liquid and swallowed with a grimace. Then she laid her head back and closed her eyes again.

"I don't like taking medicine unless it's absolutely necessary."

"Why not?"

Alyssa opened her eyes again and stared up at the ceiling.

"I guess I've seen too many patients who've had doctors prescribe medication too quickly, when it really didn't address the issue that person was having. These people finally come to me when they realize that the medicine they're taking is just a bandage that masks the real issue. Sometimes my patients just need someone to talk to. Someone to give them constructive, workable ways to handle the events of their lives."

"You enjoy helping people."

"Yes. But I don't try to tell them how to live. I help them develop tools to live a happier life."

"Like that man's wife?"

Christian asked the question gently, softly. But it got her attention. She lifted her head and stared at him. She knew immediately who he was referring to. Her attacker. He had mentioned his wife leaving him.

"Yes," Alyssa admitted. "I don't know his wife personally, but obviously she read my book and decided to take action. That's one of things I talk about in *Balance*. The need to, not only acknowledge the reality of your situation, but to also do something about it. If that man's actions tonight are any indicator of what he's like, I have a feeling he was verbally and physically abusing her. I could feel the anger emanating from him in waves. Each one felt like a punch to the stomach. He not only wanted to kill me, he wanted to do it in such a way that caused me immense pain."

"What do you mean, you *felt* it?"

Christian looked very interested. Alert. Carefully waiting for her response. Did she share this with him or not? Her ability to pick up on other's feelings was something she didn't talk about to many people. She searched his face and decided she was ready to tell him. After all, he was a vampire. You couldn't get much more off-the-wall than that.

"Whenever I do my speeches, or whenever I see a patient who has very strong emotions, I can feel what they're feeling. During my speeches, I think, because there are just too many people, I can't help but pick up on it, especially if many of them are feeling the same thing. And some of my patients, because often their emotions have been bottled up for so long, they just come pouring out of them like a damn bursting."

"I see. So you're an extremely sensitive empathic." Christian's voice sounded serious, thoughtful.

Alyssa thought about that for a minute. Sensitive empathic. Is that what she was? She had never given a name to it before, but that sounded about right.

"I guess you could say that, yes."

Jonathan jumped up onto the couch, surprising Alyssa, and her thoughts scattered. He sauntered over to her, climbed onto her lap and began purring. Alyssa smiled and began petting him. She scratched under his chin. He lifted his head so she could scratch more and closed his eyes. His purring grew even louder.

"I take it this is your cat?"

She saw a bemused grin curl Christian's lips as he watched Jonathan.

"Yes. This is Jonathan."

"Is he always so demanding?"

Alyssa returned his smile with her own wry grin.

"Jonathan lets me know when he needs attention. He's not shy about it. And he is such a lazy lap cat," she said affectionately. Jonathan lowered his head and she scratched between his ears. That was a particular favorite of his. "He'd lay with me the whole day, if he could."

"I can understand why."

Christian said the words quietly, but they hit her hard.

Alyssa's gaze flew to his. The desire and longing in his eyes burned her.

He stood up abruptly and held his hand out to her.

"Alyssa, it's time."

Chapter Ten

Christian held his hand out to Alyssa.

"Time?" she asked.

He heard the question, the vulnerability and the desire in her voice. He wanted to answer the question and reassure the vulnerability. Most of all he wanted to satisfy the desire. But now was not the time. She had just experienced a frightening evening and had a good-sized cut on her head to prove it.

"Yes. It's time for you to get some sleep. As I promised your aunt, I'll stay with you tonight and make sure you're okay. If you need me for anything, I'll be out here on the couch. I'll leave before dawn. Your aunt should be here shortly after that to see you. And don't forget to see your regular doctor tomorrow."

He saw the heat in Alyssa's eyes fade and he cursed himself a hundred different ways. Another time, another place and she would be his right now. But he would not risk her health. That was more important than anything else.

Alyssa gave him one last searching gaze, then put Jonathan down on the couch. She stood up without taking Christian's hand. Anger replaced the desire in her eyes.

Her voice sounded clipped and tight.

"I can manage going to bed on my own, Christian. It really isn't necessary for you to stay the night either. I feel fine. And now, thanks to you, the stalker has been caught. I don't have to worry about that any longer."

"I hope you're right. I hope the threat to you is over. But as far as your head injury, remember what the paramedics said. You need to be watched overnight. To make sure there are no further complications. So I'm staying. I made a promise. And I honor my promises, always, Alyssa. Keep that in mind."

She lifted her chin proudly and held his gaze.

"How could I forget that, Christian? You wear your honor wrapped around you like a knight's armor."

She walked around him and headed into her bedroom.

"Good night. I hope your honor is a comfort to you tonight," she muttered angrily under her breath right before closing her bedroom door.

Staring at the door with a grim smile, he wondered the same thing.

The door opened again. Without a word, Alyssa threw a pillow and light blanket at him. He caught it. But before he could thank her, she slammed the door.

No, she was not happy at the moment.

At least they had that in common.

He put the pillow and blanket down on the couch. He wouldn't be using it. His time to wander the world was at night. He would sleep come dawn.

Instead he looked through Alyssa's bookshelf. She had several books on therapy and psychology, but also various fiction books. He chose one and sat down to read it. It was a practical guide to Feng Shui. He had very little use for such philosophies, but as he read through the book, then studied her apartment, he realized how much Alyssa followed it.

He had traveled to Asia with Vlad. In fact, he and Vlad had traveled much of the world together before settling in Arizona. He had learned much from his friend, especially about mankind. Vlad not only showed him different countries, he had made sure they immersed themselves in the culture and environment of each one. He claimed that by letting Christian experience humanity all around the world, he would better understand how mortals and vampires needed to find a balance with each other. That they could co-exist, even help each other.

Over twenty years ago, they had visited Arizona and decided to stay. Considering that Phoenix was also called "The Valley of the Sun", it was ironic that vampires would settle here. Yet there was something that appealed to both Vlad and Christian. At that time there was still a sort of wildness about the place that one couldn't find anywhere else. Arizonans had their own "wild west" code of behavior that was independent of the rest of the states. Combined with the fact that Arizona was so open and spread out at that time, it was perfect for their kind. Over the years, many vampires as well as other immortal creatures had visited and decided to stay there.

Christian put the book down on the coffee table and strode over to the sliding glass door leading out to the balcony. He opened it and walked outside. The hot evening wind brushed over him. One more reason he liked Arizona. Warm summer nights. Sometimes he would close his eyes on a particularly hot evening and imagine it was a summer day with the sun shining bright. Though it had been hundreds of years, he still remembered what the world looked like during the day. He kept that image locked inside his mind. He could bring it up anytime he wanted to remember.

He looked out into the night. His thoughts grew as dark as the moonless night surrounding him. He thought about the man who had tried to attack Alyssa. He was now in police custody. Christian should have felt relieved, but he wasn't. Bazhena was still out there. And he needed to find out what she was up to. Tomorrow night he would visit Twice Charmed again to see what else he could learn about her activities.

What was The Light she was looking for? Which legend had she discovered? He still needed to ask Vlad about it. Christian would call him on his mobile phone right now, but knew he was in the middle of his own case. Usually Vlad turned his phone off when he was on the job. He claimed it was a distraction. He had his two-way and beeper, but those were only for emergencies.

It would just have to wait until tomorrow night. He would speak to him then.

His pondering was interrupted when he heard Alyssa's sharp cry. In an instant he was in her room. She was still in bed, fast asleep. He looked around. Opened all his senses, but felt no threat nearby.

She cried out again. Then started tossing and turning. She must be dreaming. Having a nightmare. He stood over her, waiting for the dream to pass. He tried to send soothing, comforting thoughts to her. At first it seemed to help and Christian turned to walk out of her room.

As he did so, Alyssa shot up in her bed and yelled.

"No! Mom!" Then her yell turned to almost a whisper.

Christian drew closer.

"How could you do this? How could you leave me? I should have done more, I should have done more."

Alyssa started sobbing. Christian sat down beside her. Her shoulders were shaking from the strength of her sobs. And her eyes were wide open, but unseeing as tears fell down her cheeks.

Christian wrapped his arms around her. He pulled her against his chest. She struggled for a minute and then relaxed. He began running his fingers through her hair. He sent more soothing messages from his mind to hers.

It's okay, palomita. I'm here with you now.

He continued to hold her as her tears soaked the front of his shirt.

Then he saw it, in his mind. He didn't ask for it. Alyssa just projected it to him.

A woman—Alyssa's mother—dead—lying in a pool of blood. Next he saw what he assumed was a bathroom mirror with a much younger looking Alyssa staring wide-eyed and fearful at her own reflection. She opened her mouth and a scream that sounded like a wounded animal filled his head. It went on and on—then the picture was gone.

Alyssa stiffened. She had woken up.

* * * * *

Alyssa's face was wet. She tasted salt in her mouth. She took a deep shuddering breath and breathed in deeply—spicy, dangerous and sexy. She knew that scent. Would never mistake it with another. Christian. She felt his arms wrapped around her. Her chest pressed against his. She lifted her head up and pulled back slightly. He released her without a word.

What was going on?

The last thing she remembered was slamming her bedroom door and getting ready for bed. She had been irritated, no, frustrated by Christian. She was irritated that she wanted him the way she did. And frustrated that she couldn't have him. She didn't like the fact that she seemed to be the only one who was hot and bothered, the needy one. It didn't sit well with her. Not one little bit.

Luckily the pain medication was strong and she fell right to sleep. The next thing she knew, she was in Christian's arms. She still felt groggy and more than a little confused.

"Christian?" she asked, scooting away from him. The room was dark. She couldn't see his face. But she felt his presence like a blinding beacon of light. His emotions were strong right now. Coming at her in waves. She sensed sadness—and an anger he was struggling to control.

"What is it? What happened?"

She reached out and touched his shoulder.

He immediately covered her hand with his. The silence stretched out. Then Christian finally spoke.

"You were having a bad dream. I came in to comfort you. Nothing more."

His voice sounded tense and tight. He was holding something back. Alyssa wanted to know.

"What's really going on, Christian?"

She felt him stiffen under her hand.

"Nothing. Try to go back to sleep. You need your rest after the evening you've had."

He started to rise, but Alyssa stopped him.

She scooted closer and grasped his arm. The muscles rippled and tensed beneath her fingers. The feel of it caused a little flutter in her stomach that embarrassed her. Since when did muscles turn her on so much? This man was leaving her too unbalanced, too unsure. Her next words came out a little gruffer than she meant them to.

"You're not going anywhere. I know something is bothering you. Quit being the strong, silent type for a minute and tell me about it."

Christian settled back down on the bed.

"The strong silent type?" Amusement laced his voice.

Alyssa knew that if the lights were on, she would see that satisfied smirk on his face that irritated her to no end. Exasperated, she tried to hold onto her patience.

"Yes. You know what I mean, lots of inner turmoil, but calm on the outside. Never revealing a thing."

"Is that the therapist talking or the woman?"

"What do you mean?" It was Alyssa's turn to feel uncomfortable.

This time Christian was the one to slide close to her. Alyssa pressed back against the bed's headboard to put some distance between them. He moved closer.

"I think you know what I mean, Alyssa. What are you really asking me?"

As he spoke, he reached around her and turned on the bedside lamp. Alyssa's eyes narrowed. It took her a minute to adjust to the light. But once she did, she wanted to be in the dark again.

All her grogginess disappeared as Christian's hot gaze burned her up. She felt the need to squirm under his intense stare. She fought it. Struggled to maintain a calm she didn't feel. He focused his attention on her lips.

She couldn't speak at that moment if her life depended on it.

Placing his thumb on her bottom lip, he began rubbing it lightly back and forth. Her mouth parted in a gasp of pleasure. He took the opportunity to delve inside, wetting his thumb. Then he rubbed the moisture on her bottom lip, then the top.

Her lips swelled from his touch.

"Your lush lips are calling to me. I crave to taste them. I need you."

Abruptly, he pulled his hand away.

"No. What I need is to get out of your bedroom. You must rest."

Alyssa closed her eyes. She felt dizzy from desire. His seductive voice added to the pleasure. Then he took it away.

Her eyes flew open.

Christian started to stand up. She grasped his arm again.

"Don't go."

She began running her fingers up and down his arm, caressing the contours of his muscles.

Christian sat back down. He tensed under her touch. He stared down at where her hand stroked him. Then he raised his head and their gazes met.

Alyssa watched the myriad of emotions cross his face, like restless clouds gliding across a stormy sky, anger, sadness, frustration and then desire. They were all fervent, but the last singed her with its intensity. His jaw clenched and unclenched. He looked as if he was fighting some sort of inner battle.

"Stay with me." As she spoke, she took her hand off of his arm and placed it on his knee. Then she began sliding her fingers up and down his muscled thigh. The feel of him left her dizzy.

Alyssa knew the second he lost the battle. Intense satisfaction coursed through her. A sense of feminine power like she had never known filled her. She had won. Christian would be hers. He turned to her, grasped her waist and dragged her close to him. Growling low in his throat, Christian lowered his face towards hers. Almost, but not quite touching her lips with his. She could feel his breath as he whispered.

"I'm going to kiss you now. I have to. I need to touch you, just as I crave your touch. I don't want to wait any longer. Does that tell you what you need to know, *palomita*? Is that what you wanted to hear?"

Alyssa couldn't answer. She trembled with need. Each word he spoke brushed across her wet lips and stoked the fire of desire building up inside her.

"This is my one and only warning. If you don't want this, tell me now because I may not be able to stop once we start."

Alyssa's heart leapt at his words. He wanted her, craved her, just as she hungered for him.

She closed the small distance between them. She pressed her lips to his and was lost.

Christian was lost. The feel of her soft lips, moving hungrily over his was incredible. He had wanted to stop. Wanted to let her rest after her injury. But his will became hers when she touched him. He could feel her desire and need pushing at him, surrounding him and immersing him in her sensual heat. It was too much.

He hardened to the point of pain. Gently grasping her shoulders, he laid her back on the bed. He followed her down, leaning his body over hers. Her lips clung to his, needy and bold. Her desire inflamed him. Lust engulfed him. He plunged his tongue into her mouth, demanding a response. She met each thrust with her own. Their tongues entwined and danced, until they both were moaning with need.

Tearing his lips from hers, he moved down to her chin. Such a pert chin, he gave it a nip and was rewarded by Alyssa's gasp. Raining kisses down her throat, he soon found the neckline of her tank top. The images of her wearing nothing more than the little top and the scrap of silk barely covering her womanhood were driving him crazy.

He slid his lips over the fabric until he found a hardened nipple. He flicked it with his tongue and then covered it with his mouth. Alyssa's moans grew louder as he sucked deeply and then rolled her nipple in his mouth. Christian worshipped the other breast in the same way until she squirmed under him. Thinking something was wrong he lifted his head.

Alyssa grabbed the hem of her shirt and lifted it off over her head. Then she laid back, closed her eyes and arched her back in invitation.

"Touch me. Please Christian. I need you."

Her beauty awed him. Looking down at her moist parted lips, her delicate neck and her breasts offered up to him was like a feast he couldn't resist. Her berry-red nipples were swollen and glistening from his attention. His mouth watered. Her body called out to him. It was time.

He couldn't get his clothes off fast enough. Her hungry eyes watching him seemed to make everything take longer. After removing the last scrap of material from his body, he grasped her waist and lifted her slightly, so that her back was arched higher. He lowered his mouth to her upthrust nipples and suckled each one in turn. Alyssa groaned and ran her fingers through his hair, grasping strands of it as he suckled her harder.

Christian moved his attention lower. He nuzzled her soft stomach. Breathed in the scent of green apples. He dipped his tongue into her belly button and felt her shudder beneath him. Kissing his way down, he came to the waistband of her panties. He nipped it, lifted it with his teeth and ran his tongue underneath the silky material. Alyssa's fingers tightened in his hair. She tilted her hips up and released a needy moan.

His answering growl was his only warning. He slid her panties down her legs, following their path with his tongue.

After slipping them off, he worked his way back up her legs. When he reached her sweet thighs, he lifted his head and thought he would burst from the sight of her. Her beautiful body seemed to glow with warmth, life and desire. Her eyes were closed and her wet lips parted. Her silky hair was spread around in a shiny mass of raven color. She looked like a woman ready to be loved.

He was more than ready. But he wanted to make sure she was. He slid his hand up her thigh to her center. He played with her soft curls. Alyssa sucked in a breath and opened her thighs for him. Softly he delved between her swollen lips. He stiffened. Her moist heat made him want to plunge deep inside of her, but he knew he needed to be patient. Alyssa opened her thighs further. He explored her hot slickness until she was dripping with need. She tossed her head back and forth, whispering his name over and over again. When he delved one finger inside, her whispers turned to soft mewling sounds. She lifted her hips to each thrust of his hand.

Unable to wait any longer, he removed his finger from her. She gasped in protest. Her eyes flew open. He met her lust-filled gaze with his own determined one.

"I'll have you now, Alyssa. There's no turning back. You're mine," Christian gritted between his clenched teeth.

Grasping her waist he tilted her hips up and plunged deeply inside. Her sweet, moist, warmth surrounded him. He froze because he knew he might lose it at any moment if he moved. After a few deep breaths, he slowly slid out of her, until the tip of him was at her entrance and then slipped back inside her, hard and fast. He repeated the motion over and over again. The soft sounds of pleasure she made were almost his undoing. His pace grew more frantic and her moans of pleasure louder. He covered her mouth with his, wanting to take her sounds of pleasure into his body.

He could tell when she stiffened that she was as close to the edge as was he. His need was about to explode. Yet another kind of hunger shimmered to life inside him. Lust overtook him. He tore his mouth from hers and worked his way down to her breasts. He laved and suckled one of her nipples, until it was stiff and engorged, full of blood, full of Alyssa's sweet life.

Their minds connected.

I need you, Alyssa. I need your sweetness.

Yes.

That was all she said as she arched her back, pushing her breast deeper into his mouth.

It was enough.

His teeth sank deep and she cried out his name, as her body convulsed over and over again. He knew, as her sweet life flowed into him and he tumbled over the edge, that her cries were from the exquisite pleasure of their joining, not pain.

* * * * *

Alyssa woke to the feel of sunshine warming her. She peeked through her lashes then clamped her eyes shut again. Sunlight glared in through her open window. Why hadn't she closed the curtains last night? Rolling over onto her stomach, she pulled the blanket up over her head and tried to go back to sleep. Her alarm hadn't gone off yet, just a little bit longer.

It was no use. She couldn't go back to sleep. Pushing herself up, she sat on the edge of her bed. Two things hit her at once. Her body hurt. And there was one place in particular that ached, which had nothing to do with her fall at the hotel last night. It had more to do with her tumble in her own bed. Memories of last night's encounter with Christian came pouring back.

Alyssa stretched her arms towards the ceiling. A secret smile curved her lips upward. She lay back on the bed with a sigh. Her mind slid over the image of Christian loving her. So intense, so caring—so sexy! She admitted it. His lovemaking had been incredibly erotic and satisfying. Especially in the end, when his mouth was tugging strongly at her breasts in time with each thrust of his powerful body. That had left her panting. But what had really sent her over the edge had been when he bit her.

Bit her? Bit her!

She remembered now. He had asked for permission. She had agreed. The sharp pain of his teeth pricking her skin had been mild compared to the exquisite pleasure that soon followed. Her orgasm had come swift and strong. So powerful it went on and on, until she lay totally exhausted in Christian's arms. Then fell fast asleep.

Alyssa jumped out of bed and ran to the bathroom. She looked at her chest in the mirror. Nothing. Not a mark. Not a scar. How had he done that? Had he actually bit her? Yes, she remembered the feel of his teeth piercing her flesh, first a slight sting, then a liquid heat spreading throughout her body. He had done it twice since they'd met. It was a feeling she would never forget. One that created a pleasure-pain like she'd never experienced before.

What was wrong with her? She met her own gaze in the mirror. The horrified expression on her face said it all. This wasn't—it wasn't normal. She should not find this erotic or pleasurable. A vampire was sucking her blood, for crying out loud! And she had asked, no, demanded his touch and wanted his bite. Images from last night came back to her and filled her with embarrassment, her bold hands, greedily running over his body, begging for his touch. Making sounds like she had never made before. Crying out in ecstasy as his teeth sank deep and loving every minute of it.

He was taking control of her mind. That was the only explanation. He was using mind control. Like she had read about in the books and seen on the videos. Vampires had this power. Yes. That had to be it. Why else would she find such pleasure in his actions?

Alyssa made up her mind. She had enough parental manipulation while growing up. She didn't need or want someone who had the ability to make her lose control of her body and mind like this. She succeeded in pushing aside the incredible feelings his lovemaking had aroused in her as she showered and dressed.

Alyssa walked out of her bedroom and stopped short at the sight that greeted her. Her emotions came crashing back to her. A large bouquet of deep red roses sat in a beautiful vase on the counter. An envelope with her name scrawled in skillfully scrolled writing lay at the base of it. It amazed her that a man as hard and tough as Christian could write so beautifully. And she had no doubt they were from him. Who else would have left her flowers in the middle of the night? Picking up the note, she hesitated before opening it. What would it say? Did she want to know? The thought of Christian sending her roses warmed her, but made her wary at the same time.

She carefully opened the envelope. She read his words once, then again. They caused her heart to do a little flip-flop.

Alyssa,

You have lifted me out of the darkness, into the light of your soul and brought daylight to my life once again.

Cristobal

His words, so heartfelt, so romantic, surprised her. She just didn't expect it of him. When she had told him that he was the strong silent type, she meant it. What he expressed in the note and how he wrote it, left her in a quandary. Her angry, resentful feelings were still there. But so was the caring that was getting stronger with each passing day. She didn't want someone taking control of her life. At the same time she did want this man to be part of her life.

The doorbell ringing broke her reverie.

She walked to the door and peeked out the peephole. Her Aunt Joyce. Alyssa glanced back at the roses indecisively. She'd like to put the flowers away because she knew her aunt would drill her about them. She didn't know if she was ready to talk about her feelings for Christian to anyone.

Aunt Joyce knocked again.

"Alyssa. Are you there, dear? It's Aunt Joyce."

Sighing in resignation, Alyssa unlocked the door and let her aunt in.

"Hi." Alyssa gave her a peck on the cheek.

Her aunt gave her a concerned once over.

"How are you feeling, sweetie?"

"I'm fine. Come in and sit down," she assured her aunt as they sat side by side on the couch. Her aunt took Alyssa's hands in hers.

"Are you really okay?"

"Yes. A good night's sleep has a way of making me feel better." Knowing that sleep was not all she did last night, Alyssa practically choked on her words.

"When I saw that man lunge towards you at the reception, my heart stopped. And then when you fell and hit your head, well, I was so worried. I thought—"

Her aunt stopped speaking. She was looking over Alyssa's shoulder with interest. A satisfied smile curved her lips up.

Uh, oh. Here it comes. Alyssa knew just what Aunt Joyce was looking at and what she was going to ask next.

"Who are those lovely flowers from, dear?"

Alyssa thought about lying, thought about just telling her aunt they were from one of her colleagues at work.

"Coffee?"

"What?" Her aunt looked confused for a moment.

Good. Now if only Alyssa could keep her that way, or distract her.

"Coffee," she repeated. "I haven't had any coffee or breakfast yet. Would you like me to make you a cup?"

Her aunt stood up immediately.

"No. You sit down. I'll make you coffee and breakfast. You need to rest today." Then her aunt looked at the way she was dressed.

"You aren't going to see patients today, are you?"

"Yes. I have to. It's been almost two months since I saw most of them. Luckily it's summer and a lot of them go away on vacation, but I still need to get back to them. I only have one more speaking engagement. The stalker has been arrested. What better time for me to go back?"

Her aunt moved into the kitchen. She started the coffee as she spoke. Hoping she would forget about the flowers, Alyssa let Aunt Joyce take over.

"I don't know, Aly. You had a terrible experience last night. Don't you just want to take it easy today and recuperate?"

"No. I feel fine, honestly. I think going back to my practice will be the best thing for me."

Her aunt put bread in the toaster and took eggs out of the refrigerator. She set a pan on the burner, sprayed it with nonstick spray and turned on the stove. Once it was hot enough she cracked two eggs into it.

"Well if you're sure. I just don't want you to do too much. Come sit down. Everything's ready. "

Her aunt buttered the toast, put a piece on each of their plates, then placed a fried egg on top. While Aunt Joyce put the plates, utensils and napkins on the table, Alyssa poured each of them some coffee and added milk and sugar to both cups. Her aunt and she both enjoyed their coffee the same way, sweet and light.

They sat down and began to eat. Her aunt said nothing. Just ate her food and stared at Alyssa with anticipation written all over her face. The silence stretched out until she couldn't bear it anymore.

"They're from Christian," Alyssa blurted out.

"Mr. Galiano? How nice."

Aunt Joyce's nonchalance didn't fool Alyssa. She knew her aunt was very interested.

"I take it he watched over you last night? He seems like a man of his word. I knew that if he said he would stay with you, he would."

"Yes, he stayed with me." Alyssa didn't say anything else. She hoped her aunt would change the subject.

Wishful thinking on her part, of course.

"And did he have to give you some?"

Alyssa almost choked on her coffee.

Chapter Eleven

ꟺ

She coughed so hard her eyes watered. The coffee had gone down the wrong way. Aunt Joyce stood up and pounded on her back.

Fearing her aunt would try the Heimlich maneuver next, she waved her away and spluttered aloud, "I'm fine."

That was all the energy Alyssa could expend. The remainder went to clearing her throat and taking gasping breaths. Obviously assured she could now breathe, her aunt sat back down in her seat.

"Are you sure you're okay, dear?"

She ignored Aunt Joyce's second question. She was more concerned with the first. The one that nearly choked her.

"Did he give me some *what*?" Alyssa asked incredulously. She knew her mouth hung open, but couldn't help it.

Her aunt looked at her in confusion for a moment. Then her face cleared as understanding dawned.

"Some of your medicine, dear. I thought the paramedic told Christian to make sure you took the pain medication he gave you, if you needed it."

Alyssa mouth snapped shut.

"What did you think I meant?" Aunt Joyce asked.

Alyssa tried not to look guilty.

"I, uh, wasn't sure."

"I see." A wide smile spread across her aunt's face.

She didn't say another word, but Alyssa felt like crawling under a rock. The knowing look in her aunt's eyes said it all. She decided to change the subject.

"So, I'm going to start seeing my patients again today, tomorrow night is my last speaking engagement and then, hopefully, my life can get back to normal."

"What about Christian?"

Alyssa felt a headache coming on. She massaged her right temple. Her aunt just didn't give up.

Jonathan jumped onto the table and interrupted their conversation, meowing pitifully while studying their food. Aunt Joyce gave him a stern look and then proceeded to cut her egg into small pieces and feed it to him. Jonathan gobbled it down and began purring loudly when Aunt Joyce petted him. Alyssa smiled as her aunt took the cat in her arms and laid him on her lap. Jonathan settled down immediately, looking like a king on his throne. Though Aunt Joyce continued to pet him, her eyes focused expectantly on Alyssa once more.

Her cat's arrival had given Alyssa a moment's reprieve from her aunt's interrogation. She thought about what exactly her aunt was asking her. What about Christian? She tried to answer honestly.

"I'm not sure. I don't know where a relationship with him could possibly lead."

"What do you mean? He's obviously a reliable, honest and responsible man. And he's got a great face and body to boot."

Alyssa laughed out loud. Her aunt appeared quiet and demure to those who didn't know her. She was quite petite and had the kind of face that reminded people of their grandmother. Looks were deceiving in this case though. Her aunt was an outspoken woman, always had been. And she wasn't afraid of what other people thought of her. She lived her life the way that she felt it should be lived. And she was always honest with Alyssa, sometimes too honest.

Unfortunately, in this case, Alyssa couldn't reciprocate. She tried to imagine telling Aunt Joyce that Christian and Vlad were vampires and that the agency employed mystical creatures such as elves. Her aunt would think she had gone crazy. It wouldn't be pretty, not pretty at all.

She tried to think of an alternate explanation to dissuade her aunt from pursuing the notion that she and Christian might have a future together. She would have to come up with something that stopped all further speculation. The idea hit her like a brilliant strike of lightning. Why hadn't she thought of it earlier?

"The reason there can't be anything between Christian and I is because of Tom."

"Tom? Tom who?" Her aunt's eyes narrowed with suspicion.

"You know Tom Hardly. The therapist I share office space with?"

"Oh, *that* Tom," her aunt said with a dismissive wave. "What does he have to do with this?"

Her aunt was watching her closely. She had to make this look and sound good.

"Well, you know how we've dated a few times?" Alyssa didn't wait for an answer. She didn't want to give her aunt a chance to protest. "He and I have decided to see each other exclusively."

"Since when? I thought you didn't like Tom in that way? You told me he was too wimpy for you."

Alyssa lifted her chin stubbornly. Her aunt was making this difficult. She just wanted to tell one little white lie to get her aunt off of her back. Instead she had opened a whole new can of worms.

She had met Tom when she was looking for office space to rent. She had just finished her appointment with the leasing agent when he showed up to view the same property. The agent introduced them and they hit it off immediately. They eventually decided to share space and had been friends ever since. He was a kind, intelligent man, who was somewhat attractive in a preppy, suburban, white bread kind of way.

Alyssa felt absolutely no attraction to him. They had dated a couple of times, but both agreed that there wasn't any chemistry between them and they should stay just friends.

"I never said wimpy. I said he and I didn't seem to click in that way. Since the last time we discussed this, I've changed my mind. I've decided to give Tom a chance. He's a nice man who I can have an interesting intellectual conversation with. We enjoy each other's company."

"If that's the case, then what happened last night with Christian?"

Alyssa had enough. She didn't want to discuss this with her aunt any longer. She was a grown woman and didn't need to explain her actions like this. Tamping down her frustration, she pasted a pleasant smile on her face.

"That was a mistake. It should never have happened. Now, can we please talk about something else? I have to leave for the office soon."

Her aunt studied her a little longer, than finally nodded.

"Okay, Aly. If that's what you want. But I think Christian is a much better man for you."

"Thanks for your opinion. But I've made my choice. Now tell me how much money you raised last night at the charity event. There seemed to be a good turnout."

They talked for a little bit longer as Alyssa finished her breakfast. Her aunt insisted on washingthe dishes. Alyssa made sure Jonathan had plenty of food and water before she and Aunt Joyce walked outside together.

Her aunt gave her a big hug and Alyssa hugged her back. She started to pull away but Aunt Joyce held her close a moment more.

"You know the reason I'm so nosy is because I care, don't you, honey?"

Alyssa gave her aunt another squeeze.

"I know, Aunt Joyce."

"I just want you to be happy, really happy. You deserve it."

"I know."

Aunt Joyce released her. As she pulled back, Alyssa saw there were tears in her aunt's eyes. She wiped them away quickly and then gave Alyssa a wobbly smile.

"You have a good day. Take it easy, don't do too much and be careful, okay?"

"I will. And thanks. I love you."

"I love you too, sweetie."

Alyssa drove down Scottsdale Road. She didn't notice the traffic congestion, or the fact that it was already 100 degrees, even though it wasn't even noon yet. Her thoughts were not focused on the drive to work.

She pondered the conversation she had just had with her aunt. She dwelled on the man responsible for that talk. And, as Alyssa was finding to be the case whenever she spoke about Christian, or even if she were just thinking about him, she just couldn't seem to make a concrete decision about the man.

She arrived at her office in Old Town and found her parking space taken. Releasing a sigh of frustration she smiled and shook her head. She loved working in this part of Scottsdale because of the unique character of the place. But it was a tourist haven. Parking was a nightmare, even if you had your own reserved space. The roads were almost always congested and during the fall, winter and spring the sidewalks were full of tourists shopping for southwestern gifts, taking pictures of the old wooden cowboy standing tall, or just strolling around sightseeing. Beautiful Native American jewelry made by the renowned jewelry designer Gilbert Ortega could be found in his large gallery off Scottsdale Road. Giant bronze statues of horses, Native Americans, or cowboys could be seen outside one popular gallery in particular. The old Southwest feel of the place attracted people from all over. The fact that the Grand Canyon was only a few hours drive away also added to the tourist trade.

But there was another side of Old Town. The artistic, free-spirited side of it, where artists of every ilk displayed their wares and were sometimes onsite to greet and talk to customers. The new age crowd was also alive and well in the area. Their shops and art galleries were scattered throughout Old Town. And there were little hideaway cafes that locals frequented because of the great food and atmosphere. And Mexican food. Arizona was known for it. Alyssa couldn't go more than a week without it. Julio's Barrio was her favorite. Their rich green chili, fresh fish tacos, or lime-infused shrimp fajitas were the best in town. The family who owned it had been making and serving fantastic Mexican food in the state for over thirty years.

Among all of this was the political heart of Scottsdale. City Hall, the Department of Revenue and many other city government offices were located in Old Town. So if one was looking for an area mixed with the old and the new, the serious and the fun, this was the place. It was a mishmash stew of people and sights, brimming with life. For Alyssa, the best part of Old Town was that everyone felt comfortable and almost reveled in their individuality, despite the contrasting mix.

The worst part was the parking.

After finding a parking spot not too far away, Alyssa walked into her office and smiled at her receptionist.

"Good morning, Stella."

Stella had been working for them since the day she and Tom opened their office. And she was very efficient at keeping their appointments organized and running the office smoothly. More importantly their patients felt comfortable with her. They were lucky to have her.

Every year since Stella turned sixty, she talked about retiring. It had been three years and so far the woman had stayed with them. She and Tom knew that Stella really enjoyed working and was the type of active person who couldn't just sit at home, but they humored her. Each year they begged her to stay, told her how invaluable she was to them and persuaded her to keep working for one more year.

"Ms. Edwards. How are you? I saw what happened on the news last night. Is everything okay?"

From her expression, she knew Stella had been truly worried about her welfare.

"Yes, Stella. Thanks for asking. I'm fine and the man who attacked me is safely behind bars. Hopefully I won't have to worry about him ever again."

"Let's hope not. I'm glad you're okay. And it's nice to have you back. Your patients missed you."

"Thank you. It's nice to be back. Uh, exactly how much did my patients miss me?" Alyssa narrowed her eyes suspiciously.

Her receptionist laughed as she handed Alyssa a large pile of message slips.

"They missed you *this* much."

Alyssa tried not to groan as she saw the amount of callbacks she had to make."I'll be buried under this mountain of messages for most of the day if you need me."

"Ah, the price of fame," Stella sighed, holding the back of her hand to her forehead.

Alyssa chuckled.

"Thanks a lot."

Stella ignored her sarcasm.

"Anytime. Your first appointment is at ten."

"Right." Alyssa nodded as she walked into her office. "I'll try to get a few calls in before then."

Alyssa spent most of the day seeing patients and returning calls. When lunchtime came, she snacked on soy nuts, raisins and diet soda while driving to the police station to give her statement. Luckily, Vlad had already informed the police about most of the incidents, so Alyssa confirmed what they already knew and added information that was missing. It wasn't a pleasant way to spend her lunch hour, but luckily it didn't last long. Soon she was back at her office. She peeked her head in the door and waved to Tom when she returned, but they didn't get to talk until the end of the day.

Alyssa called her aunt to let her know she would be home late. Aunt Joyce was so protective normally that she knew she would be even doubly so now. If she didn't call, her aunt would worry. And after the fiasco the other night at The Plaza, she didn't want to put her through any more stress than necessary. Even though she was tough as nails, Aunt Joyce was no spring chicken. And as each year passed, Alyssa kept a closer eye on her.

Alyssa had meant to see her doctor today about her head injury, but between running down to the police station and seeing a few extra patients who couldn't wait to see her, she didn't have time. Luckily the cut hadn't bothered her all day. It was close to eight o'clock before she finished with her last appointment. There were more calls to make, but since she had already returned the most urgent ones, she decided the rest could wait until tomorrow. Some of her friends had left very pointed messages about her failure to call them and their worry over her last public attack. She felt bad about not speaking to any of them, but things were just too hectic. After tomorrow night, hopefully she would be able to get her life back to a normal routine again and go out with her friends.

As her office door closed, she leaned her head back against her chair and sighed with relief. Her door opened again. She looked up as Tom walked in.

"See what happens when you get famous?" Tom teased. "May I have your autograph now or later?"

"Ha, Ha. Very funny." Alyssa's voice dripped with sarcasm, but her smile was genuine as she stood up and gave Tom a hug.

"How are you really? I heard about the attack last night. Are you okay?" Tom released her and sat down in the chair opposite her desk.

"I'm fine. I tripped over my own clumsy feet and bumped my head. Other than that, I'm just glad they finally caught the guy," Alyssa explained as she sat back down.

"So am I."

"How were things while I was gone?"

"A little hectic. I offered to see a couple of your patients like you suggested, but most of them declined. They knew I tend to specialize in children, so I think many of the adults felt I just couldn't deal with their issues."

"If they only realized how serious and dangerous some of those children's issues are, I think they would change their opinion pretty fast. You really do an amazing job, Tom. I've seen you change children's lives."

"Thanks. You're not so shabby yourself, sister." Tom did his best Humphrey Bogart impression.

Alyssa laughed. Tom liked to do impressions and he was pretty good. But the way he scrunched up his face when he did this one, always looked so funny.

"Is Stella gone?" Alyssa asked after she finally got her laughter under control.

"Of course. You know Stella. If she doesn't get home by six, she says Bernie throws a fit."

Stella and Bernie had been married since high school. They were the type of couple who complained about their spouse to everyone, but who couldn't live without each other. When people saw them together, they knew the two of them were still deeply in love, even after being together for so long. Alyssa admired their relationship, because she knew how rare it was.

"Are you done for the day?" Alyssa asked.

"Pretty much. I have some notes I'd like transcribed, but it can wait. How about you?"

"Let's see. I've been gone almost six weeks. What do you think?" Alyssa said with a wry smile.

She knew she needed to stay and transcribe notes as well, but she couldn't seem to keep her attention where it belonged. Alyssa had been so busy today that fleeting thoughts of Christian had only briefly skittered across her mind from time to time. But ever since sundown, the image of his face leaning close to hers as they made love last night kept popping up. His intense stare and sexy mouth called to her.

"I think you need to slow down." Tom suggested. "You just started back to work and you have one more speaking engagement tomorrow night. Give yourself time to adjust. You can't do everything in a day. Start fresh tomorrow."

Alyssa knew Tom was right. She had purposely not scheduled any appointments for tomorrow, because she wanted to relax before her last speaking engagement. Maybe she would use that free time to catch up on her notes. She knew her brain wasn't going to cooperate tonight. Christian's presence in her mind was getting stronger, more demanding. She had to find a way to see him.

"I guess you're right. Maybe I will call it a night and play catch up tomorrow." Alyssa stood up and stretched. Her body ached from sitting so long.

"Good. Let me get my things together and I'll walk you to your car."

She heard the bell ring on the front door and wondered who it was. Neither of them had any more appointments for the day.

"I'll get it. You finish packing up."

She could just make out Tom's voice as he spoke to their visitor, but couldn't hear what he was saying. Then everything was quiet. Alyssa gathered her paperwork. She had enough cases to keep her busy well into the afternoon tomorrow. Stuffing her briefcase until it bulged, she managed to get everything in. She shut the light off in her office and went to find Tom. He had less to take home than her. What was taking him so long?

She walked down the hall towards his office. Had someone turned the air conditioning on ultrahigh? It felt like she was walking in a giant freezer. As she reached Tom's closed door, the hair on the back of her neck stood on end.

Suddenly she didn't want to open Tom's door. Something horrible was behind that door. She didn't know how she knew that. But she did. It was the same feeling she had as a teenager before she walked into the bathroom and found her mother lying dead in a pool of blood. A struggle ensued inside her. It pulled her in two different directions. Danger. Her friend. Her body and mind were screaming for her to back away from the door. She took a couple of involuntary steps backwards. Then she stopped. Tom. She couldn't leave him. She had to go inside and help him.

Go back. Open the door. Tom needs you. It would be okay. Everything would be okay. Don't be afraid. There's nothing to be afraid of.

The soothing voice in her mind was strong. Yet it calmed her. Helped her move forward towards the door once again, to save her friend. Yes. She needed to save her friend. She placed her hand on the doorknob.

The other voice in her head was yelling at her to stop. It was screaming in her mind.

Danger.

Stop.

Don't move.

It even sounded like Christian's voice. She hesitated.

Open the door. Tom needs you.

Don't go inside. It's dangerous.

Alyssa tried to clear her mind, but it was impossible. Her thoughts were filled with these two opposing voices. She took her hand off the knob and covered her ears. Trying to block out the sound. But it was no use. The voices were inside. She couldn't stop them.

Suddenly, Tom's image came to mind, his kind, smiling face. How could she leave him in danger?

Before any other thoughts filled her head, she reached down, twisted the doorknob and pushed open the door. The sight that greeted her almost brought her to her knees. Tom. Lying on the ground. A deep gash slashed across one side of his neck. Blood pumped out of it at a dangerous rate. It spilled to the floor and started to pool around him. What happened? Alyssa felt like she was about to pass out. She pinched her arm as hard as possible. The pain helped her dizziness fade.

Tom needed her now. She had to help him. Moving forward, she sank down to her knees behind Tom's head. Lifting him up so that his neck was above his heart, she rested his head against her chest.

Removing her suit jacket she bunched it up and pressed it to the gash on his neck. She had to stop the blood from flowing out so quickly. If it didn't stop soon, she knew he would die. No one lost that much blood and lived. She spied the phone on Tom's desk. She would have to move with him to the phone so she could call an ambulance. Why hadn't she done that first?

She knew why. She had to stop the blood. She remembered how the doctors told her father that if someone had found her mother earlier and stopped her from losing so much blood, she might have lived. One more thing Alyssa felt guilty about. She wasn't about to let the same thing happen to Tom. She would just have to slide his body along the floor on her lap and get the phone. There was no other way.

But before she could start to move, the office door slammed and a familiar voice from behind her spoke.

"Well, aren't you the good friend? Poor Tom. I guess he just couldn't take my, uh, ravenous attention." Bazhena's mocking tone made Alyssa's heart speed out of control in fear.

She swung her head around. Bazhena's evil leer was smeared with blood.

"He's quite tasty, I must say. A good year, I think." Bazhena smacked her lips in appreciation. "Don't bother trying to save him, Alyssa. I really don't think he's going to make it."

The nonchalance in Bazhena's voice horrified Alyssa. This creature had no compassion and no regard for human life.

"Now that I've had my snack, how about some dinner? That's you of course, my sweet little thing," Bazhena said as she slowly stalked forward. "Let's find out what Cristobal finds so wonderful about you."

"Why do you want me?" Alyssa lifted her chin proudly, even though she knew it was quivering with fear. She needed to stall Bazhena in the hopes that she could stop Tom's bleeding. She felt blood soaking through the material even as they spoke.

Bazhena stopped moving forward while she considered her question. She looked surprised by it. Alyssa tried not to show her immense relief.

"You? Why do I want *you*? Because of The Light, my dear."

"The Light?"

"Yes. The Light is the last puzzle piece I need to solve the legend and gain immeasurable power. Once I have it, the world will be mine. I must join The Light and The Dark together with the various other pieces I've acquired around the world. Then the spell will be complete."

"What do you mean the world will be yours? In what way?"

"Curious little human, aren't you? I'll answer your questions. Then, once I satisfy your hunger for knowledge, you will satisfy my hunger for you," Bazhena said with an evil leer. The sharp points of her teeth shone in the light of the room. Making them look even more deadly.

Alyssa tried to keep her face bland, but her whole body shook with fear.

"I found some old scrolls a year or so back during my travels through Egypt. I've traveled the world many times, but that particular area holds a special place in my heart. Anyway, I found these scrolls in an old decrepit shop in Cairo and read though them. They contained the one prize I have always wanted, always dreamed about."

Bazhena's eyes became glazed with some far off memory.

"What prize?"

Bazhena didn't answer right away. Her eyes grew sad, as she got lost in her thoughts. Then she shook her head, as if to clear it.

"The best prize of all. Becoming the most desirable being on the face of the earth. To have creatures of every ilk want to do my bidding. Crave to stay with me forever. Die in their effort to please me. No one would be able to resist me. I've had a taste of that as a vampire, but it's not enough. Never enough. I want more. I need more. No one will ever turn me away again. That is true power. Once I have that, I will rule the world."

Alyssa was shocked. Could there actually be such a legend? Could someone hold that much power? Alyssa knew that if Bazhena accomplished her evil plan, the world would not be a better place. She shuddered at the thought of what it could become.

"There you are, human. I've shared my secrets with you. Unfortunately you won't be around to see the world once I rule. Because I'm going to suck every last drop of blood from your body while you scream in agony and ask for mercy. I won't give you any, of course. Only when I hear that last beat of your heart, will I be satisfied."

Bazhena stalked forward.

Alyssa gently set Tom's head down, leaving her jacket pressed against his neck. She hated leaving him there, but her own life was in serious danger. Scooting backwards on her bottom, she saw Bazhena transform before her eyes. A moment before, she was a beautiful, but evil-looking woman. But now, her face lost all expression. Her teeth elongated and protruded sharply out of her mouth. Eyes that moments before held evil amusement, turned cold and predatory.

"Usually I like to give my victims pleasure as I eat them, but not you. You I will eat the old-fashioned way. I think your blood will taste best while you're screaming out in pain. Yes, that would be perfect." Bazhena practically purred out those last words as she drew closer.

Alyssa scooted back until she hit the wall behind her. She had nowhere else to go. Then her hand encountered something. As she felt around, Alyssa realized it was Tom's miniature *Zen* sand garden. She had given it to him for Christmas last year. He hadn't been overly impressed with it, but nevertheless kept it in his office so her feelings wouldn't be hurt.

Bazhena was almost on her. Alyssa did the first thing that came to mind. Grabbing a handful of sand, she threw it in the vampire's face. Bazhena recoiled with a shriek and tried to claw the sand from her eyes. Seeing this as her only chance at escape, Alyssa stood up, opened the door and ran out. She sprinted down the hallway, but glanced back when she heard a deafening roar.

"You will pay for that, human!"

Alyssa turned back around. Keep moving. Don't stop. She couldn't let fear overwhelm her. She had to find help. She had to get away.

She didn't see the figure standing in the hallway until she ran straight into him. It felt like she smashed into a solid brick wall. She fell backwards and hit the floor, hard.

Dizziness assailed her, before everything went black.

Chapter Twelve

ཀ

Christian barely had enough time to move Alyssa out of the way before Bazhena launched herself at them. He turned sideways. She slammed into the wall. Her head punched through the other side. She shrieked in rage, trying to pull it out, but couldn't.

Christian pulled a metal stake out of his jacket and approached Bazhena. He twisted her body so that she was facing up instead of down. She screamed out in pain as the jagged edges of the wall cut into her neck. Blood streamed out of the deep wounds. Christian pushed her down so that her body was held back against the wall. This would have broken the neck of a human. Snapped it and killed them instantly. But Bazhena was no human. And she was still alive. Injured, yes, but far from dead.

"Now you'll die, Bazhena," Christian growled. "Your real death is long past due. You're an abomination, even to our kind. It's time you left this world."

He raised the stake. Prepared to sink it deep into her heart, to finally rid the world of her evil. Then he made a mistake. He hesitated. His time spent with Vlad had made him loath to kill unless absolutely necessary. His hesitation lasted only a few seconds. But it was enough. One minute Bazhena was there, the next she was fog, slipping through his fingers.

Christian roared his outrage as she drifted away into the night. Her mocking laughter filled his head. He was amazed that she had the strength to transform in her condition. Vlad had been right. Bazhena was more powerful than he imagined. He should go after her. He knew she would be vulnerable. Weak from her injury, blood loss and the energy it took to transform. But Alyssa needed him right now.

He turned and lifted Alyssa into his arms, then carried her to her office. Gently laying her down on the couch, he felt her pulse. It was strong and steady. She would be okay. He walked to Tom's office. When he studied the unconscious, bleeding man, he wasn't too sure about Alyssa's friend.

Her friend. Christian knelt down beside Tom and began his repair. First things first, he ran his tongue over the man's wound, healing it with his saliva. Tom's blood flow immediately slowed as it coagulated. Almost gagging, Christian spat out the taste of Bazhena that still remained on the man's skin. It reeked of evil, decay and death.

Next, Christian made a small slit in his arm with his nail. He carefully lifted Tom's head and brought his mouth to the now bleeding cut. He sent a mental suggestion and the man immediately latched onto his arm. He drank until Christian felt it was enough to replenish the blood loss and then he urged Tom to stop drinking and sleep. Alyssa's friend immediately obeyed, falling into a deep slumber, as Christian gently lifted him and laid him down on his couch. He ran his tongue over his own wound. It would be healed before morning, as would Tom's bite.

Christian implanted the idea into Tom's mind that he had fallen asleep at the office, erasing all memory of Bazhena. Tom would remember saying goodnight to Alyssa, staying late at the office and falling asleep on the couch. That would be it. He would remember nothing more.

Yet there was so much more. Once a human drinks from a vampire, his or her physiology changed. What Alyssa's friend might wonder about is why he suddenly can read without his reading glasses, why he's slightly stronger than before and why he will end up living to almost one hundred years old. Tom would also have one other special trait. He would live the rest of his life as Christian's human slave, if he should decide to make use of him. That meant that if Christian called to the human, he would have no other choice but to obey him, completely. He found this last detail abhorrent and would never make use of it, unless it came down to a life or death situation.

Next Christian considered how to cover up what had really happened. Damage control was one aspect of their business that Vlad insisted upon and had taught all the employees of Sundown Security. Eliminate all incriminating evidence.

Christian kept all the tools he needed either on him, or in his car. He put toppled furniture back where it belonged. Because he couldn't do much to repair the hole in the wall, he hit it a couple of times, to make a crack appear from the ceiling. Then he tore out more pieces of the wall, so that it stretched to the floor. Now the damage looked more like a structural fault than a vampire or human one.

It was the best he could do. He would let Tom and his receptionist come to their own conclusions about the damage.

Christian used the various chemicals he had on hand to clean the blood from the office. Afterward he removed Tom's shirt and pants and cleaned them too. He spread the clothes over a chair. They would be dry by morning. Tom would wake up in his underwear, but that was just too bad. Christian grinned with satisfaction at the image of Alyssa's receptionist finding Tom undressed in his office tomorrow morning.

As he studied Alyssa's unconscious friend, Christian grew serious. Anyone observing him would think he held no feeling other than bland boredom. They would be wrong. Dead wrong. Now that he had done what he swore to do so long ago, protect human life, his fingers curled with the need to wrap them around Tom's neck and squeeze until his face turned blue, his eyes bulged out of his head and his struggles ceased. These savage thoughts filled his head as one fact slammed into him again and again. One thought tore at his mind. Alyssa was in love with this human. That knowledge cut him like a knife. Jealousy raged through his body, as did the instinct to kill.

Alyssa's aunt had told him all about Tom. When Christian awoke this evening, he had quickly satisfied his hunger on a homeless man, then erased his memory of the event and sent him to a shelter for the night. Afterwards, he went directly to Alyssa's apartment. He wanted, no, he had to see her. Making love to her the night before had only wetted his appetite. He needed to be with her. Right or wrong, she completed him. Filled a void inside him that he had never known was there.

When he discovered that Alyssa wasn't home, he paged Vlad and found out where her aunt lived. Though she was probably fine, he needed to know for sure. It was his job. He was supposed to protect her. And until the last event tomorrow night was over, he would do just that. He tried to ignore the voice inside his head that told him his feelings involved so much more than just protection or sex.

When he arrived at Joyce's house, she welcomed him into her home without a problem. For some reason, Alyssa and her aunt's warm welcomes bothered him. They both needed to be more careful whom they let into their home. He should know. Under other circumstances, he would not be someone they should allow into their house, or into their heart.

Christian slammed the door shut on that thought. Alyssa didn't have room in her heart for him, it was already occupied by Tom. Joyce had told him how Alyssa and Tom had shared this office for several years. How they became friends, then lovers.

"Well, Christian. I don't know what to say. If Alyssa is staying late at the office, it's probably for two reasons."

"What reasons?" Christian eyes had narrowed suspiciously.

He hadn't known about Tom then. Or that Alyssa shared an office space with someone. He should have known, he should have found out. His job was to not only protect his client, but also to find out as much as possible about them so that he could protect them in every way.

"One reason is because she is so backed up returning calls and seeing clients. My niece is a workaholic. She works until she's exhausted. Oftentimes she works so hard she doesn't take time to eat. Or she eats snack food when she remembers. I've told her again and again to slow things down, but she doesn't listen. She always has to strive high and work hard. I think she got that from her father. He was in the military, you know."

"I heard," Christian said. "But what's the other reason she would stay late?"

"The other reason?" Joyce had looked at him with wide, innocent eyes, yet Christian had felt like she wasn't telling him the complete truth. He knew enough about the lady to know that she was very capable of manipulating people to do her bidding. Her motives were pure, but nevertheless she did try to control other people's lives. What was she up to this time?

"The other reason she's working late?" Christian had reminded her.

"Oh yes." Joyce's eyes had suddenly lit up as she paused and studied Christian. "Are you sure you want to hear this?"

Alarms had gone off inside Christian's head. Whatever she was about to tell him, wasn't good. He could sense it. He slowly nodded anyway.

"Tell me."

"The other reason Alyssa may be staying at the office late is because of Tom." Joyce had seemed to get much pleasure out of her words. When she stopped speaking, she looked at him with anticipation-filled eyes.

Christian had felt the hairs on his neck raise up. His body tensed. A growl from low in his throat rumbled softly.

"Tom? Is he a patient of hers?" Even as Christian had asked the question, he knew what her answer would be.

Joyce shook her head.

"No. He and Alyssa have known each other for years. Tom's also a family therapist. He's the man who shares her office space. And soon, I think, her bed."

Jealousy crashed into Christian. He had clenched his hands into fists. His growl grew deeper. He clamped his mouth shut to hide the incisors he felt elongating. His first instinct was to kill Tom. To rip his throat open and watch him die. Alyssa belonged to him. Nobody else. She was his.

Christian had managed to rein in the beast. Barely. The urge had been so strong that it left him shaking.

I am in control, not the beast. Only me. I decide, not it. I am not a monster.

Christian had to say the words over and over inside his head until the beast became little more than a growling, hissing whisper in his mind.

"Are you okay, Christian?" Joyce's voice had brought him back to himself. Her concerned expression told him that she was genuinely worried about him.

"Thank you for your concern, Joyce, but I'm fine," he had assured her with a smile. "I think I'll go check on Alyssa."

"I think you should also." Christian hadn't missed the smug smile on Joyce's face.

"Even though the stalker was caught last night, it's still my job to protect your niece until tomorrow night. I'm just doing what I'm paid to do."

Christian had winced as he heard the defensive tone of his own voice.

Joyce had given him a knowing smile and nodded.

"Of course you are, dear. And you're doing an admirable job of protecting Alyssa."

After an awkward goodbye, Christian had left in search of Alyssa. He followed the directions Joyce had given him to her office. He had tried to stay calm as he drove, but the thought of Alyssa with another man was almost too much for him. He imagined her naked in bed, her head thrown back in ecstasy as someone other than him brought her to her peak, again and again. He pictured her luscious mouth worshipping another man's body and his body rocked with rage. Jealousy had started to overtake him once more until he pulled into the parking lot of her office.

His jealousy and rage disappeared in an instant. Fear had replaced it. Alyssa's fear. He felt it coming at him in waves, as if she stood right beside him. Christian had sent her messages designed to soothe her and a command to stay where she was. Sensing her confusion and resistance, he had searched her mind. He wasn't the only one inside Alyssa's head.

Bazhena.

Her presence filled the air with its malevolent stench. He had streaked into the office as fast as his superhuman speed allowed. As he heard Bazhena's screech of rage, he knew he was just in time.

* * * * *

The sound of Alyssa stirring brought Christian's thoughts back to the present.

What was it about her that touched him so? Why her? Alyssa brought out thoughts and feelings inside him that had been buried for over two hundred years. Why now? He hadn't cared about someone like this since Elena.

Elena.

Her name brought her image instantly to mind. They had met as children when both of their families still lived in Spain. His father and hers were good friends. They decided early on that Elena and he would marry. It had all been arranged.

When they were children, they didn't know of such things. They met and became fast friends. But even back then, Christian had felt a certain protectiveness towards Elena. She had been so little, so soft and quiet. He had been many years older, bigger, stronger and smarter, according to her. She always listened when he told her what to do. And she asked for his advice whenever she wasn't sure about something.

The two of them spent many childhood days giggling, running and playing together. They always pretended that he was the noble hero and she the lady in distress. She would call for help and he would come to her rescue.

And when he rescued her, Elena would stare up at Christian with adoration and say, "I knew you would save me. I knew you would come."

Those words would forever haunt him. In the end he hadn't saved his Elena. He had actually caused her death. He was to blame for giving in to temptation, for arrogantly tossing Elena aside and for pursuing Bazhena like a dog in heat. Granted she was a vampire and had seduced him with her powers, but his love for Elena should have been stronger.

He should have been stronger.

But he hadn't been. He had been weak. And Elena had been viciously murdered because of that weakness, because he had been unable to control himself.

Never again.

Christian had made a vow to himself after he and Vlad met. He would never let himself get out of control again. He would be the master of his own fate. He would decide when and where. No one else. Only him. And he would control the monster inside him with everything he had. Never again would he lose himself to the power of his emotions.

Christian's thoughts came crashing back to the present again when Alyssa's eyes fluttered open. He stared into her crystal blue gaze and was lost. All his vows and promises drifted away like a soft breeze on a warm summer night. Whatever it was that made him feel this way, it was done. Choice was nonexistent. She was his now, whether she realized it or not. And no one was going to take her away from him. Ever.

* * * * *

Alyssa woke to find herself staring into Christian's beautiful eyes. The look on his face took her breath away. It was hot with desire and intense with possession. She lost herself in the power of his gaze. Her body tingled with awareness, her heartbeat sped out of control and her breath grew short. She tried to breathe deeply to calm herself, but the sexy, dangerous scent of him drifted seductively in the air, enflaming her further.

Then another odor intruded. It was strong and overwhelming. Blood. She smelled blood. Her memory came crashing back. Nausea swept over her. Her stomach rolled in protest as images filled her head.

Tom.

Bazhena.

Alyssa bolted upright. Until her face was inches from Christian's. She grabbed his shoulders. Frantically she looked around the room.

"Tom? Where's Tom? We have to get some help. Bazhena attacked him. He's bleeding and I—"

Christian's face darkened with anger, but he laid a finger gently against Alyssa's lips to quiet her.

"He's fine," he assured her through clenched teeth.

Alyssa wasn't convinced. She saw the way Tom had looked before she passed out.

"Are you sure?" Tom had been in grave danger from too much blood loss. She needed to know he would be okay, that his fate would not be the same as her mother's.

"He's lost a lot of blood, Christian. I think he needs to go to a hospital."

Alyssa noticed Christian's face grow tight and tense.

"Tom will be fine, Alyssa. I have taken care of his wound and his lost blood has been replenished."

Alyssa let go of Christian's shoulders and then sagged with relief. Tom was fine. He would be okay. His blood loss had been taken care of. Replenished. Alyssa felt tense again. Exactly what had Christian done to Tom?

"Replenished? What do you mean replenished? How did you—?"

Christian's face exploded with emotion. The anger in his eyes made her shrink back against the couch. She had never seen him this way. So furious, his feelings emanated in waves from him. Each one struck her like a blow. Battering her emotionally rather than physically.

"Enough! I don't want to talk about your lover right now." Christian growled deep in his throat and his eyes began to glow. Alyssa's eyes widened in fear as she saw his sharp teeth elongate before her eyes.

"I want to talk about the danger you're in. You will come with me now. I need to keep you safe until I find out what's going on with Bazhena. She wants you for some reason. Until I discover why, you need to be kept under my tight protection. And don't worry about your boyfriend. He'll be okay. He'll wake up in the morning on his couch, thinking he fell asleep at the office."

Alyssa shook her head slowly. Anger was starting to replace the fear his transformation had caused. She would not be treated like a child. She was an adult. Christian needed to understand that.

"No."

"No?" His voice was deadly. Quiet, but more threatening than if he had screamed at the top of his lungs.

Alyssa refused to be intimidated.

"I'm not going anywhere until I know that Tom is okay and you tell me what's going on." She folded her arms across her chest and waited.

Christian's expression hardened until his face became so emotionless it looked like it was etched in stone. Yet his gaze burned with fury so strong it shot daggers straight at her. She struggled to hang on to her own anger, but common sense and self-preservation were screaming for her attention. Unfortunately, she might have realized it too late.

Christian grasped her shoulders and pulled her forward. Her face was inches from his. Their eyes met and clashed. They held each other's gaze, both refusing to look away. Alyssa thought she saw admiration kindle in Christian's eyes, but then he moved and she wasn't sure. Turning his head sideways, he pressed his cheek against hers and whispered in her ear.

"Do you know what you're doing to me, *palomita*? Do you understand the consequences of your actions? I am not in a state to be played with right now. I would not play nice, I promise you that. The smell of blood is everywhere, filling my senses, tempting me. The odor of another man is on you, stirring up my anger and my beast. Your seductive scent is also calling to me, drawing me closer." Christian punctuated his words by running his tongue first down, then up her neck. When he reached her ear again, he gave the lobe a little nip with his teeth and sucked on it gently. The pain-pleasure of his mouth caused shivers to run through her and the breath to hitch in her throat.

"My beast is close at hand. Ready to take over, ready to take you if I let it. And it would not be a gentle joining. Don't push me right now. Just trust me and do as I say." Christian's last words sounded deep and hoarse.

He slid his mouth down and grazed his teeth over her neck. Then he sucked on the spot where his teeth had been. She was going to have one hell of a hickey tomorrow morning. The strong pull of his mouth started an ache between her legs that made her knees weak. He stiffened, squeezed her shoulders almost to the point of pain, then shuddered. Slowly, she felt his body relax until finally he released her.

He was having trouble controlling himself. Alyssa had kept her body completely still until he released her. Somehow she sensed that if she moved too much, his restraint would be unleashed. He moved away and she sighed in relief. Okay. Now was definitely not the time to challenge him. She would just have to trust him.

Trust him. Hmm.

That was a tough one.

Definitely not her strong point. Especially when it came to this man. One who was strong and controlling, like her father. One who had an emotional hold on her.

She admitted it. There was something more than physical attraction between them. Strong feelings were involved. But she didn't want to deal with them right now. One thing at a time. They would have to reach a compromise.

Alyssa waited until Christian composed himself and turned back to her. His face still looked tight, but his eyes were calmer. No longer glowing. His fists unclenched and he held them loosely by his side as he stood up.

"We need to go now, Alyssa." Christian held out his hand to her. His eyes remained shuttered as he gazed down at her, showing no emotion. But she could feel the tension in him as he waited.

She didn't take his hand.

His eyes narrowed dangerously.

She spoke quickly.

"I'll go with you, but only on one condition."

He began clenching his jaw.

"What?" The word came out little more than a growl.

"Please let me see Tom, so that I know he's okay. I won't ask for any more answers and I'll go with you without a fight."

Christian looked like he was about to deny her.

"Please, Christian. I need to see for myself that Tom will live. It's very important to me."

He nodded.

"Okay. He's in his office. Come with me. We don't have much time."

He held his hand out to her again. This time she took it. His hold was gentle as he led her to Tom's office. She gasped when she saw the cracks and hole in the hallway wall.

"What happened?"

Christian continued walking as he explained.

"Bazhena. She got a little irritated when I tried to show her the door." Christian's mocking tone was not lost on Alyssa, but she could also sense an underlying concern in his voice. She was surprised and a little frightened that someone as powerful as Christian was troubled.

She stopped short when they entered Tom's office and she saw him lying on the couch in his underwear.

"Why is he in his underwear?"

Christian shrugged negligently.

"I had to clean the blood off his clothes. One of the services I perform in this line of work is eliminating the evidence. We can't leave proof of our paranormal activities around for the world to see. That would be pushing our luck," Christian explained as he pointed to the clothes draped over the nearby chair. "His clothes will be dry by morning."

"I see."

Alyssa dragged her gaze to Tom's neck. She remembered the bloody tear from earlier and didn't relish seeing it again. Her mouth formed a perfect "O" when she saw that the bleeding gash now looked like little more than a deep cut that had already started to close.

His recovery was amazing. She felt the pulse at his wrist and was pleased that it beat steady and strong. He was going to be okay. The tightness Alyssa felt in her chest slowly released.

"How?" she asked as she studied Tom.

Christian knew just what she was asking.

"Vampires have a healing compound in their saliva. His cut will be gone by morning. And don't worry. Your lover won't remember a thing about this night, other than the fact that he worked late and fell asleep on his couch."

"Well, let me at least cover him with a blanket," Alyssa said, opening a cabinet and pulling out a lightweight blanket. She laid it over Tom, then froze as something finally clicked in her mind. She turned back to Christian.

"Why do you keep calling Tom my boyfriend? What makes you think we're lovers?"

Christian's eyes ignited with fury once more. He stalked towards her. Towering over her, he glared down at her. A growl rumbled low in his throat. Alyssa's eyes widened in fear as she craned her neck up to look at him.

"You told me no more questions. You didn't keep your word, Alyssa. I've wasted enough time here. We're leaving. Now."

Alyssa bristled at his domination.

"Wait just a minute. I'm not—"

"Sleep."

Christian interrupted her with only one word. It was spoken softly, but the moment Alyssa heard it, everything grew fuzzy. She tried to fight it, tried to keep her eyes open, but her eyelids felt like they weighed a thousand pounds. She struggled to hold on to her thoughts but they scattered into a thousand pieces as Christian spoke again.

"You will sleep now, *palomita*. Sleep."

Then everything went dark.

Chapter Thirteen

ꙮ

Christian carried Alyssa to his car. He drove out of the Old Town Scottsdale area and headed west on Camelback Road. They were going to his side of the tracks this time. He glanced over at Alyssa sleeping in the seat beside him. A primitive and savage satisfaction filled him. He was bringing his woman back to his lair, where he would make her his once and for all. She belonged to him. Not that weakling human, Tom. Christian let his anger roll over him as Arcadia's green, lush, resort-like neighborhood changed to the high-end Biltmore area, to the office buildings of the shakers and movers of the Camelback corridor.

Alyssa made a small sound and he glanced at her again. Some of his triumph faded as he stared at her beautiful face. She looked so innocent, so vulnerable while she slept. He returned his gaze to the road. Guilt. That's what he was feeling. He didn't like using mind control on Alyssa. It wasn't fair. But his emotions had gotten the better of him. Jealousy had reared its ugly head. Every time she had mentioned Tom's name, the image of her and Tom making love crashed into Christian's mind. He imagined her voluptuous body entwined with Tom's and her cries of passion filling the air. It had been too much. Her denials had fallen on deaf ears. Christian's baser emotions had taken control.

One instinct took over.

Make Alyssa his.

Fully. Completely. So that no doubt remained for either of them.

Once they reached the downtown area, Christian headed south on Central Avenue. This part of the city was quiet at night compared to farther south, where investors with a lot of money were trying to revitalize the city around the sports arena. Run down buildings had been replaced with lively new clubs, restaurants and well-known chain stores. As a result, more people were not only starting to frequent the area at night, but many were also moving into the newly built condos surrounding the renovation.

Christian headed west, towards Fifteenth Avenue and the historical Encanto District. That was his neighborhood. The older residences and large green gardens in this section of town appealed more to him than some of the new, more sanitized, desert landscaped housing developments in Scottsdale. The fact that the houses were spread apart on large lots and offered privacy to their owners was something Christian favored. Having a tall security wall surrounding his property also added to its appeal.

After punching in his private code on the keypad, the gates swung open and he drove onto his property. A sense of relief welcomed him immediately, as it always did when he arrived home. Here he could be himself. This was his refuge. The property had been paid off years ago, so was completely his. His castle. And now he was bringing home his queen.

Christian frowned in consternation.

His queen? Where had that come from?

He tried to ignore that last thought. But as he lifted Alyssa into his arms, he felt it. Possession. He wouldn't deny it. He had won his lady and was bringing her home. Where she belonged. He brought her into the house and carried her upstairs to his bedroom. Laying her on his bed, he sat down beside her. Skimming his fingers lightly over her soft cheeks, he sent her a mental push. It was time for Sleeping Beauty to awaken.

* * * * *

Alyssa reveled in the feel of Christian's hand against her cheeks. This was a wonderful dream. She sighed with pleasure.

His hand was like the rest of him—strong and sexy. She practically purred when he ran it gently through her hair, massaging her scalp along the way. He had very talented hands. She knew that from experience.

He worked his way to her neck and tingles ran up and down her body. He drew little circles along its curve. Alyssa tilted her head to the side, so that he could have better access.

A seductive chuckle was her first indication that maybe she wasn't asleep. Christian's next words confirmed it.

"You better be careful, little girl, or this big bad wolf might be tempted to eat you."

Alyssa's eyes snapped open. Christian looked down at her with amusement. Yet the fire in his eyes was unmistakable. She felt pinned in place by his powerful stare. Burning desire left her breathless. He held her gaze a moment longer then looked away as he got off the bed.

Where was she? She sat up and looked around her. She didn't recognize anything but the fact that she was in a bedroom. It was a modern room. Decorated in black, gray and tan, very masculine, but at the same time very tastefully done and extremely neat. There were no clothes or papers strewn about. Everything was where it should be.

The room would have almost been completely cold and impersonal if one item didn't stand out like a sore thumb. It caught her interest and held it. It was a portrait hanging on one wall. It was large, with an ornate frame and was very, very old. Alyssa was not an antique expert, but she had been to enough antique shops and viewed enough portraits to know this one was done long ago. It didn't go with the room. It was put there as if an afterthought, without any regard for the rest of the room. It looked like a family portrait.

Alyssa got distracted when she noticed that Christian was watching her closely.

"Where am I?"

He smiled. But his eyes remained wary, searching hers, as if looking for something.

"Welcome to my home, Alyssa. You're the only human, other than my personal assistant, to enter it and leave…"

Alive. Alyssa ignored the voice in her head that finished the last word of his sentence. The one he purposely left unsaid. She was the only human to enter his home and leave *alive.* Instead of fear, she let curiosity get the better of her.

"Your home?" she asked.

"Yes. I brought you straight from the office to my house. After the attack on you and Tom at the office, I don't think you'll be safe at your place, at least not until morning. Bazhena was injured, but one never can tell with a va—"

"Tom!" Alyssa interrupted, jumping up from the bed. "What about him?"

Alyssa saw Christian's eyes harden.

"As I told you earlier, your boyfriend will be fine. I don't think Bazhena planned on or expected to see him last night. And since she is in a weakened state, I can't see her using her remaining strength to go after him tonight instead of you. It's you she wants for some reason. Everyone else is just a side dish."

Alyssa shuddered at the memory of Bazhena licking her lips and looking at her like she was food. Her ability to follow through on that look was unmistakable when she recalled the way Tom had looked. She would never forget the sight of the tear in his throat, or the blood spilling endlessly out of it. He had been badly injured, but his uncanny recovery, thanks to Christian, made her believe that her friend would be okay.

She released a sigh of relief. "Thank you for helping Tom. He means a lot to me and—"

Her words cut off abruptly as she found herself pressed backwards and pinned to the bed. Christian lay over her, his face inches from hers. A growl rumbled deep in his throat. He kept his weight balanced on his elbows, so he wasn't hurting her, but there was no way she was going anywhere until he let her.

"I don't want to hear about you and your lover," he said through clenched teeth.

Alyssa knew she should be scared by the fury in his eyes. Knew she should be in shock over everything that had just occurred. But, instead, she felt really, really irritated. Her little encounter with Bazhena had been enough for one night. She didn't need this from him right now.

"He is not my lover, or my boyfriend," she bit out, trying to push herself up.

Her struggles didn't faze Christian.

"Your aunt told me a different story." His eyes narrowed dangerously.

"My aunt told you whatever she could to get you to do what she wanted you to do."

Christian still looked disbelieving.

Alyssa blew out an exasperated breath.

"Tom and I are and have always been just friends. End of story. Now will you let me up?"

Alyssa managed to squeeze her hands between them and give Christian's chest a little push. He ignored her actions as he searched her eyes. He looked uncertain now. As if he finally realized all may not be what it seemed.

The feel of his solid chest against her hands made her want to flex her fingers to test its hardness. Suddenly he invaded her senses. His closeness. His strength. The way he stared so deeply into her eyes. The spicy, seductive scent of him. The feel of his hard contours pressed against her curves. Her body kicked into overdrive. Her nipples hardened against his chest and a pulsating ache began between her thighs.

"You and he are no more than friends?"

Alyssa stared into Christian's mocha-colored eyes. She wanted to lose herself in those eyes. Her irritation faded as desire burned through her. Deep, dark, silk sheets in the middle of the night desire. The kind that would leave her panting for more.

"Alyssa?"

"Huh? What?"

An arrogant looked filled Christian's face and he gave her a knowing smile. His uncertainty from a moment ago was gone. His deliberate smirk ruffled her feathers. He was just a little too sure of himself. He knew what she was thinking. That she was his for the taking. Alyssa steeled herself against the lust that was threatening to overtake her.

"Will you get off of me now?" Alyssa tried to sound impatient and irritated, but instead her voice came out husky and soft.

His smile widened.

"Gladly. But first you need to answer my question," he said easily.

Too easily.

"Question? What question?" she asked, narrowing her eyes in suspicion.

Instead of answering, Christian brought his mouth close to her ear. He blew softly into it and chills ran down Alyssa's body.

"Are you mine to take, *palomita*?"

His words rocked her. There was no other word for it. As the last syllable left his lips, Alyssa's body became his. She sucked in a gasp as the fire he ignited inside her flamed out of control. Her body became sensitive to every point they touched. She reveled in the feel of his hard chest under her flexing fingers. The press of his hips against hers was unbearably light. Tilting hers upward, she strove to bring them closer.

"I sense your desire, *mi amor*. I feel it too. The scent of your body is calling out to me. Can you deny it?" Christian asked before he captured her earlobe with his mouth and sucked on it lightly.

His teeth grazed along the edge as he pulled away and looked down at her once more. The passion and possession in his eyes were undeniable. It left her shaking with need. It left her wanting to be possessed by him, completely. So completely that she was sated to the point that she could barely move. Yet she hesitated. Could she let herself go? Open herself like this? Need him so?

Christian must have sensed what she was going through. Though his face remained tight with passion, tenderness filled his eyes. It was the tenderness that got her. It was like a soft breeze running over her in the midst of a raging heat wave. The intense desire she felt was still there, but it was different now. The gentleness in his eyes told her what his words hadn't. Her heart was safe with him. He would handle it with care.

Something blossomed inside her. The knot in her chest she never realized was there loosened and released. A smile she couldn't hold back if her life depended on it spread across her mouth. Then the tears came. She didn't want them, not now. But they didn't listen. They slowly slid down her cheeks unchecked.

Without a word, Christian leaned closer and kissed one as it fell. She continued to cry and he continued to rain kisses all over her face. He murmured soft words in Spanish in between each touch. She didn't understand what he was saying, but somehow they made her feel better. The tears slowed and eventually stopped. Christian's mouth drew closer and closer to hers with each kiss. Once he reached them he hesitated, hovering just above her lips, no more than a whisper away.

Alyssa needed this. She needed him, now. Her hunger could wait no longer. Lifting her head slightly, she tried to press her lips against him. Christian pulled slightly up and away from her.

"Say you want me, *palomita*. Say the words I crave to hear." Christian's voice was hoarse with need.

Alyssa didn't hesitate.

"I want you, Christian. I need you, only you."

A groan sounded deep in his chest as he slanted his lips over hers. His expert mouth possessed hers, claimed her as his. Alyssa moaned when she parted her lips and he delved inside. He plundered her mouth ruthlessly, taking and demanding more from her. She gave as good as she got, meeting each touch of his tongue in a dance as old as time.

Christian couldn't get enough of her. She was his. She wanted him, just him. He used no coercion, no powers beyond those of human attraction. She had made the choice of her own free will. He knew it hadn't been easy for her. He had seen the vulnerability and uncertainty in her eyes. She was scared. He understood.

He would never forget the moment when Alyssa's eyes changed. When she looked at him with warmth and welcome instead of guarded passion. In that instant he had felt like he could do anything. Be anything. The guilt that ruled his life had faded under her warm gaze. She made him feel like so much more than he was, so much better. And he wanted to be that, for her.

When she finally spoke the words he needed to hear, Christian released the passion he had barely held in check. He delved into her mouth again and again, wanting to taste her completely, totally. He couldn't get enough. When she met his tongue with hers he almost exploded. The silky feel of it made him imagine other parts of his body enjoying her touch. His pants grew even more painfully tight as desire burned through him. He dragged his mouth down her neck, laving her pulse point on the way. Taking small nips of her collarbone, he started to unbutton her blouse the rest of the way.

When Alyssa placed her hands over his, he thought she wanted to stop him. He couldn't have been more wrong. She gently pushed his hands aside and quickly unbuttoned it herself. When she undid the last button, he spread her shirt apart and slid his fingers over her soft stomach. She quivered from his touch. He covered her mouth with his again as his hands skimmed over her belly button and worked their way up. The tips of his fingers touched the edge of Alyssa's bra and she shivered under his touch. Christian undid the front clasp with an ease that told much about his experience with women.

Arching her body upwards, she made it clear that she wanted his touch. But Christian hesitated. His hungry gaze devoured her beauty and softness. He had been with many beautiful women during his life, but not a single one could measure up to the woman he now held beneath him. No, he had no trouble finding his way around a woman, but tonight he felt like a green boy. Worried he would not please her, as she deserved to receive pleasure.

He looked down at his hands and realized they trembled. Alyssa moaned with need and lifted her body again so that his hands covered her breasts. Christian ran his fingers back and forth over her nipples and watched as they darkened and pebbled under his touch. They looked like sweet ripe berries. He needed them in his mouth. Bending over her, he worshipped one breast with his mouth while continuing to caress the other. Alyssa's soft sounds of pleasure were killing him. He took turns drawing each nipple into his mouth. Sucking them gently until they hardened and tightened from his attention.

Alyssa's fingers gripped his hair and pulled his head closer. The tug of his mouth became more demanding until she was writhing under him, moaning his name over and over again. He skimmed his hand down, along her smooth stomach to the button of her slacks. Unbuttoning and unzipping them, he slid them down as she lifted her hips obligingly. All the while he continued to suckle her breasts. Her moans grew louder and more needy.

Christian pulled away to look at the little scrap of silky peach cloth she wore. It barely covered her womanhood. He smiled at her sexy choice of panties. Unable to help himself, he slid his fingers along its edges. Alyssa made soft mewling sounds in her throat. When he laid his hand over her core, he could feel her moist heat through the cloth.

Alyssa lifted her hips and gasped.

"Christian, please."

"Easy, *palomita*. I know what you need. And I'll give it to you."

Christian slipped his fingers underneath her panties. His fingers delved into her sweetness. Alyssa hissed and her hips jerked with each stroke of his fingers. He found her tender spot and gave it the attention it deserved. Over and over he caressed her, felt her harden from his touch. Her lips spread apart as they swelled with passion-filled blood.

Christian tore her panties off. He needed to see all of her. He stared down at the perfection that lay before him. Her voluptuous curves made him harden to the point of pain. Her soft skin made him hunger to taste it. And her body's responses to his touch made him want to plunge deep inside her and lose himself in her softness. But still he held back. He wanted her pleasure to come first.

Alyssa's moans became pleas for more. Christian gently spread her thighs and stared down at her womanhood. She was so beautiful. Swollen and wet with need, the scent of her desire made his mouth water. He lowered his head and took her in his mouth. Alyssa's hips rose up to meet him. He ran his tongue over the center of her, flicking it over and over. Quivering from his touch, she gasped his name as he plunged his tongue inside her. Then he drew her nub into his mouth, again and again, until she screamed her release.

Christian lifted his head and watched as she gave her body up to passion. It was so incredibly erotic that he almost lost it then and there. She stilled as the last vibration overcame her, then lay with her eyes closed, a smile on her face. After quickly undressing, he began kissing his way back up her body. She giggled when his mouth ran over certain parts of her. He gave her teasing nips in those spots and then continued his way up.

He lapped at her stomach then delved his tongue into her belly button. Her giggles soon turned into gasps of pleasure. He slid his mouth up to her swollen breasts and devoured each wet, pebbled nipple in turn. When Alyssa started moaning and squirming restlessly underneath him he knew she was ready again.

Spreading her thighs wide, Christian kneeled on the bed poised above her. He tilted his hips forward until his hardness pressed lightly against her softness. Alyssa kept her eyes closed, tightly closed. The feel of her was so unbearably good that his next words were no more than a hiss between his clenched teeth.

"Open your eyes, *palomita*. I want to look into them when we join."

Alyssa immediately obeyed his command. Her eyes fluttered open. Glazed with passion and need, her blue irises glowed against her long, dark lashes. Her full red lips were parted from each panting breath she took. She bit her bottom lip and tried to lift her hips higher so that he entered her. He pulled slightly back so that he remained just out of reach.

"Christian!" Her needy gasp filled him with savage satisfaction. Good. She was as hungry for him as he was for her. It was time.

He plunged deep and sure.

Now it was his turn to gasp with pleasure. The feel of her tight wetness surrounding him made his self-control slip dangerously low. His strokes began slow and long. Each one brought him almost out of her before he thrust deeply inside again. Alyssa's passionate cries grew louder and louder. His strokes grew faster and harder. He felt her stiffen below him and knew she was getting close. Gritting his teeth, he held himself back, waiting for her to tumble over the edge. She arched her back, tilting her hips up to take him more fully. Her breasts jutted up, like an offering he couldn't resist. His body raged out of control. Christian captured one of her nipples with his mouth and drew hungrily on it.

Alyssa cried out and pushed herself more fully against his lips. Passion consumed him, but another hunger also surfaced. Unable to stop it, his teeth lengthened. One grazed against her blood-engorged nipple. The beast broke free. It wanted to feed.

It would not be denied. His teeth sank into the soft skin of her breast. Her sweet nectar flowed into his mouth and he drank deeply. Alyssa screamed her release and her body convulsed wildly beneath him. Christian lifted his head and roared as he exploded inside her a moment later.

After the last wave of orgasm rolled over him he lowered his head and ran his tongue over Alyssa's bite. It would heal quickly. Laying his head on her chest he listened to her heartbeat as it slowed. Her breathing became even and he knew she dozed.

He was not so lucky.

He laid his head across her chest, careful not to put all his weight on her. But he didn't sleep. What he had just shared with Alyssa had been the most wondrous experience of his entire life. He had made love so many times over the hundreds of years of his existence, that he'd lost count. His partners had been mostly worldly women who knew their way around a bedroom. Alyssa affected him like no other. He could tell from her actions as well as the tightness of her woman's core that she had not been with many men. Yet each soft, needy sound that left her lips, each tilt of her hips, each touch of her fingers had seduced him more completely than any courtesan he had ever been with. They had joined as more than two bodies. They connected in mind as well as body. They had touched each other inside and out.

He lifted his head and gazed at Alyssa's sleeping face. He gently ran his hand through her hair. As he started to pull it away, a single curl wrapped around his finger and clung to it. A surge of protectiveness like he had never known rose up in him. This woman belonged with him and to him. No one would ever hurt her. Not without answering to him.

She was so beautiful in sleep, like a fallen angel. Her silky raven tresses spread wildly around her heart-shaped face. Thick, dark lashes brushed against her ivory skin. Her soft cheeks were flushed from their lovemaking. Lush, red lips swollen from his kisses. His gaze moved down the graceful curve of her neck to her chest. The sight of her berry-tipped breasts stirred him.

Made him want to take her again. But the sight of his bite marks stopped him in his tracks.

Shame washed over him. He had let the beast go. He had completely lost control of himself. How could he? After all these years of keeping tight rein on it, he'd failed to keep the beast in check. What if he had killed her? What if the beast had wanted all of her, all her blood, until her heart stopped beating? The hairs rose on the back of his neck as he realized that it could have happened. His beast could have taken her from him.

He had not bitten a woman while making love since he broke away from Bazhena. He was always under tight control. He had let himself feel the physical pleasures of lovemaking, but always held part of himself back, enough to keep the vampire in check. Hundreds of years had gone by and he had never had this happen. Something about Alyssa called to his beast. Made it want to rage out of control. Made it want to totally consume her.

Christian carefully pushed himself up and away from her. He continued to stare down at her sleeping form while he dressed. Her lushly curved body called to him, but he steeled himself against it. This was the last time they would make love. If he couldn't trust himself with her, then he had no business making love to her. It would not happen again. He couldn't risk the horrors his beast could claim, or Alyssa's well-being.

It was time to call in the reinforcements.

Chapter Fourteen

Alyssa woke up. She'd just had the most erotic dream. She stretched and then rolled over onto her side. Reaching down in search of her blanket, she felt all around her but couldn't find it. The sheets felt different, silky and smooth. Not like her usual one hundred percent cotton thread. That was strange. Yawning, she thought about forgetting about the blanket and going back to sleep. But there was a definite chill in the air. She must have set the air conditioner too high. Reluctantly she opened her eyes. A gasp escaped her lips as she encountered Christian's intense mocha eyes inches from hers. He was bent over her on the bed.

It hadn't been a dream!

"Time to awaken, *palomita*." The tenderness in his eyes was unmistakable as he ran his index finger gently down her cheek. He looked longingly into her eyes for a minute, then straightened and walked away.

The seductive softness in his voice washed over her, making her recall their passionate lovemaking. Alyssa cringed as she thought about how wild she had acted with him. She definitely wasn't a virgin, but she had never let herself go the way she had done with Christian tonight. The things she had done, the noises she had made. It was like she had become a totally different woman. One who'd just let her inner self-free and enjoyed the moment with everything she had.

Hmm. Maybe it hadn't been so embarrassing after all. She distinctly remembered Christian keeping up with her pace for pace. The desire that burned in his eyes had been her undoing. The whole experience had been incredible. The best she had ever experienced. She had never felt as close to someone as she had when Christian plunged deep inside her.

As he walked across the room, Alyssa couldn't help admire the way Christian moved. Like a panther, dangerous, yet graceful, beautiful, but deadly. When he abruptly swung around, his face no longer looked gentle. Instead it was shuttered. His eyes cold.

"Get dressed. I'm taking you home." His voice was brusque and unfeeling.

The temperature in the air grew colder. Christian's gaze remained fixed on her. The nakedness she had reveled in only moments before now left her feeling vulnerable. As if reading her thoughts, his eyes ran insolently down her body. His face became tight and angry, as if what he saw was not to his liking.

"Get dressed, now."

Alyssa leaned up on her elbows, but didn't get up.

"What's going on, Christian?"

Her eyes narrowed with suspicion. What kind of game was he playing? They had made the most incredible love, then he woke her up tenderly and now he had suddenly become Mr. Arrogant Jerk.

"Can you just do what I ask without an argument for once, Alyssa?"

His voice sounded resigned, as if he was tired of talking to her.

Anger bubbled to life in Alyssa. She sat up and grabbed her clothes. Walking arrogantly towards Christian, she glared at him. If he wanted to act like an ass, she would treat him like one. She paused right before walking by him.

"If this is some sort of Buffy the Vampire Slayer and Angel the Vampire after-they-make-love-for-the-first-time kind of thing, I'm not liking it at all. Get over yourself, Christian."

He continued to look straight ahead. The only acknowledgement that he had heard what she said, was a tightening of his jaw. Alyssa wanted him to feel something. Needed to get something from him other than coldness. She couldn't take that. Not after everything they had shared.

Standing up on her tiptoes, she leaned towards him. Placing her mouth by his ears, she whispered the one thing she hoped would get his attention.

"It wasn't that good."

Alyssa wasn't disappointed.

Before she could blink an eye, Christian lifted her up by the shoulders and backed her against the wall directly behind her. He pressed his body against hers to keep her pinned there. His eyes flared to life. Anger and something else shined bright.

"Not that good? Are you sure about that, Alyssa? Are you *sure*?"

Grasping her thighs, he spread them wide so that they wrapped around his hips. Even through his pants, she could feel his hard manhood pressing against her core. He flexed his hips once, then again, brushing against her womanhood. Alyssa bit her bottom lip to keep the whimper of pleasure buried in her throat from breaking free.

"How about if we put your words to the test?"

Christian devoured her mouth without warning. She tried to push him away, but he easily held her hands against the wall on either side of her head. She grew dizzy from the onslaught of his lips. His kisses started out hard and demanding, but soon became soft and seductive. He sucked on her bottom lip until she couldn't help but part them for him. He delved in and out of her mouth, teasing her with his tongue. Alyssa moaned and tentatively met his touch. He pulled back slightly, so that she was forced to probe deeper. When he continued to tease her, she began boldly exploring his mouth.

Christian eventually broke their kiss and rained kisses down her neck to her breasts. Without hesitation he wrapped his mouth around one nipple and drew on it. The hard tug of his mouth left her squirming with desire. She arched against his mouth so that he could take more of her. Christian switched to her other breast with a low growl and she stiffened in pleasure. His mouth was working magic on her body, while he continued to flex his hips against her. When he finally lifted his mouth from her breasts she was panting with desire.

Alyssa didn't notice that he had let go of her hands until she heard him unzip his pants. He pressed his hardness against her opening and she almost screamed from pleasure. He grasped her bottom and pulled her closer to him. The feel of his hands holding her in place was driving her wild. She squirmed against Christian, but he didn't budge.

"Now, what were you saying?" Christian said through tightly clenched teeth.

Alyssa couldn't respond. All she knew was desire. She wanted him inside her, now.

Christian slid one hand around to the front of her and cupped her womanhood. He pressed his thumb near her most sensitive spot and began making circles around it. She felt her wetness coat his finger until it felt slippery against her. Closer and closer he circled until he almost touched her center. Then he hesitated.

"Christian!" she hissed.

Alyssa's hips tilted involuntarily towards his touch.

"Is this what you want?" he asked arrogantly.

Before she could answer, Christian flicked his thumb against her nub.

Alyssa couldn't stop the small sob of pleasure that erupted from her mouth.

"When it comes to pleasure, you are just a baby compared to me, *palomita*. Never forget that."

Then he plucked at her center, playing her over and over again, until her orgasm overcame her. She screamed his name and her hips convulsed helplessly over and over again. Before her last convulsion shook her, Christian growled low in his throat then sunk his hardness deep inside of her. Holding her behind with both hands, he pulled her towards him and plunged into her over and over again. Yelling her name, his release came swift and strong.

Christian leaned his forehead against the wall beside her head as his heaving breaths eventually slowed. Alyssa would have slid to the floor if he hadn't been holding her up. She waited for her own breathing to become normal before lifting her head off of his shoulder. As she did so, he pulled himself straight and carried her towards his bathroom. The feel of him moving inside her as they walked sent tingles of pleasure through her. He walked to the sink and set her down on it. Looking deeply into her eyes, he leaned down and kissed her thoroughly. Then he pulled away and walked out of the bathroom without a word.

Alyssa sat in stunned silence until she heard Christian return. He handed her the bundle of clothes she had been holding.

"Please get dressed."

Alyssa felt like she was in a daze as she met Christian's arrogant smile. His way too masculine smile woke her up. It was the kind of satisfied smile that said he knew he had pleasured her well. Alyssa sat up straighter and lifted her chin proudly. Well, at least he had said please this time.

"I'll be right out."

"I'll be waiting with baited breath, *palomita*." Christian's knowing smile made her want to throw something at him. But the door shut before she could find anything suitable.

Once Alyssa finished cleaning up and getting dressed, she quietly opened the bathroom door. She stopped short at the sight that greeted her. Now dressed, Christian stood looking out the large window that took up almost one wall of his bedroom. Her eyes ran over him. This man took her breath away. She had never understood what that term meant until now. Just looking at him made her feel like someone had punched her in the stomach, knocking the breath from her body.

His long hair was neatly tied back. She hadn't had a chance to free it during their lovemaking. Her fingers itched to do so now. She remembered the silky texture of it under her touch.

His broad shoulders strained against the tight black T-shirt he wore. Even in stillness, she could see his muscles bunched beneath the material. Her gaze ran down past his slim hips to his behind. Christian had one of the finest butts she had ever seen. The faded jeans he wore clung to every hard curve of it in just the right way. She would love to walk up behind him and run her hands all over his magnificent body. Considering the fact that he had brought her to her peak three times made no difference. She couldn't get enough of him.

Alyssa remained silent as he continued to stare out into the night. He had to be very deep in thought not to notice her standing there. The man had senses like she had never seen. What was he thinking about?

There was something about the way he stood looking out the window that pulled at her heart. He was a man who proudly faced the world no matter what it gave him. And he faced it all alone. If what he had told her was true, he'd been living this kind of life for over two hundred years. How could he bear it? Wasn't he lonely?

An ache pounded at her chest. She wanted to reach out to him. Need filled her. Need to help him. Need to touch him. Need to make all the hurt, all the loneliness he ever felt go away. She wanted to fill his nights with happiness and contentment instead.

She slowly walked towards him. She had to touch him. Reassure him that she was here. Make his loneliness go away, for just a little while. As she drew closer she saw him stiffen. He had finally become aware of her. She stretched her hand out towards him. But before she could touch him, he swung around and took a step back. Their gazes met. Christian's eyes looked haunted. He shook his head slowly back and forth.

"No, Alyssa. It's time for you to go home. Time for you to get back to your real life. And time for me to get back to mine."

Alyssa slowly dropped her arm back to her side. She had to fight the urge to go to him. Something about the way he spoke reinforced her need to help him. He was standing proudly in front of her, yet she sensed his need, his hurt and his loneliness.

"Christian, I—"

He pressed his fingers to her lips. His eyes filled with pain and something else. Was it longing? Before she could figure it out, he shuttered his expression. His stare turned hard and cold.

"It's over. I can't do this. Let's go."

He dropped his hand, turned away from her and walked from the room.

* * * * *

Christian drove her home. Neither of them spoke. Alyssa sat stiffly in her seat and stared straight ahead. The frown on her face told him she was deep in thought and that she was perplexed by his actions. He wasn't sure he understood them himself.

After they had made love the first time that night, Christian had made a decision. But Alyssa had sidetracked him from that and they made love again. The second time had been wild and intense. It had confirmed his weakness. And strengthened his resolve. This woman was a danger to him. She made him long for things he shouldn't. She made him want to forget about his guilt, forget about his anger and forget about his promise to make up for the horror and death he had reaped on so many. Apples and sunshine. She made him want to live again. And he could never do that. He had chosen his path and he had to stay with it. For Elena, for all the humans he had viciously killed and for himself.

When they reached her condo she unlocked the door, then turned slowly towards him.

"Do you need to come in?"

Alyssa's voice was cold and distant. She would not reach for him again. He'd made it clear back at his house that he didn't want that. Didn't want her. Alyssa had her pride, as she should. She held that around her now as she faced him.

"Yes." He said nothing else. Didn't need to. They understood each other completely.

She walked in first and he followed close behind.

She sat down on her couch and waited the several minutes it took him to check all of the rooms and windows in her condo.

When he was finished, he came and sat down on the chair facing Alyssa.

"I've called a, uh, friend to watch over you the rest of the evening. I have to find out what Bazhena's up to, but I can't do that if I stay here with you. You can trust the guy who's coming over. He may seem kind of rough, but he won't hurt you. And he's very good at his job."

Alyssa frowned at his words. She wasn't happy with his decision. But she clamped her mouth tightly together and nodded her head.

She stood up abruptly, walked towards the door and opened it halfway.

"Well, that's everything then. I guess you better go," she said, facing him coldly with her chin held high.

Christian stood up at her words.

"I can't leave until my friend gets here. I'm not leaving you alone, Alyssa."

She wanted to scream!

She was so angry she could barely keep it in.

Christian infuriated her. First they have one of the most passionate, moving lovemaking experiences she'd ever had and then he just dropped her like a hot potato. As if she meant absolutely nothing to him. He didn't seem like the love 'em and leave 'em type of guy, but maybe she had been wrong about him.

He hadn't ever actually said he cared about her. His actions had made her believe he did, but who knows? The guy was a vampire. Maybe his wiring was different. Maybe immortals didn't feel the same way mortals did. Whatever it was, it left her feeling very confused.

And extremely furious.

Alyssa should just take him at his word. He had said it was over. So it was over. Isn't that what she wanted in the first place? She didn't need a man in her life right now. Things were going pretty well for her. Her stalker had been caught. Her last speaking engagement was tomorrow night. After that she could get back to her life, her practice and maybe even write another book. Other than the fact that a crazy vampiress had tried to kill her, her life was great.

So what if he made her feel cherished. So what if just the sight of him made her heart skip a beat. So what if she felt a connection with him that she had never felt with another person. He didn't want her. It was over.

Well she wasn't about to beg. No way. She would never do that. She wouldn't stoop to the level her mother had. Never. She didn't need him that much.

The jerk.

Alyssa felt tears sting her eyes. She bit her lip to hold them back. Anger ate at her. She wanted to yell at him. Ask him what the hell he was doing, but she wouldn't do that. Her pride wouldn't let her.

Be patient, be patient, be patient. He's leaving soon.

The chant helped a little. Alyssa took a couple of deep, calming breaths. She began to calm down.

She started to shut the door again, when Christian growled low in his throat. She swung her gaze to him. Their eyes met and locked. She couldn't look away. His stare had become cold and distant. He cocked his head sideways, as if studying an insect. The chill that went through her had nothing to do with the weather. At that moment, Christian looked inhuman. He looked…like a vampire. The hackles rose in her as he swiftly strode towards her. He suddenly seemed to double in size.

It wasn't necessarily that he grew taller. He grew…fuller, more threatening. His presence took up all the space in the room. It was menacing, there was no other word for it. His lips parted into a snarl and his sharp, elongated teeth were exposed. She felt herself cringing even as she struggled to maintain her composure. Reality hit her like a semi running into a tree. This was no ordinary man, this was a creature who, from everything she had read, could crush her like a bug.

But habits die hard and Alyssa forced herself to stand in the face of his oncoming rush. He drew nearer and nearer, until she could see the red of his eyes glowing bright. He reached her quickly. Then placed his hands around her waist and lifted her up as if she weighed nothing.

Christian studied the door to make sure his eyes weren't deceiving him. Alyssa partially blocked his view, but there was little doubt in his mind about what he saw. Bazhena had been here. While he searched through Alyssa's condo, lost in his own thoughts, she had been here. She wasn't as weak as he had thought. He cursed under his breath. She was taunting him. Flaunting his carelessness in his face. She had left her trademark symbol on the door. Christian remembered Bazhena telling him about it when he had first been turned.

"I leave this symbol at every kill scene as a reminder to all men that death is close at hand. To let them know that it's just as easy for a woman to kill a man as it is for a man to betray a woman. Look well at it, Cristobal, so that you will remember what I do to the men who betray me."

Back then, the sight of her handiwork had left him nauseous. At first he could only stare at it, wondering at the fate of the victim. He soon learned that Bazhena reveled in killing men. And it was rarely quick. She didn't like quick deaths. She wanted it to be long and drawn out. She wanted her torture to make a man scream for his own death, scream with the last breath he had. "Cristobal, you're special. You remind me of my one true love. The one who said he loved me, but left me for another," she said, petting his head softly.

Christian shook with revulsion. He needed to escape. At that time, Bazhena's will was strong and his power undeveloped. She controlled him through pleasure and mind control. She only allowed him to feed when he was completely weak from hunger. And she made him feed off of her.

"I am everything to you now. I decide whether you live or die. Never forget this," she softly crooned.

He knew one day he would fight to leave her, but only when he was strong enough. Until then he could do nothing. So he bided his time, planning his revenge.

Christian brought himself back to the present. He closed the remaining distance between he and Alyssa, reaching her before she could turn around. He lifted her up and thrust her behind him. His clear view of the door did little to comfort him.

This was no coincidence. Bazhena meant to kill Alyssa. Her message was clear. And Christian knew that he would never let that happen. Not again. This time he had the power and the discipline. This time, he would finish things with her once and for all.

"Did I miss the party?"

Alyssa moved from behind Christian and gasped at what she saw. She fought the urge to step back. The stranger standing in her doorway was one of the largest men she had ever seen. He was well over six-feet and he had a weightlifter's build. Muscles mounded over muscles. Her gaze scanned his body and returned to his face. He lifted one eyebrow in question. Alyssa felt her face flush with embarrassment. She had practically devoured the guy with her eyes! His gaze heated up as he did a slow perusal of her. When his eyes returned to her face, intense interest filled his stare.

Christian's growl diverted her attention.

He placed his arm possessively around her waist.

The men's gazes locked and clashed. The testosterone in the air practically choked her. Something unspoken passed between them, but she wasn't sure what it was. The stranger finally broke his stare and glanced back at Alyssa. His gaze had faded to one of impersonal regard. He nodded his head towards her.

"I'm Jason."

"Jason is going to stay with you until morning." Christian explained, sliding his arm from her waist.

"What's this?" Jason asked, pointing his thumb at the door.

"Bazhena," Christian responded grimly.

Alyssa hadn't noticed the outside of her door until that moment. When she had opened it earlier, her gaze had stayed firmly on Christian, urging him to leave. She followed Jason's gaze and nearly gagged from the sight of her door. Now she knew why Christian's eyes had turned red and his teeth had elongated. Blood. The smell of it registered immediately. She was suddenly becoming an expert on its scent. Her mind tried to deny what she saw, but it was useless. Pieces of what must be someone's intestines hung from the doorway. Skin and hair lay on the floor in the hallway. Alyssa thought she saw an eyeball through the long dark hair, but she couldn't bring herself to look closer.

Nausea rolled over her. She covered her mouth and ran to the bathroom. Slamming the door behind her, she barely made it to the toilet. The entire contents of her stomach emptied in seconds. She continued to gag for a few moments longer, as the image of what she had seen branded her mind. But there was nothing left to come up. She flushed the toilet, washed her hands and face, then brushed her teeth.

Closing the lid of the toilet, Alyssa sat down on it. Resting her head in her hands, she struggled to get herself under control. She took several deep breaths. Tried to think about anything except the door. But it kept popping up in her mind, like some horrible, grinning jack-in-the-box toy.

* * * * *

Christian glared at Jason.

"Don't get any ideas. She's mine. Watch over her. Protect her. That's it."

"I'm not the one who expressed interest first. Your woman practically ate me with her eyes."

Christian bared his elongated incisors.

Jason shrugged his shoulders.

"Whatever. She's not my type anyway."

Christian snorted.

"You're a gargoyle. What *is* your type?"

"That's for me to know and you never to find out, vampire. You just go do your job and I'll do mine. Your woman is safe from me, unless she wishes otherwise. I've never been one to turn down a lady."

The gargoyle's cocky grin made Christian want to smash his fist into the creature's face. He held himself back.

"Keep dreaming, gargoyle. The lady's wishes are mine and mine alone," Christian replied with a tight smile.

He didn't have time for an ego contest. He had to find out what Bazhena was up to.

He strode towards the door. "I'll clean this mess up before I head over to Twice Charmed. Vlad's meeting me there. I'll have my pager and phone on if you need to contact me."

"Later."

Christian hesitated before walking out the door. Swiveling his head around, he stared at the closed bathroom door. He should say goodbye to Alyssa. He should make sure she was okay. But he already knew she was. He could sense that her thoughts were slowly returning to normal. He wanted to check on her anyway, reassure her that she would be safe, that he wouldn't let anything happen to her. But he didn't.

He couldn't bare the sight of horror and repulsion that was most assuredly written all over her face. Alyssa finally understood. This was no romantic fairy tale. He was a monster. He hid it well behind a civil exterior. Nevertheless, he still had the beast inside him, fighting to claw its way out of him and rage at the world.

He pinned Jason with his gaze.

"Stay with her until first light. Her aunt will be here come morning. Protect Alyssa with your life, gargoyle. Because if anything happens to her, you're dead."

"I'm shaking in my boots," Jason replied, sarcasm lacing his voice.

Christian narrowed his eyes and growled low in his throat.

"I don't need you to tell me how to do my job, vampire. I've managed just fine without your advice for hundreds of years."

Christian nodded. "Good, we understand each other."

He closed the door without another word. After cleaning up and removing all evidence of Bazhena's handiwork, he drove to Twice Charmed. It was time to clean up a bigger mess. Bazhena.

Chapter Fifteen

ꝏ

Alyssa was in way over her head. If she didn't know it before, she understood it now. This wasn't a fairy tale told to frightened children. This was real. There were elves and vampires in the world. They existed. And they weren't happy campers. Bazhena was one of the unhappy ones. She was an extremely pissed off vampire. And she was after Alyssa. That thought made her want to vomit all over again.

The sound of her apartment door slamming shut caught her attention. She should go out there. Face whatever she needed to face. She wasn't a coward. She never had been. But if what she had to deal with tonight was an inkling of what she would encounter in the future, she didn't know if she could handle it. Alyssa jerked her head up at the sound of someone by the door.

"Alyssa. You can come out. Christian's cleaned everything up."

Jason's deep, gruff voice sounded calm and reassuring, but she wasn't sure about this man who had been assigned to watch over her. She was almost positive he wasn't mortal. Something about him didn't seem right or normal. An aura or energy recognized now that she'd spent time in the company of immortals. She wouldn't want to be around Jason when he was angry. That much she understood.

"I'll be out in a few more minutes. I need a little more time," she called out.

"I understand."

After that, she heard nothing. A few minutes passed and Alyssa finally decided she could get up and leave the bathroom. The nausea had passed and she had managed to calm down somewhat.

Opening the door, she walked out and saw Jason sitting on her couch reading a magazine. Jonathan was curled up beside him, purring away as if they were lifelong friends. He put what he was reading down and slowly turned towards her. His expression was grim.

She glanced around, but didn't see Christian.

"Where's Christian?"

"He had to go."

Go? That's it. The guy just leaves without a goodbye? After everything that had happened? Anger bubbled up inside of her. Her body shook from the fury that engulfed her.

"Left? He just left?"

"That's right." The man went back to reading the magazine as if it their conversation bored him.

Jason certainly didn't use an excess of words. In fact, she got the distinct impression that he didn't even like talking to her. She guessed, in his book, hitting on her was fine, but talking was kept at a minimum. Alyssa felt like throwing something.

"That's great. Just great."

Jason didn't respond.

Without another word, she strode into her bedroom.

Jason looked up and grinned as the human woman slammed the door behind her. The vampire didn't realize how deep he was into this. He had sensed the bond between Christian and Alyssa almost immediately. He might struggle on the hook for a while, but the vamp was well and truly caught. She had him exactly where she wanted him. Poor guy.

* * * * *

Christian drove down Van Buren Street. As he got closer to Twenty-Fourth Street the area changed. Became seedier. Rundown shops lined the road. With the mental hospital nearby it wasn't the most desirable place to hang out. For humans. For immortals like himself, it was perfect. Down here, people tended to ignore the strange and unusual. They minded their own business. Just tried to survive.

Twice Charmed came into view and Christian grinned at all the cars lining the street and filling up the parking lot. Didn't mystical creatures have anything else to do? It wasn't even the weekend and the place was packed. Christian eventually found a parking place, about as far away as possible.

As he walked up to the club, he saw Vlad pull into a parking space near the entrance. Christian ground his teeth in irritation. How had he found a space so easily and so close?

Christian walked up to him as he got out of his car. Vlad locked the door and turned towards him with a grin.

"Patience, my friend, patience. This time of night, people are coming and leaving all the time. You just have to wait it out."

Christian grunted his reply as they walked into the club. The bouncer, a gargoyle they both knew, let them in without question. With a quick nod, he waved them past.

"I don't have a lot of patience lately, Vlad."

"I noticed."

Vlad chuckled as amusement filled his eyes.

"Women. What can I say? It doesn't matter if they're mortal or immortal. They just seem to have this way about them that drives men crazy. Sometimes in a good way," Vlad said grinning wolfishly. "Other times in a damn frustrating way."

Christian scanned the room as they found a table and sat down. Most people were on the dance floor, moving to the sound of the latest gothic rock band. If the air didn't crackle with immortal energy, this place would seem like almost any other hot nightclub. But the aura was unmistakable. The majority of the patrons here tonight were immortals or other mystical creatures.

"You asked me about The Light. After doing some research, I found the answer."

Christian swung his interested gaze back to Vlad.

"And?"

"And it seems our friend Bazhena has an ego bigger than we originally thought. Not only is she determined to attract and kill men. She has decided that she wants to attract all men. Every single one of them."

"What do you mean?"

"She's found an ancient spell that's designed to make her the most desirable creature in the world. If she succeeds, no one, human or immortal, will be able to resist her."

"Is that possible?"

"According to the legend, yes. But first she must collect certain items to make the spell complete. One of the most important items on that list is The Light.

Christian frowned in consternation.

"That brings me back to my original question. What is The Light'?"

Vlad paused before answering.

"What?" Impatience laced Christian's voice.

"The Light is a soul who is devoted to helping others, a person who can empathize with others, to the point of almost knowing their thoughts. A person who has experienced pain and death and is determined to save others from that pain, even at the risk of his or her own life. A person convinced that it's his or her job to save the human race. In other words, a hero, or heroine."

"Alyssa!" Christian hissed.

Vlad nodded his head slowly.

"Bazhena must have found out about Alyssa from her national tour and best selling book. When we ran into her that first night at our office, she wasn't there to see us, as she claimed. She must have been following Alyssa. It's her she's wanted all along. She fits the description completely."

"Is there only one Light? Surely other people fit that description."

"More than one Light exists. But, as you can imagine, they are in the minority. Bazhena must have just decided to go for Alyssa because she had caught her attention. And once she saw Alyssa had a connection to you, it probably made the pot sweeter for her. Acquire The Light and have her revenge on you for leaving her," Vlad explained.

Christian's eyes narrowed dangerously.

"Bazhena will never have Alyssa. I won't allow it. She'll have to kill me first," Christian vowed.

"Do you have a plan?" Vlad asked.

"Like I told you earlier, I had her where I wanted tonight. I almost killed her. A moment's hesitation cost me that opportunity. But she escaped in a truly weakened state. Dammit! If I hadn't stayed to care for Alyssa I know I could have killed her."

Vlad looked at Christian shrewdly.

"If you could go back now, knowing what you know, would you truly have left Alyssa alone and gone after Bazhena?"

Christian struggled within himself for a moment, then released a frustrated breath.

"No. That's become my bane. Alyssa means too much to me. She is my weakness."

"If you look deep inside yourself, my friend, you'll realize that she is so much more to you than that. She's also your strength."

Christian didn't want to face that issue right now. He would handle this as he'd handled everything in the past. Analyzing the issue step-by-step, never getting ahead of himself. At the moment, Bazhena was the problem he needed to deal with.

"Bazhena is still in a weakened state. Dawn is close approaching. I can't see her doing anything else until the next nightfall. Even then, she may not be at her full power. But I still wouldn't underestimate her. She left a personalized message for me today at Alyssa's condo."

Vlad's eyes narrowed dangerously and fury changed their color to red. Christian knew just how much he hated Bazhena.

"What kind of message?" Vlad demanded.

Christian explained about the head on Alyssa's door and the significance of Bazhena leaving it there.

"She is insane. Even for a vamp. Do you have a plan?"

"Yes, but for it to work, I'll need you to watch over Alyssa tomorrow night at her last speech. Even though I'll be close tc both of you at all times, I don't trust her with anyone else."

Vlad agreed.

"I'll be there. What are you going to do?"

Christian laid out his plan to Vlad.

"It sounds good. But I'm bringing backup with me, just ir case. I want to end Bazhena's existence as much as you do Nothing is going to get in the way of that this time," Vlac promised.

"I have no problem with that. Just keep them downwind oi Bazhena. I don't want her thinking anything is wrong."

"Right. I know just which guys to use."

Before Christian could ask Vlad who, Amy walked up tc them.

She was the human he had gleaned information abou Bazhena from the last time they met. Maybe she could help hin again. He remembered her boyfriend was acting as emissary tc Bazhena while she was in the city. He also remembered tha Amy wanted "the change", she wanted to become a vampire But her boyfriend kept refusing.

"Hi, handsome." Amy smiled seductively as she sidlec closer to Christian. "Haven't we met before? I don't think I'c forget a face like yours, or yours for that matter," she said glancing heatedly towards Vlad.

"You boys look, uh, hungry and bored. Maybe I could interest you both in a little snack and play?" She brushed her hair over her shoulder, exposing her creamy white neck to both of them. She had bite marks on her neck. They were faded, almost completely healed, but still discernable to another vampire.

Christian's beast stirred. The woman's blood called to him.

Christian wrapped his arms around Amy's waist and slid her back between his long legs. When her bottom bumped into him, she released a moan of pleasure.

Grinning wolfishly at Vlad, Christian raised one eyebrow in question.

"I'm up for a little snack and play. How about you, bud?"

Vlad looked deeply into Amy's eyes. Christian released her with a knowing chuckle as she moved away from him. She slid between Vlad's muscular thighs. She gasped at the contact. He ran his fingers slowly down her bare arm to her fingertips. Lightly grasping her hand he lifted it to his mouth. Turning it over, so that the fleshy part of her palm was exposed, he pressed his mouth to it. His eyes remained locked on hers. When he began running his tongue over the tender spot, Amy let out another moan of pleasure.

Vlad gave her palm one last kiss before lifting his head and smiling seductively.

"Your beauty and delectable offer truly tempt me. Unfortunately, I'm obliged to be elsewhere. I'm sure Christian will have no problem satisfying you."

Vlad grasped Amy's waist and pressed her away from him. In a matter of seconds, she was all over Christian. Vlad smiled ruefully. His friend never had trouble with the ladies, with or without the use of power. He got up off of the barstool and prepared to leave.

Ignoring her frustrated sigh, Christian set Amy away from him. Then he sent her a mental command to stay.

Vlad and Christian walked slightly away from Amy. Just out of listening distance.

"She is the one you mentioned talking to previously?" Vlad asked immediately.

"Yes. I erased her memory of our previous encounter. I'll see what else I can find out from her."

"Be careful."

"Always."

Vlad gave him a doubtful look.

"See you tomorrow night. Good luck."

Vlad glanced back at Amy one last time with desire and regret evident in his stare.

"It's a tough job, but someone's got to do it," Christian replied with a cocky grin.

"Tell that to Alyssa."

Christian's smile slipped and he frowned angrily.

"What the hell is that supposed to mean?"

"I'm sorry, my friend. My comment was uncalled for. I know you're an honorable man. My current project with Little Miss Princess has left me very frustrated and, uh, unsatisfied. I'm jealous of the time you get to spend with a beautiful woman. What more can I say?"

Christian's expression relaxed.

"That bad?"

Vlad nodded his head, a pained expression on his face.

"Yes."

Christian could see that Vlad was deeply troubled by his situation.

"Can I help you with anything?"

"No. This is something she and I need to come to terms with very soon." Vlad changed the subject quickly. "If I don't hear from you, I'll assume that whatever you learned tonight isn't important to our plan. I'll see you tomorrow night."

"Right. See you then."

* * * * *

Alyssa punched her pillow. She had to do something. She was angry and frustrated. He left without saying goodbye! After everything they had shared that night, the coward couldn't even face her to say goodbye! Well, that was just fine. The next time she saw Christian, she was *so* going to let him have it.

She gave the pillow one last punch and set it down. As she lay back on her bed, staring at the ceiling, her mind wandered over the last few days. She had been stalked, threatened and attacked. She had met preternatural creatures of different kinds and a vampire had bitten her on more than one occasion. Not her everyday life, that's for sure.

She could handle the first part, the threatening, stalking and even attacking. It wasn't pleasant or something she wanted repeated, but she had always been a fighter. Taking what life gave her and dealing with it the best she could. However, the preternatural creatures and vampire bites were more questionable. It wasn't just the danger from Bazhena that worried her either. Although that was scary enough, it was her feelings towards Christian that left Alyssa floundering.

She was in love with him. She knew that now. Finally admitted it to herself. It happened so quickly that she couldn't trace the exact moment when it became a reality. Despite this, it was true. Now what was she going to do about it? She had just made the most incredible love with Christian and he left her without a word. She felt empty without him. Why couldn't he have at least said goodbye?

Alyssa panicked. It was happening. She was becoming like her mother, needy and dependent. Revolving her thoughts and feelings completely around one man. Fear engulfed her. What was she going to do?

When Jonathan jumped on her bed and snuggled next to her, she absently petted him. His loud purring comforted her. She concentrated on the silky feel of his fur. Her thoughts grew less frantic.

"What am I going to do, Jonathan?"

The cat raised his head at the sound of her voice and stared into her eyes. He looked at her with complete understanding. His yellow eyes seemed to urge her to speak.

"I can't, won't be like my mother. I don't want to live that way." The desperation in her voice was obvious even to her. "But I do love him."

As if sensing her distress, Jonathan stood up and meowed sharply. Placing his front paws on her chest, he settled down half on top of her, half off. He nuzzled her hand as she started to pet him again. He began purring and Alyssa could feel the soothing vibration of the sound against her chest. Her mind raced for a few minutes, but the calming sound of Jonathan's purring soon lulled her to sleep. Her dreams were filled, fittingly enough, with a sexy vampire whose mocha-colored eyes made her melt into a puddle of desire.

Loud voices woke her up some time later. Alyssa bolted up in her bed as she heard her aunt yelling. Jonathan had to jump off her chest as she did so and he gave a loud meow of complaint. She gave him a quick pet in apology as she listened to the voices that came through the door loud and clear.

"Who are you and what have you done with my niece?"

"Your niece is safe," She heard Jason growl back menacingly.

Alyssa scooted off the bed and strode towards her door. Opening it quickly she walked out and stopped in her tracks.

Aunt Joyce stood on tiptoes, hands on her hips, glaring up at Jason. Her face was screwed tight with anger. She seemed unconcerned with the gigantic size of the man in front of her, or the fact that his body language was far from friendly. His fists were clenched tightly at his sides and his body rigid as he loomed over her aunt.

Alyssa needed to diffuse this situation immediately.

"I'm okay, Aunt Joyce. Jason is a friend of Christian's. He's just keeping an eye on me, while Christian's, um, away."

"Hmph." Joyce gave Jason one last glare, before she walked over to Alyssa. Her expression transformed from anger to worry in an instant.

"How are you, dear? How's your head? You look a little frazzled." Joyce placed her hand softly against Alyssa's cheek.

Alyssa smiled.

"I'm fine. Last night was just a little, uh, hectic. I'll make some coffee for us and tell you all about it."

"I'm glad you're okay, dear."

Her aunt slid her hand from Alyssa's cheek as her expression changed again, this time to irritation.

"I wish someone had told me what was going on. I got a call from Christian, requesting that I meet you here early this morning, but nothing about this man," her aunt said glancing back at Jason. "Someone should have told me."

The reproof in her voice was unmistakable.

"You'll have to take that up with Christian. I had nothing to do with it," Alyssa said with great relish. Christian could just face the music for leaving without saying goodbye to her, or explaining anything to her aunt.

Alyssa noticed Jason staring strangely at the two of them. It was as if they were some alien species he didn't quite understand. When she walked towards him, his expression cleared. Arrogant boredom replaced his perplexed expression.

Alyssa held her hand out to him.

"Thank you for watching over me, Jason."

Jason did not hold out his hand. He just stared blankly at her. Alyssa dropped her hand slowly, wondering what to do next.

"Would you like to have some coffee with us?" Alyssa finally asked.

Jason's eyes widened at her words. He looked surprised by her offer. Then he seemed to get a hold of himself and cleared his throat loudly.

"Uh, no. I have to go now. Before it becomes full light."

Without another word, he strode to the door, opened it and left.

Alyssa locked the door, then turned back to her aunt. They looked at each other in confusion. Then her aunt shrugged her shoulders and started making coffee.

"That was a strange man, Alyssa. There was something different about him."

Alyssa nodded in agreement.

"Yes, very different."

Alyssa said nothing more to her aunt about it. She knew she had just met another creature of the night, but she wasn't sure what he was. He wasn't a vampire. She was starting to learn what it felt like to have a vampire in her presence. And Jason didn't give her the same sense. But he definitely didn't have the same "feeling" as a human either.

As soon as the coffee was ready, her aunt poured each of them a cup. She and Aunt Joyce sat down at her small kitchen table.

"Okay. Tell me everything. What happened to you last night? And why did Christian leave a message asking me to come here so early this morning?" Her aunt asked.

Alyssa had to be careful. She couldn't tell her aunt too much. She didn't want to risk Christian's life. She didn't think her aunt would ever purposely try to hurt Christian. But if she learned the truth about him and Sundown Security Agency, there could be trouble. This was a situation most people didn't encounter everyday of their lives and she wasn't sure what her aunt would do if she found out that Christian was a vampire working for a security agency made up of preternatural creatures.

"I was attacked last night." Alyssa wanted to leave Tom out of this as much as possible because Christian had erased his memory of last night's events.

"What!" her aunt gasped.

"Luckily, you sent Christian to my office. By the way, we need to talk about that afterwards."

"Talk about what?" Joyce tried to look innocent and failed.

"You inciting events to further your causes."

Her aunt looked like she was about to protest. Alyssa held up her hand to stop her from talking.

"We will talk about this. I promise you. Later."

Her aunt nodded sheepishly.

"So I was leaving my office and someone attacked me, um, on the way out."

"Where was Tom?"

"He had to stay late to finish up a few things."

"Why didn't he walk you out?" her aunt gazed suspiciously at her.

"I didn't feel the need. He was very busy and my car wasn't too far away. So, even though he offered, I declined." Alyssa felt miserable as the lies rolled off her tongue. She hated lying. To anyone, but especially to someone she cared about.

"That wasn't very smart of you dear. Especially in light of everything that's happened to you recently," her aunt admonished.

"I know," Alyssa agreed. What could she say? Her aunt was right.

"So I was walking to my car and I heard someone behind me. I didn't stop to look back and see who it was. I just began running. The next thing I knew, I ran straight into Christian."

"Then what happened?"

"Christian went after the guy. Unfortunately, before he could get to him, the man disappeared."

"He just disappeared?"

"Yes. You know how Old Scottsdale is packed with buildings and cars. There are a lot of places to hide."

Aunt Joyce nodded her head.

"After that, Christian took me to his house. We talked and, um, rested a bit, then he brought me home." Her aunt gave her a dubious expression at that part of her explanation, but Alyssa chose to ignore it and continue.

"Then he told me he wanted to go back to where I had parked my car and check out the area. He wanted to look for evidence, I guess. But he refused to leave me alone. Since it was the middle of the night, he didn't want to wake you up, so he called his friend Jason. He agreed to watch over me until you came over this morning."

As the last word of her lies left her lips, Alyssa had to swallow the large lump of guilt that filled her throat. At least her aunt looked satisfied with her explanation.

"You have had quite a night," her aunt said sipping her coffee.

Alyssa relaxed a little and took a sip of her own coffee.

"But I'd like to know a little bit more about the resting part at Christian's home," her aunt asked with a mischievous smile.

Alyssa choked on her coffee.

Chapter Sixteen

ꙮ

Amy didn't stand a chance. She told Christian everything she knew. If there was one thing he had learned over the years, it was the art of seduction, with and without using his powers. Amy was starved for attention. Her boyfriend must be so busy helping Bazhena that he had little time for her.

He slowly backed Amy into a dark secluded corner, whispering promises into her ear as he ran his hands up and down her quivering body. Guilt and the image of Alyssa filled his head, but he struggled to ignore it. He had to rid the world of Bazhena before she could complete the legend. By the time he had Amy where he wanted her, he knew she was ready for him. He could have taken her there and then in the club and she would have welcomed it.

She began massaging him through his pants. She nipped his earlobe with her teeth, then whispered to him.

"Please, Christian. I'm ready. I've told you everything I know. Take me now and I'll make it one of the most enjoyable rides you've ever had. And I want you to take me completely. You know what I mean. Let everything go. Sink your hardness and your teeth into me. Take your pleasure and my blood. I want it all. I can take it, baby. I know what you need. Do it and you won't be sorry."

Amy rubbed herself against his hardness. She kissed his neck and took small bites of his skin. The smell of Amy's blood filled his senses. The sound of it rushing through her veins called to his vampire. His incisors elongated. Christian pulled away from Amy. The beast roared its outrage, but he had no trouble controlling it. He didn't want this woman.

She moved close to him again. Tried to press her body against his. He set her away from him and held her there. Amy whimpered and struggled in his hold.

"Sorry, Amy. You're a very beautiful woman and I appreciate all the information, but I don't think it's going to work between us. There's someone else in my life."

As Christian said those words aloud, he finally realized how true they were. Alyssa was now the most important thing in his life. He loved her. And didn't want to live without her. They would have to find a way to make things work. He was not giving her up.

For a moment, Amy looked furious. Her eyes filled with rage. Then they cleared and became calm. She smiled serenely.

"I understand," she said easily. "Will you at least walk me to my car? I'm suddenly feeling very tired."

Christian nodded.

"Of course."

He'd walk her to her car and then clear her mind again. Once he erased her memory, he would plant the idea into her head that she was sick of vampires and that she needed to find a nice normal guy. She would no longer have the urge to come to this club. Instead she would meet a mortal man and start a family. She was a beautiful woman and he was sure she would have no trouble finding a husband.

As they walked towards the exit, Christian spotted Eric. The dragon slayer was leaning negligently against a wall, watching the crowd around him with his usual cynical smirk. Women seemed to hover around the guy, but he ignored their attention as he scanned the crowd. He must have a quarry tonight.

They nodded at each other as their eyes met. Then Eric glanced at Amy and waggled his eyes suggestively at Christian. They gave each other a knowing look that only two males in their prime could share. Eric's said, "You lucky dog" and

Christian's said, "Eat your heart out, pal". Eric turned back to the crowd as Christian and Amy left the club.

Amy stopped at a little red sports car. She leaned back and rested her elbows against the hood. Christian could see anticipation and desire enflame her eyes as she stared up at him. She licked her lips with her small pink tongue.

"How about one last good night kiss?" Amy purred.

"Gladly." Christian smiled.

Resting a palm on the hood on either side of her, Christian leaned over. He pressed his hips to hers. Amy gasped from the contact and licked her lips again to moisten them. Amy didn't know it, but there would be no kiss. It was time to make her forget about him and move on with her life.

Preparing to clear her mind, he almost didn't notice her eyes dart quickly to his right. Something had caught her attention. Sensing danger, he turned around. Something slammed into his head. He staggered to his knees. Before he could stand up again, he felt a painful prick to one arm, then the other. He shot to his feet, knocking down whoever had been by his sides.

Christian saw five vampires standing around him in a circle. The two men, who had been by his side, got to their feet and joined the others. They stood at the ready, waiting for him to attack. One of them was Amy's boyfriend.

He sneered at Christian knowingly.

"You have an appointment with my mistress. Bazhena is very anxious to meet with you."

Christian swung his gaze back to where Amy still leaned nonchalantly against the car.

"I told you if you had just given me what I needed you wouldn't be sorry. You should have listened to me," she said with a careless shrug. "Now Bazhena will make me immortal."

Suddenly, Amy's image grew fuzzy and dim. She and the vamps around him began to laugh. The sound grew softer and softer as Christian felt his knees grow weak. Anger and frustration filled him. He tried to fight, tried to move, but he couldn't. His body refused to respond. The prick he had felt earlier? They had injected him with something! Why had he been so stupid? So careless? His last thought was of Alyssa as he slid to the ground. Then everything went dark.

* * * * *

Alyssa coughed for almost a full minute. The coffee had gotten into her air passage and just didn't want to get out. Her aunt stood up and tried to pat her back. Again.

Alyssa held up a hand to stop her.

"No-stop-I'm fine," she choked out. She drew in a deep breath, immensely glad her air passage had finally cleared.

Her aunt sat back down and waited patiently for her to speak.

Alyssa shook her head.

"No, Aunt Joyce. This is between Christian and I. I'm not prepared to share this kind of information with you at the moment."

"Whatever do you mean, dear?"

Her aunt's attempt to look innocent didn't faze Alyssa.

"I think you know exactly what I mean. Now can we talk about something else?"

Her aunt sighed, but nodded her head in agreement.

"Fine. What do you have planned for today?"

Planned? Alyssa was still trying to recover from last night. Things were completely unsettled with Christian. And she had her last speaking engagement tonight. She would see Christian this evening. They would sit down and talk about this, no matter what. She loved him. She admitted it now. But she wasn't sure where their relationship could go from here. He was a vampire. She was mortal. Did she want to spend her life with a gorgeous guy who never aged, while she grew older and older? A guy who drank blood and couldn't go out during the day?

Did she want to be with someone who made her feel cherished, beautiful and powerful? A man who was so sexy she wanted to rip his clothes off every time she was with him? Who made the most incredible love to her she had ever had?

What did she want? Right now, just a bath. That was all she could deal with at the moment.

"First I'd like to take a bath," she told her aunt. "Get cleaned up and just soak for a little while. I really appreciate you coming over so early, but I don't think you need to stay with me. I'm really fine. And Christian will be picking me up after sundown."

"I'm staying with you. Christian felt it was important that you remain in your apartment today and not go out. He also said that I needed to stay with you until he picks you up tonight. So I'm staying."

Alyssa started to protest, but her aunt shook her head.

"I know how stubborn you can be dear. You get that from your father, by the way. And your mother, come to think of it. But I'm sure Christian knows what he's doing. If he feels you're still in danger and need to stay at home, then that's exactly what you're doing. Do you have any patients scheduled for today? If so, you need to cancel them. If you'd like, I can call Stella and tell her."

"That's not necessary. I told her I wasn't taking patients today. And since it's so close to the weekend, I had her postpone any more scheduling until Monday."

"Great. Then it's settled. You go take your bath and I'll wash out the cups and coffeepot."

"I really don't—"

"Go, Alyssa. I'm staying and that's that." Her aunt pointed towards the bathroom, giving her the no nonsense frown she used to give Alyssa when she was a child.

"Fine." Alyssa stomped off to the bathroom. She knew she was acting like a child, but she couldn't seem to help herself.

The minute she sank into the hot bath water scented with lavender, her mood improved dramatically. She closed her eyes and moaned with pleasure. Making love with Christian had given her body some aches she hadn't had for quite a long time. The heated water relaxed her tight muscles.

Leaning her head back against the rim of the tub, Alyssa closed her eyes as images of she and Christian rolled through her mind. She and Christian making love. Him protecting her from her stalker, then holding her in his arms as he flew her home. Then there was him protecting her from Bazhena. The images went on and on like a slide show. Lastly, she remembered how he had looked last night. Standing in front of his large bedroom window, looking out into the darkness, like a solitary man up against the world.

Alyssa had ached when she saw him like that. She had wanted to go to him, comfort him. So that he wouldn't feel alone ever again. Is this what her mother had felt? An uncontrollable need to help her mate no matter what? A driving need to make him happy? Was she finally becoming what she was always destined to be, her mother's child? A woman so obsessed with a man that everything else fell to the wayside, even her own life?

Isn't that what was really bothering her? The vampire thing was just an excuse, a very strange and extraordinary excuse, but still an excuse. She looked deep into her heart and the answer was there. She wouldn't have made love to Christian if she hadn't already accepted him for what he was. It all came back to her fears. Could she give so much of herself to someone else without losing who she was?

Tonight. It would be settled tonight. They would talk. It was their last evening together as bodyguard and client. She would be honest with him about everything and she would expect the same thing from him. That included Bazhena. Alyssa wanted to find out exactly what that insane creature wanted with her. And how they could stop her once and for all. Yes, tonight.

Alyssa's mind raced a while longer, then finally settled down. The lavender-scented bath calmed her. The image of Christian appeared in her mind and she smiled. He leaned his shoulder against the doorframe. He wore no shirt and his half buttoned jeans rode low on his hips. A wicked smile curled the corner of his lips up. His eyes were hot and hungry for her. His hair was loose.

Her fingers curled into fists. She wanted to run her hands through his soft tresses. Feel it whisper across her body as they made love. Her eyes ran hungrily over him. His powerful arms flexed under her stare. His muscular chest tapered down to a narrow waist.

Christian's ribbed stomach looked like a six-pack commercial. His golden skin made her mouth water. She licked her lips in anticipation of tasting him. He looked good enough to eat. Alyssa's gaze moved lower, following the light sprinkling of hair leading into his pants. Her hands itched to unbutton his jeans the rest of the way, to explore where her eyes roamed.

Christian chuckled softly.

Her gaze flew back to his face. He gave her a smile so sexy her body tightened instantly.

"You look like you want to eat me, little girl."

Alyssa gasped. Was he reading her thoughts again? She didn't care. Not anymore. Instead of retreating, she did something she had always wanted to do. She told him exactly what she wanted to do to him.

"I do want to taste you, Christian, every inch of your skin, from top to bottom and back up again. I want to dip my hand into your pants and touch you. I want to run my fingers up and down the length of you until you're panting. Then I want you to taste and touch me until I'm crazy with desire. After that, I want to feel you inside of me, filling me completely. Plunging deep over and over again until we both reach the precipice. Then do you know what I want?"

Christian's eyes had darkened with desire.

"Tell me, Alyssa. Tell me everything." The deep timbre of his voice told her just how affected he was by her words.

"When we're so close to the edge, almost ready to explode, I want you to sink your teeth into me. I want you to take me completely and totally without holding anything back. Only then will I scream with pleasure as we climax. You'll come inside me, your hips helplessly convulsing from the power of it, as my woman's core constricts around you while I shake uncontrollably from the strength of my release. That's what I want Christian."

By the time she was done, Christian was panting. The passion in his eyes singed her. He pushed away from the doorway and stalked towards her.

"Your wish is my command, *palomita*."

Someone knocked on the bathroom door. Christian's sexy image evaporated. Alyssa gasped from the loss.

"Alyssa, how are you doing?" Aunt Joyce called from the other side the door.

"I, uh, I'm fine. I'll be out in a minute."

Alyssa sank deeper into the water with a groan. Her body still hummed in anticipation of Christian's touch. Great, now she needed a cold shower.

* * * * *

Christian had never desired another woman like he did Alyssa. The image of her in the bath, with bubbles barely covering her delectable body was bad enough. But when she described in detail what she wanted to do to him, he almost lost it. Her words left him hard and throbbing. He craved to fulfill every one of her requests. When her image faded he wanted to yell his outrage. His body throbbed painfully for her. That ache eventually faded as his body calmed, only to be replaced by a different kind of pain.

Daggers shot through his body. He woke up and would have doubled over from the intensity of it, if he weren't tied up.

He opened his eyes and found himself in what looked like an old warehouse. His hands and feet were spread apart and bound by chains and metal clamps to two large posts. He felt a slight burning sensation where the binds touched his skin.

Christian was undressed. That was of little concern to him as another wave of pain splintered through him. It felt like little pieces of glass were cutting him from the inside out.

"Unpleasant, isn't it?"

Christian swung his gaze around to find Bazhena standing in the doorway. She slowly slid her eyes over him. Stopping at his manhood. She stared at it intently for a moment and licked her lips before meeting his gaze once more.

He gritted his teeth, ignoring the pain racking his body and glared at her.

"Of course, the pain you caused me last evening was also quite unbearable for a time, Cristobal. I think you were actually considering killing me, weren't you?"

"What do you think?" Christian asked mockingly.

Bazhena's eyes flared with anger, but she ignored his question.

"Those little painful pricks you're feeling are an experiment of mine. Actually, they're the result of many experiments and many deaths. I had to find just the right balance of holy water and human blood to injure a vampire, but not kill him, to render him unconscious, but only temporarily. It was quite frustrating actually. You would not believe how fragile the vampire body can be, even with just the smallest difference in quantities. And I had so many willing participants, all men, of course. As you know, I only turn men, never women. I wouldn't want the competition. Besides, you remember how much I enjoy, uh, *working* on men. Don't you, Cristobal?"

Bazhena smiled, exposing her sharp, elongated teeth. She slowly strode towards him. The sway of her hips, her parted lips and the blaze in her eyes told Christian she was hungry—for sex—and for him. He could almost smell her desire and hunger.

She hadn't fed yet. Memories came rushing back. He had been in this position before with Bazhena, during his fledgling years, when she owned him body and soul. When his very existence was based on her whim. He swore he would never let that happen again. Never let himself be so dependent on another.

Christian tested the bonds holding him, but found them completely unyielding. And he couldn't shape shift. His body was too weak from the painful concoction he had been injected with.

"The bonds won't break. I also had them especially designed just for you. Made from a mixture of blessed crosses and metal. Just enough to hold you but not enough to burn."

"What do you want, Bazhena?" Christian asked through gritted teeth. The pain seemed to be increasing as the time passed. In small increments, yet he could feel the difference with each knew wave.

"Want?" Bazhena's throaty laugh filled the room. "I want so many things, Cristobal. Where do I begin?"

Christian ignored the seductive sound of her voice. She was trying to get to him. He could feel her mind pushing into his.

"Why are you here?" Christian tried again. He needed more information. He needed to know what she had planned.

"I'm here because my one true love betrayed me. He claimed to love me, but left me for another." Bazhena began pacing back and forth in front of him. Her voice grew louder, more distressed as she ranted. "I was crazed with grief and did something no woman, no woman should ever have done. I did it all because of a man. Your weak and puny gender formed me. Made me into what I am today. And so, I seek my vengeance again and again. So many men have died over the years, yet it still isn't enough. I am the *Wendigo*. I am the Weeping Woman. Different names, but both exist for the same purpose. Revenge. Mankind must pay for what he did to me. But why am I telling you? You know all of this. Just as you know you are special. The one man I couldn't kill. You remind me too much of him, you see. But then, you left me too." Bazhena suddenly stopped pacing and turned to face him. The crazed look on her face faded as she ran her eyes possessively over him once more.

"Now, at last, I have you back again. It's ironic actually." Bazhena gave him a wry smile.

"What?" Christian needed to know what was going on in her crazed mind. He needed to know so he could save Alyssa.

"That the one man I couldn't kill is the one who is going to help bring about the rise in my power and the ruin of all men. I knew there was something special about you, Cristobal. From the first time I saw you so long ago, you had a way about you that was so different from all the others I had met. I was definitely attracted to you. Of that I'm sure, but it was so much more than that. It was as if we were destined to meet."

Christian stiffened when Bazhena sidled next to him. She ran her long red fingernail down his cheek, under his chin, then back up the other cheek. She stood on tiptoe so that her mouth was parallel to his ear. She sucked on the lobe for only a second then ran her tongue down his neck. He arched his back when she sank her teeth deep. She moved away as the blood dripped from his ear to his shoulder. Bazhena eyed it hungrily but didn't drink it.

"Your blood would taste so sweet on my tongue, Cristobal. I've missed it. I've missed you. Isn't it time you came back to me, my pet? Isn't it time you belonged to me once again?"

He would never be her slave. Not again. Never again.

As she spoke, she ran her hands down his body. She circled his nipples with her nails, then plunged lower. She splayed her fingers over his taught stomach and sighed.

"You always were so beautiful. I don't know how I survived giving you up."

Her hand slid down, fingers delving through his hair before wrapping around his manhood. He was fighting her touch, fighting the desire she was trying to push at him. A spasm of pain wracked his body again and he almost lost it.

Bazhena chuckled low into his ear.

"Fight me, Cristobal. Fight me. You know how much your struggles turn me on. In the end, you'll beg me for it, just like you always did. And I'll have you just the way I want you, every last drop of you. I'm going to lap you up, lick by delicious lick."

As if to emphasize her words, Bazhena ran her tongue up and down his neck, found his other earlobe and sucked hard. He waited for her to bite that one too, but she didn't. She just continued sucking while she caressed him. Christian fought her, but he could feel himself slipping. Her desire was pushing at him. Her mind control had grown over time. And she was throwing everything she could at him. He groaned aloud as he grew hard from her touch. His body and mind were betraying him.

"You won't win, Cristobal. You know you want me, just like you've always wanted me."

She was whispering inside his head now. She had gotten to him.

He tried to push her out, but the pain hit him again and this time almost brought him to his knees. Bazhena gave his ear one last lick before she slid her mouth down over his chest and suckled his nipples in turn. They pebbled beneath her tongue and she laughed low and husky.

His manhood grew beneath her touch. He closed his eyes and attempted to find another place, as he used to do, so long ago. Alyssa's sweet face suddenly came to mind. Her image filled his head and then nothing else mattered, everything, the pain, the pleasure, it all faded as he thought about Alyssa. He let her fill him completely. Her goodness, her light, it soothed his mind and his body. He was still in pain, but the desire that Bazhena created paled to nothingness. He softened under her touch, until he lay limp in her hand.

Bazhena screeched and her hand tightened painfully around him.

"No! You will not think about your human now. Not now, Cristobal. You are mine!"

But Christian could barely hear her. He was remembering everything about Alyssa. Replaying the moments they had spent together. The pain faded as his mind reached out to her. He called her name in his head over and over again.

"She will pay for this. That bitch will pay!" Bazhena snarled as she pulled back from Christian and stalked angrily out of the room.

He tried to break the bonds again. Fought the pain and darkness threatening to engulf him again. He could not let Bazhena hurt Alyssa. He reached out to her with his mind. Tried to warn her, but the darkness finally won. He slumped forward as his consciousness started to fade. Her injection was poisoning him.

* * * * *

Alyssa dressed carefully for the evening, while her aunt sat in the other room watching TV. True to her word, Aunt Joyce had stayed with her the whole day, entertaining her and keeping her mind on everything but tonight. The only reminder she had was a phone call from Tom. He had told her about the cracked wall and falling asleep at the office.

"I never fall asleep here. It was really strange."

Alyssa was relieved to hear her friend's voice. Relieved to know that he was okay. She pushed the image of his torn throat and pale face from her mind.

"I guess you're working too hard. Maybe it's time you took a vacation?" she suggested lightly. "Or maybe it's those late nights with the ladies. They're finally catching up with you," she joked, chuckling for his benefit.

It sounded forced to her ears, but he didn't seem to notice. Tom spoke a bit more about getting the wall fixed.

"I'm having someone from the management company come take a look at it today. All I can think of is that the building did a major resettling during the night. But usually that's a gradual process, not all at once. You wouldn't believe how big the crack is."

"I'm sure I'll get a nice long look at it on Monday."

"Yes, you will," he agreed with a chuckle.

Tom wished her luck with her last speech.

"I know you'll do a great job. As usual, they'll be eating out of the palm of your hand."

They both laughed and wished each other a good weekend before hanging up.

Alone now, in her room, Alyssa could think of little else but seeing Christian again. She stared out her window into the slowly darkening sky. They would talk tonight. They would find a way to be together or they would separate forever. There could be no in-between for her.

Giving herself one last look in the mirror, she picked up her purse and headed into the other room. But before she could open her bedroom door, an intense pain like she had never felt before left her bent over, clutching her stomach. She took some deep cleansing breaths to gain relief, but it did little good. The pain seemed to spread throughout her body, like pins sticking her from the inside out. Then she felt him in her mind. Christian. He plowed into her thoughts without invitation. And he kept repeating the same thing, over and over again.

Alyssa. Beware. Alyssa. Beware. Alyssa. Beware…

His voice rang over and over in her head. She fell to her knees from the pain engulfing her. Her head felt overloaded from the intrusion of his thoughts. Dizziness assailed her. She was sure that she was about to pass out, when suddenly the pain ceased. Christian's voice in her head stopped. Both were gone in a second, simultaneously. As if they had never been.

Alyssa slowly straightened. What had just happened? Why was Christian's voice in her head? Where had that excruciating pain come from? She opened the door and walked into the other room. Her aunt looked normal. She briefly looked away from the TV to smile at Alyssa and then returned to watching her program.

Alyssa stilled. She listened. Trying to pick up any unusual, or threatening feelings. She remembered what Bazhena's presence in her mind had done to her in the past. She felt none of that now. Just nothing. Normal. Yet unease filled her. She wasn't sure what it was, but there was something wrong. She couldn't name it, but nevertheless the discord was there, deep inside her.

The knock on her door made her jump.

Aunt Joyce got up and calmly headed towards the door.

"Wait."

Her aunt stopped and turned back to Alyssa. Her face was filled with question and concern. Her frown deepened when she saw the look on her niece's face.

"What is it, dear?"

Alyssa didn't know why she stopped her aunt. She just felt like it was necessary to be cautious right now. They needed to know who was at the door before they opened it. The air around her seemed to grow thick with energy. It felt oppressive, almost choking her with its pressure.

"Please don't go any closer to the door. Just ask who it is before you open it."

Aunt Joyce gave her a quizzical look. But did as she asked.

"Okay." Her aunt turned back around, but didn't walk the remaining distance to the door.

"Who is it?" she called out.

"It's Christian."

Joyce closed the distance to the door and reached up to unlock it.

"No!" Alyssa cried out sharply.

Aunt Joyce glanced over her shoulder at Alyssa in question.

"It's Christian, dear."

Alyssa shook her head.

"No. It isn't. Ask again," Alyssa whispered. She knew Christian's voice. She knew what it felt like to be with him. She could feel his energy, feel him. Whoever, or whatever was on the other side of the door wasn't Christian.

She cleared her throat and spoke louder this time.

"Who is it?"

This time no one answered. After a minute, Alyssa thought whoever was there had left. Then she noticed the doorknob turning slowly. First one way then the other.

Alyssa reacted immediately.

"Move away from the door, Aunt Joyce."

"But—"

"Just move away from the door. Walk backwards, towards me."

Her aunt slowly moved back to stand beside her. It seemed difficult for her. As if she were struggling against something. By the time she reached Alyssa's side, her face was red from exertion.

"I think we should open the door, Alyssa. We really should."

Her aunt's voice sounded strange, dreamy almost. And her eyes looked dazed. Someone or something was trying to get to her.

"No. We'll wait."

Alyssa's voice sounded calm, although she felt anything but that. Something unnatural and evil lay on the other side of her door. Its presence suddenly hit her like a punch to the stomach. It had covered up its hatred and malevolence until this moment. She had no doubt that whatever was standing in the outside hallway meant her harm.

"Go into my bedroom. Open the first drawer of my nightstand. There's a large cross in there and a vial of holy water. Get both and bring them out here as quickly as you can."

Her aunt didn't respond. Alyssa reached out and gave her shoulder a little shake. Joyce seemed to snap out of a daze. She shook her head, then glanced at Alyssa. Her eyes looked wide with fear.

"Huh? Holy water? A cross? Shouldn't we call the police?"

Aunt Joyce looked at Alyssa like she was crazy. She started to protest when the turning doorknob started rattling violently. The sound of a low growl reached her ears. Whoever was out there was getting impatient.

"Do it now!"

Her aunt let out a small squeak then ran into the bedroom. Alyssa kept her eyes on the door. A minute later, Aunt Joyce came back with both items. Alyssa took them from her. Reaching into her own blouse she pulled a necklace out. It was a gold chain with a cross on the end of it. She unclasped it and handed it to her aunt without letting her gaze leave the door.

"Take this. Go into my bedroom, lock the door and call the police. All the windows are locked, so you should be safe. Stay in there. No matter what you hear, don't come out. And only open the door for me—no one else. If anyone other than me gets into the room before the police come, hold the cross in front of you and pray. That will be your only protection."

When her aunt just stood there, Alyssa spared a glance her way. Aunt Joyce met her eyes stubbornly. She clenched her jaws tightly together and shook her head.

Alyssa would not allow anything to happen to her beloved aunt.

"You need to listen to me. We don't have much time."

As if to emphasize her words, her apartment door started to shake, making loud rattling, splintering noises. It wouldn't hold much longer.

"No," her aunt said crossing her hands stubbornly over her chest. "I don't know what's going on or who's out there, but I won't leave you alone, Aly. I'll call the police, but I'm staying with you to face whoever you're facing."

Frustration filled Alyssa. She wanted to yell at her aunt. Tell her that she didn't understand. It wasn't *whom* she was facing. It was *what*. Whatever was on the other side of the door wasn't human.

Chapter Seventeen

ജ

The rattling stopped. Alyssa swung her gaze to the door. It was no longer shaking. She glanced at her aunt. Her eyes were wide with fear and she seemed to be having trouble breathing. She grasped her Aunt Joyce's hand and squeezed it reassuringly.

"Hang on. It's going to be okay."

Her aunt nodded, but said nothing.

Alyssa stared at the door. Holding her breath, she waited to see what would happen next.

It wasn't what she expected.

She jumped as a loud screeching filled the air. The noise was soon followed by a moan and then a whimper. A hissing sound and the scent of burnt flesh soon followed. Nausea hit Alyssa strong and hard. She released her aunt's hand and covered her mouth, attempting to stop the smell. It did no good. It seemed to permeate everything. She turned to her aunt, about to tell her to go into the bedroom again, when the elderly woman crumpled to the floor in a dead faint.

Alyssa wasn't sure how long she stood frozen in place, her hand covering her mouth. Her eyes glued to the door. Waiting. Not knowing what would come next. Her heart beat out of control and her breath came in short pants.

"Alyssa. Open the door. It's Vlad Maksimovitch. I've taken care of your unwanted visitor. You're safe now. Christian couldn't make it tonight, so I'll be taking you to your speaking engagement."

Alyssa started. Then her shoulders sagged with relief as she recognized the comforting sound of the After Sundown owner's voice. She walked towards the door intent on opening it, but stopped short before doing so. What if it wasn't really him? She had read that vampires could shape shift. What if this creature had changed into the form of Vlad? Was it possible?

"How do I know it's really you?"

"Look through your peephole. Who do you see?"

Alyssa did as he suggested and saw Vlad standing on the other side of the door. The urge to open the door was strong. But the instinct to survive was stronger.

"How do I know it's really you?"

There was silence on the other side of the door for a moment. Then Vlad cleared his throat and spoke.

"Remember the first time we met?"

"Yes."

"I offered you tea. You chose chamomile. You said it helped you relax."

Alyssa let out the breath she was holding. Only Vlad could tell her that. It had been only the two of them in the room when that happened.

Alyssa undid the bolt and opened the door. She covered her nose in preparation of that terrible flesh burning smell hitting her full force. Yet there was nothing. The horrifying scent had all but disappeared. She looked around her and saw no evidence of, well, of anything strange, just Vlad standing in the doorway, looking very normal.

"How did you do that?" Alyssa's eyes narrowed suspiciously.

"It's part of my job. Clean up and remove evidence."

"What about the other people living here? They had to hear that terrifying scream and smell that burning smell."

"As I'm sure you've come to realize, we have the ability to project thoughts. It's a very powerful tool. I just changed your neighbors' perspectives a bit. They think they heard a cat screeching into the night. And the odor they picked up, just smelled like someone had burned their dinner."

Alyssa nodded silently as she listened to his explanation. No wonder very few people knew about these preternatural creatures' existence. They were too good at covering up their actions.

"Aren't you going to invite me in, Alyssa?"

Alyssa met Vlad's polite smile with startled eyes.

"What?"

"I can't come into your home without permission. That is one hard and fast rule of the vampire. We cannot enter someone's private abode without an invitation. Once humans make a place their own in one fashion or other, it becomes theirs. The power of that is something not even a vampire can undo. That's why your earlier visitor could not open your door. He could shake it and twist the knob, but he couldn't open it without you inviting him in first."

Alyssa digested that bit of information and logged it with the other tidbits she was learning about vampires. It was amazing how so many of the movies she had seen and books she had read portrayed this information correctly. Alyssa looked down at the cross and holy water in her hand.

"Does this work?" She held the items up in front of her. Vlad took a cautious step backwards.

Most definitely. Now please put those items down and invite me in so that we can talk.

The sound of Vlad's voice was inside her head suddenly. It seemed to sweep through her. And before she knew it she had put the cross and holy water down and invited him in.

"Please come in, Vlad."

"Thank you."

Vlad walked in and shut the door behind him. Alyssa took one step backwards, then another. What had just happened? One minute she was just standing there and the next she did something without thought or awareness.

Vlad must have seen the confusion on her face.

"I'm sorry, Ms. Edwards. I had to use compulsion on you. We don't have much time. We need to talk about this evening," Vlad explained. "Christian had to handle a situation that needed his immediate attention. Otherwise he would have been here tonight. I'll take you to your speech. You'll be safe with me."

Alyssa only half heard Vlad's explanation. He had controlled her with his mind! She was about to tell Vlad what he could do with his compulsion, when she heard a soft moan coming from behind her. Her eyes widened in alarm and she swung around.

"Aunt Joyce!"

Alyssa strode quickly to her aunt's side. She was starting to wake up.

Vlad was beside her instantly.

"Your aunt has been through much tonight."

Alyssa bent over and knelt by her aunt. Vlad did the same.

"She stood by my side. She didn't know what was happening, but she refused to leave me."

"She is a very strong, loyal and brave woman. I can see where you get it from."

"She means so much to me. I couldn't bear it if anything happened to her. I need to call an ambulance."

Alyssa started to reach for the phone. Vlad grasped her arm. She stopped at the contact. She looked down at where he touched her, then back up at him. Vlad nodded in understanding and released his hold on her.

"I sense no physical injury to your aunt. She was just so shocked by what happened that she fainted. Unlike you, she has had no experience with creatures of the night. It was too much for her. However, she'll be fine."

Alyssa gently brushed her fingers across her aunt's cheek.

"How do you know that? Don't tell me, another vampire power."

"Yes. Vampires are very sensitive to the physical state of humans. We can hear the blood rushing through your veins if we want. We can sense injury or trauma to the body. Detecting physical weakness is an ability all predators have become adept at. It helps us hunt. But it also can help us in a situation like this."

"I see," Alyssa said quietly as she added one more bit of information to the vampire record in her mind. She shuddered when Vlad mentioned "the hunt" part, but she was glad for that ability in her aunt's case.

"I can ease her mind, if you let me. But you must decide quickly, Alyssa. We have a lot ahead of us tonight."

"Ease her mind? What do you mean?"

"As I said, she's had to deal with a lot. Bazhena sent the creature outside your door. He was completely evil. This creature could have filled her head with all sorts of images that she is better off not remembering. I can replace those memories with more mundane, acceptable ones."

Alyssa considered his words. She didn't want her aunt haunted by this event either. Despite her spunk, her aunt was getting up there in age and she was worried about her.

"What kind of memories?"

"What were you two doing before he came to your door?"

"My aunt was sitting on the couch watching TV. I had just come into the room when the creature knocked on the door. Once I heard that, a distinct feeling of unease and discord overcame me."

"Usually these creatures are very good at covering themselves up from human perception. How is it that you felt his evil?" Vlad's eyes narrowed suspiciously.

"I don't know. Sometimes I can just pick up other peoples' feelings, especially if it's a large group feeling the same thing, or a particularly strong thought by an individual."

"You're an empathic?" Vlad's eyes widened with surprise.

"That's what Christian called me. I guess I am. But another reason I was suspicious was that I picked up on Christian's thoughts."

"His thoughts?"

"Yes. I think he projected a warning to me. I kept hearing his voice saying 'beware' in my mind."

"I see," Vlad said thoughtfully. "Yet you didn't pick up on the evil compulsion of the creature trying to get to you. Because of your empathy, you seem to have the ability to filter out and sort through information that is being projected telepathically to you. Your mind must have sensed the danger and blocked out his thoughts. You must have a strong will. Most humans don't have that ability. Your aunt doesn't. Let's take care of her and then we can discuss this further. May I ease her mind?"

Alyssa hesitated. She hated the thought of someone using any kind of mind control on her aunt, but on the other hand, she wanted her to be okay. When Tom had called her earlier in the day to tell her about the damage to the wall and about falling asleep at the office, he sounded fine. He had no memory of what had happened last night with Bazhena. She was relieved by that, glad he didn't have to live with such a horrifying memory. Her aunt deserved the same.

"Yes. Do it."

Alyssa stood up and turned away from the picture of Vlad leaning over her aunt. She paced the floor for a few minutes.

"It's done. She will have no memory of what truly happened here tonight."

"What will she remember?"

"I erased the old memory and implanted the memory of her watching TV and falling asleep. You will leave her a note that I came to pick you up, but that you didn't want to wake her. I've compelled her to sleep until morning. We'll lay her on the couch and turn the television on. When she wakes up that will be her memory."

Alyssa felt disturbed and relieved at the same time. But in the end, she knew her aunt would be happier not remembering.

* * * * *

Christian sensed the moment Bazhena entered the room. He had lost consciousness a couple of times while she was gone. During that time, he had dreamt about Alyssa. Pictured the time they spent together from the first time they met until tonight. But now he was totally aware of Bazhena's presence. Despite the pain that now pounded at him endlessly, he felt her evil immediately. Gritting his teeth, he lifted his head and faced her. Her eyes glowed with rage.

She stopped inches from him. Without warning she slapped him across the face. The force of it caused him to almost lose consciousness. Somehow he managed to stay standing.

"Do you know what your friend Vlad has done?" Bazhena didn't wait for his answer. "He's killed my loyal minion. A creature that stood by my side for ages, dutifully doing all I commanded. Your friend killed him. This is personal now."

"And it wasn't personal when you tried to kill his father?" Christian asked mockingly.

She slapped him again. Consciousness was slowly slipping away. Pain was becoming all he knew. He could barely keep his head up.

"Vlad will not live to see another sundown. Neither will your little human girlfriend."

Bazhena's voice was soft, like a gentle caress. Christian wasn't fooled. She was furious. The underlying tremor in her voice was caused by her effort to control herself. Christian saw her hands curl into claws. She would kill him now. He could see it in her eyes.

He pulled at the bonds once more. It was no good. His efforts only intensified the burn of the metal against his skin. He wouldn't break free this way. He had to think of another plan. His mind quickly ran over his available options. There really was only one left. It filled him with disgust and self-loathing, but it was the only thing that might save Alyssa.

Once Christian was truly dead, Bazhena would kill her. He had no doubt of that. Bazhena's search for power was insatiable. Whatever it took to make that come true, she would do. Alyssa's face rose in his mind like a beacon in the dark. Yes, she was his apples and his sunshine. She was the guiding light of his existence. And Christian loved her with everything he was. Without her his life would not be worth living. If he had to end his own life to preserve hers, then so be it. He would have to do whatever it took to save Alyssa.

Even reliving his worst nightmare. Belonging to someone. Tying himself to someone so completely that he didn't know where he ended and she started. Losing the power to even decide if he lived or died. That's what life with Bazhena had been like before. And it would be like that again. This time for the rest of his existence. She wouldn't let him out of her clutches twice.

But Alyssa would live. She would have the life she deserved. He didn't deserve anything but pain. Though he had tried to save human lives. Tried to pay for all the killing and pain he had caused others. But he always knew that it would never be enough, that his debt would never be paid. That redemption could never be his. He was the undead, a creature of darkness. There would be no happily ever after him. He understood that. Had always known that.

He met Bazhena's gaze squarely.

"I offer you an exchange."

Bazhena's eyes lit with interest and wariness.

He struggled to stand upright.

"An exchange? What do you mean, Cristobal?"

"I offer you my servitude in exchange for Alyssa. I will give myself completely to you without a fight and will stay with you as long as you wish. In exchange, you will not kill Alyssa, or Vlad. And you will leave Arizona."

"Hmm, interesting. What about the legend? What about the last key?"

"I know about the legend. As you know, there are other 'Lights' in the world. Alyssa is not the only one."

Christian watched Bazhena carefully as he spoke. Her eyes became inscrutable when he mentioned Alyssa. She turned away from him and began pacing the floor in front of him.

"So, you're willing to become my slave again just to save Alyssa and Vlad? Interesting. Such devotion from you, Cristobal," Bazhena said mockingly.

She stopped pacing. Stood right in front of him. Grasping his chin, she studied his face. Then she looked deeply into his eyes.

"You are still a very desirable man, Cristobal. But could you give me the kind of devotion you show the human girl? I wonder. Can you forsake all others and do my bidding, regardless of the cost to you, or them?"

Christian didn't hesitate. He knew what was at stake here. Ignoring the fear and repulsion that crawled over him, he nodded his head.

"Yes. I will live for you, only you. And I will do all that you ask of me."

Bazhena smiled. She looked delighted by his words.

"I like the sound of that, Cristobal. You will live for me, only for me. Yes, that sounds just right." Bazhena slowly released his chin. "And I suppose I can find another 'Light'. We will leave Arizona tonight. Vlad and your human will keep their precious lives."

Christian wanted to sag forward and drop his head. His strength was almost at its end. Alyssa was safe. Now if he could only rest. Escape the pain for a little while. But he knew it wasn't possible. He needed to follow through. Make sure Bazhena followed through with her word. He squared his shoulders once more.

"I request a blood exchange to seal our deal." His voice sounded weak, even to his own ears.

Bazhena looked surprised by his request.

"You know what that means, don't you? Once that's done, there is no going back. No changing your mind. You will be fully and completely mine, Cristobal." A blood exchange between vampires to seal a bargain was considered irrevocable. Once done, neither vamp could renege on the deal. It was an unwritten law.

"I understand. Just do it."

"I would truly love to, but I can't."

Christian snarled at her.

"There is a reason. Despite how you're feeling right now, your blood is starting to rejuvenate itself. Past experiments have shown that it will return to its normal state within the next hour. That's why I made these special bonds for you. I knew your strength would come back and I needed something else to restrain you," Bazhena explained. "Until then, I can't taste you, or the mixture will enter my bloodstream."

Christian looked at her in disbelief. He felt like his body was slowly tearing itself apart inside. Could she be telling the truth?

"I see the doubt on your face. Believe what I tell you. I've enjoyed the death of many men to get the proportions just right. I even made sure I used vampires who were of the same age as you. As you know, the older we get, the more powerful our blood is. With enough time it can overcome almost anything. Dying will not come so easy to you, Christian. I have big things in store for you before that happens." Bazhena chuckled as she strode towards the door.

"I'll return in one hour to make the blood exchange," she called over her shoulder.

Christian stood stiffly upright until she left. The minute he lost sight of Bazhena he sagged forward. The image of Alyssa swam before him. A smile curved the corners of his mouth up as consciousness slipped away.

* * * * *

Alyssa finished writing the note for her aunt. She propped it up on the coffee table by the couch where her aunt was sleeping peacefully. Jonathan had joined her there. He sprawled his upper body over Aunt Joyce's chest and his lower body on the couch. She couldn't help but think he looked like he was trying to protect her or watch over her in that position. She softly scratched his head.

"You watch over her, Jonathan. And I'll buy you a great big bowl of Teriyaki Chicken when I get back," she said tenderly.

Jonathan meowed softly, then started to purr. He looked up at Alyssa and she could have sworn he winked. She was sure they had a deal.

Neither spoke as they left her apartment and Vlad led her to his car. It was a sleek and smooth-looking black Jaguar. It suited Vlad perfectly. Smooth and put together, but also dark and mysterious at the same time. She got in the car and enjoyed the luxurious feel of the interior.

Vlad turned to her before starting the engine.

"Please tell me more about your empathic ability."

Alyssa sighed. She really wasn't comfortable talking about it.

"Please, Alyssa. This is very important."

"It's really nothing. I can pick up on strong feelings from other people or large groups of people. It sometimes aids me when I talk to my clients and more recently it's helped me gauge the audience at my motivational speeches.

"What did you feel tonight?"

"I already told you."

"Tell me again."

Vlad's voice brooked no argument.

Alyssa sighed.

"I was getting ready to leave. Suddenly I heard Christian's voice in my head. He kept saying, 'beware' over and over again. Then it just stopped."

"That was it. All you heard was his voice in your head. No feelings?"

Alyssa suddenly remembered the terrible pain that had engulfed her. It had been so intense. She had thought she was going to die from it.

"Pain."

"What?"

"I felt intense pain. It hit me first, making me double over. Then his voice rang loud and clear in my mind, telling me to beware."

"How long did the pain last?"

"It lasted until Christian's voice stopped. That was the strangest thing about it. The minute his voice was no longer in my head, the pain stopped."

Vlad said nothing.

Alyssa glanced at him. He looked worried.

"What is it?"

Vlad hesitated.

"What?" she asked again. She didn't like this. Not one little bit.

"Has Christian taken blood from you?"

Alyssa suddenly felt embarrassed. She didn't want to answer his question. It was none of his business what Christian and she did.

"This is important, Alyssa."

"Yes! Okay? Christian drank my blood more than once."

Alyssa folded her arms across her chest defensively and glared at Vlad.

"Thank you. That explains it. You and Christian share a strong physical and mental connection. That's why you could feel what he was feeling and read his thoughts."

Alyssa's jaw dropped.

"You mean Christian is the one feeling that excruciating pain?"

Vlad slowly nodded.

"I think so. I haven't been able to reach him by phone or pager. I believe he's in trouble. He was going to gather as much information as he could about Bazhena last night, after he left you. We came up with a plan. I was supposed to take you to your speaking engagement, some of my men would do surveillance and Christian would stay in the background. He was setting a trap for Bazhena. And you were the bait."

"Me—Bait? I don't understand."

"Yes. Bazhena wanted to use you for an ancient ceremony she's trying to recreate."

Alyssa nodded in understanding.

"I remember her talking about this last night in my office, something about being the most powerful woman in the world. But what does that have to do with me?"

"Bazhena needed someone whose life was totally devoted to helping others. A person who felt it was their duty to make people's lives better. Someone like you."

"I see," Alyssa said, but she still didn't understand what was going on.

"So, what do you think happened to Christian?"

Fear and worry engulfed Alyssa. She had thought of Christian as all-powerful. She couldn't imagine anything happening to him. What had Bazhena done to him?

"I think Bazhena discovered him snooping around and managed to capture him somehow. He thought she was too weak from their encounter at your office, but she obviously wasn't. Either that, or she had some of her friends help her out."

"That creature actually has friends?"

"More like groupies who will do her bidding for a chance to better themselves. Vampire society is made up of a hierarchy just like any other. The most powerful vampires, usually the oldest ones, are at the top. And it goes down from there. Bazhena is quite old, so if she visits a city and demands help with something, lesser vampires jump at the chance to help her. The best example of this in human society is to compare these lesser vamps to social climbers."

Alyssa was only half listening to Vlad. It was back. The pain. The one she felt in her bedroom earlier. It was slowly starting to build. She held her stomach and bent forward in the seat.

"Alyssa? What's wrong?"

"The pain. Again. Like before," Alyssa gritted out between clenched teeth.

But this wasn't like before. It was worse this time. And now instead of Christian's voice, she was seeing images. The two of them together, scenes from the first time they met. Their encounter at the Plaza Hotel. Making love at Christian's home. It all flashed before her eyes like a movie. And with each image, her pain deepened.

Suddenly Christian's voice whispered through the corners of her mind. He sounded weak and in pain, yet his voice was comforting, like cool water on the burning ache in her body. He told her how much she meant to him. How much he loved her. And he told her to never forget that.

I love you, Alyssa. I never thought I would be able to feel that for anyone ever again. But I do for you. No matter what, please never forget that. I—

His voice got cut off. Something slammed into Alyssa's face, hard. All the images in her mind instantly disappeared. Her head flew back against the seat from the impact. It felt like someone had just hit her.

With a truck.

Chapter Eighteen

ꟷ

"Alyssa? Can you hear me? Ms. Edwards? Wake up. You want to wake up. You want to see me. It's time."

Vlad's hypnotic voice broke through her dazed state.

It sounded comforting. She was drawn to it, like a beacon in the mist. She moved towards it. Little by little, climbing out of the fog she had been in. Knowing she would feel better if she did. Knowing it would bring her peace.

Alyssa's eyes fluttered open to find Vlad leaning over her. She must have passed out. The pain she had felt had been worse than anything she had ever experienced in her whole life. And now she knew without a doubt, that Christian was the one actually living through that torture.

Bazhena.

She was responsible. Alyssa knew that with every fiber of her being. And powerful vampire or no, she was going to pay for hurting him.

Alyssa sat up. Vlad moved back to his seat. She turned to him and met his gaze squarely.

"We need to find Christian, now. He doesn't have much time."

Vlad started the car.

"I understand. And I know just who to ask."

Vlad took the 101 Highway West to Highway 51 South, while Alyssa called her publicist. She told him a family emergency had arisen and she wouldn't be able to make the speech. He wasn't happy about it, but agreed to let the function coordinators know and reschedule for another date.

They were heading towards Central Phoenix.

"Where are we going?"

"There's a club called Twice Charmed. It's located around Twenty-Fourth Street and Van Buren. I know some of the people who frequent the establishment quite often. They may be able to tell us where Christian is."

Alyssa wondered just what kind of club it was. The area he spoke about was seedy, to say the least. It was known as the place to find prostitutes and strip joints. Was Twice Charmed a strip club? At this point she really didn't care.

They needed to find Christian and they needed to find him fast. She remembered the weakness in his voice. And that hard blow to her face that echoed Bazhena hitting him. For some reason he was trapped in Bazhena's hold. And he couldn't get away. No, it didn't matter where they were going. If it meant saving Christian, she was ready to go to hell and back if necessary. She didn't question her feelings now. They just were. She needed to accept them until there came a time when she could analyze them fully. Now was not that time.

Vlad pulled into the parking lot of a large building. It looked like some sort of warehouse. As he parked the car and came around to her side to open the door for her, she hesitated. This didn't feel good. There was something wrong about this place. Something that screamed for her to leave and go far, far away. To never return.

She sat frozen in her seat. Vlad squatted down by the open door, so that he could look at her.

"It's okay, Alyssa. This place has a security spell on it."

Alyssa didn't want to move, but Vlad had caught her interest. She forced herself to look at him. What was he talking about?

"A security spell?"

"Yes. Many preternatural creatures come here. It really is not a place for humans, unless they are under protection. The owners discourage humans from coming here by sending out a subconscious danger signal. Humans pick up that warning and avoid this club as much as possible. That's what you're feeling right now. But it is only an illusion. You will be safe with me. Now come, we don't have much time. Christian needs us."

At Christian's name being mentioned, Alyssa broke out of her frozen stupor. Shaking her head, she got out of the car. *It's only an illusion. It's only an illusion. It's only an illusion.* She kept the chant up as they walked towards the entrance of the club, but her dread continued to build. As they approached the man standing by the door, Vlad took her hand.

"I must pretend you are with me, or they will not allow you in. Please play along," he whispered, giving her hand a reassuring squeeze.

Even if she hadn't felt this uncomfortable feeling before, the sight of the large, formidable looking bouncer would have done it for her. He gave Vlad a cursory glance then settled his stern gaze on her.

"What does she want?" he asked. Though he was addressing Vlad, his eyes never left Alyssa's.

"She's with me," was all Vlad said, but it seemed to satisfy the man. He gave her a quick once over then nodded his head.

"You two can go in, Vlad."

"Thanks, Dominic."

Alyssa felt the bouncer's gaze follow her as they walked into the club. Yet her attention was soon diverted by who she saw. Or rather what.

The outside of the club looked like an old, rundown warehouse. The inside was opulent. That was the only word for it. Despite the dim lighting, she noticed almost all the fine details. High domed ceilings with art relief carved into it. There were bar stools and high tables, but there were also leather couches and beautifully scrolled wood tables. The floors looked like marble. And there was one large bar spanning the entire wall of one side of the club. Behind the bar there were what she assumed were espresso and cappuccino machines. They looked shiny and clean, reflecting the dim lights on their smooth surfaces. There were other machines she didn't recognize and bottles of liquids she couldn't begin to name.

Then there were the customers. Everyone looked human, yet she could sense they weren't. The air practically hummed with magic. There was a lot of it here. Surprisingly though, she picked up on mostly happy feelings. The people here, on the whole, seemed to be having a good time.

Vlad silently led her across the room. She could feel eyes following her. And she sensed some interested curiosity on the part of those who looked at her. Many of them must be able to tell that she was a mortal human, just as she sensed that they were not.

Vlad stopped abruptly in front of a woman wearing a form fitting black dress. The spaghetti straps that held it up were slipping down her shoulders, as the woman huddled over the drink in front of her, but she didn't seem to notice. Vlad reached up and touched her shoulder. The woman stiffened immediately, then slowly turned to face them.

Alyssa couldn't stop herself from gasping. The woman was absolutely gorgeous, but that wasn't what surprised her. It was the large bite mark on the woman's neck. It looked like someone had tried to take a healthy chunk out of her skin. Although it appeared to be healing, Alyssa could still see blood glistening on the puncture wounds. And she had a bruised cheek that was so swollen; her eye on that side was forced partially shut.

The woman didn't seem to notice her. Instead her eyes fixed on Vlad and widened with fear. She made as if to move away, but Vlad's other hand snaked out and grabbed her upper arm before she could go anywhere. She tried to break away, but soon realized she wasn't going anywhere until Vlad let her.

"Amy. What a pleasure to see you again." Vlad said the words pleasantly as he led the woman to a secluded table in the corner. But as Alyssa followed close behind, she knew Vlad was feeling far from pleasant. He was furious.

"L-leave me alone." Amy's voice quivered with fear. She tried to move away again, but Vlad forced her to sit down by his voice alone.

"You will sit, Amy. Now."

His voice brooked no argument.

Vlad sat her down beside him and Alyssa joined them on the opposite side of the small table. What had happened to this woman? What did Vlad want from her? She didn't like to see the woman frightened. But did she know something about Christian?

"I don't want to talk to you," Amy said.

"Why not? Just last night you wanted to do more than talk. Why the change of heart?"

The woman licked her lips nervously. Her gaze darted to Alyssa then back to Vlad. Then back to her. Her eyes turned pleading.

"Please don't let him hurt me. I didn't mean any harm. I just wanted to become immortal. They told me they would do that if I helped them get Christian."

Alyssa's eyes widened in shock.

"You know Christian?"

Amy nodded.

"We met last night. I made sure I caught his interest, like my boyfriend wanted me to. He said, if I helped distract Christian and got him alone in the parking lot, they would finally turn me," she explained fearfully.

"What happened? Where is Christian now?"

Alyssa noted the hypnotic sound of Vlad's voice. It was compelling, pulling at a person to answer whatever he wanted. Amy wasn't immune to this. She started talking immediately.

"My jerk boyfriend didn't turn me. He, his friends and I brought Christian to Bazhena's place. Then he gave me up to that bitch vampire. She practically tore my throat out feeding on me." Amy reached up and fingered the spot on her neck where the deep puncture wounds were still visible.

"When she was done, I asked her if she would turn me. She slapped me across the face and knocked me down. She and my boyfriend laughed in my face. Then she said she never turned women. It wasn't good for business, she said. She told me to leave. She said to never come back or I was dead. Really dead."

Alyssa was shocked. Vlad didn't hesitate.

"You will take us to where Bazhena is."

Amy started to protest.

"But, I can't. She'll kill m—"

"You want to take us, Amy. You need to lead us there. Your body aches to be with your boyfriend again. You know he's with Bazhena. If you don't see him soon, you'll go crazy. You must take us there."

Vlad's hypnotic voice went on and on, lulling Amy into acquiescence. She shook her head adamantly at first, but soon that changed. Soon she was looking at Vlad with eagerness and anticipation.

"Yes, I must take you there. I must see him. I can't live without him."

"Let's go, now." Vlad stood up and Amy immediately complied.

Alyssa started to follow close behind as Vlad led Amy towards the exit.

She didn't notice the large man approach her, until he silently took her arm and started to lead her away. She tried to twist out of his grasp, but his hold only tightened. He wasn't hurting her, but he wasn't letting her go either. She dug her heels firmly in the floor and resisted the man's pull until he finally stopped and turned towards her. Alyssa gasped at how handsome he was. His face would turn heads in a crowd. The only thing interrupting his good looks was a wicked-looking scar that ran down one side of his face. It started at the corner of one eye and ended at his jaw line. Yet somehow it only added to his wicked attractiveness, giving him a dangerous edge.

He was not only a tall man, he had a warrior's build. That was the only way she could describe it. His tight-fitting T-shirt and jeans revealed an extremely muscular body. This guy worked out, a lot.

Alyssa did one of the few useful things her father had taught her. She brought her knee up and hit the guy between his legs.

The man winced and bent slightly forward, resting his free hand on his thigh. But he didn't release her. She twisted around, hoping to loosen his grasp, but he held on tightly. She struggled until he stood up straight again and stared down at her. His eyes had a dangerous glint they hadn't before. He held her stare a moment. Just long enough to let her know who was in charge. Alyssa lifted her chin defiantly and met his gaze.

Something close to admiration flashed in the man's eyes for a minute. Then he slowly ran his gaze down her body. By the time his eyes came back to her face, she felt like he had completely undressed her with his eyes. The look he gave her was so hot it felt like she was going to burn up. In response, she put her free hand on her hip and gave him her best scolding look. A wide grin spread across the man's mouth. Amusement lit his emerald green eyes.

"Christian mentioned you were feisty."

Then his gaze moved past her in question.

"Vlad?"

Alyssa turned around. Vlad was standing right behind them holding Amy by his side.

"Alyssa, this is Eric, uh, Dragonslayer. He works for me. You must go with him now. We don't have much time. Bazhena wants you dead. It wouldn't be safe for you to go to her lair."

Alyssa yanked her arm away from Eric. Surprisingly he let her go with a knowing chuckle. She gave him one last glare before turning back to Vlad.

"Sheesh! Are all the guys working for you good-looking? Is that a prerequisite or something?" Alyssa asked in a huff.

Vlad just lifted one eyebrow and stared silently at her.

"I'm going with you, Vlad. I will *not* stay behind knowing Christian is in such a state of pain. You may need me. I'm in touch with his feelings in a way you're not. I may be able to help you because of that."

Alyssa knew she was grasping at straws, but she couldn't sit back while someone else rescued Christian. She had to know she had done everything she could to help him. She could do no less.

"No, Alyssa. You're The Light that Bazhena wants. She would do anything to get a hold of you. That's probably why she's torturing Christian right now. She's trying to lure us to her, so she can get to you. It's a trap. You are the key to her power. If you're anywhere in her proximity she would become even more dangerous, because she wants you at all costs."

"You're wrong." Amy said the words so quietly. They almost didn't hear her.

"What did you say?" Vlad asked as he leaned closer to her. Eric and Alyssa followed suit, forming a tight circle around Amy.

"I said you're wrong."

"What do you mean?"

"I mean that this woman is not the key or The Light Bazhena seeks," Amy said, looking at Alyssa.

Vlad's eyes narrowed suspiciously.

"If she isn't, then who is?"

"Christian. He is the one. He is the key to the legend."

Vlad's eyes widened in shock.

"How do you know that?" Alyssa asked as her mouth fell open in disbelief.

"When we brought Christian to her, she and my boyfriend spoke quietly to each other. They thought I had lost consciousness after Bazhena fed off of me, but I hadn't. I heard their whole conversation," Amy explained with a shrug.

"Bazhena said how happy she was to have the key, but how sad it would be that Christian would have to die because of it. She told my boyfriend how she wished she could keep Christian as her pet, as she had before, but how it would be impossible if she were to attain full power. She said that the only way she could attain full power was through his death."

They all stood in stunned silence for a minute. Alyssa was the first to move into action. She grabbed Amy's arm and started pulling her towards the club's exit.

"You are taking us to Bazhena, now. Let's go."

"But I don't want t—"

Alyssa stopped short, swung around and stuck her face as close to Amy's as possible.

"Tough. You either take us there now, or I kill you myself. Got it?"

The deadly calm in her voice brooked nor argument.

Amy just silently nodded her head in agreement and let Alyssa lead her outside.

Alyssa missed the look of male amusement that passed between Vlad and Eric as they followed close behind and got into Vlad's car.

Amy gave directions to Vlad as they drove. She was the only one who spoke. Eric was looking blankly out the window and Vlad was closely following Amy's direction. Alyssa was too lost in her own thoughts about their new discovery. Christian was The Light? That meant that Bazhena could have killed him already. That thought scared her and left a void in her that she didn't even want to consider. But wouldn't she have felt something? She and Christian were connected. They had a bond like she had never experienced before. Why hadn't he reached out to her again?

Maybe it was time for her to reach out to him. Closing her eyes, she brought the image of his handsome face to mind.

* * * * *

Christian woke up. He felt much better. The gut-wrenching pain inside him had all but disappeared. He lifted himself up, so that he stood straight once more. The bonds burned his skin slightly, but that was minor.

"Feeling better, my pet?" Bazhena's mocking voice filled the room.

Using the powers of their kind, she moved close to him so quickly it was little more than a blur. She was close enough for him to see the desire flaring bright in her eyes, but not near enough to touch.

Christian strained against the chains, but it was no use. Though the pain was gone, his body was still too weak to break his bonds. He needed to recuperate. He needed blood. The hunger was beating at him now. It was time to feed.

As if reading his thoughts, a slow smile curved the corners of Bazhena's lips up.

"Hungry, Cristobal? Let's take care of that immediately."

She clapped her hands. The vamps he had seen back at Twice Charmed came into the room. They were dressed in some sort of hooded ceremonial robes. Christian watched them warily as they each took a position around him. He felt his fangs elongate as anger filled him. He snarled at the men around him, but they ignored him. They only had eyes for Bazhena.

"It's time, Cristobal. First we'll exchange blood, then you will be mine." Bazhena gave him a seductive smile as she opened the long silk robe she was wearing. Her bare body was revealed beneath. Christian couldn't help staring at her. Her body was made to please a man. That was one thing he would never forget.

When she ran one of her nails across one breast, barely above her nipple, blood immediately came to the surface, beading along the cut. Christian's mouth watered. He remembered the rich, heady taste of her. She was a very old vampire. And she had taken so many lives. Her blood was filled with their essence, powerful and rich. His beast roared with joy. It knew her taste. Knew the power it held. She slowly closed the remaining distance between them. As she did so, her men also closed in around him and held him back, restraining his movements. He growled low in his throat.

"Don't worry about them, my pet. This feeding is just for you." Bazhena moved forward so that her chest was in easy reach of his mouth. She leaned her head back and held her arms out on either side of her. "Only for you. Drink from me, Cristobal."

Christian didn't hesitate. He needed his strength if he was deal with Bazhena. He had to make sure she kept up her part of the bargain—him in exchange for Alyssa and Vlad's life. It was the only way. He clamped onto Bazhena breast and suckled her.

She cried out with pleasure. Grasping his head in her hands, she pressed him closer. He drank ferociously. Despite her evilness, her blood was ancient and it filled him with a surge of power. As he felt her nipple harden under his tutelage, felt her blood's sweetness run into his mouth, he recalled the times they had spent together. His body tingled with pleasure as all the erotic images came to mind.

Mind.

She was trying to control him even now. He could feel her seductive presence winding through his brain. Touching him, luring him, teasing him. He growled low in his throat and pressed his mouth harder against her. He drank as quickly as he could. Trying to get as much of her power as possible. Trying to ignore the passion-filled haze she was wrapping around him.

"Enough!"

He barely heard Bazhena's voice. He was too lost in the taste of her blood, the pleasure it brought him. Before he knew what was happening, he was pulled away from her. His hunger was barely sated. He needed more. He leaned forward, but was held back by her vamps.

His eyes snapped up to meet Bazhena's. Her eyes were bright with desire as they ran hungrily over his body. He could tell she would like nothing better than to have him then and there. Longing, then regret filled her face.

She turned away from him for a moment. When she finally faced him again, Christian could tell she had gotten her passion under control. Her face had once more become cold and unfeeling.

Too bad, maybe he could have used it against her.

"Now that you have drunk from me first, we can finish the ceremony."

"Ceremony?" Christian asked suspiciously.

"Yes, Cristobal. The ceremony is almost complete. I just need to say the last few words and take your blood, then it will be done."

Warning bells went off in Christian's head.

"What are you talking about Bazhena?"

"Well, it's very simple actually. I've pursued a legend for some time—a legend of untold power. I had collected all of the necessary parts of the puzzle, except one."

"The Light," Christian said.

"Yes, The Light. Now I have it, so I can finish the ceremony. Soon I will be the most powerful creature in creation. None will be able to refuse me, so I will rule over humans and preternatural creatures alike. The world will be my oyster."

Bazhena's eyes glazed with triumph and something not quite sane. Christian ignored it as her words finally sunk in.

"You have The Light?" Had Bazhena gotten to Alyssa without him knowing about it? Had his efforts been for nothing? But wouldn't he have felt it if she was hurt or in trouble?"

Bazhena's husky laugh filled the room. Her vamps laughed along with her. Christian frowned in confusion. What the hell was going on? The laughter finally died down. Bazhena's eyes turned crafty.

"Yes, I have The Light. He's standing right in front of me. You are The Light, my pet." She stared at him with anticipation in her eyes. Waited for a response, as if she relished the moment.

Christian ignored her. Him? He was The Light? How was that possible?

"You're wrong, Bazhena. The Light is somebody who has devoted their life to helping others. Who feels it's their duty to do so. I've done no such thing."

"Haven't you?" Bazhena smiled almost tenderly. "I seem to recall a fledgling vampire who had once been in my power, he had everything before him. He could have killed and fed to his heart's desire and have a beautiful woman by his side. He and I could have ruled the world together, but he turned against me. He forsakes the pleasure of the hunt, the pleasure of drinking from victims so frightened their blood was sweet and rich with adrenaline. And he gave up the pleasure of the kill. Of feeling his victim's puny little hearts slow and eventually stop as he took their life force. He tasted of all of this, yet he turned his back on it. He silenced and muzzled the proud beast inside of him that so often tempted him. That roared for release. That screamed to live its life as it was meant to. Instead of plundering mankind, he decided to help and protect it. He made it his duty. He devoted his life to it. And has followed through with that devotion for many, many years. He became a hero to mankind."

Bazhena said the last words with distaste, as if they were dirt in her mouth.

Christian shook his head back and forth. No. It couldn't be.

"You have the wrong guy. I'm no hero and definitely not The Light. I appreciate the feed. I can't deny that your blood is a heady treat. But I'm not the one you're looking for." He smiled mockingly.

Bazhena's eyes grew angry at his mocking tone.

"Oh, I think you are, my pet. But either way we'll see, because I plan to finish the ceremony right now, then suck every last drop of blood from your body. If it works, then you will be dead and I will become the powerful goddess I wish to be."

"And if it doesn't?" Christian had to keep Bazhena talking. He had to stall her as long as possible, so he could figure out what to do.

An evil grin spread across her face.

"Then I will go with my second alternative. Your lovely little human will make a tasty snack—or your brave friend, Vlad. I'll kill them both as a consolation prize until I can find another Light. But I don't think it will come to that. You are the key to my power, I have no doubt."

Christian growled and tried to lunge at her, but the vamps held him back.

"We had a deal. Me in exchange for Alyssa and Vlad."

Bazhena rolled her eyes.

"Oh that. Well, it would be a deal, except for the fact that you're going to be dead in a few minutes, so you really can't hold up your end of the bargain, can you, darling?"

Christian roared. He struggled violently against the men holding him. He threw a few of them off, but there were just too many. Holding him in place, they pulled his head back, so that his neck was vulnerable and exposed.

One of the men closest to Bazhena handed her an ancient looking scroll. She unrolled it and began reading it aloud.

"The Light shall fill me with its purity. I take its essence into me. I leave nothing behind. Its power becomes my power. And so it shall be done."

As she spoke she moved closer to him. He strained against the chains, but the vamps held him in place. He saw Bazhena's eyes light with anticipation as her incisors elongated in her mouth. She placed her lips near his ear.

"I'm sorry to lose you, my pet. But this power is all I've ever wanted. Now all mankind will pay for what they did to me. No one will ever turn away from me again." She slid her mouth down his neck. Her teeth grazed his skin once, then again. "I will make this as pleasant as possible for you, Cristobal. You deserve that, at least. Goodbye."

Bazhena's teeth sank deeply into his skin. He could feel his blood pouring from him to her as she took great gulps of it. Yet he felt little pain, she made sure of that. She kept sending soothing thoughts to him, but he continued to struggle. The vamps around him held on tightly. He fought with all his strength, but soon even that failed him. He felt weakness start to seep into him as Bazhena continued to take his blood. Everything around him started to grow fuzzy and dim.

That's when he heard it. Christian was sure it was just a hallucination, but he strained to hear it again.

Christian? Please hold on. We're on our way to you. Don't let go. Vlad and I are almost there. Fight it, my love, fight it. I'm with you now. Can you feel it? I won't leave you. Stay with me.

Joy rushed through him as he heard Alyssa reach out to him in this way. They truly were bonded. True mates.

But it was too late. He wouldn't last much longer.

It's too late. Stay away. I'm sorry I failed you. I love you, palomita. Goodbye.

With the last of his strength he sent her his thoughts. Then everything grew dark.

Chapter Nineteen

ꕤ

"No!"

Alyssa scream filled the car.

Everyone's eyes turned to her.

"What is it, Alyssa? What's wrong?" Vlad asked as he pulled into the parking lot of another rundown, abandoned building.

Alyssa's eyes were wide with fear.

"He's fading fast. Bazhena's close to killing him. We need to hurry. It's almost too late."

Alyssa started to get out of the car.

Vlad held her arm.

"You must stay with me, Alyssa. You don't know what kind of powers are at work here."

"Then let's move it, Vlad. I told you, it's almost too late. Christian can't hold out much longer."

Alyssa jumped out of the car. Vlad followed.

Eric and Amy also climbed out.

Vlad turned to back to them.

"No, Eric. You take the car and drive Amy back to the club. It's only a few minutes from here. Then come back and park on the street. Whatever you do, do not come inside. If Bazhena succeeds with her plan, she'll be able to control all mankind. That means you too. And I wouldn't want to have to kill you." Vlad gave Eric an arrogant grin.

"You wish," Eric said as he and Amy got back in the car. "Good luck."

Vlad nodded, then turned back towards the building.

"Let's go."

He and Alyssa approached the entrance.

"Bazhena will know we're here, won't she?

"It depends on how involved she is in the ceremony. If she is totally focused, she may not. Let's hope that is the case because surprise is just about the only thing we have going for us."

Getting into the building was easier than either of them thought. The front door was open. They walked right in. No one was around. Alyssa closed her eyes and tried to *feel* Christian. She didn't know how she did it, but she could.

"He's back here," she whispered to Vlad as she walked down a hallway towards where she sensed he was.

Vlad followed without a word. They reached a closed door. Alyssa grabbed the knob, then turned back with a questioning look.

Vlad nodded silently.

She twisted the knob and slowly pushed the door open. What she saw stopped her in her tracks. Icy fingers of fear wrapped around her heart. Bazhena in all her naked glory was bent over Christian. He was on his knees in chains. His head was thrown back, a pure look of ecstasy written all over his face as Bazhena gorged herself on him.

Alyssa moved into the room. Suddenly four men appeared. They circled around her, growling menacingly.

One of the men smiled evilly, showing his sharp teeth. He ran his gaze hungrily over Alyssa. Then he licked his lips with anticipation in his eyes.

"Great. A snack. I'm starving."

Alyssa's eyes widened with fear.

She swung around as she heard a surprised yelp behind her. Vlad picked one of the men up by his hair and threw him across the room. He hit the wall with a loud thud, slid to the ground and didn't move.

"I'm hungry too," Vlad said with a leer. "Who would like to be my first course?"

The other vamps looked at Vlad with surprise and more than a little fear.

"Beware, he is an ancient one," the vamp who had threatened her said to the others. They all nodded as they watched Vlad warily.

Alyssa took advantage of their inattention to slip beyond them. She strode towards the spot where Bazhena leaned over Christian. But before she reached them, Bazhena stood up and slowly turned around.

Alyssa gasped and took a step back.

Bazhena glowed. There was no other word for it. Her body looked illuminated with an energy that surrounded her. It reminded her of some of the holy scenes she had seen on the beautifully stained glass at St. Paul's church in New York City. Prominent figures were haloed in a holy light. Bazhena had that light around her. But Alyssa knew it was far from holy. It was evil. It was corrupted power that filled the vampire.

Bazhena laughed triumphantly, ignoring the blood dripping from her mouth. Christian's blood. She looked down at herself and flexed her muscles. She was fixated on the power that surrounded her.

"It is done. I am the most powerful creature on earth. No one will be able to deny me." Bazhena laughed again. It sounded almost crazed. This time she punctuated her words by swinging her arms around and smashing the two poles holding Christian chained. Alyssa turned away, shielding her eyes as wood splintered everywhere.

When she swung back to face Bazhena, she was gone. Turning full circle, Alyssa scanned the room. When she finally saw Bazhena, she couldn't believe her eyes. All the vamps in the room, including Vlad were bowed on one knee in front of her. She stood tall, looking down on them with a satisfied smile and an insane look in her eyes.

"Hmm. How nice. You all are bowed down to me, as you should be. Now whom should I begin with? Vlad, I think I'll save you for last. Your death will be slow and painful, of course." Bazhena chuckled as she pointed to one of the other vamps.

"You. Come to me," she commanded.

When the man started to stand, Bazhena stopped him.

"No. Crawl to me like the dog you are."

"Yes, mistress." The man obeyed, crawling to her.

"Now kiss my feet."

"Yes, mistress." Again the man obeyed without question. Alyssa noticed all the men had sort of a crazed look on their faces. They also were looking at Bazhena with intense desire, as if they all hungered desperately for her.

The legend!

Bazhena had completed the ceremony. Now all mankind would do her bidding and find her totally irresistible.

Alyssa started to back away as she gave the man another order.

"Good. Now kill yourself. Take that piece of wood next to you and pierce your heart."

Alyssa watched in horror as the man did her bidding without question.

"Yes, mistress." He crawled to the piece of wood she pointed to, picked it up and drove it through his own chest.

He squirmed on the floor few a few seconds, then lay still.

Bazhena's insane laughter filled the room.

"Goody." She clapped her hands like a child at a candy store. "Now you. Crawl to me."

The vamp she pointed to did so without hesitation.

Alyssa turned back to where Christian lay. Maybe she could help him. Find some way out of here before Bazhena could get to them. She knew she wasn't thinking clearly, but she thought that if she could just get Christian out of here, everything would be okay. She needed to get Christian out.

She slowly moved towards him, glancing back at Bazhena every few seconds to make sure she hadn't noticed her. Alyssa finally reached Christian. Looking down at him, everything froze inside of her. A small puddle of blood had formed around him. It was coming from the puncture wound on his neck. Barely. There was obviously so little left in his body that the blood was only coming out in slow, small, reluctant drops.

Her surroundings faded away as Alyssa's memories came rushing back. Her mother dead on the floor, just like Christian, in a pool of her own blood. No. Not again. She was too late again. Too late to save Christian, just as she had been too late to save her mother.

Too late, too late, too late…

Alyssa didn't even realize she was screaming until Bazhena appeared by her side. Alyssa clamped her mouth shut and looked at the woman with fear. She waited for the vampire to speak, waited for her to utter the words that would make Alyssa unable to resist.

Bazhena studied Alyssa curiously, like an insect. Then she glanced down at Christian. When she glanced back up, regret was in her eyes.

"If he wasn't The Light, I think I would have spared him, he was one of the few men I actually cared about. But there was no other way. If I was to gain true power over the world, then Cristobal had to die. I *will* miss my pet."

Alyssa was surprised by the regret in the vamp's words. But before she could dwell on it, Bazhena's expression changed from regret to evil delight in an instant.

"I think I will take care of you now, pitiful human. All but Vlad are dead and he and I have a personal issue to settle before he dies. It may take a while." Bazhena's face lit with anticipation.

Alyssa glanced across the room. All the men were on the ground. Dead. Except for Vlad. He still knelt on one knee, bowing.

"I really don't know what Cristobal saw in you. You look weak and frail to me. I guess I'll never know. It's of little consequence now anyway," Bazhena said with a shrug.

"Bow down to me now, pitiful mortal. Bow down to your mistress."

Alyssa waited for the words to overcome her, for her to fall to her feet enthralled by the spell and Bazhena.

But it didn't happen. Alyssa felt nothing. Her eyes widened in surprise as she continued to meet Bazhena's gaze. The spell wasn't working on her. Why? How could that be?

Bazhena's eyes narrowed dangerously.

"I said bow down."

Alyssa obeyed Bazhena's command. Only so that she could have a moment more to think. For some reason the spell wasn't working on her. She didn't find Bazhena irresistible. And she didn't feel compelled to do whatever the vamp told her.

"Ah, that's better. Obviously you have some spirit. That's what Cristobal must have seen in you. But now you are nothing compared to me. Just a fly that I'll squash and forget about."

Alyssa kept her head bowed, not moving. Trying to figure out a way to escape Bazhena's plan for her.

"Look at me."

Alyssa obeyed immediately.

"I know you're only mortal, not a vampire, but I'm sure a stake through your heart will kill you just as easily. I'm bored with you already. I want to get to the fun," she explained, glancing over to where Vlad still kneeled.

"Pick up that stake," Bazhena said impatiently, pointing to the splintered piece of wood close to where Christian lay.

Alyssa did as Bazhena bid. She noticed the large splintered piece of wood had sharply pointed ends on both sides. A plan formed in her mind. She was frightened, but when she glanced at Christian's still form as she picked up the stake, her heart hardened and her resolve solidified. She had to do this. For Christian. It was too late for anything else.

"Now stand up. I want to see your face as you die. Otherwise it will be no fun."

"Yes, mistress," Alyssa said copying the male vamp's toneless response she had heard earlier. Alyssa tried to look dazed and out of it. She must have succeeded because Bazhena smiled with satisfaction.

"Good. Now take that stake and plunge it through your heart. Kill yourself."

Bazhena moved right in front of Alyssa, close enough to reach out and touch her, but far enough to allow Alyssa to place the stake between them. Perfect.

"Yes, mistress," Alyssa replied tonelessly.

But instead of plunging it into her own heart, she pushed it forward straight into Bazhena's chest, hoping her aim had been true. Bazhena was so shocked by Alyssa's actions that she fell backwards from the force of the blow. Alyssa fell on top of her and plunged the stake deeper, past the resistance of her ribs. Until she felt it hit the floor beneath the vamp.

Bazhena looked up at her in shock. Her eyes widened, blood poured out of her mouth and nose and her body started jerking. Alyssa closed her eyes against the terrible sight, but kept all her weight on the stake until the woman stopped moving. She opened her eyes and met the vamp's blank stare.

Bazhena was dead. Not undead. But truly dead.

Alyssa let go of the stake and rolled over onto her back. She closed her eyes and released the breath she had been holding. She felt numb.

"Thank you, Alyssa."

Alyssa's eyes shot open. Vlad leaned over her, a smile curving his lips up at the corner.

"What just happened? Why wasn't I affected by Bazhena's power spell?"

He held out his hand to help her up. She took it and stood up.

"I'm not sure, but I believe you've just saved the world."

She went immediately to Christian and knelt by his side.

"I may have saved the world, but I couldn't save Christian."

Tears formed in her eyes and she let them fall without shame. This man who had entered her life so suddenly, was now gone just as suddenly. No longer would she hear his sexy laughter, see his eyes light with passion as they stared at each other. Feel his arms around her. Never again. And never would they have the chance to spend time together, loving each other.

Alyssa lifted her head up and screamed. All the frustration, sadness and anger came out. She raged at fate until her voice grew hoarse.

Bending down, she kissed Christian's cold lips.

"I'm sorry I couldn't save you, my love."

"I think you can."

Vlad's voice was soft and hesitant as he spoke, but his words caught her immediate attention.

Alyssa's head snapped up and she narrowed her eyes suspiciously.

"What do you mean?"

"There is a way, but you must be willing. You must trust Christian completely. You must hand your life over to him, just as his life is now in your hands. If you can do this, then he will live again. Truly live, no longer a vampire, but a mortal human like you."

Alyssa gasped and her eyes widened in shock.

"What? How?" She didn't know what questions to ask first.

"I am an ancient, Alyssa. One of the earliest vampires to walk this earth. I know how we began, our origins. There is a way to bring Christian back. He is almost completely drained of blood, but there is still enough in him that he has a chance. What I'm about to tell you can go no further than this room. No one must ever know about this, do you understand?"

"Yes." Alyssa nodded and waited.

"Human blood has always been stronger than vampire blood. It is a little known fact, but true nonetheless. That is why vampires crave it. We need the blood to exist because our blood is different. It needs host cells. In other words, it can't exist on its own. It must constantly have human blood cells to convert and make into vampire blood cells. And the process works without fail most of the time. Thus we exist and create other vampires," Vlad explained. "Are you following me so far?"

"Yes. Please continue." Alyssa hadn't done well at biology in school, but she found Vlad's words fascinating.

"As you may or may not know, when we turn a human into a vampire, we must almost completely drain them of blood before we let them drink from us. That is the only way the conversion can take place. The human blood must be so minimal as to barely be there or it won't work. Human blood is full of defenses and with enough of it in the body of a vampire, it can easily break up and dissipate the vampire blood to the point that it is negligible. The vampire cells are weak without a host and the human body instantly recognizes them as alien. They are seen as an enemy and are easily destroyed by the defense system present in human blood."

"Like an infection?"

Vlad nodded.

"Something like that."

"So you're saying that I have to let Christian take almost all the blood from my body? Then he'll come back to life as a human."

"Yes, the conversion is painful, but he will become human again."

"But why can't we just go get some human blood at the blood bank and give him that?"

"No. There is more to this than physiology. There is also the magic and mystical part of being a vampire. For those who know of it, this ceremony has always been described as the "Redemption". The human participant must be bonded to the vampire. He or she must accept the vampire for everything he or she was and is, without judgment, without resentment and with complete forgiveness. For it to work, the two people must be in love. Their mind and bodies must recognize each other. They must have exchanged thoughts, been in each other's minds. And they must have already made an exchange of blood."

"What happens if they aren't connected in this way?"

"Then the process becomes deadly. The human blood overwhelms the vampire blood too quickly. The body becomes human before it has a chance to recover all the necessary blood to function. The heart starts beating before there is enough blood to run through it. In other words, the vampire becomes human, then dies moments later."

Alyssa shuddered at the horrible image his words brought to mind.

"It's a terrible thing to witness," Vlad explained. "I know other vampires who have tried this with humans they haven't bonded with. It has failed every time. The only way this works is between two people who are connected through love in mind, body and soul."

"So how does this bond between the two make the conversion a success?"

Vlad shrugged.

"It's hard to say. Perhaps the blood recognizes each other and works together to ease the process somehow. Maybe it is something else completely. Remember, being a vampire is more than just physiology, just as being human is so much more. There is magic and the unknown in both cases."

Alyssa took less than a second to think about it. She would do it. She loved Christian without any doubts or fears. She wanted him back.

"Fine. Let's do it."

"Wait. There's one more thing."

Alyssa let out an exasperated sigh.

"I don't like the sound of that. The 'one more thing' I've heard in all the movies never bodes well for the hero or heroine. What is it?"

"What is your blood type?" Vlad asked.

"My blood type?"

"Yes your blood type."

"A positive, why?"

The serious look on Vlad's face made her wish she had never asked.

"Once you are almost drained of blood, Christian won't be able to replenish it with his. He'll be undergoing the transformation and will need all the human blood he has inside of him. So, we may be going to the blood bank after all, Alyssa. For you. I want to make sure you receive the right blood type. You'll need a transfusion quickly. I'll make sure you get it," Vlad explained. "Eric is parked outside. I'll leave him here to remove the evidence and clean up this mess while I take you and Christian to someone who will help us."

Alyssa frowned.

She didn't like the fact that she had to put her life in the hands of others. She had always had a hard time with that. She glanced over to Christian's still form. In that moment she knew that the decision was out of her hands. If it saved the man she loved, then so be it.

Alyssa raised her head proudly and met Vlad's intense stare.

"I'm ready."

Vlad took his shirt off, rolled it up and laid it on the floor next to Christian's head. Alyssa couldn't help but notice the scars marking his back. She started to ask him about it, but the forbidding look on his face stopped her.

"We must move quickly. Christian is fading fast. Lay down here, next to him."

Alyssa obeyed without a word.

"This may hurt a little. I'm sorry, but I will try to make it as comfortable as possible."

One minute Vlad was talking, the next, he was slitting her wrist with his nail. The cut was deep and her blood swelled up immediately.

"Hold your wrist over Christian's mouth."

Alyssa lifted her hand and placed it in the air over Christian's face. Vlad held it there with his free hand. Blood dripped rapidly into his mouth. At first Christian did nothing. Vlad began massaging his throat, trying to get him to swallow. He continued to do that for a few minutes, until Christian's eyes flew open. Alyssa saw they were glowing red.

There was no life in those eyes, only death and hunger.

Vlad moved Alyssa's hand to the floor by her head. Christian snarled, rolled over and covered Alyssa's body with his. Then he grabbed Alyssa's arm. As he brought her wrist to his mouth, his teeth elongated and sharpened. She closed her eyes, waiting for the pain, but it never came.

You will be fine. Be at peace. There is no pain.

Vlad's voice filled her head with soothing thoughts. She didn't hear the hungry gulping noises Christian made as he devoured her blood. Soon everything became fuzzy and soft around the edges. She knew she was losing too much blood, but she didn't try to pull away. She trusted Christian, as she had trusted no one for a very long time.

Thank you, palomita. Thank you for your trust.

The voice drifted into her head like a soft breeze, caressing her with its tenderness. Alyssa reveled in the sound of it. Christian. He would be okay. Relief filled her even as everything grew dim around her. She pushed one last thought back to him.

I love you.

Then the darkness came. She fell headlong into it.

Chapter Twenty

ℵ

Christian opened his eyes. He was lying in his bed at home. Everything looked familiar, yet something was different. He rolled to his side and froze. Alyssa lay sleeping next to him. She looked so pale. He touched her pulse point to make sure that she was still alive. It beat slow and steady against his fingers. His heart slowed from its frantic beat. It had sped up when he thought something was wrong with Alyssa.

Wait a minute. His heart? It had never beaten before, unless he willed it to. If he didn't know better, he would swear he was— No!

Memories came rushing back to him. Last night. Bazhena. He thought he had died. Alyssa had given him her blood. She had saved him. She had sacrificed herself for him. Put her trust completely in him. He knew that must have been difficult for her. He ran his finger down her soft cheek. She stirred slightly, then stilled again.

He was tempted to touch her again. Then touch her some more. But she needed to sleep. He wouldn't wake her. Getting out of bed, he pulled some pants on and walked to the window. Staring out into the night, he tried to piece together last night's events.

I love you.

Christian remembered Alyssa's last thought before he felt darkness surround her. She had said that she loved him. His apples and sunshine loved him. He had reveled in those words. Played them over and over in his head until the darkness had also taken him.

What had happened last night? What about Bazhena?

"Feeling better, my friend?"

Christian swung around. Vlad leaned negligently in the doorway. An amused smile curved the corners of his mouth."

"Yes. Thanks to you." Christian grinned right back at his friend.

"Your lady deserves the credit. She has a lot of spirit and courage."

"She'll receive my thanks when she wakes up. I can promise you that," Christian vowed.

"Without her we would both be dead. As would much of the male population in the world, if Bazhena had gotten her way."

"What happened? I remember Bazhena draining my blood and I remember waking up and finding Alyssa giving me blood to save me. But nothing in between. How did you know what was going on. How did you find me?"

"I remembered your friend, Amy. Alyssa and I found her at Twice Charmed. She wasn't very cooperative, so Alyssa threatened to kill her if she didn't help us."

"What?" Christian glanced back at Alyssa doubtfully.

"You know what they say about dynamite coming in small packages," Vlad replied with a knowing grin and a shrug.

"Do I ever." Christian chuckled and a wolfish grin spread across his face. Alyssa was definitely dynamite. "Alyssa is a strong, independent and spirited lady."

"I noticed. You're a lucky man."

"I know," Christian said quietly as his face grew serious once more. "What happened next?"

Vlad told him everything up to Alyssa killing Bazhena.

"Alyssa killed Bazhena?" Christian was stunned and angry. "How could you let her risk her life like that? Do you know how easily Bazhena could have killed her? But wait a minute, why didn't Bazhena's powers work on Alyssa?"

"I'm sorry, my friend. If I had any control over myself, I would never have let Alyssa close to Bazhena. But I didn't. My body and mind were no longer mine. As far as Bazhena's power over Alyssa, I read over the legend several times last night. It seems Bazhena missed one very important part of the wording. It says she will be found irresistible to *mankind.* It says nothing about *womankind.* Her power only applied to men. It had no affect on women. And since Bazhena assumed she had the legend's power over Alyssa, she never tried to use vampire compulsion on her."

"A lucky misunderstanding for all of us."

"True." Vlad nodded solemnly. Then he stared intently at Christian.

"What?"

"Do you feel any different?"

"Different? Not really. Why?"

"We need to talk." Vlad's face looked grim. Whatever he wanted to say, it wasn't going to be pleasant.

Christian glanced back at Alyssa. He walked to the doorway leading into the hall.

"Fine, but let's go to my library and talk there. I don't want to wake Alyssa. She's been through enough."

* * * * *

Alyssa peered through her lashes after the door slammed to make sure both men had left the room. They were gone. Opening her eyes fully, she sat up in the bed. She had woken up halfway through Vlad and Christian's conversation and unabashedly eavesdropped. She smiled when she thought about how proud Christian had sounded when he spoke of her. Exasperated by her risk taking, scared for her, but also very proud of her.

Her smiled drooped, however, when she thought about why Vlad needed to talk further to Christian.

He didn't know. Christian wasn't aware of the fact that he was no longer a vampire. She wondered how he would take it.

Would he be glad, or would he be angry? Would he be sad that he was no longer immortal? Would he feel relief that he no longer needed to drink blood to survive? Would he miss the powers he once had?

All these thoughts ran through her head as she sat in his bed. In his bedroom. In his house. What would happen now? She loved him and she knew he loved her. But would it be enough? Would the loss of the kind of existence he had known for hundreds of years turn him away from her? He had thanked her for helping him last night, but would he come to resent the fact that she had made the conversion with him without his consent?

Too restless to sleep, Alyssa got out of bed and slipped on the clothes that were lying by the foot of the bed. She wasn't thrilled that someone had undressed her, but in the overall scheme of things, she dismissed it as unimportant. Her thoughts skimmed over the events of last night again and again as she paced. She had done what she thought best. She didn't want Christian to die. She couldn't bear the thought of being without him.

Did that make her weak, like her mother? No. She didn't think so. As she lay there letting Christian drain her of blood last night, somehow knowing that everything would be okay, she came to a realization. Real love was based on trust. Without it, there was nothing. Her parents didn't trust each other with their love. Unfortunately, that had lead to pain for both of them.

Alyssa swung around as the bedroom door opened. Christian walked in and Alyssa's breath caught in her throat. How was it possible that a man could look so yummy just getting out of bed? His slightly tousled hair gave him a boyish air, but the burning desire that flared in his eyes told her he was all man. She wanted to take him back to bed.

Alyssa's eyes slid helplessly down his body. His hard chest rose and fell with the deep breaths he was taking. The muscles rippled enticingly with each movement. Her eyes lowered further. His jeans weren't buttoned all the way up, so they rode low on his hips, giving her an enticing glimpse of his hard abs covered in a trail of soft hair leading down. She followed the trail to where it stopped and swallowed hard. She suddenly wished she had x-ray vision.

"X-ray vision, *palomita*?"

Alyssa's eyes flew back to his face and her mouth fell open.

"How did you-uh, I thought you didn't have—"

"I guess Vlad forgot to mention one very interesting part of the reverse conversion process. It's true I'm no longer a vampire. I'm no longer immortal and no longer require blood to live. However, the conversion doesn't take away everything. The powers I had as a vampire remain intact. It seems my work at Sundown Security is still wanted. In fact, Vlad wants me as a full partner now. He told me the fact that I can operate during daylight hours with my powers would be a great addition to our business."

"So you *can* read my mind?" Alyssa was glad Christian would be able to continue the work he found satisfaction in, but right now she wanted to know more about this mind-reading business.

"Yes, among many other things." Christian gave a very masculine chuckle.

His eyes met hers with complete knowing and arrogance. The look in his gaze was all male. He told her with that one glance that he knew he could have her right then and there, if he wanted to. And she would welcome it.

For once, Alyssa didn't care that he knew how much she wanted him. She met his hot look with a passionate stare of her own. Then she offered him the kind of seductive come-hither smile women have been giving men for ages.

"Many other things? Hmm. Sounds promising," she said in a teasing voice.

Christian growled low in his throat as he slammed the door behind him and closed the distance between them. He pulled Alyssa into his arms and lowered his mouth to hers. His kisses were hungry, demanding everything from her. Alyssa didn't hesitate. She stood on tiptoe to have more of him. It felt so good to be back in his arms.

The next thing she knew, he picked her up and carried her to the bed. Laying her down on it, he slowly undressed her, then followed close behind. He pressed his body over hers. The feel of his hot hardness pressed against her sent tingles of anticipation through her body. Hot? This was the first time that she had noticed Christian was hot. He felt sizzling in her arms. She pressed up against his heat, welcoming it as it surrounded her.

"You're hot," she said breathlessly as Christian moved his kisses over her chin and down her neck.

He raised his head and smiled with amusement dancing in his eyes.

"Thank you."

"No, uh, I mean you *are* hot and all, but what I'm saying is your body temperature is hot," she stammered.

Understanding dawned in his eyes as she spoke, but his grin grew wider.

"Thank you again. And I'm sure a thermometer will measure my body temperature at a normal 98.6 from now on. But at this moment, I think my body heat is rising." Christian's eyes were half closed with desire as his gaze burned a trail from her face, to her neck, to her breasts. They rested there and he licked his lips. "You make me very, very hot, *palomita*."

Alyssa gasped as Christian lowered his head and ran his tongue around one nipple. He did the same with the other and she felt them harden under his touch. With a groan he latched onto one. The suction of his mouth made her hips rise against his in invitation. He continued to worship each one in turn, until she was squirming and practically panting. She splayed her fingers through his hair, tried to pull him back to her needy mouth, but he resisted. Instead his lips slid lower. Over her quivering stomach, stopping to delve his hot tongue in her belly button before moving on.

When his mouth grew close to her center, she moaned with need. She couldn't help but tilt her hips up as she felt his warm breath against her. When his mouth found her, she practically jumped off the bed from the pleasure of it. Soon he had her gasping and moaning with need.

"Please, Christian. I need you now."

As if he had been waiting just for those words, Christian rose above her. He gently grasped her thighs, spread them wide and perched his hardness against her core. Alyssa closed her eyes as desire swept through her. She could feel the heat of him pressed against her, yet he didn't move.

"Christian!" Her needy voice filled the silent bedroom.

"Yes, my love. But first you need to look at me. I want to look into your beautiful eyes as I plunge deep inside you."

Alyssa let her eyes open and met his hot stare.

Christian grasped her hips and thrust deep. She gasped from the pleasure. She wanted to close her eyes as the rhythm of their bodies took her to another place, but Christian held her gaze with his. It was incredibly erotic. She watched his face grow tight with passion. She struggled to keep her eyes open as she grew closer and closer to the edge. His hands were everywhere, adding flames to her already out of control fire. He slid his hand between them and rubbed her tender nub. The combined friction of his fingers and each plunge into her body was too much. She began to splinter into a thousand pieces.

"Keep your eyes open, *palomita*. I want to see you come to your pleasure," Christian demanded.

Alyssa couldn't refuse him. He held her eyes as she peaked. It intensified everything. She had never experienced anything so passionate. And she knew watching her drove him over the edge. His eyes flared wide and he gasped. She felt his body explode as he came inside her.

Christian rolled over onto his back, bringing her with him, so that she lay sprawled on top of him. Lethargy took over and she fell asleep in his arms.

Some time later, Alyssa woke up. It was daytime and Christian was no longer under her. In fact he wasn't even in the bed. She sat up and immediately found him with her eyes. She remained quiet.

Christian stood in front of his large window. The drapes were open wide. Sunlight streamed into the room. He was naked, but this didn't faze him as he stared outside. After a minute he seemed to sense her perusal. He slowly turned around.

The emotion in his eyes was almost too much for her to bear. He looked like a little boy who was enjoying his first Christmas. His gaze was wide with wonder and joy. He opened his mouth to speak, but couldn't seem to get the words out immediately.

When he finally did, they weren't the words Alyssa expected.

"Thank you," he said as he strode to where she sat on the bed. "Thank you for giving me my life back."

Alyssa felt tears sting her eyes. She didn't try to stop them. Not with this man. Never with him. She never needed to hide from him. She knew that now.

Christian sat beside her on the bed and tenderly brushed away her tears with his finger.

"I love you, Alyssa. Bazhena was wrong about her choice for the legend. You *are* The Light, the guiding light of my existence. All that I ever wanted and needed. I just didn't realize it right away. My apples and sunshine. I couldn't ask for more."

"Apples and sunshine?"

"Yes, one of the first things I noticed about you is that you always carried the scent of apples on you. It drove me crazy with need. You represented everything I didn't have, everything I wasn't. I was darkness and death. You were sunshine and life.

So, whenever I thought about you, the words apples and sunshine always came to mind. I craved that, craved you from the beginning."

Alyssa couldn't speak. Christian's words sent an arrow through her heart. Left her aching with love. This incredible man loved her and needed her as much as, if not more than she needed him. And he loved her enough to tell her. She could do no less. Swallowing hard, she said the words that she had been so afraid to say in the past.

"I need you too, Christian. You are everything to me. I love you so much my heart aches with it every time I see you. I can't and don't want to imagine my life without you. How would you like to spend the remainder of your short mortal life with a little bird?"

Christian's grin grew wide. He kissed the tip of her nose and chuckled.

"So you found out what *palomita* means?"

"Yes. My curiosity got the better of me. I went online and looked up the English translation for *palomita*. The words "little bird" came up immediately."

Christian nodded his head.

"That's right. You're always so full of energy, always fluttering around doing one thing or another. Yet you are so feminine and soft. Like a little bird," Christian explained with a tender smile before continuing.

"And I would consider it an extreme honor and pleasure to spend the rest of my life with you, little bird. Whether it is five or five hundred years, it would never be enough time with you. But I promise you that I will make the most of every second of it, if you let me."

Alyssa watched Christian's eyes darken with desire and knew that he meant to keep that promise. Good. She would hold him to it. With pleasure. Christian lowered his mouth towards hers. She rose up to meet his kiss. Joy swept through her as their lips touched.

This was her man. Her partner. Her love. Alyssa would give him everything and she knew Christian would do the same for her. Just as it should be.

The End

Enjoy an excerpt from:

All Night Inn

All Night Inn

ꕥ

"Ms. Colson." Jonathan came upon her so quietly she startled, dropping the rag. He watched silently as she recovered her composure. "You did well tonight. I have no objection to continuing your employment." He eyed the cloth on the counter then turned his intense blue stare back to her. "What are your feelings about it?"

Shaken, but not deterred. With a boldness she didn't feel, she stared back at him. "I still want the job."

Just for an instant a smile slipped across his lips. "Very well." He inclined his head, and pointed to the hallway leading to his office. "That way, please."

She preceded him inside. It wasn't a large room. Jonathan's desk took up the bulk of the space in the middle. In one corner was a brown leather couch, easily six feet long, with a colorful striped blanket spread across the back. A mini-fridge sat next to it, doubling as a lamp stand. For a moment Sharon speculated as to what kind of drinks her future boss kept cold. Little plastic bags from the local blood bank, perhaps?

Heart pounding, she eyed the couch and waited. Jonathan followed her gaze, hesitated, and apparently decided against the intimacy that would afford. He directed her toward the top of the desk with an elegant wave of his hand. "If you will sit there, Ms. Colson?"

She did as he instructed, facing him as he approached. For the first time since that brief caress in the bar, he touched her, placed his hands on her shoulders. She'd thought they'd be cold, clammy, but there was perceptible warmth to them. She felt it through the thin material of her blouse. Not warm enough to be human, but there.

For a moment he studied her face. "You're sure about this?"

Sharon closed her eyes and steeled herself for the sensation of his mouth on her throat, the prick of his teeth piercing the skin. She hated pain. She was the kind to insist on local anesthesia before allowing a splinter to be removed.

"Just do it," she whispered.

He did nothing. She opened her eyes and his blue stare bore into her. "You must look into my eyes and let me into your mind, Ms. Colson. I'll take the fear from you and make it easy."

He wanted to link minds with her? Panicked, Sharon shook her head. "No, not that. I won't let you do that."

He frowned. "You don't understand. I can block what you feel and make it pleasurable for you. Without a mind link there will be pain."

"I do understand. I expect the pain. I can deal with it."

He shook his head, displeasure infusing his expression. "I'm not in the habit of causing discomfort. I enjoy feeding..." One long finger traced the vein in her neck. "I'd rather you enjoyed it, too."

"It isn't important I enjoy it," she said, her voice desperate. How could she make him understand? Sharon took a deep and ragged breath. "There was a man I met who did a mind link to me once." She shuddered at the memory. It had been...awful. She'd felt like she'd been ripped apart and afterward...no, she couldn't think about the "afterward."

"It was months before I could think straight. I'm willing to let you feed off me, but I can't let you into my mind."

He let go of her and stepped back, disappointment in his face. "I'm very sorry, Ms. Colson. I would have enjoyed having you here...but the role of a companion requires my being able to touch your mind."

Moving to the door, he gestured to her. "Come with me to the bar, and I'll pay you for this evening."

"No!" Nervously, she licked her lips. "Please...can't you make an exception? I really need this job."

Frustration showed in his face. "Exception to what? To the mark, no, it's too dangerous for me to have unmarked humans here."

Desperation made her bold. "What about the link, then? Just this once? Maybe when I know you better, can trust you more…I promise I'll let you into my mind."

For a moment she thought he was going to give up and send her on her way. Then she caught the hungry look in his eyes and the way he studied her neck with a possessive stare. She could tell he wanted this, to taste her, to mark her as his own. He might not ever take her blood again, but he wanted it this time.

The way he licked his lips told her that he wanted it bad enough to forego his principles and bleed her without the mind link.

"As you wish, then." The vampire returned to her and took a different hold with his hands. One moved to the back of her head, the other to just below her shoulder blades. It was a more intimate embrace than the one he'd taken before—and more secure. His hand caressed her hair, pulling it back, baring her neck. It might have been the prelude to a kiss.

Piercing blue eyes stared into hers. "I will hold you to that promise," he whispered.

His arms tightened and he moved so fast that she didn't have a chance to say anything, couldn't have pulled away if she wanted to. Held in his vise-like grip, sharp pain stabbed through her as his fangs plunged into her neck, unerringly locating the artery. A burning sensation followed as strong lips drew the blood through the tiny holes.

Pain. It was worse than she'd imagined. Sharon wanted to cry out, but couldn't. He held her so close she was crushed into his chest. His throat rippled as he swallowed and she felt his heartbeat stutter then pick up pace, growing faster, almost matching the furious pounding of hers.

She hadn't expected him to take so much, just a few swallows, a taste. This was more like a banquet for him as he guzzled her life's blood. Fear grew inside her…fear of what she'd promised, of what she would become at his hands.

A vampire and companion linked minds—it was "required". How was she ever going to deal with that?

As her body chilled, his grew warmer. A rushing noise sounded in her ears and dizziness encompassed her. She grew weak and faint and still he took from her until she began to wonder if he intended to stop feeding at all, or if her life would end in his arms.

Was she going to die?

A gasp of fear and pain escaped her. Abruptly his mouth stopped moving and simply rested. He breathed heavily, the heat of his breath scorching her throat. The worst of the pain ended at the same time, but the relief from it put tears into her eyes.

His grip eased, and he allowed her to pull back, but only briefly. "A moment," he whispered. "I must stop the flow." He pressed down, covering the aching places where his teeth had pierced the skin.

She felt the touch of his tongue move across the holes, sealing them but not healing. He gently licked the rest of her neck, cleaning the remaining blood and soothing her skin. The throbbing abated under his tender ministrations.

The vampire drew back, a warm possessive glow in his eyes. An odd thought slid into her mind. *He was a neat eater.* Only the smallest amount of blood lingered at the corners of his mouth, and as she watched his flitting tongue removed even that evidence.

Deep amusement laced his voice when he spoke. "Congratulations, Ms. Colson. You have the job."

Why an electronic book?

We live in the Information Age—an exciting time in the history of human civilization, in which technology rules supreme and continues to progress in leaps and bounds every minute of every day. For a multitude of reasons, more and more avid literary fans are opting to purchase e-books instead of paper books. The question from those not yet initiated into the world of electronic reading is simply: *Why?*

1. ***Price.*** An electronic title at Ellora's Cave Publishing and Cerridwen Press runs anywhere from 40% to 75% less than the cover price of the exact same title in paperback format. Why? Basic mathematics and cost. It is less expensive to publish an e-book (no paper and printing, no warehousing and shipping) than it is to publish a paperback, so the savings are passed along to the consumer.
2. ***Space.*** Running out of room in your house for your books? That is one worry you will never have with electronic books. For a low one-time c ost, you can purchase a handheld device specifically designed for e-reading. Many e-readers have large, convenient screens for viewing. Better yet, hundreds of titles can be stored within your new library—on a single microchip. There are a variety of e-readers from different manufacturers. You can also read e-books on your PC or laptop computer. (Please note that Ellora's

Cave does not endorse any specific brands. You can check our websites at www.ellorascave.com or www.cerridwenpress.com for information we make available to new consumers.)

3. ***Mobility***. Because your new e-library consists of only a microchip within a small, easily transportable e-reader, your entire cache of books can be taken with you wherever you go.
4. ***Personal Viewing Preferences.*** Are the words you are currently reading too small? Too large? Too... ANNOYING? Paperback books cannot be modified according to personal preferences, but e-books can.
5. ***Instant Gratification.*** Is it the middle of the night and all the bookstores near you are closed? Are you tired of waiting days, sometimes weeks, for bookstores to ship the novels you bought? Ellora's Cave Publishing sells instantaneous downloads twenty-four hours a day, seven days a week, every day of the year. Our webstore is never closed. Our e-book delivery system is 100% automated, meaning your order is filled as soon as you pay for it.

Those are a few of the top reasons why electronic books are replacing paperbacks for many avid readers.

As always, Ellora's Cave and Cerridwen Press welcome your questions and comments. We invite you to email us at Comments@ellorascave.com or write to us directly at Ellora's Cave Publishing Inc., 1056 Home Avenue, Akron, OH 44310-3502.